REIGN

THE SAINTHOOD-THE BOYS OF LOWELL HIGH BOOK THREE

USA TODAY & WSJ BESTSELLING AUTHOR

SIOBHAN DAVIS

Original Paperback edition © July 2020

This edition March 2023

ISBN - 978-1-959285-40-3

Editor: Kelly Hartigan (XterraWeb) editing.xterraweb.com

Cover design by Shannon Passmore www.shanoffdesigns.com

Sainthood logo and angel logo graphic design by Robin Harper of Wicked By Design.

Stock imagery © depositphotos.com

Formatting by Ciara Turley using Vellum

Everything changed after the attempt on my life, and now, I'm more determined than ever to crush my enemies until they lie in pieces at my feet.

Sinner believes he has pushed me into a corner, but he underestimates my thirst for revenge.

Nothing will stand in my way.

And I'm no longer in this alone. Saint, Galen, Caz, and Theo have won my trust and my heart. Together, we are an unbreakable team and an unstoppable force.

Staying one step ahead of the game is critical to our success, so we've little choice but to partner with the most unlikely of allies. The situation is tense and fraught with danger, and it's not just our lives at stake.

Everything rests on finding the evidence that links The Sainthood to Daphne Leydon's kidnapping and murder, and we're running out of time.

Sinner thinks war has already come to Lowell. But he has overlooked his deadliest enemy and the challenge that comes from within.

We won't stop until he's defeated and we have taken his crown.

Sinner is going down.

Note From The Author

This is a dark reverse harem romance, and it is not suitable for young teens due to mature content, graphic sexual scenes, and cursing. The recommended reading age is eighteen-plus.

This is the third book in the series, and it cannot be read as a stand-alone.

REIGN

Gang Structure & Control

The Sainthood (Prestwick & Lowell)

President: Neo/Sinner

Junior chapter leader: Saint Lennox

Junior chapter second in command: Galen Lennox

Junior chapter members: Caz Evans, Theo Smith, Bryant Eccleston.

The Arrows (Prestwick)

Leader/President: Archer Quinn

Sergeant at arms: Diego Santana

Junior chapter leader: Darrow Knight

Junior chapter second in command: Bryant Eccelston (Sainthood spy)

The Bulls (Fenton)

New Leader/President: Marwan

Lowell High School gang

Leader: Finn Houston

Second in command: Brooklyn Robbins

Finn's girlfriend: Parker Brooks

Parker's bestie: Beth McCoy

LOCATIONS

Prestwick: birthplace of The Sainthood and The Arrows.

Lowell: where Harlow lives and where the new chapter of The Sainthood has been established

Fenton: birthplace of The Bulls

SCHOOLS

Prestwick High – The Arrows reigns supreme

Prestwick Academy – The Sainthood reigns supreme

Lowell Academy – A private school Harlow used to attend

Lowell High – The new school Harlow and The Sainthood now attend. Finn Houston used to reign supreme until The Sainthood took charge.

KEY CHARACTERS

Harlow Westbrook – 18, MC.

Giana Westbrook – Harlow's mom.

Trey Westbrook – Harlow's dad (deceased.)

Saint Lennox – 18, MC

Galen Lennox – 17, MC. Saint's cousin.

Caz Evans – 18, MC.

Theo Smith – 18, MC.

Alisha Lennox – Galen's mom.

Diesel – Harlow's friend/trainer & VERO employee

Sariah Roark – Harlow's best friend.

Emmett – Harlow's friend.

Sean – Sariah's boyfriend.

Lincoln – work associate of Trey Westbrook.

Howie Young – DEA Agent

Randall Solice – Head of VERO

Taylor Tamlin – Parker's half-sister

Ashley Shaw – Harlow's friend

Jase, Chad – Ashley's boyfriends

Chapter One
Harlow

The fog clouding my brain refuses to clear as the sounds of whispered arguing rouse me from slumber. I attempt to move, but my heavy body won't cooperate. It's as if I'm superglued to the warm, soft surface I'm lying on.

"She needs to wake up in her own time."

The deep voice is familiar. *Caz.* My lovable, giant teddy bear of a man.

"She'd want to be there," Saint retorts in his usual belligerent manner, but I hear the strain in his voice.

"Saint is right. She'll never forgive us if we take this choice away from her," Theo agrees, always the voice of calm logic.

"What choice?" I croak, blinking my eyes open and wincing as bright light stabs my retinas. My eyes shutter again, affronted by the blinding light.

"Princess." Shoes squelch on the floor as Saint approaches. His warm hand lands on top of mine, and I force my eyelids to open again. "There's my girl." Troubled blue eyes lock on mine, and there's so much emotion written on his handsome face as he pins me with an intense stare.

The cuts and grazes on his cheeks and forehead are new, as is the thicker layer of stubble on his jawline, confirming I must've been out of it for some time. I quickly take in my surroundings, not surprised to discover I'm in a hospital room. "How long have I been unconscious?" I ask, recalling the car bomb that put me here.

"It's Sunday," Theo supplies, coming up on the other side of my bed.

What the hell? "I've been out of it for three days?" I cringe at the hoarse tone of my voice.

"You've woken up briefly a few times," Saint confirms, rubbing soothing circles on the back of my hand with his thumb. "But you were in pain, so the staff has been feeding you a steady line of morphine."

"Do you want some ice chips?" Theo inquires, and I twist my head around to face him. His sexy dirty-blond hair is pulled up into a tight bun on the top of his head, showcasing his stunning face. With his high cheekbones, expressive hazel eyes, and full lips, he could easily grace the catwalk for a living, but that would be a waste of his sharp brain and shrewd intellect.

My man is the full package, and I'm a lucky bitch.

Little scrapes and cuts line his face too, and he also looks like he hasn't shaved in days.

I move to turn on my side, and a strangled groan slips from my mouth as pain batters my body from all angles. "Yes," I rasp, ignoring how much I'm hurting when I notice how parched my throat is. My dry, chapped lips crave something cold and soothing, and I attempt to sit up, hissing as a throbbing ache spreads across my upper body.

"Careful, babe." Caz appears from behind Saint, pressing the button on the bed to elevate it so I'm in more of an upright position. Caz gently eases me forward as Theo stuffs a couple more pillows behind me, propping me up more comfortably.

"How bad does it hurt?" Saint inquires, threading his fingers in mine.

"Like a bitch," I truthfully admit, opening my lips as Theo pops some ice chips in my mouth.

Caz perches on the side of my bed, brushing hair back off my brow as Theo administers ice chips in short, measured stints and Saint holds my hand.

"Where's Galen?" I ask, shaking my head when Theo brings the plastic cup to my mouth again.

Panic churns in my gut as the events that landed me in here swarm to the forefront of my mind in vivid Technicolor. Galen was with me when the bomb went off, and I know he tried to shield me from the worst of it, which does nothing to reassure me now. My gaze darts wildly around the private hospital room, my worried eyes flitting between the guys as I seek him out.

"Relax, Lo. Galen is fine," Saint says. "He's sleeping in the room next door."

"Thank fuck." My head drops back on the pillows as air whooshes out of my mouth in grateful relief. "I want to see him," I bark, scowling at Saint. "And why are you all in here? Galen shouldn't be left alone."

A familiar smirk pulls up the corners of Saint's mouth.

"There's our ballbuster." Caz grins, his tone laced with amusement. He presses a kiss to the tip of my nose in an unbelievably sweet gesture. "Missed you, babe."

"Stop deflecting. Take me to Galen."

"Alisha is with him," Saint says. "And we've been taking it in turns, ensuring neither of you are alone."

"Saintly got thrown out the first day when they refused to

put you both in the same room," Theo explains, gently cupping one side of my face.

"Still causing trouble," I murmur, fighting a smile as I squeeze Saint's hand.

The door opens unexpectedly, and a pretty woman in blue scrubs steps into the room. "It's good to see you awake, Harlow," she says, striding to my bedside. "How are you feeling?"

"Like someone has just gone to town on my body with a bat."

She pins Saint and Caz with an ice-cold look, and they glare at her. "I need to get close to Ms. Westbrook to check her vitals, so scoot."

A giggle bursts from my mouth as my two alpha-holes reluctantly step aside, still glaring at the nurse, and I wonder what happened that they're so salty.

"Are they always this territorial?" She probes my head with gentle fingers.

"They're usually much worse, so count your blessings," I joke.

She shines a light in my eyes, takes my blood pressure, checks my chart, and tops up the saline drip hooked up to the back of my hand. "Everything looks good, Harlow." Her warm smile is genuine. "We're scaling back your pain meds, but if it hurts too much and you need more, just press the button."

"I'm good," I lie, because I need to get the fuck out of here. "The pain is manageable."

"You're lucky your injuries weren't more extensive."

"So, I can leave?"

"That's up to the doctor. You've suffered a mild concussion and bruised a few ribs, so he may want to keep you under observation for another twenty-four hours."

Hell to the no. I don't give a fuck what the doctor says—I'm leaving today.

"Can't you just give me pain meds and let me recuperate at home? I'd rather be in my own bed." I hate hospitals with a burning passion. It reminds me of the time I spent in the hospital after my kidnapping.

"You can discuss it with the doctor. He's with Mr. Lennox, so he'll be right with you."

"How is he?" I blurt, reaching out and grabbing her arm as she prepares to walk off.

She pats my hand before replacing it on the bed. "I can't discuss another patient with you even if he is your boyfriend. While Galen's injuries were a little more serious, he is on the road to recovery. You were both very lucky you got far enough away to avoid the full impact of the blast." She pats my hand again. "I hope the police find the person responsible."

Saint growls. Caz's eyes narrow. Theo sighs, plopping down into the chair and pulling it up closer to the bed.

The nurse leaves, and my gaze bounces between the guys. "What have you found out? Was it Taylor?" I remember the flash of long blonde hair just before Galen shoved me away from the car, which makes Taylor Tamlin—Parker's half-sister and a girl who has connections to The Bulls and The Arrows—the most likely suspect.

"That fucking bitch is dead," Caz spits out, confirming the truth.

"As soon as we locate her," Saint agrees.

"We pulled footage from the front of the school," Theo explains, lacing his hand in mine. "Taylor put the bomb under the car parked alongside yours and waited for us to show so she could activate it remotely."

She's clearly pissed I killed her half-sister Parker. "She did her homework." She is obviously aware of the safety features of my custom-built Lexus and knew it had an explosion-mitigating floor.

"Bitch is smart," Theo says.

Saint harrumphs, glaring at Theo across the bed. "She's dumb as shit, dude. She messed with *us*. And there's only one way that story ends."

"Damn fucking straight," Caz agrees, reclaiming his spot on the edge of my bed. He drags a hand through his hair, stifling a yawn. He too is sporting superficial wounds and more stubble than usual on his face.

"Are you guys okay?" I ask. "And have any of you slept?" I reach out, running my fingers through the bristly hair on Caz's right cheek.

"We're fine." Theo offers me a reassuring smile. "Don't worry about us. Just focus on getting better, sweetheart."

"We were far enough away to avoid any serious damage," Saint adds. "We got hit with some debris, but we can cope with a few minor cuts."

"How bad is Galen? And don't even attempt to sugarcoat it." I drill him with a warning look.

"Don't sweat it, Lo." Caz tweaks my nose, flashing me a wide grin. "That pretty face you love is still intact."

"You can see for yourself in a bit," Saint says as the door opens, and a tall, thin man with salt-and-pepper hair enters the room.

The doc looks at my stats and asks me a few questions before agreeing to release me later today provided my prognosis hasn't changed.

I fling the covers off the instant he leaves the room, pulling my body around in the bed so my legs dangle over the side, biting the inside of my cheek to stop myself from crying out as pain pummels me from every angle. "Fuck."

"This is madness," Caz says, beseeching me with his eyes. "Stay in bed, babe."

"I've been in bed for three fucking days. I'm done sleeping." I push to my feet, ignoring the wave of pain that washes over me, clasping Caz's shoulder to steady myself. "I want to see Galen and…" I falter as my best friend's face forms in my mind's eye. Blood rushes to my head, and my heart pounds in my chest. "Sariah," I whisper, tears pricking the back of my eyes as that part of the day returns to haunt me. We were only leaving school because Vice Principal Pierson had received a call confirming Sariah was being taken off life support. "Is she…"

The three guys share an anguished look, and I drop back on the bed as a different kind of pain settles on my chest. My breathing stutters, and my chest heaves as pressure bears down on me. A pulsing pain throbs in my skull, and my heart aches as if someone has a hand around it, squeezing it tight. "Please tell me it was a lie," I whimper. "A ruse to get us out of school. Please tell me that's all it was." My heart thumps frantically behind my rib cage as I cling to straws.

"Princess." Saint sits down on the other side of me, gently sliding his arm around my back. "She's gone, babe. I'm so sorry."

"What?" Tears spill out of my eyes and down my cheeks before I can stop them. "No!" I cry as intense pain whips through me, sucking all the air from my lungs, making breathing difficult. "No! Not Sariah!" I sob.

Saint gently pulls my head onto his shoulder as Caz takes my hand, holding it firmly in his warm grasp.

"She can't be dead, Saint. Sar never hurt anyone. This is all wrong," I say in between sobs. Parker and her cronies attacked Sariah at school, because they couldn't get to me, beating her so badly she ended up in a coma.

Liquid pain churns in my gut and swirls up my throat, blocking my airway as I give in to the tsunami crashing and tumbling inside me. I break down completely, and the noises ripping from my throat don't even sound human. My tortured cries bounce off the walls as I self-destruct. Theo moves around the bed, kneeling in front of me, taking my free hand and showering it with soft kisses.

"Her funeral is in a couple hours," Theo explains when my cries have died down. "We were planning on waking you up. We knew you'd want to be there."

So that's what the whispered arguing was about.

"How did Taylor know?" I sniffle, needing to focus my brain on anything but the fact I'll never see my best friend's bubbly smile and beautiful face again.

"We spoke to the vice principal," Saint says, pressing a kiss to the top of my head. "We thought Pierson might've been involved, but she's clean."

"A neighbor of Taylor's is an orderly here," Theo supplies, rubbing my hand in a soothing gesture. "He was keeping her updated, and she got a heads-up on the news. She called Pierson, pretending to be a nurse, and set the whole thing in motion."

"That's how we knew it was a setup," Saint adds. "Sean called Theo when he couldn't reach you. He hadn't asked anyone to call the school to pass you a message."

"That's why you hung back as we were leaving school that day."

"We should've made you hold up too." Pain blares in Theo's eyes.

"Then we'd probably all be dead." I pull my hand from Caz, swiping at the moisture under my eyes. "That was obviously her intent." If it'd just been about taking me down, she had any number of opportunities to attack me as I was entering or leaving the hospital to visit Sar. The fact she waited tells me she wanted to take the guys out too.

"She's going to regret coming after us," Saint growls.

"I have software recognition set up," Theo says. "And we put the word out on the street."

"She can't hide forever," Saint adds. "And when she surfaces, we'll grab her."

"She's mine," I seethe, fire burning in my belly. "Mine and Galen's."

"No one argues with that," Saint agrees, piercing me with that intense lens of his.

I nod, drawing a deep breath and urging my body to relax. Holding on to Saint, I push awkwardly to my feet. "I need to see Galen. Take me to him now."

Chapter Two
Saint

Lo clings to me as Caz opens the door to Galen's private room. Theo has gone back to the house to grab clean clothes for all of us. We'll freshen up here as there isn't enough time to go home before the funeral service begins.

"Hey." Lo's voice is soft as Galen's eyes flicker open and his head turns toward her. Alisha—Galen's mom—is conked out on a chair, softly snoring.

"Angel." Galen's voice is gruff and sleep heavy. He's been sleeping most of the past three days as well; although, he's been awake for longer periods in between, refusing extra pain meds because he's desperate to get back on his feet.

I have never been as scared as I was back at the school. We thought we'd lost them.

The scene was a fucking mess. Debris strewn everywhere. Billows of acrid smoke stinging our eyes. Our ears ringing from the noise of the detonation. The bomb drew everyone from school outside, and it was pandemonium. When we finally got to Lo and Galen, they were unconscious on the ground, covered in shit from the explosion.

Because they were closer to the car than us, they suffered the brunt of the damage. Galen was lying on top of Lo, his body shielding hers from the debris, but I worried he'd broken her pelvis or forced all the air from her lungs. Waiting for the EMTs to show up was excruciatingly painful, because we were afraid to move either of them, and we honestly didn't know if they were going to make it.

"You're my hero," Lo tells my cousin, bending over him to plant a light kiss on his lips. "You saved me. Saved us."

"I've been so worried about you," Galen admits, inching to the side of the bed and opening the covers. He pats the space beside him. "Come here."

Caz helps Lo up beside Galen, and my chest tightens as her gown opens at the rear, exposing the multicolored bruising covering her back, distracting from the gorgeous ink on her skin. Caz and I exchange a look before flopping into the empty seats by Galen's bed.

I know the guys feel the same way I do. I want to gut Taylor Tamlin from head to toe, slice layers off her skin, gouge her eyes from their sockets, and rip her insides to shreds, until she's nothing more than a nonexistent bloody mess on the floor.

How fucking dare she come after us.

How dare she attempt to take the only girl who has ever mattered from us.

Lo cautiously snuggles into Galen's side, her fingers lifting to the sling on his arm and then on to the myriad of cuts and bruises marring his pretty-boy face. "You got hurt protecting me." She looks directly into his eyes. "I won't ever forget that."

"You're evenity now," Caz says, his lips twitching.

"Evenity isn't a word," I deadpan, humoring him because we could fucking use it.

"It is according to the *urban dictionary*." He lowers his tone so it's almost reverential.

Dude's got issues.

"I like that one," Lo proclaims, grinning at him as she lifts her arm for a knuckle touch. "And for the record, we were already evenity." She returns her gaze to Galen, and they share a moment. "Galen doesn't have anything to prove to me."

Galen lightly clasps her face, kissing her. They engage in a whispered conversation, in between kissing, and I stand, walking to the window, affording them some privacy. I shove my hands in my pockets as I glance out the window. Caz comes up alongside me, his eyes studying me. "What?" I ask.

"I thought you were past the jealousy."

"I am," I admit, and it's not really a lie. I *have* learned to share her, and it pleases me they were able to move beyond Galen's sick betrayal, but I'd be lying if I said I wasn't dying to kiss her and hold her and tell her how I feel.

The first twenty-four hours after the explosion were a nightmare. Lo was heavily sedated, and the longer she slept, the more I worried she wouldn't ever wake up. That she wouldn't know how deep my feelings run. I made a promise to myself I'd tell her the first opportunity I get.

I want nothing left unsaid between us. *Nothing.*

"I'm giving them some alone time," I add when Caz doesn't look convinced. "And I'm looking forward to some alone time of my own."

Caz smirks, and I elbow him. "Not like that, asshole. She's injured."

"Bet she's still as horny as ever." He waggles his brows. "And we've got to look after *all* our girl's needs."

Now it's my turn to smirk. "Well, when you put it like that. Can't let our girl down." My cock twitches at the thought of Lo's gorgeous, sexy body, and I adjust myself in my jeans as blood rushes south and my dick hardens. Caz chuckles as the door opens, and Theo slips into the room.

Alisha wakes, kissing her son goodbye and tossing us a wave before she leaves. She has been here every day, and she appears to be making an effort to stay sober for her son although we all know it won't last long. At least, she's trying.

Giana has been here every day too, but she doesn't linger, and I'm grateful because with Giana comes Sinner, and none of us want my prick of a father around our girl. He turned up the first day, but it was just for show. He's probably wishing Taylor Tamlin had succeeded in eliminating Lo as a threat and solving one problem for him. But hell will freeze over before I let that asshole harm one more hair on my girlfriend's head.

If there is anything good to come from this, it's that Sinner's twisted plans to enjoy Lo with his creepy buddies is on ice. I intend to exaggerate her injuries for as long as we can get away with it, hoping it'll buy us enough time to come up with a way of extracting her from that aspect of her initiation.

I stay behind to help Galen shower while Theo and Caz go back to Lo's room to help her do the same.

After we've cleaned up and changed our clothes, I force my cousin to eat some of the shit they pass off as food in this joint while I sweet-talk one of the nurses into getting a script for Galen and Lo. Doc told Galen he wanted him to stay here until tomorrow, but fuck that shit. We're bailing now. Between us, we can take care of them, and none of us wants to spend another goddamned minute in this hellhole.

Galen is finishing the slop on his plate when I walk back into his room. "Got a script," I say, holding up the two pieces of paper in my hand.

"Good." Galen pushes the plate away with a grimace. "I want to talk to you about something." He adjusts the sling around his neck supporting his sore, previously dislocated, shoulder, as I plonk down on the bed beside him.

"What's up?"

"I think I have a solution which keeps Lo out of Sinner's grabby hands."

I straighten up, leveling him with a solemn stare. "Let's hear it."

I'm still mulling over Galen's suggestion as I drive us to the Catholic church on the outskirts of Lowell, where the service for Sariah is taking place. Everyone is quiet in the car, and the mood is somber. Lo is seated between Theo and Caz in the back seat, the latter fussing over her the entire journey. It's funny to see this side of Caz, because all he's known for is his role as the muscle behind our plans. Lo has brought out a softer side to him, to all of us, and it's changing us in ways we never expected.

"We're going to be late if you don't step on it," Galen grumbles, glancing at the time on his cell.

"I'm taking it easy on purpose, dickwad." I gesture toward the dazed, injured girl in the back. Lo has been lost in thought the entire trip from the hospital. She hasn't cried since she broke down when I first told her the news, but she's teetering on the edge. There's a haunted look on her face and a tortured glimmer in her eyes that highlights her pain, even if she's doing her best to numb herself to the emotions.

We all see it.

This has devastated her.

"Put the pedal to the metal," Lo says in a monotonous tone,

empty of feeling. She stares absently out the window, as her chest heaves and air expels from her mouth in a loud rush. "I don't want to be late."

We rock up to the red-and-gray-brick church ten minutes later. Mourners stream through the doors as I park the car at the side of the road. Galen hisses through his teeth when he slides out of the passenger side, clutching his sore ribs. Theo lifts Lo down from the back seat, and she doesn't mouth a word of protest, standing stiffly, staring off into space. Theo and I trade another concerned look, and it seems to be all we're doing these days.

"Galen," Lo calls after my cousin. "I need you."

We step back as she grabs hold of Galen's hand, and they walk ahead of us, toward the church. It's hard to step aside and let someone else comfort her when all I want is to bundle her into my arms and keep her safe, but I've got to let her call the shots. Her head is a mess right now, and we're all treading on eggshells, wanting to help her but not fully understanding how to do that.

"It's good they're getting closer," Theo murmurs, as if he's read my thoughts. "Out of all of us, Galen needs her the most."

I'm not sure I agree, but I'm not up to arguing as I prepare to step foot in a church for the first time in my life. I'm a little on edge, which surprises me because there are few situations I can't handle. I'm not convinced my black soul won't be struck down the instant I walk inside, and a healthy dose of fear mixes with curiosity and skepticism as I prepare to enter the building.

But damnation doesn't rain down on me as I follow Galen and Lo up the center aisle. We attract our fair share of inquisitive glances, but I ignore them, keeping my gaze trained on the girl who has flipped my world upside down.

Galen and Lo take a seat in the first pew, beside Sariah's grandma Lorna, and Sariah's boyfriend, Sean. Emmett, Sean's friend, and the guy who wants into our girl's panties, is also there. I try to restrain my uncharitable feelings toward the dick, but it's challenging because the dude annoys the fuck out of me.

The three of us slip into the pew behind them as organ music starts and the congregation stands. I pay attention to the ceremony at first, because I have a natural curiosity, but the priest loses me during the homily when he starts talking about God's will and death being a test of faith for those left behind.

How the fuck could this be God's will?

Sariah's grandma has lost everyone she loves, and I'm baffled that she still supports a God that has taken so much from her. Maybe I'd feel differently if I was religious, but I struggle to wrap my head around it because it's nonsensical to me.

Galen comforts Lo with his free arm wrapped around her shoulders as he holds her tight to his body. The sounds of open grieving surround us, but our girl doesn't cry, and that worries me.

Lo was here six months ago, burying her dad, and I know she's still mourning the man she idolized. Now, she's lost her best friend, and with so much shit on her plate, I see what she's doing. Burying her emotions so she's numb to all feeling.

Internalizing her pain isn't a good thing. I should know, because I've been denying my emotions for years, and it twists a person up like you wouldn't believe.

When the service concludes, we follow the chief mourners outside to the small graveyard attached to the church.

Ashley Shaw approaches us as we walk to the graveside. She's holding hands with her boyfriend Chad, and his best friend Jase—aka Ashley's other, secret, fuckboy—is in tow, hands shoved deep in his pockets. Ashley takes Lo to one side, whispering in her ear as she swipes tears from her eyes.

Chad and Jase nod at us. They got their first shipment a few days ago, and our business arrangement is running smoothly. We have Lowell Academy in the bag. That should please my prick of an old man.

"This sucks, man," Chad says.

"I didn't know Sariah well, but she was cool," Jase adds.

"She didn't deserve this," Caz says, his fingers twitching with the craving for a cigarette. Caz and Galen have been trying to kick the habit, because Lo never stops busting their balls.

The girls finish their conversation, and we walk to join the masses surrounding Sariah's resting place. Lorna is sobbing her heart out, enveloped in Sean's arms, as she mourns the loss of her beloved granddaughter. Silent tears stream down Sean's face, and I hurt for the dude.

This shouldn't have happened to Sariah.

She was attacked because Parker couldn't get to Lo, and Lo was a target because of her association with us. Guilt slaps me in the face, especially for the selfish thought lingering in the back of my mind, grateful it's not Lo in that coffin. I'm an asshole for thinking it, and the lump clogging my throat is painful. It's no secret I don't do well with emotions, and the virtual outpouring of grief around the graveside rattles me.

Lo hangs her head, fidgeting with her hands, her body shaking with the effort involved in holding it together. She glances around, and her bloodshot eyes meet mine. Pain radiates from her every pore like an aura, and I want to absorb it, to free her from suffering. She gravitates to me, keeping one hand firmly in Galen's grip as she leans into my side. I kiss the top of her head as my arm snakes around her back, uncaring how this must look to a bunch of do-gooder Holy Joes. I've got zero fucks to give, because this is all about my girl.

After the graveyard, we head back to Sariah's grandma's

house, joining the throng of bodies crowded into her small living room, before Sean pulls us out to the backyard, leaving the oldies inside. Theo and Caz sit on a wobbly wooden bench while Galen and I take a couple of patio chairs beside Ashley, Chad, and Jase. Lo gingerly lowers herself onto my lap, and I carefully wrap my arms around her.

She's wearing a fitted black dress that clings to her enviable curves with black tights and her beloved black biker boots. Apart from the raised, bruised, scabbed-over grazing on her left cheek and the fact she's a little hunched over in pain, you'd never know she was injured, or that she just narrowly escaped death.

A familiar red haze sweeps over me, and I fucking hope we find that slut Taylor sooner rather than later.

I'm itching for payback—Sainthood style.

Forcing those murderous thoughts aside, I focus on the beautiful, sad girl on my lap. "You need any pain pills, princess?" I whisper in her ear. I charmed the nurse into giving me a few to tide us over until we can fill the script at a pharmacy.

Lo shakes her head, and waves of her glossy dark hair tumble over her shoulders. "I'm okay." Her lips pull into a smile, but it doesn't meet her eyes.

My girl is hurting, and I hate I can't do anything to help. I rub my thumb along her plump lower lip, choosing not to call her out on the lie. Our eyes connect, and simmering chemistry pulses in the air between us reminding me there is one thing I can do, *we* can do, to help, but it requires privacy and the new big bed Theo had delivered to the barn yesterday.

I brush my lips across her lips, because I can't go another second without tasting her, but I pull back before it develops because this isn't the time or place. Lo sighs, settling her ass back into me, and my cock instantly stirs to life. A devilish glint flashes in her eye, and I bring my mouth to her ear. "Is my dirty girl entertaining dirty thoughts?" I whisper.

She leans down, running her fingers through my shorn blond hair as her mouth hovers millimeters from mine. "Always," she rasps. "Never doubt that."

Her sexual confidence, and the way she makes no apologies for her appetite, is one of the things I love most about her.

She pulls back as Emmett emerges from the house with a bucket of beers. There is no love lost between me and him, but I set my personal feelings aside and nod affably as he offers me a beer.

"I can't believe she's gone," Sean says, his eyes downcast as Emmett passes beers around. Galen declines, unsurprisingly, but Lo accepts one, and I subtly shake my head at Theo when I see his lips parting to say something.

Lo needs this, and we're not her dad. If she wants a fucking beer, she can have one.

"Me either," Lo adds. "I hope they throw Beth and those other bitches in a cell and they never see the light of day again." The girls were already arrested and charged with assault, which will now automatically get upgraded to a murder charge. They will get what's coming to them, and I hope it's the maximum sentence.

"You can fucking bank on it, Lo," Sean says, his eyes full of hatred. "They will pay for what they did to my girlfriend." He chokes on a sob at the end, and tears pool in his eyes. I bleed for the guy. If this was Harlow, I would lose my fucking mind. Scorch the Earth and burn all the motherfuckers responsible.

Tense silence filters through the air until Lo extracts her cell. "Sar wouldn't want us moping." She looks at Sean. "She would kick our asses if she saw us right now." Sean nods, and there's a hint of a smile on his mouth. Lo glances at Theo. "There's a loudspeaker in Sar's room. Would you grab it?"

"I'll get it," Sean says, standing. "And you're right. Sar would hate this. Let's get fucking drunk and dance and remember how fucking amazing she was, because she was a girl in a million." He hangs his head as emotion threads through his words, and I share a look with the guys.

I know we are all thinking the same thing and feeling guilty for our selfish thoughts.

Sean comes back with the speaker, and Lo hooks up her cell, playing one of her and Sariah's playlists, and we hang back, swapping stories about Sariah over a few beers.

Day turns to night, and Lorna joins us when the rest of the oldies have gone home. Lo sings along to Sariah's favorite songs, her eyes glistening with unshed tears. Theo takes my place when I need to go inside for a piss, and I seize the opportunity to grab some water, handing the bottle and a few pain pills to Galen. He's quiet, not complaining, but the sweat beads on his brow attest to his pain. His ribs were already fucked before they took another battering, so it's obvious he's hurting.

I'm just about to suggest we head home when my cell vibrates in my pocket. I pull it out and read the text message from one of the junior chapter members.

"We've got to go," I say, repocketing my phone.

"What is it?" Lo asks as Theo gently lifts her off his lap.

I lower my voice so none of the others hear. "Taylor's been found. The guys are holding her for us."

For the first time all day, the veil of sadness lifts from Lo. Her jaw tenses as her eyes glimmer with determination. "Let's do this." She grabs Theo's hands. "It's time to take that bitch down."

Chapter Three
Harlow

We pull up to an enclosed property in Prestwick, and Saint kills the lights as we approach the high iron gate. Putting the engine in park, he extracts his cell and taps out a message.

"Why aren't we going to the warehouse at Landing's Lane?" I ask, because I was told it was their main interrogation place, and I presumed that was where we were headed.

"It's too open after the fight," Saint shares as the gates creak open. He puts the car into gear, and we move forward. "That place is retired now."

I don't say another word as we drive over the bumpy road toward the large brick warehouse in the near distance. I know The Sainthood has a number of secret warehouses scattered about and that all the locations are a heavily guarded secret.

Saint drives his Land Rover around the back of the struc-ture, parking it to the right of the door. Theo helps me out of the car, pressing a kiss to my temple when he puts my feet on the ground. I wrap my arms around his neck, pulling him to me, needing his familiar smell and the feel of his toned body against mine, to ground me.

Today has been one of the worst days of my life, and it's not over yet. The few beers I inhaled back at Sariah's house have taken the edge off my heightened emotions, but I'm still tense, still feeling out of sorts, grappling with the multitude of emotions flooding my system as I struggle to deal with the loss of my best friend. I'm trying to numb myself to feeling, but it's not as easy as it used to be, because I'm no longer desensitized.

Opening my heart to the guys has lowered my resistance, and I'm feeling far too much. I can't function like this, and I desperately need to lose myself in my guys to remember who I am. To remind myself why life has to go on even though I will never forget the bubbly blonde who brightened up my world in so many ways.

Sar would hate to see me like this, and I owe it to her to live my best life, but it's all too raw.

I guess this is what true grieving feels like. I've never let myself go there before, and a pang of guilt surges through me as the thought lands in my mind. I'm feeling more today than I did the day of my dad's funeral, and it makes me feel like I let him down. Like I should have let it in more, because Dad meant the world to me, and it feels wrong now that I was so closed off to my emotions that day.

Theo hugs me to him, and I cling to his warmth and his comfort like he's my favorite blanket. "You're going to be okay, beautiful," he whispers, threading his fingers in my hair. "We will be with you every step of the way."

"I hate feeling like this," I whisper, conscious the other guys have stalled by the door, waiting for us. "It feels like I'm losing myself."

He places his mouth on mine, kissing me sweetly before pulling back and clasping both sides of my face. "We will never let that happen. We'll never let you forget." He kisses me again. "I love you, Lo." He presses his forehead to mine. "And I'm never letting you go. Never."

"I love you too," I murmur, gripping his toned waist. "I love all of you," I admit out loud for the first time.

"Have you told them?" he asks, easing his head back from mine.

"Not yet, but I will." My own sense of mortality is screaming at me. I came so fucking close to death, and I'm not out of the woods yet. If my time should come, I want to leave this world with no regrets and I want my guys to know how much they mean to me.

I shuck out of Theo's embrace, pushing those sentiments aside for the time being. We are here to teach this bitch a lesson, and it can't wait.

Saint nods as I approach with Theo at my side, and I return the gesture. The guys have scarcely taken their eyes off me all day. I see the concern in their eyes, and it warms all the frozen parts of me, but I need to remind them—and me—that I'm not some broken shell of a girl.

I'm Harlow fucking Westbrook.

Survivor.

Queen.

Some two-bit ho isn't getting the better of me.

We step into the warehouse, and it's a lot like the one at Landing's Lane. This level is empty save for a few bikes parked haphazardly in one corner and a couple long tables at the far end. A few crates rest on top of the tables, and an unfamiliar guy with a bushy gray beard and an overhanging belly slouches against the wall, smoking a cigarette. Saint and Galen head in his direction, and he straightens up, tossing his cig to the floor, stomping on it with his dirty boot.

"Who found the bitch?" I ask.

"One of our snitches," Caz confirms. "She put up one hell of a fight, and it took three of them to get her into the van."

Pulling up the side of my dress, I unstrap my Strider from its sheath, enjoying the feel of the cool blade under the palm of my hand. "It will only require one of me to take her down," I say, flashing Caz a steely grin.

"You don't have to do this," Theo says.

I lock eyes with him. "I know. But I want to."

His features soften, and I see nothing but love and concern shining in his eyes, but this shit ends now. "I'm not going to break, guys. I'm stronger than this. Today's been hell, but I'm not some fragile little doll you need to handle with kid gloves."

"We know that, babe," Caz says.

"Then stop looking at me like I'm about to fall apart!" I snap. "It's fucking insulting."

He chuckles. "Sharpen those claws, princess, and channel them in the right direction."

I flip my blade over and over in my hand, keeping one eye on Saint and Galen as they talk to the dude with the beard. "I don't need a pep talk. I know exactly where to channel my rage."

Sounds of approaching footfalls end our conversation.

"Let's go," Saint says, walking past us toward the other end of the building.

"You hanging in there?" I ask Galen, falling back to walk alongside him. Truth is, the guy looks like shit. We have similar injuries, but his are more serious, and he was already nursing a few broken ribs before the explosion. Sweat plasters his flattened hair to his brow, and his eyes are red-rimmed and bloodshot. He's bent over as he walks, his shoulder supported in a sling, and he's holding his upper torso with his free arm, as if he's holding himself together.

"I'm okay. Took a couple pills back at the house, so the pain is easing up. I just want to get this over and done with so we can crash at the barn."

"Amen to that."

"How do you want to play this?" he asks, as we step through the single door, following the guys down a flight of stairs to the basement level.

"We inflict pain to get the answers we need, and then we gut the bitch."

A muscle clenches in his jaw as he nods. "I'm down with that plan."

The others are waiting at the bottom of the stairs in front of the closed door. "This is your show," Saint says. "But if you aren't up to it, just say the word."

"We're up for it," I hiss, unfairly taking my pissy mood out on him. "And you can all quit with the babying." I push past them with Caz's deep chuckle following me as I yank the door open and enter the basement.

Lights are low down here, and the space is largely empty except for a few chairs, a long steel gurney, and a table that houses a myriad of weapons and instruments of torture. Another older guy, with a neater, shorter beard, wearing one of The Sainthood's leather cuts, stands guard at the side of the room.

I stalk across the concrete floor, eyes blazing as I glare at the petite blonde strapped to the chair in the middle of the room. Taylor's hands are tied behind her back around the chair, and her ankles are securely fastened to the legs of the chair. A trickle of blood seeps from a gash on her forehead, and there's dried blood on a cut on her lip. Her long hair hangs in stringy, matted strands around her heart-shaped face as she tips her chin up to glare at me. Her nostrils flare, and her eyes burn with hatred as I approach.

Lifting my leg, I ram it into her stomach, pushing her to the floor with a loud thud.

Not gonna lie, that maneuver has me sweating bullets as pain rips across my torso, my body protesting the motion. But fury trumps pain, and I straddle her chest, locking my hands around her neck and squeezing. I don't want to kill her, at least not yet, but I do want to set the tone for this meeting.

"Fucking...slut," she rasps, her eyes burning a hole in my head as she glares at me.

I tighten my hands around her throat, digging my nails into her flesh and drawing blood. "You're not in any position to throw shade," I say, smiling as tears leak involuntarily from her eyes and a bluish tinge appears on her skin. A gargled sound erupts from her throat, and I remove my hands from her neck before I accidentally kill her. This bitch isn't dying before we get to the truth.

Caz extends his arm, and I take his hand, letting him help me to my feet.

Saint grabs a fistful of Taylor's hair, yanking her off the floor. She screams in pain as he uses her hair to pull her body, and the chair, into an upright position. When he lets go, long strands of her hair are wrapped around his fingers. He wipes his hands like they're diseased, until all the hairs are gone, and I smirk.

Galen and I stand in front of her with the others at our back. "Here's how it's going to go." I flip my knife repeatedly in my palm. "We're going to ask you questions, and you're going to answer. If you refuse, I'll cut you. If you continue disobeying, I'll kill you." I lean down into her face, ignoring the sharp stab of pain in my ribs. "Trust me, it won't take much to push me there."

She spits in my face, and I slap her hard a few times on each cheek, relishing the way her head whips back. I step aside, taking the tissue Theo offers me, using it to wipe her disgusting spittle from my face. "You're already trying my patience, and that doesn't bode well for you."

"Like I give a crap, whore!"

I punch her square on the nose this time, and she roars as blood gushes from her nostrils.

"I'm guessing you give a crap about your little sister, so, unless you want her to join your other sister in the ground, I suggest you lose the attitude and get with the program."

"Don't you fucking touch her, you cunt!"

"That's it," Saint snaps, pushing past me. "I've had enough of her disrespect."

He grabs her chin, forcing her head back at an awkward angle. "You talk to our girl like that one more time and I'll cut your cunt into tiny pieces and feed it to you one piece at a time."

"Come on, Taylor. I thought you were smarter than this," Galen says, shaking his head in disgust.

Saint glares at her one final time before dropping her chin.

"I'll tell you what you want to know if you promise you won't touch my sister," she spits out. "She's innocent in all this."

"Agreed," I say, because I had no intention of doing anything to her sister. "But if you double-cross us, all bets are off."

She nods, and her eyes betray her resignation. Perhaps she is smart.

"Who ordered the hit on us?" I ask, leaning against Saint when he presses up against my back.

Her lips curve into a smug grin. "No one. I did that all by myself."

Galen scoffs, rolling his eyes. "We heard you were smart, but you're as dumb as a bag of hammers."

"I'm telling the truth," she yells. "I came after you for Parker." She drills me with a poisonous look. "You killed my sister, and I wanted revenge."

"She tried to kill me first, and it was self-defense."

"I don't fucking care! It wasn't enough to kill her. You had to set her on fire and try to frame The Bulls for her murder. Do you have any idea what that did to my father?"

"Do we look like we give two shits about your father?" Galen coolly replies.

"And if you think we're buying this bullshit, you're sorely mistaken." I purposely look over at Theo. "Pull up the girl's location. I think we'll be paying little sis a visit after all."

"No!" Taylor shrieks, panic entering her tone. "I swear I did this alone."

I lean down into her face. "Liar," I hiss.

She sighs, squeezing her eyes shut for a split second. "Look, it was me and my dad, okay? The club had nothing to do with it."

"So, Ruben wasn't coming after me because I killed Luke McKenzie?" I probe.

"Yes. He wanted you dead for that, and that stupid asshole Corr was supposed to take care of you at the training facility, but that was before Ruben was arrested and the club came under new leadership. The order went out that you weren't to be touched, forcing us to take matters into our own hands."

My eyes meet Galen's as I try to work out if she's telling us the truth or not. His gaze suggests he's as suspicious as I am.

"If you wanted revenge for your sister's murder, why target the guys?" I ask.

"They weren't innocent either. They used Parker's intel to burn the drug house down, and then they tossed her aside like she hadn't helped them."

"Parker was a conniving cunt who was playing every

angle," Galen says. "She turned up at the fight on the losing side. That was her choice, not ours."

"It doesn't fucking matter!" she shouts, nostrils flaring again. The chair screeches as she squirms on the seat, her arms straining in obvious pain. "You dragged her into this mess in the first place."

"Wrong, bitch." Caz grabs her by the throat. "That honor was Finn's. He used her as his lackey. He was the one who put her in harm's way. Your anger is misplaced."

"Don't worry. I was gunning for him next."

"You know where he is?"

She shakes her head. "Pussy took off with his number two. Dad's trying to find them, but so far, they're hiding under a rock."

She reached the same conclusion we did that Finn and Brooklyn took off because they know they have fucked up and made enemies on all sides.

"Were you behind the shootout at the diner?" I ask, moving on to the next topic.

"Yes, but I should've just done it myself. Those assholes couldn't do anything right."

"You were at the party at Galen's during spring break," I continue. "Why?"

"Ruben asked me to broker an arrangement between The Arrows and The Bulls."

"So, Tempest *was* the conduit?"

She laughs. "Oh, please. That trailer-trash dumb bitch couldn't fucking sell oil to the Arabs. She helped me get close to Darrow Knight, and that's about as useful as she was."

A throbbing pain in my temples has me swaying a little on my feet, and Saint slides his arm around me, keeping me steady.

Taylor laughs. "Having trouble standing, Harlow?"

Galen darts forward, slapping her viciously. A flash of pain races across his face, and I know that cost him. "You're lucky you're still breathing, cunt. Don't push your luck."

She spits out a mouthful of blood, sending daggers in all our directions. "I've answered your questions. Now let me go."

We burst out laughing, angering her further. She hisses, narrowing her eyes, and the chair wobbles as she struggles against her restraints to no avail.

I slip out of Saint's hold, putting my face all up in hers. "Who the fuck said anything about letting you go? The deal was we wouldn't go after your little sister, and we'll stick to our word."

"Just kill me already then," she snaps. "Put a bullet in my skull and be done with it."

That had been the original plan, but now I'm rethinking things. I straighten up, smoothing a hand down over my hair. "Nah." I shake my head. "There's no fun in that." Honestly, if I wasn't so dead on my feet, I would gladly stay here and torture the bitch for a couple hours, but I'm barely keeping my eyes open, and Galen is about to conk out, so we'll have to put it on ice.

"You!" I click my fingers at the guy hanging by the wall. He's been watching the whole thing go down, but he hasn't interfered, letting us handle our shit, like a good little soldier.

He walks to my side. "Ms. Tamlin needs to be reminded why the Saints are not to be messed with. Be creative in relaying the message, but I want her alive." I grin maliciously at her. "We'll be back to finish up in the morning."

The bearded dude infuriates me when he casts a glance over my shoulder, looking to Saint to rubber stamp my decision.

My asshole doesn't let me down though, storming over to the guy, grabbing him by the throat and shoving him into the wall. We walk toward them. "Did my girl not speak clearly enough?" Saint's eyes rip through the older dude, and he shoves him a couple more times before letting him go.

"Understood, Saint, and it'll be handled."

"Don't tell me," Saint snaps, cracking his knuckles like he'd love to ram his fist in the jerk's face. "Tell Harlow."

"And while you're at it," Galen adds, coming up on my other side. "You can apologize for disrespecting her."

"I'm sorry, Harlow," the guy says, his cheeks reddening in anger. "You can trust me to carry out your command."

Taylor laughs, claiming our attention. "Da fuck? You must have some magical pussy, slut. This shit has to be seen to be believed."

Caz punches her in the face. "What the fuck were you told about spouting that shit?"

But she doesn't respond, because she's out cold, and we exit the warehouse, all of us more than ready to head home.

Chapter Four
Harlow

"What do we do with her?" Theo asks, when we reach the guy's barn a half hour later. Someone switched the heating on while we were en route, and it's toasty warm as we trudge inside. We are all beat and ready to hit the sack.

"Princess." Saint tosses his keys on the kitchen counter, scrubbing at his prickly jaw. "Your call."

"I don't know," I truthfully admit. "And my brain's too tired right now. Let me sleep on it."

"Sounds like a plan," Saint agrees.

"You two head upstairs," Theo says, gesturing toward me and Galen. "We'll grab some supplies and follow you up."

Galen and I drag our weary bodies up the left-side stairs, gawking at the new addition to the first bedroom. The new bed Theo had delivered is a monster that stretches from one side of the room to the other. It would probably sleep eight, so there's more than enough room for all of us, but I'm a little worried about an elbow to the ribs during the night, and it seems Galen is on my wavelength.

"I can't wait to test that bed out," he says, shooting me a wicked smile. "But I'm likely to kill one of those motherfuckers if they touch me during the night."

"It can wait," I agree, taking his hand and pulling him into the second bedroom where a comfy king-sized bed awaits us. "We'll sleep in here tonight." I help Galen get undressed first before changing into my sleep shorts and flimsy tank. Then I brush my teeth, comb my hair, pulling it back into a ponytail, and climb into bed beside him.

Saint and Theo appear in the room, carrying a tray loaded with bottles of water, pain meds, additional bandages, and a bowl filled with chopped fruit. "Thanks," I whisper as Theo sets it down on my bedside table, conscious of the soft snores rumbling from Galen's chest. He's already out for the count, and it won't take long for me to follow him to the Land of Nod.

I lean up on my elbows because the movement isn't as jarring on my sore ribs, dutifully opening my mouth for Theo to pop a couple pills in. He brings a bottle of water to my lips, tipping the cold liquid into my mouth, washing the pills down. Then Saint feeds me some of the fruit, and I smile at both my guys, my heart swelling with their tender care of me. They each drop soft kisses on my lips, and I could get used to them looking after me.

Caz appears behind them, dressed in a pair of gray sweats that hang loose off his hips, highlighting the defined V-indents I love so much. Saint and Theo pull back, letting Caz in closer. He leans down, planting a firm kiss on my lips. "Liking what you see, babe?" he teases, rubbing his nose against mine.

"Always, dude. Never doubt that," I say over a yawn.

"Sleep, princess." Caz tucks the covers around me. "Sweet dreams." He blows me a kiss as my eyelids flutter, and I'm vaguely aware of them tiptoeing out of the room before my mind shuts down.

I wake the following morning groaning as pain slices my head in two and spears through my ribs. It feels like I'm burning from the inside out, and I hate feeling so weak. Galen is still asleep, his face contorted in pain even in slumber. I press a soft kiss to his cheek before hauling my aching body out of bed and into the shower.

The cool water is a welcome balm to my overheated skin, and I feel a lot better after I've dried, freshened up, and changed into fresh pajamas.

Poking my head over the railing in the bedroom, I look down at the main level, but it's deathly quiet downstairs. The others are obviously still sleeping. I sneak a peek at the bedroom next door, smothering a giggle when I find Saint stretched out in the big bed all by himself. I'm guessing the other two slept in their bedrooms across the other side of the barn.

"What's so funny?" Galen asks from behind me, his voice deep, and I turn to find him blinking his eyes and yawning.

"Your cousin is spread-eagled across the big bed, looking like all his wet dreams have come to life," I joke as I slide back under the covers. I grab a bottle of water and the pill bottle, swallowing a couple before offering them to my bed buddy.

"He probably spent half the night imagining all the dirty shit he wants to do to you in that bed," Galen says before knocking back his meds.

"Speaking of dirty shit." I move my hand under the covers, placing it on top of his cock. He is hard beneath his boxers. "You want me to take care of that for you?"

"Aren't you sore?" he asks, but he can't disguise the hungry look in his eyes.

"Yep, but I can manage," I reply, stroking him through his boxers. The honest truth is I need this with him, with all of them, to help me feel like myself. And we could all use the distraction. Sex is one of my go-to coping mechanisms, and a mild concussion and a few bruised ribs won't stop me from getting my rocks off.

Galen's eyes roll back in his head when my fingers slip under the band of his boxers, meeting his soft velvety flesh. I give him a few quick pumps before withdrawing my hand and pulling the covers aside along with his boxers. "I won't be able to blow you because it hurts too much to bend over, but I can give you a hand job." I'd love to ride him, but it's out of the question because we're both too injured, which fucking sucks.

"We can sixty-nine," he suggests.

"Or I can take care of our girl while she takes care of you," Saint says, drawing both our gazes to where he stands, buck-ass naked, in the doorway between the two bedrooms.

I look at Galen, and he nods. I smile at Saint. "Get your sexy butt over here."

Saint saunters toward the bed, his erect cock jutting proudly from his hot body, licking his lips and devouring me with his eyes. "Lose the clothes, princess," he demands, placing one knee on the bed and leaning down to kiss me. My mouth opens for him, welcoming his greedy tongue, and I whimper into his gorgeous mouth as he stokes my arousal to dizzy heights in no time. Desire pools low in my belly, and I groan when Saint nips at my lower lip as Galen runs his fingers up and down the exposed skin on my arm.

Saint helps to remove my top, flinging it on the floor as I lean down to kiss Galen, while his cousin drags my sleep shorts and panties down my legs. Galen ravishes my mouth, his urgent need for me matching the growing heat building between my legs. We settle our heads on pillows, angling our faces so we can kiss as my fingers wind around his wide girth and I begin stroking him again.

"That's it, princess," Saint purrs as he spreads my legs.

"Pump his cock. Rub your thumb over the tip," he commands, and I break away from Galen's lips to watch my thumb dragging along the glistening precum resting on the crown of his cock.

"Fuck." Galen drags out the word, softly jerking his hips up as my hand glides up and down his hard length.

Saint is sweeping his fingers up and down my legs, getting close to the apex of my thighs.

"Agh." I cry out the second Saint's fingers slide inside me and his hot tongue flattens against my clit.

"That feel good, angel?" Galen asks, tilting my face around to his as his fingers knead my breast.

"So damn good," I rasp, crashing my mouth down on his as I kiss him with everything I'm feeling.

I quicken my pace, pumping Galen in long, fast, measured strokes until he's moaning into my mouth, yanking fistfuls of my hair, rolling my nipples between his fingers, and bucking into my hand. "I'm going to come, angel. Don't stop, babe. Keep going, just like that."

Saint curls his fingers inside me, hitting just the right spot, and I cry out as I feel my climax building in intensity.

I rip my lips from Galen's, working his shaft harder, and all three of us watch as his balls lift, and he blows his load, spraying ropes of salty cum across his toned abs and over the sheets, coating my fingers in the sticky substance. Galen flops back on the bed, grabbing my face and kissing the shit out of me, as Saint continues working me over from between my legs.

When I cry out into Galen's mouth and my hips arch, almost lifting off the bed, Galen releases my lips, caressing my face as he urges me to come. "That's it, angel. Come all over Saintly's face."

"Come for me, dirty girl," Saint croons, his voice thick with lust. "Ride my face. Take what you need."

I explode all over his face and his filthy mouth, screaming as the most intense orgasm lays claim to my body. My ribs are burning as I writhe on the bed, but I barely feel the pain over the waves of heavenly pleasure shooting through me.

"Damn, you are the hottest thing I've ever seen," Galen admits. "I can't fuck you, but my cousin can."

I open my eyes, staring at Galen as he stares at Saint.

"What do you say, princess?" Saint asks, climbing up the bed and biting my earlobe as his hands move to my bare chest. "You want me to fuck you, dirty girl?" He fondles my breasts while planting hot openmouthed kisses all over my neck.

"Hell, yeah."

Needing no further encouragement, he carefully slides me down the bed until my legs dangle off the edge. He nudges my legs apart, lining his straining cock against my entrance.

"Fuck me, Saintly," I demand, reaching my hand up to his chest. "No treating me like I'm a doll. Fuck me hard and fast. Make me soar to the stars."

"Your wish is my command, princess," he says, slamming into me in one rough thrust.

I scream, and there is no way Caz and Theo aren't awake now.

Saint pounds into me like a madman, holding my legs around his hips as he takes possession of me. Behind me, Galen's grunts claim my attention, and I watch as he repositions himself lower on the bed so he can kiss and touch me. His hand is stroking his cock as he plays with my tits, pinching my taut nipples, sending pleasure-pain sensations rippling all over my body.

Galen jerks himself off as Saint fucks me, both roaming their hands over my body until we're all damp with sweat, our skin flushed from exertion, close to the edge.

"You close?" Saint asks Galen, and he nods.

"Angel?" Galen sucks my lower lip into his mouth.

"I'm almost there," I rasp, moaning as Saint shoves harder and faster inside me. He drops one of my legs, using his free hand to vigorously rub at my clit, and I'm scaling the mountain faster and faster.

We come together, moaning and writhing, as we all milk our pleasure until we're sated.

Saint collapses on my other side, curling his long, hot body around me as Galen kisses me softly.

"Hmm." A dreamy smile ghosts over my mouth, and my gaze flits between both guys. I caress their faces at the same time, gently cupping their cheeks. "I dreamed of a Lennox sandwich so many fucking times, but nothing compares with reality."

Saint's lips lift in a smug grin as Galen buries his nose in my neck.

"Get used to it, princess." Saint brushes his fingers against my hip. "Because that definitely won't be your last Lennox tag-team fuck."

Chapter Five
Harlow

"Have you decided what to do with the slut?" Saint asks an hour later when we are all seated at the dining table. Caz and Theo set plates piled high with eggs, bacon, hash browns, and toast in the middle of the table, and the guys descend like vultures who haven't been fed for a week.

"I have a plan," I say as Theo sits beside me, scooping up food and depositing it on my plate. I smile, kissing his cheek as Caz distributes mugs of steaming-hot coffee. Angling my head back, I offer him my mouth, and he drops a quick kiss on my lips.

Saint clears his throat, because he's an impatient fuck, and I toss him a smirk. "We should let her go," I say, savagely biting into a piece of crispy bacon.

"Why the fuck would we do that?" Galen stares at me like I've lost my mind.

"Because this vendetta her family has against us must end now. We have bigger fish to fry, and the Tamlins will only distract us."

"I agree with Lo," Theo says.

Caz snorts. "Course you do."

"What the fuck does that mean?"

"It means you can't say no to her." Caz holds up his palms. "Don't shoot the messenger for telling the truth."

"If I don't disagree with Lo much, it's because she usually speaks the truth and her decisions are always solid. That's the reason, asshole, not because I'm trying to suck up, if that's what you're implying."

"Wow, dude. You're making a big fucking deal out of nothing. It was just an observation."

"Well, it's a fucking wrong observation," Theo barks, and I look between the two of them wondering what the actual fuck is going on.

Has something happened I don't know about?

Saint clears his throat again. "You two pussies done snarking at each other?"

A muscle clenches in Theo's jaw, and I slide my hand under the table, placing it on his thigh. He flinches, and I stare at him, silently asking the question. He grips my hand as I move to pull away, linking his fingers in mine.

"You sure about this?" Saint asks me, pretending like the atmosphere isn't thick with tension.

"No, but it's the smart way to play it."

Honestly, I want to go nuclear on that bitch's ass. She tried to murder us, and she deserves to die. But if we take her out, her daddy will come after us with everything he's got. We're currently weakened with Galen and me injured. Plus, I still have my initiation tasks to deal with, along with discovering the identity of the mole within The Sainthood. We're hoping the mole can help us uncover the evidence we need to put Sinner and the board away for the kidnapping and murder of Daphne Leydon, the police commissioner's wife, a woman who was also the niece of the current US president. And I'd really like to stop Saint's dad before he marries my mom.

Those are our priorities—not that vengeful bitch.

"We have enough on our plate right now," I add.

"And it doesn't mean we can't come after her later for payback," Saint suggests, onboard with the plan.

"I think we knock her about a bit and then return her to her daddy with a warning," I say, squeezing Theo's hand. He's here, listening to the conversation happening around him, but not really here. I cast a quick glance at Caz, and he looks pissed. Something has definitely happened, and I need to get to the bottom of it.

"I say we go one step further," Galen adds, swallowing his last mouthful of eggs. He's ditched the sling, and he's wincing every time he lifts the damn fork to his mouth, but I don't bother calling him out on it, because he's stubborn as fuck and he won't listen to a word I say. "We'll call the new president of The Bulls and tell him what they tried to pull. Let him dole out punishment."

I nod, liking that plan more.

A beeping sound echoes from the wall-mounted panel by the door, claiming our attention. "What's that?" I ask as the guys trade wary expressions.

Theo is already on his cell, stabbing buttons. "What the fuck?" he mumbles, his eyes darting to mine.

"What is it?"

"It's your mom," Theo replies. "She's at the front gate."

"My mom is here?" My jaw slackens.

Saint straightens in his chair. "How da fuck does she know about our place?"

"I haven't told her."

"We know, angel." Galen rushes to reassure me so I know they aren't accusing me.

"Maybe your dad told her," I suggest.

Saint shakes his head. "He doesn't know the location. He must know we have our own place, but he's never asked, and I've never offered."

"That doesn't mean he doesn't know," I say, watching Theo text Mom the code for the gate.

"I guess we're about to find out." Caz stands, heading toward the kitchen.

I climb awkwardly to my feet, walking out with Saint to greet her.

"You okay with this?" he asks as we wait outside for Mom's car to appear.

"It's not like I have much choice."

"You still don't trust her."

"Do you?" I peer into his blue eyes, seeing my answer there. "Exactly. I don't like this. This is your safe place. Your sanctuary. I hate she knows where it is."

"It makes me wonder what else she knows." Saint folds his arms across his impressive chest.

"Yeah, me too." My brows pucker. *What the hell is Mom playing at?*

"You're still worried about her," Saint adds, and it's a statement, not a question.

I give him a terse nod. Mom has disappointed me so much these past couple of months, and I've lost faith in her, but that doesn't mean I want anything bad to happen to her. I don't know what her motives are, but Sinner's are pretty clear—he wants to punish both of us for what he perceives to be a betrayal. No matter what has happened between us, she's still my mother, and I can't let him hurt her, because it's the right thing to do and because my father trusted me to keep Mom safe.

"I've been getting daily reports from the guy I have at the

house." Saint shoves his hands in the back pockets of his jeans. I forgot he'd hired a guy he knows and trusts from within The Sainthood ranks to do "odd jobs" around the house, under the guise of keeping an eye on Mom. "Sinner hasn't been around a lot, but when he has shown up, he's pissed, and that's never a good thing."

"I know. I'm scared he's going to kill her." The asshole is deranged and depraved enough to do it even though he claims to love her.

"We won't let that happen, and Giana is stronger than you give her credit for," he says as Mom's car rounds the bend, heading our way.

"Maybe." I'm being noncommittal on purpose. Lately, Sinner's been beating her up and doing nothing to disguise it, which worries me, along with the fact Mom appears to be letting it happen. That doesn't instill confidence.

I step forward as Mom parks in front of the barn and kills the engine. She hops out, making a beeline for me. "You shouldn't be outside, Harlow," she chastises me, gently pulling me into her arms. "You should be resting."

"Why are you here, Mom?" I ignore her so-called concern.

"I want to make sure you and Galen are all right."

"You couldn't just call?"

Hurt skates across her face, and I feel like a bitch. Until I remember all the lies she's telling me, and my tinge of remorse evaporates.

"I know you think I don't care, Harlow, but that couldn't be further from the truth."

Yeah. Whatever. She barely even visited me in the hospital from what the guys have said.

"Let's talk inside." Saint scans the grounds with suspicious eyes before he opens the door, gesturing her inside.

"I came alone," she volunteers, sliding past him into the barn.

Saint plants his hand on my lower back as we follow her inside, closing the door behind us.

"Wow. I love what you've done with the place." Mom looks around, smiling widely until her eyes land on the framed posters of nude chicks on the walls. She hastily looks away, and Saint and I share an amused grin.

It reminds me of something I had planned, and I make a mental note to follow up on it.

"Coffee, Giana?" Theo asks, handing her a mug as Caz comes up on my other side, grasping my hand.

"Thank you, Theo." She smiles before spotting Galen leaning against the edge of the table, and it fades from her face as concern replaces it. "Galen. You should be in bed too." She clucks her tongue at him.

"Don't worry," Caz says. "Harlow and Galen got plenty of rest in bed, among other things," he adds, under his breath, and I elbow him in the ribs.

"No sex for you for a month," I hiss in his ear. He pins me with a horrified look, and a burst of laughter pushes up my throat. "I'm joking," I whisper. "Kind of."

"Don't torture me like that," he whispers back as I watch Mom quizzing Galen out of the corner of my eye.

"Why don't we sit in the living room and talk?" Mom suggests, circling her arm around Galen and herding him forward.

"She did come here for a reason," I murmur. Caz keeps a firm hold of my hand, leading me over to the couch.

I sit beside Caz and Saint while Mom sits on the other couch with Galen and Theo takes the chair. "Why are you really here?" I inquire, watching her knotting her hands in her lap and chewing on her lip with growing trepidation. "And how did you know about this place?"

"Don't be mad," she says, "but I followed you here one time." I grind down on my teeth in frustration, and a muscle ticks in my jaw.

I'm calling bullshit on that.

There is no way she tailed us here without us knowing. The guys are way too smart for that, and I've never come here alone. She didn't put a tracker on us either, because we've been checking daily.

Why the fuck does she keep on lying? I could call her out, but she'll just deny it, so what's the point in even going there. I don't believe a word that comes out of her mouth anymore.

"I knew the guys must have another place as they didn't always stay at the house," she continues, pretending she doesn't feel the wave of hostility emanating her way. "I wanted to ensure you were safe and resting up."

"Did you tell him?" Saint asks.

She shakes her head. "I didn't see the need to."

Well, that's reassuring. *Not.*

"I'd prefer it's kept that way," Saint says, placing a warning hand on my knee. He can tell I'm seconds from implosion.

"I'm betting Neo already knows," Mom replies. "There isn't much that gets past him."

Which is pretty much the conclusion we've already drawn. But I'm sure she didn't come here to talk about the barn. "What is it, Mom? Just tell us."

"I know what he expects of you, Harlow." Her pained eyes meet mine, and I can't work out if she means his plans to gang-rape me with his buddies and call it initiation or that he wants me to assassinate the commissioner.

"Which is?" I prompt.

She twists her hands in her lap. "I know he wants to fuck you. He taunted me with it last night." She raises a shaky hand, pulling it through her hair, and her long-sleeved blouse moves down her arm a little, revealing heavy bruising around her wrists.

Acid crawls up my throat. "He hurt you again." I glare at Saint. So much for his spy. This is what I was afraid of.

Her cheeks flush red, and she waves her hands about. "It's nothing, Lo."

"Just more rough sex, huh?" I bite out, because I'm getting sick of her dismissing his treatment of her. Fuck. I can't deal with this today. My emotions are veering all over the place, and I can't handle it.

"Harlow." Her tone brooks no argument.

"Say what you came to say, Mother," I snap. "You're pissing me off now."

"I'd like you to get out of town for a while. Just until he calms down and I can find a way to keep him away from you."

Saint and Galen lock eyes, and my curious gaze bounces between them.

"You don't need to worry about that," Galen says. "We have a way to ensure that doesn't happen."

"You do?" I blurt, because this is news to me. From the expression on Caz's and Theo's faces, it's the first they're hearing of this too.

"We'll discuss it later," Saint says in that commanding tone he likes to use.

Mom's shoulders visibly relax. "I knew I could trust you boys to take care of my daughter."

"Lo doesn't need us to take care of her," Theo says. "She's very capable without our interference."

"That I know as well." Mom's smile is tinged with sadness. "Lo's had to grow up way too fast."

"Why are you with him, Mom? Please tell me." I've asked her before, and she usually deflects.

She tilts her chin up, and all hint of sadness disappears, replaced with a steadfast confidence Mom used to always convey. "Don't go there again, Harlow. As much as I want to give you answers, I can't. Just trust that I know what I'm doing, and don't worry about me. Focus on looking after yourself."

That is the closest she has come to telling me she's working some angle. The conversation I had with Saint and Theo in my closet returns to the forefront of my mind, and I drop the subject even though I'm tempted to push her buttons to try to get her to open up. The guys are right. If Mom has an agenda, she's keeping me out of it for a reason. I've got to let it go and concentrate on dealing with my own shit.

"Okay, Mom. I won't ask you again." My tone is devoid of emotion because I'm so done with this.

Her shoulders relax again. "I'd still like you to get out of town. Neo is unpredictable right now, and I want you out of his crosshairs. He's furious someone tried to take you all out, and he's seething that The Arrows ambushed his delivery. Who knows what he'll do when he's like this. I've never seen him so angry. It would give me peace of mind to know he can't vent that anger in your direction. Staying here is too risky, but he doesn't know about your father's cabin. Go there for a few days."

My mouth hangs open, and I stare at my mom in complete shock. "You know about it?"

"There's a lot I knew that your father wasn't aware of," she cryptically replies, standing. "And don't ask, Harlow. You agreed."

I absently nod, thrown for a loop. I want to ask her if she knows it was Sinner who kidnapped and tortured me, but I'm also afraid to ask, because if she confirms it, I have no idea how I'll stop myself from murdering her with my bare hands.

"Have you contacted the school?" Saint asks. "Or do you need us to cover it?"

"I've spoken with Vice Principal Pierson. It's handled." She stands in front of me. "Walk me out, darling?"

Caz helps me to stand, and I follow Mom outside.

"I'm so sorry about Sariah, Harlow." She holds my face in her palms. "I know how close you two were."

I gulp over the fresh lump in my throat, beseeching Mom to drop it.

She nods briefly before clearing her throat. She releases my face, clasping my hands in hers. "I know I'm asking a lot, but I need you to trust me and believe me when I say you are the most important thing in my life. Everything I have done is to protect you. I almost lost you too." Tears well in her eyes. "I nearly died when Saint called me." Tears stream down her face. "This is not the life I wanted for you, and I can't stand by while others try to harm you."

"It's okay, Mom. We know who's responsible, and we're dealing with it." Although, I'm far from safe, but articulating that point won't help either of us.

"I'm so proud of you, Harlow." Her eyes shine with the truth of her words. "You never stop fighting, no matter how many times life tries to drag you down. I always thought you were more like your father, but I think there's more of me in you than I realized, but you're stronger than we were at your age."

"Was it real, Mom? Did you really love Dad?"

"Oh, honey." More tears pool in her eyes. "Trey Westbrook was the love of my life, and I loved him with my whole heart and soul. I miss him so much."

Tears gather in my eyes. "Me too. He was the best dad."

"He was, darling, and he loved you so much. He was incredibly proud of you." She kisses the top of my head, and we stand there, without speaking, both lost in our heads, but it's not awkward, and the burst of angry frustration I was feeling inside dies out. I didn't realize how badly I needed to feel Mom's love or how deeply it cut me believing she didn't care enough. I don't understand why she's doing what's she's doing, and I hate she is concealing so much, but I believe her now, and I hope we can find a way to permanently repair our relationship once that bastard is out of the picture.

"Take those boys and get away from this mess for a few days," she says, breaking the silence. "When you return, we'll talk properly." She kisses my brow. "I love you so much, honey. Never doubt that."

"What about you, Mom? Who's going to protect you?"

She tucks my hair behind my ears. "I'm a big girl, Harlow. I know how to take care of myself, and I know the inner workings of Neo's mind. I know how to play him, so don't waste a second worrying about me." She kisses my brow again. "Go. Rest. Eat. Heal. We'll talk when you are back. I promise."

I wait until she has driven out of sight before heading back inside, trying to figure out what the heck just happened.

"She gone?" Saint asks, and I nod.

"I *think* she's on our side." I lower myself on to the couch beside Galen.

"She's definitely working an angle," Saint agrees.

"And she's doing it for you," Theo adds. "That was crystal clear today."

"What's this cabin she mentioned?" Caz asks.

I wet my lips, preparing to eat humble pie. "I was going to tell you about it. It's a cabin that's been in my dad's family for generations. It's where we went once a month to train."

"Wait! Granddad knows about it?" Saint looks seriously unhappy.

I walk over to him, climbing into his lap, ignoring the stab of pain that shoots through my ribs. "Don't do that. Diesel knew about it because it's where we trained. Period."

"Why didn't you tell us?" Theo asks.

I drag my lower lip between my teeth, trying to find the right words to explain it. "The cabin was something Dad and I did together. Our secret, or so we thought. After he died, it became my retreat from the world when things threatened to become too much. I planned to take you there, but we've only recently cleared up our differences, and with everything going on, there hasn't been time."

Saint peers into my eyes, and I let him see the truth. He nods, brushing his thumb against my lower lip, and a relieved sigh escapes my mouth.

"How far away is it?" Theo asks.

"It's about a two-hour drive from here."

Saint lifts me off his lap, placing my feet on the ground as he stands behind me. "So, what are we waiting for? Let's make a move."

Chapter Six
Harlow

We deal with Taylor first, adding a few more cuts and bruises to her pretty face, and I enjoy her anguished screams as I hack off her long blonde hair with my knife, leaving her with short, jagged ends that will take some time to grow back. I want that bitch to look in the mirror every day and be reminded of me and the danger she's placed her family in by coming after us.

After her little makeover, we dump her on her father's doorstep. We make it clear to him that we're letting her live on the understanding they drop their vendetta. Taylor's father is a member of The Bulls, so he understands we've shown leniency, and he's clearly no fool, because he gives us his word that this ends now. Still, we're taking no chances, and Saint makes the call to Marwan, the new Bull's prez, ensuring he's aware of what's gone down.

"What do we do about Sinner?" I ask when we're on the highway, heading toward the cabin.

"We can't tell him the truth because he'll start an all-out war with The Bulls," Theo says.

"Not if we present it as an opportunity to ensure they are kept firmly under his thumb," Saint muses while he drives. "I'll call him from the cabin. Explain how we handled it and why."

"He'll kill her old man," Galen pipes up from the back seat. "His daughter tried to take us out. He'll never let that slide."

"That can't happen," I say. "Taylor will come after us with all guns blazing if her dad dies."

"We need to give Sinner something else to worry about," Caz proposes.

"Maybe we give Darrow something," I say, mulling it over in my head, before it comes to me. I glance over at Saint. "The location of the supplies warehouse."

Deathly silence greets my suggestion.

"It's too risky," Galen says after a few tense beats. "That secret has been kept for generations. Sinner would go postal, and he won't stop until he discovers who leaked that intel. We can't take that chance."

"What if we do this in reverse," Saint suggests, and all eyes dart to him.

"Explain," Theo says.

"We get the location of The Arrows supply warehouse and feed that to Sinner. Give him a project to occupy his mind."

"How?" Caz asks. "That's as well guarded as our warehouse, and if Bryant knew anything, he'd have already told Sinner."

"Valid point," Galen admits. "We need a quick win."

"Has anyone heard from Bry recently? Has he planted the hidden camera in Archer Quinn's office yet?" I ask.

"He's due to update us," Saint says. "I'll call him and see if it's done."

"That could be our best shot. If he can get details of the next Arrows shipment, we could feed that to Sinner and let him have at it."

"I'll make it happen," Saint says. "And I'll call Marwan and tell him to sit tight on the Tamlins so Sinner doesn't hear about it before we're ready to tell him."

"I love it when a plan comes together," Caz says, rubbing his hands in glee. "And I love going on a mini vacay with our sexy princess even more." He pokes his head through the gap in the front seats, pinning me with a shit-eating grin. "Are we nearly there yet?"

We pull up to the cabin, late in the afternoon, after making a pitstop to grab some groceries and beer. Saint jumps out, inputting the code I gave him, and the gates open to grant us entry.

"Wowzers," Caz says as we drive along the road leading to the house. "You own all this land?" His nose is pressed to the glass, and his eyes are out on stilts.

"Yep. It's mine now." Dad left the property to me in his will, although it was only disclosed to me after the main will had been revealed. He thought of everything, and he was still protecting Mom from the grave.

"I noticed the barbed wire and security cameras at the gate," Theo says, looking left and right as we drive past the dense forest that surrounds the land on both sides. "It seems private and secure."

"It is. Dad gave every consideration to my safety. The entire twenty-acre site is enclosed with high walls and barbed wire, and there are numerous cameras everywhere linking to screens in my dad's study. I've spent a lot of time here alone since he died, and I've never felt scared, because if anyone managed to breach the security systems, I would know about it before they made it to the house. He also has a secure panic room in the basement that is impenetrable."

"I vote we hole ourselves up here forever and let Sinner seal his own fate," Caz quips.

"I wish it were that easy." I rest my head against the window, peering across the empty fields into the forest as we draw closer to the cabin.

A few minutes later, Saint pulls the Land Rover to a stop in front of the familiar two-story wooden structure.

Caz whistles under his breath as we climb out of the car. "Nice, babe. Very nice."

I rest my head on his shoulder as Saint and Theo grab our bags from the back. "I love it here. It's so peaceful. When I need to clear my head, I come here."

"I can see why." Galen comes up on my other side.

He's hunched over, in obvious pain, and I press my hand to his brow, frowning at the heat radiating from his flesh. "You need to take more medication and grab some sleep."

He takes my hand, bringing it to his mouth, kissing the back of my knuckles. "If you want to play nurse, you won't hear me complaining."

Caz snorts. "I can guess why."

Galen flips him the bird, smirking. "Jealous, much?"

"Nah." Caz carefully tucks me under his arm. "I'll be the one taking care of our girl tonight."

I was planning on sleeping with Theo so I can ask him what's up, but I won't deny Caz—if he wants me in his bed tonight, he's got it.

"Asshole," Galen mutters as I step up to the cabin and unlock the door.

I walk inside, moving to deactivate the alarm while the others stream through the door. Theo dumps our bags on the floor in the hall while Saint deposits the bags of groceries on the kitchen counter, and Caz and Galen set off exploring. I let the guys wander around by themselves while I unpack the groceries, fire up the Keurig, and make some sandwiches.

"This place is the shit," Caz says, sweeping into the kitchen as I'm plating our food. He wraps his arms around me from behind, nuzzling his nose into my neck. "I already feel right at home here."

"I can't believe you have a game room, a bar, and a gym back there," Saint says. "I'm beginning to agree with this idiot." He nudges Caz out of the way with a smirk. "Maybe we should just stay here and never leave." He snatches the plates from my hands, taking them over to the table.

My eyes skim over the open-plan kitchen, dining, and living room area, looking for the others. "Can you grab glasses from the cupboard there?" I ask Caz, pointing behind his head, as I walk to the refrigerator and grab a large bottle of water. Rummaging in my purse, I find the pill bottle, washing a couple tabs down with water. Then I fill a fresh glass and walk into the living area where Galen is lying on the couch. Theo sits across from him in my dad's chair, tapping away on the tablet perched on his lap. "Hey." I sit on the floor at Galen's side, reaching out to brush strands of his dark hair off his brow. "You look like you could use these." I open my palm, revealing the pills.

"Thanks." He takes them from my hand, and a jolt of electricity zips up my arm when his fingers brush against my skin. I hand him the glass of water, watching his throat work as he swallows, wondering why I find it sexy as hell.

"You should go up to bed," I suggest. "You look beat."

"I'll doze here," he says, resting his head on the fluffy cushions.

Theo puts his tablet aside, walks to my side, and helps me to my feet. "You should be resting too."

"I'm fine." I shoot Galen a cheeky wink. "Guess I have a higher pain threshold than pretty boy here."

"You're not human," Galen grumbles, his green eyes flickering open and shut, but there's no heat behind his words.

"Damn straight." I flash him a grin. "I'm a goddess among men."

Theo smiles adoringly at me, and time stands still. His hazel eyes hold hidden depths I'm dying to get lost in. His hair is down, just how I like it, all shiny and glistening, framing his gorgeous face. I thread my fingers through the strands, and he hums, leaning his face into my palm. "Theo," I whisper, feeling our connection all the way to the tips of my toes.

He pulls me close, tenderly and carefully slanting his mouth above mine and drinking from me. There is no urgency to this kiss, and he takes his time worshiping my lips, but there's a tinge of desperation I don't understand.

When we break apart, I rest my forehead against his. "What's wrong?" I whisper over his mouth. "And don't say nothing, because I know you. I can tell you're upset."

"I—" He bites down on his lip, looking over his shoulder at the others. "Can we talk later? In private?"

"Of course, and I know just the spot." I tug on his hand, leading him to the table.

Galen sleeps on the couch while we devour the sandwiches, and after we've finished eating, Caz and Saint take off to explore the grounds.

"Come with me," I say, leading Theo into my father's study. I had intended to take him out to the little seated area at the edge of the garden for our chat, but I don't want to leave Galen here by himself, in case he needs something, and there's no point in wasting this opportunity.

Closing the door, I gesture toward the two large armchairs in front of the fireplace. I ease myself into the chair while Theo kneels before the fire. Wood is stacked in the open grate, something Dad always did, and my heart throbs behind my chest as I watch Theo light the fire. We don't speak, and I sense he's preparing to unburden himself. When he's done, and flames are flickering in the hearth, he sits across from me, sighing. He runs his fingers through his hair in a familiar nervous tell.

"You know you can tell me anything, Theo. I'm a judgment-free zone, and whatever you tell me will stay between us."

"You're the best secret-keeper, Lo. I already know that. This is hard to say because then it's making it real and..."

"And?" I prompt after a beat of tense silence.

"And I have to confront it, only I'm not sure I'm ready."

"This is about Caz, right?" I softly ask.

He nods.

"Did something happen last night between you?"

He worries his lip between his teeth.

"You know it's okay if it did?" I reassure him. "I have zero issue with you two hooking up."

"It wasn't like that," he blurts. "Fuck." Groaning, he leans forward on his elbows, burying his head in his hands. "I'm a mess, Lo." He looks up at me, and my heart hurts when I see the conflicting emotions written all over his face.

"Come sit in front of me. I need to touch you." I should've waited to have this conversation someplace more intimate where I could console him.

He drops to the floor in front of me with his back against the legs of the chair and his knees tucked into his chest. I place my hands on his shoulders and begin kneading. "What are you afraid of?"

"I've spent years imagining what it would be like to be with a man, and now it's within reach, I'm terrified, Lo." He looks back at me, and I brush my fingers across his brow and down over his cheeks. "What if it's not what I want after all? Or what if I'm no good at it? Or what if I want something more and he doesn't? I don't want to mess up my friendship with him or the others, and I don't want anything to come between us or for anything to damage our relationship." He grabs my hand, struggling to contain the heightened emotion in his tone. "And what if Galen and Saint hate me for this? Or they think I'll hit on them next or—"

"What exactly happened?" I ask, interrupting him on purpose before he gives himself a heart attack.

He squeezes my hand before letting it go. "We were talking one minute, and then we were kissing, and it felt great, fucking amazing actually"—he looks back at me again, and his eyes are alive, sparkling with happiness, until his mouth drops and the mood changes—"but the instant he put his hand on my thigh, I freaked the fuck out. Told him to get out, and I pretty much haven't stopped freaking since," he admits.

"Why do you think you freaked out when he touched you?" I ask, continuing to unknot the boulders in his shoulders as we talk.

"I don't know." He sighs heavily. "Maybe I'm not ready. Maybe that's why I'm so fucking terrified."

"You need to talk to Caz, Theo. You need to tell him what you told me. He will understand."

"What if he doesn't?"

"You won't know unless you tell him how you are feeling. He's probably confused too. I'm guessing it was a big deal for him as well."

I know Caz has been with guys before, which is probably why he was the one making the move, but I don't mention that as Caz told me it in confidence and I'm not sure if Theo knows or whether it would help or hinder. All I know is I love both these guys, and I see the attraction between them, and I want nothing more than for them to figure it out.

It's tempting to interfere. To act as the middleman. But I can't get dragged into this. They need to figure this minefield out for themselves, and if Theo is truly scared, then he needs to find his courage to go after something he's desired for years or work out whether his desires have changed. I can't make that choice for him.

"He's angry with me," Theo says.

"It could be hurt," I suggest.

"I don't want to hurt him." Theo twists around so he's facing me. "That's the last thing I want."

"Just talk to him." I wind my fingers in his hair. "You know Caz. No matter what the outcome is, he'll be cool with it. But he needs to understand what's in that beautiful head of yours. I have faith you two will work it out."

"And you're truly okay with this?" His voice elevates with his disbelief.

"Are you kidding me?" I laugh a little. "You're mine and Caz is mine, but the thought of the two of you together?" I fan myself. "That is seriously fucking hot, and it makes me horny as hell." I squirm on the chair as need pulses in my groin.

"You really mean that." He blinks profusely.

"I really do. And as much as I love thinking about you two getting down and dirty, there is nothing hotter than seeing you finally get your heart's desire."

Chapter Seven
Harlow

"**H**as anyone spoken with Diesel?" I ask later that night as we watch back-to-back scary movies in the living room. It's Halloween and the first time in years I'm not out partying up a storm. I'm lying lengthways on the big couch with my head on a cushion on Theo's lap, and my bare feet are resting on Saint's thighs. A soft blanket covers my body, and I'm toasty warm and content.

"Granddad called the instant I messaged him the day of the explosion," Saint says, rubbing my feet under the blanket.

"He was freaking out," Caz adds from his spread-eagled position on the other couch. Galen caved to his pain and went to bed a couple hours ago after popping some more pills. "I could hear him shouting down the phone at Saint." He chuckles, reminding me they are such assholes when it comes to my trainer and friend.

"He blames us for not keeping you safe. Not that I fault him for that. You got injured on our watch, which should never have happened," Theo says.

"Don't do that!" I snap, instantly losing my temper. I glare up at him. "This is not your fault. The only person responsible is that conniving cunt Taylor, and I refuse to let her occupy any more of my headspace."

"The perv's been checking on you daily," Saint supplies, ignoring my little outburst. "He's overseas doing whatever the fuck he does. He has no update on that DEA agent, but he said he'll be all over it once he's back on US soil."

"I texted him this morning, but I haven't heard anything from him yet," I admit. I had a few worried messages from him when I powered up my cell, so I'd expected him to call me ASAP, but he must be knee-deep in his latest mission.

"I'm sure he'll call when he can," Theo assures me, bending down to kiss my cheek.

I guess I drifted to sleep at some point during one of the movies because the next thing I'm aware of is waking up in my bedroom with a heavy arm around my waist, sweating like I'm in the midst of a raging inferno. Heat rolls off Caz in waves, and he's suctioned to my back, like an overheated electric blanket. I glance at my body, grinning when I spot the Pearl Jam tee I'm wearing. It's one of Caz's favorite shirts, and I love that he put me in it.

I'd like to stay here, secure in his strong arms, inhaling his comforting spicy, masculine scent, but he's too fucking hot, and his shirt is already stuck to my back like glue. Beads of sweat have plastered hair to my brow, and I need to cool down before I spontaneously combust. It takes mammoth effort to extract myself from Caz's embrace without waking him, especially with sore ribs, but, somehow, I pull it off.

I pad into the en suite bathroom and run the shower, setting the temp to low. The cold, fresh water soothes my inflamed skin as I step under the showerhead, tilting my head back and letting rivulets trickle down my face. When I'm sufficiently cool, I adjust the temperature so it's a little warmer and wash my hair and my body.

"Babe." A gruff, sleep-drenched tone booms in the silent room. "You okay?" Caz asks, stifling a yawn.

"I was too hot," I admit, turning around as the shower door opens. "I didn't mean to wake you." I've no clue what time it is, but it's still dark out, so I'm guessing it's the middle of the night.

"Well, I'm definitely awake now." He grins, stepping into the shower, fixing me with a lust-laden look.

My gaze lowers, roaming over his broad chest, sculpted abs, and the line of dark hair that runs down to his hard cock. My libido instantly rouses, and I shoot him a matching grin as I wrap my fingers around his shaft. "You sure are." I pump him in slow, measured strokes, wishing I could drop to my knees and blow him, but my stupid fucking ribs won't let me. I nip at his jawline, grazing my teeth along the layer of stubble on his chin and cheeks. "And I'm wide-awake too, so what are you going to do with me, stud?"

"Turn around and face the wall. Hands on the tile. Ass up in the air, babe." He lightly swats my butt as I put myself in position. My ribs ache a little, but the pain is bearable. I hear him lowering to his knees, and my pussy clenches in anticipation. I cry out when his hot tongue licks a path along my slit, moving from my pussy to my ass, and my cunt clenches with pure need.

I need this, *him*, so fucking bad.

He pushes two fingers inside me, slowly stroking my inner walls, and fireworks explode behind my retinas. I move my hips, riding his fingers, desperately needing more. He alternates between his fingers and his tongue, working my pussy and my clit until I'm dangling from dizzy heights. Suctioning his mouth over my cunt, he ravishes me with his wicked lips and his naughty tongue while his fingers ease into my ass.

I come apart instantly, shattering blissfully, screaming and whimpering, as my climax rips through me.

"You okay?" he asks in a deep voice as he stands, brushing my wet hair to one side so he can nibble on my neck.

"I need you inside me." I reach back, grabbing his ass cheek, feeling his throbbing erection pressing against the seam of my butt.

"You sure, babe?" Caz's hands round my body, moving up to cup my heavy breasts. He continues kissing and sucking on my neck as his fingers roll my nipples and knead my sensitive flesh, and I ache down below, needing him to fill me to the hilt.

"Yes. I need to feel you moving inside me."

He lines his cock up with my entrance, slipping into my greedy pussy little by little until he's fully seated inside me.

He is careful as he starts to move, and it frustrates me to no end, because I could use a rough, hard fuck, but I can't criticize him because I know he doesn't want to hurt me. He moves in and out of me in slow, deep thrusts while his hands explore my body and his lips trail kisses all over my back. He murmurs loving words in my ear as he fucks me, and my heart swells with emotion. I didn't think Caz had this in him, because he's all alpha in the bedroom, but the longer we make slow love, the more I fucking love it and him.

After a while, he picks up the pace, grunting into my ear as his fingers find my clit and he rubs the tightened bundle of nerves, bringing me closer and closer to heaven, until we're both ascending at the same time. His hot cum spurts inside me as his cock pulses, and I groan as my body succumbs to pleasure, climaxing again.

Caz pulls out of me, using the shower hose to wash both of us clean, and then he scoops me into his arms, pressing the sweetest kiss to my lips. My head lolls against his chest as he carries me back into the bedroom. I'm exhausted and struggling to keep my eyes open as he tenderly dries me before laying me down in the bed. Getting in beside me, he is careful to keep his warm body away from me. I smile, fighting sleep when he takes my hand, lifting it to his mouth to kiss my knuckles. "I love you, Caz," I murmur. "Thank you for taking care of me."

"I love you too, princess. So fucking much." He leans in, pressing another soft kiss to my lips, and I drift back to sleep with a massive smile on my face.

The rest of the week follows a similar pattern, and it's weird to have so much free time to ourselves. Caz and Saint keep themselves busy exploring the property and working out in the small gym. Theo joins them for a daily workout before burying himself in his tablet, trying to decode Dad's secret files on the dark web. I showed the guys the files on Tuesday, and I spent a couple hours going through my notebook with Theo, explaining the work I've done to date. He took over from there, insisting I rest up while leaving the investigative work to him.

I've been too tired, too sore, too grumpy, and too melancholy to protest, so I let him have at it.

Galen and I are partners in crime as we sleep, eat, and watch back-to-back movies, taking our meds and giving our bodies adequate rest to heal. He comforts me when the pain of Sariah's passing returns to torment me, holding me close and showering me with kisses, helping to distract me from my grief. He doesn't offer platitudes, and we don't talk about it, which I'm grateful for, because I'm not ready to confront the maelstrom of emotions just yet.

"I'm bored," I announce Friday night, when we are all in

the living room, finally reaching my breaking point. "All this sitting around is making my skin crawl. I need to be doing something." I'm an active person, and sitting around doing nothing is driving me insane. I'm well rested, and it's time to get things back on track. I point at the TV screen. "And if I watch another movie, I'm going to scream."

"I'm with you, angel." Galen wraps an arm around my shoulders. "If I see another movie, I'll puke." We must have watched twenty movies since we arrived on Monday, and I'm maxed out.

"Want to play with us, princess?" Caz asks, his eyes glinting devilishly as he turns the TV off.

I arch a brow, my fingers moving to the hem of my sleep shirt. "Is that a trick question, or don't you know me at all?"

Four sets of heated eyes land on mine as I whip my top off, exposing my breasts and rapidly hardening nipples.

Galen cups one of my tits, bending his head to suck my other breast into his mouth. Throwing my head back, I whimper as he skillfully plays with my tits while someone drags my pajama pants down my legs. I haven't bothered getting dressed all week, and I've never been more grateful for my laziness. Easier access has its benefits.

The couch dips on my other side, and my head lifts as Theo takes my face, planting his warm mouth on mine. We kiss as Galen continues working my breasts while Saint pushes my legs apart, running his hands up the insides of my legs. I cry out into Theo's mouth when Caz's fingers rub my clit and again when Saint's wicked mouth lands on my cunt, his tongue instantly plunging inside me.

I orgasm in record time, and if I was any other girl, I'd probably feel embarrassed, but I'm me, and I fucking love how fast my guys can bring me to ecstasy.

Saint stands, quickly shedding his clothes, and I lick my

lips as he reveals his drool-worthy body. Galen and Theo climb off the couch, repositioning me along the length of it while they work on removing their clothes. Caz is already naked, sitting on his favorite recliner with his legs spread, his hand stroking his hard cock, while he drags his gaze over my naked body and slyly watches Theo undress. Our eyes meet, and Caz doesn't disguise the hurt and the longing from his face. Neither of them has said anything to me the past few days, but I'm planning on taking Theo to my bed tonight, and I'm coaxing it out of him.

I'm not the only one who's noticed something is off between them although they've been making an effort to talk and act like nothing has changed. But living in such close quarters, and being as close to the guys as they are, it's impossible to hide the fact something is wrong.

Saint kneels on the end of the couch and lifts my legs around his waist as he slides inside me in one expert thrust. His eyes latch on mine as he lowers his head to kiss me, and I run my fingers along his shorn, velvety blond locks, closing my eyes as I focus on all the things he's doing to my body. He fucks me hard and fast, jolting my body as he rams into me, and it doesn't take him long to climax.

Caz thrusts inside me next, and I suck Theo off while Caz fucks me. Tension is ripe in the air, especially when Caz and Theo lock eyes while they pump into my body, and there is so much unsaid that is swirling around us, altering the atmosphere. Caz screws me like a man on a mission, his jaw firm, eyes focused, body taut and glistening, as he ruts into me relentlessly, as if it can exorcise the demons who taunt him.

Galen sits on the floor, planting kisses all over my body, before his fingers find my clit and he vigorously rubs me. I come apart as Caz spills inside my cunt and Theo shoots ropes of salty, hot cum down my throat.

The instant he's done, Theo snatches his clothes up and

races upstairs without saying a word. A muscle clenches in Caz's jaw as he pulls his sweatpants up and heads to the gym in a similar silent fashion.

"What the fuck is going on with them?" Saint asks, running a hand back and forth across his neck as he looks in the direction Caz took off.

"They'll work it out in their own time," I say, not wanting to betray either of their confidence. Although, if they don't get their shit together soon, they'll have to fess up. Galen and Saint are no dummies, and they're probably already close to guessing the truth.

"My turn," Galen says, grabbing the arm of the couch as he hauls himself up.

I move to sit up, but Galen shakes his head. "I need your pussy, angel. It's been too long." We've been kissing and making out all week, but sex has been out of the question with our mutual injuries.

"I'm yours," I tell him, opening my legs wide. "Spear me with that monster cock," I tease, licking my lips as I visually feast on his throbbing erection. Beads of precum glisten on the crown of his cock as he lowers to his knees on the couch. His face contorts painfully, and he hisses behind gritted teeth. He shouldn't be doing this yet, but I'm not about to tell him how much pain he can withstand.

"You want help?" Saint asks, coming toward us.

"Fuck off, Saintly." Galen glares at his cousin while lining his cock at my entrance. "I'm capable of fucking my girl without assistance." He eases inside me, and I moan as he gradually fills me up.

Galen fucks me hard, even though I can tell he's in pain, but he doesn't have it in him to fuck me slowly, and I know he wants to get off inside me.

"Saintly," I snap, clicking my fingers. "I need your mouth."

He crawls toward me, and our lips collide in a scorching-hot kiss as his cousin penetrates me with his hard cock. Saint slides his hand under the waistband of his sweatpants, freeing his hard-on and jerking himself off as he kisses me and fondles my tits.

Galen roars, shooting his load inside me in a combination of pleasure and pain. Never one to leave me unsatisfied, he slumps to the floor, leaning forward and pushing his fingers into my pussy. He adds another digit, roughly pumping in and out of me, and I come all over his fingers as Saint jerks off onto my tits.

"I'm dead," I moan, unable to move, my body satiated and practically stuck to the couch.

"Welcome to the club," Galen purrs, flopping on his back on the ground. "But if this is what death feels like, you can kill me any time."

Chapter Eight

Harlow

I wake up alone on Saturday, shocked when I glance at the clock to see it's one o'clock in the afternoon. The guys literally fucked me into a deep sleep. Not that I'm complaining. I grab a shower, pull on a pair of cut-off jean shorts and a lacy black tank and wander downstairs in search of my guys.

I find them in the study, huddled together, talking quietly over mugs of coffee.

"What are you whispering about?" I prop my hip against the door frame, eyeing them suspiciously.

Saint jerks his head up, Theo stiffens, Caz bites on the corner of his lip, and Galen's Adam's apple jumps in his throat, confirming my suspicions.

My eyes narrow to slits as I step into the room. "If you're cooking something up without me, you can fuck off." I plant my hands on my hips, glaring at them. "I'm not putting up with this bullshit again, so spill."

"No need to get your panties in a bunch, princess." Saint

stands, sauntering toward me with a shit-eating grin. "We were always going to tell you."

"So, tell me." I challenge him with a deadly look.

"We will. When you're less pissed."

I slap his chest, growling and snarling. "If you're trying to annoy the crap out of me, you're doing an excellent job."

"Babe." He grabs the nape of my neck, holding me firmly in place. "You trust us, right?"

"I don't know," I hiss. "Do I?"

"Princess." He shakes his head. "Don't go pissing me off because we both know how that'll end."

"With me choking on your cock?" I try to keep the hope from my tone, but I'm a lost cause when it comes to these guys and sex. I literally cannot keep my hands, or my thoughts, off them. This week has proven that. Even injured, I've been indulging my addiction several times a day.

"You are so fucking perfect, Harlow." Saint yanks my mouth to his, kissing me hard, landing a slew of drugging, bruising kisses on my lips.

"Baby." I grab his ass through his sweatpants, speaking in between kisses. "You know I hate stuff being kept from me."

He grinds his hard-on against me, and my pussy pulses with need. "We needed to discuss it first," he admits, winding his hands in my hair. "There will be occasions where we have guy stuff to discuss or occasions where you need to let us protect you. You can't bust our balls every second of every day when we're doing it for you."

"Want to test that theory?" I arch a brow, rubbing my pelvis against his, my eyes rolling back in my head as the bulge in his pants presses against my zipper. "And now you've made me horny."

"You're perpetually horny," Caz pipes up. "I fucking love it."

"You guys make me crazy wet," I admit. "It's becoming problematic."

My cell phone vibrates in my pocket, and I step away from Saint to answer it, smiling when I spot the caller. "Commander. Where are you?" I ask by way of greeting.

"At the gate. Let me in," Diesel says, hanging up before I can answer.

I can't contain my grin as I slip my cell back in my pocket. Diesel is one of my favorite people on the planet, and I've missed him.

"Commander?" Saint grits out, gnashing his teeth, letting me know he knows exactly who I'm referencing. "Man, I really fucking hate that dude."

"We know," I drawl, rounding the desk and punching the button to open the entrance gates. I stab Saint with a piercing look. "I can't decide if your jealousy is hot as fuck or irritating as fuck." I prod my finger into his bare chest. "And I haven't forgotten you owe me a conversation." My gaze bounces between the four of them. "All of you." I send them one final heated glare before I head outside to welcome my trainer and friend.

"Hey." My smile is genuine as I watch Diesel climb out of his Land Rover and stalk toward me.

Very gently, he pulls me into a hug. "It's so damn good to see you, Harlow. I was going out of my mind with worry."

"I'm fine."

His eyes probe mine. "Are you really?" He looks over the fading cuts and bruises on my arms. "How badly do you hurt?"

"I'm good. Honestly. It hurt like a bitch at the start, but it's manageable now. Stop worrying."

"That's a virtual impossibility when it comes to you."

I ease out of his hold, feeling the weight of the stares boring into my back. "You know better." I tsk him. "It'll take more than a petty bitch to knock me down." I take a proper look at him, noting the deep purple shadows under his bloodshot eyes and the extra growth on his chin and cheeks. His hair is a little longer, curling around his ears. "You look like shit. Do you ever sleep?"

"It's been a while," he admits, dragging a hand through his hair. "I came straight from an overseas mission into a messy situation in Rydeville, and now I'm here. I haven't had time to sleep."

"You're staying the night," I tell him. "And I'm cooking you a proper dinner."

He ruffles my hair, pressing a kiss to my brow. "Tempting as that is, I value breathing." He narrows his eyes, staring over my shoulder. "I don't trust that punk not to slit my throat in my sleep."

"You're smarter than you look," Saint says, and I hear the smugness in his tone.

"Saintly." I spin around, glaring at my lover. "Knock this shit off. I fucking mean it." It's getting so old.

"Stay if you want," Theo says, tugging Saint back inside. "We have lots to discuss."

"I'll take a rain check. I need to meet with the boss man, but I can stay for a couple hours."

I loop my arm in his. "Come on inside. We'll talk over brunch."

Saint yanks me away from Diesel, pulling me over to the stairs. Diesel stalls, ready to spill blood for me, and I shake my head, telling him to leave it. "What the fuck, Saint?" I ask, as he manhandles me up the stairs.

"Put a fucking bra on," he hisses, dragging me down the hallway to my bedroom. "I can see your fucking nipples, and that pervert is not getting a show."

"You are certifiably insane." I roll my eyes as I enter my bedroom. "You know that, right?"

"Bite me." Saint slams the door, leaning back against it, folding his arms, and fixing me with a stern look.

I look in the mirror, and my nipples *are* poking through my thin tank. I shrug, whipping it off. "I don't know what the big deal is," I say, wanting to press his buttons. "They're only nipples, and it's not like he hasn't seen them before."

"Don't fucking push me, princess." He rubs his temples, and I silently fist pump the air. Annoying Saint is one of my favorite pastimes. Not least because it often leads to the rough, angry sex I crave.

"Or what?" I stalk to the door, pushing my bare breasts into his naked chest. "Will you punish me, Saintly?" I nip at his lower lip. "Please punish me," I purr in a breathy tone. "Put me over your knee and slap the shit out of me." My eyes darken as I flash him a grin. "Or impale your cock in my ass and fuck me until I repent."

"Jesus. Fuck." His head slams back against the door as his hardening cock nudges against my stomach. "You will be the death of me. I'm convinced of it."

"Don't pretend you don't like it. We both know you fucking love it."

He claims my mouth in a hard, grueling kiss, and I'd love nothing more than to let him angry fuck me, but Diesel is downstairs, and he'd know what we'd done. I made a promise to myself that I would never rub my relationship in his face, because I know he has feelings for me.

Reluctantly, I pull back, grabbing a bra from my dressing table and putting it on. Saint watches me redress, his eyes glued to my tits, the bulge in his pants straining against the material.

Saint grabs me to him, cupping my boobs through my bra. "You have the best tits, princess. I'm going to fuck them later."

"Promises, promises," I tease, opening the door.

He hauls me back against his hard chest. "Damn straight, babe. I never say anything I don't mean."

We rejoin the others downstairs. Theo and Caz busy themselves in the kitchen while we sit at the table, nursing fresh cups of coffee. "Is there any update on the DEA asshole?" Galen asks, sliding his arm along the back of my chair.

"I have a meet arranged with him for later in the week, but he's still refusing to play ball," Diesel admits. "However, I did glean some new intel. I had a guy on my team run a background check on Agent Howie Young and I found something interesting."

"Do we have to drag it out of you?" Saint asks, impatiently tapping his fingers on the wooden tabletop.

Diesel ignores him, focusing on me. "Agent Young is on an extended leave of absence. As far as his superiors are aware, he's spending time with his family."

"He's gone rogue," I surmise. "You were right. This is personal for him."

Diesel nods. "It's got to be. It also means he obtained the recording of McKenzie's murder illegally."

"If that's the case, how did he manage to get The Bulls off the hook for Parker's murder?" Theo asks, setting a plate piled high with pancakes on the table.

"My guess is he fed that to a buddy who called it in legit. He couldn't have pulled that off otherwise," Diesel says, helping himself to a few pancakes and some of the crispy bacon Caz sets down.

We all tuck in as I digest this new info in my head. "So, last time you talked to him, he said he was going after The Sainthood, and Ruben was his informant, so he was using The Bulls to get to The Sainthood. Now we know he's not on official business, it can only mean that taking The Sainthood down is personal for him."

"Meaning we have a shared agenda," Saint says, quickly connecting the dots.

Diesel sets his silverware down. "You want to broker a deal?"

I shrug. "It's just a suggestion, but if we share the same goal, maybe we can work together in exchange for him giving us that recording." I don't want that hanging over my head. If that gets handed over to the authorities, I could be sent to jail.

"The guy is shady as fuck," Diesel says. "I could propose it, but we risk exposing all of you, and that makes me uncomfortable. I don't trust the guy. Who's to say he won't tell Sinner as a means of buying his way in to the organization?"

"It's too risky," Saint agrees, sighing. "But we need to get the recording back." He drills Diesel with a look. "He could hang Lo with it."

"He hasn't so far," Caz says. "Why?"

"He knows it's leverage," Theo says, sipping his coffee.

"I'll get it back. You're not going down for this," Diesel reassures me, and everyone hears what he's not saying.

Knowing Diesel would kill for me does strange things to my insides. *Good* strange things, because understanding I have strong backup reassures me more than he could ever know.

"*We'll* get it back," Saint butts in, challenging Diesel with a dark look. "Lo is ours to protect."

I roll my eyes and count to ten in my head. When I'm calm enough, I speak. "Just meet him and sound him out without committing anything or exposing us. Don't make any rush calls, Diesel, and whatever we decide to do, it must be a joint decision between all of us."

"Agreed, and I've got a man watching him. If he makes a move, we can put it to a vote then."

"Good." I shovel some bacon in my mouth, washing it down with orange juice.

"What about your initiation tasks?" Diesel asks. "Has Sinner backed off?"

"For now," Saint confirms. "The explosion bought us some time, but he'll be on our case again soon."

"Have you come up with any new ideas?"

The guys share looks around the table, and it brings me back to earlier. Whatever they were discussing was something to do with this. I'd put money on it. They had insinuated the same the day Mom came to the barn, but I'd forgotten to bug them about their comment later.

"I've thought of something," I say, already knowing the guys will not discuss whatever their suggestion is in front of Diesel—not when they haven't discussed it with me. "A plan for how to handle the commissioner's assassination. But we're going to need official help to pull it off."

"Why are we only hearing about this now?" Saint swivels in his chair, glaring at me.

I jab my finger in the air. "Pot. Kettle. Black." I pin him with a smug look as I toss my long, dark hair over my shoulders. "You're really not in any position to criticize."

His glare darkens, and a shiver tiptoes up my spine. Angry Saint turns me on like you wouldn't believe.

"What's your idea?" Diesel asks, pushing away his empty plate.

"Sinner needs to believe I've done it, because he needs to think I'm loyal to him, and it's the only way I'll get him off my back. So, what if we set up a fake assassination? We bring your boss and the commissioner into the plans. Set him up in a location that works, get him to wear a bulletproof vest loaded with fake blood, and I take him out. We put out false media reports confirming he's dead while the commissioner goes into hiding. Sinner will lower his guard because he'll think the threat has ended with the commissioner's death, but it might just draw out the person who has the evidence we need."

Chapter Nine
Harlow

Five sets of stunned eyes land on me. "What? You don't think it'll work?" I probe.

"I think it's genius." Theo waggles his brows.

"I think I'd love to get inside your head," Diesel adds, smiling.

"Among other places," Caz murmurs under his breath before I give him the stink eye, and he shuts up.

"You're not doing it," Saint barks. "It's too fucking dangerous. Any number of things could go wrong."

"And *that's* why I didn't bring it up before now." I tilt my head to the side, shooting daggers at him.

"I agree it's dangerous," Diesel says, cutting through the thick tension in the air. "But with careful planning, Lo can pull this off."

"I don't doubt that," Saint scoffs, looking at him like he's a dumb fuck. "She's a fucking lethal shot. I'm more concerned about it getting back to Sinner."

"It's widely known Sinner has contacts in high places,"

Diesel agrees, "but we'll keep it contained to a small trusted circle so there's no risk of the truth leaking."

Saint still looks unconvinced, boring a hole in Diesel's skull as he drums his fingers on the tabletop.

"I would never let Lo go through with this if I thought it'd place her in graver danger," Diesel continues. "I would take a bullet for her before I'd let anything happen to her. You can trust me on that."

My eyes plead with Saint. "You know it's the truth, so unless you have a better plan?"

Silence engulfs us, and we wait while Saint thinks it through.

"Okay," he says after a couple of tense minutes. "We'll do it, but we keep those in the know to a minimum."

"You have my word." Sincerity drips from Diesel's tone.

My shoulders slump in grateful relief.

"It doesn't necessarily mean Sinner will stop looking for the evidence," Galen says. "But it's got to relieve some of the pressure."

"And if we give him some shit on The Arrows and push him toward escalating the war between both crews, he'll be distracted enough while we try to find that fucking evidence," Saint says. He stares at Diesel. "Will your boss go for it?"

"He wants that evidence as badly as we do, and he wants to end Sinner, so I think I can sell it to him." He scrubs a hand over his prickly jaw. "It would help if I had something to sweeten the deal, because he won't like crawling into bed with the junior Sainthood." Diesel rubs the back of his neck. "Asking him to trust all of you with something like this is a big ask."

My chair scrapes as I stand. "I'll be right back." I glance at Theo. "I need you." Theo rises, following me out of the open living space, down the back hallway, and into Dad's study.

"You're giving him the coded files," he says, correctly guessing where my mind has gone.

"It's all we've got to offer, and, let's be honest, we're never going to crack that code." I've spent months going through them with no success.

"I might be able to find something on the darknet," Theo says. "But it'll take time, and even if we uncover the code, there is no guarantee whatever is in those files will be of any use. We have no clue where your dad got them. If he knew what was on them, or if he knew there was something important on them, he would've used them himself."

I gather them up, dumping them in a paper box. "Exactly my thoughts. Let's see what Diesel thinks."

Theo carries the box out of the study, placing it on the table, while I explain to Diesel.

"*Trey* had those files," he says, disbelief underscoring his tone, when I've finished updating him.

I nod. "You know what they are?"

He stands, lifting the top of the lid and pulling out a couple files. He rifles through them, cussing under his breath. "These are highly classified Homeland Security files that were stolen from an operative's house in January. Guy was found dead. His house ransacked. The head of Homeland Security reached out to VERO to help recover the stolen files."

"What's on them?" Theo asks, plonking into the seat beside me.

"Intel on terrorists that had national security implications. That's all I know." He puts the files away, replacing the lid.

"Why did my dad have them?"

He leans his elbows on top of the box. "It was widely believed The Sainthood was behind the killing and the theft, so my guess is your father stole them from Sinner."

"Is this why they killed him?"

"Honestly, Lo. I don't know." Strain is etched across Diesel's face. "I can't help feeling there is more to this than we think. That it's way more complicated and it goes deeper than we suspect."

"Should we keep them here?" Galen asks.

"Fuck no." Diesel vehemently shakes his head. "That'd be like sitting on a volcano that's about to erupt." He stares at me. "Handing these to VERO is the right call, and it will buy us goodwill. I'll say you only just found them, and you came straight to me."

"Are you sure this is the right play?" Saint asks, worry etched upon his handsome face.

"I wouldn't suggest it otherwise." Diesel drills him with a look.

"Okay. Do it. Set it all up, and we'll keep you posted as soon as Sinner puts things in motion," I say.

"What about your other tasks?" Diesel asks.

"Lowell Academy is done, and Sinner won't be getting his grabby hands on Lo because we have a solution," Saint supplies.

A solution I still know nothing about.

Diesel arches a brow, and Saint smirks. "You don't need to know the specifics," he says. "Trust we have it handled and focus on doing your part."

A muscle clenches in Diesel's jaw, but he refrains from lashing out, which I guess is progress. "Walk me out?" He stares at me, and I nod.

"You sure you want to do it like this?" he asks after he's put the box in the back of his vehicle.

"I don't see how we've any other choice. Things are escalating with Sinner. He's reckless and unpredictable, and he'll hurt Mom even more if I don't look like I'm playing ball."

"He's hurting her?" Diesel asks, concern blazing in his eyes.

"He's hitting her, and she's letting him."

He shakes his head. "You want me to talk to her?"

"No. She won't thank me for interfering. What you're doing now is the best way to help."

"Okay, but if anything changes, you let me know." He wraps his arms around me, and I rest my head on his chest. "Take care, sweetheart." He kisses the top of my head before letting me go.

"You too." I step back, waving as he drives away. I turn around, unsurprised to see Saint standing in the doorway.

"I hope we've done the right thing," he says, looking even more worried than before.

"Me too," I concede, because there are no guarantees.

He opens his arms, and I fall into them, closing my eyes as he cradles me to his chest. "I can't bear the thought of anything else happening to you," he admits, holding me close.

"I feel the same way about all of you." I look up at him, palming one cheek. "But our world is a dangerous one. There will always be risks and times where we're gambling with our lives."

"Not if I can help it," he says, pressing his lips to my brow, his mouth lingering there.

"What do you mean?" I slide my hands up his chest, holding him closer.

"Have you thought about after this is all over?"

"Not in a while," I truthfully admit. "Before Dad died, my goal was to graduate with a strong GPA and attend college at Brown. I couldn't wait to see the back of this place, but now there's a lot more at stake, including you guys and my mom."

"Wherever you go, we go," he simply says, pulling my mouth to his for a kiss. "None of us want to stay here anymore."

"You don't?" I can't contain my surprise. He shakes his

head. "I thought you wanted to take over The Sainthood and mold it into a legit organization?"

He shrugs. "That was always the plan, but plans change, and it's not like we couldn't join a different chapter if we move or rejoin the Lowell chapter if we return at some point in the future."

"You've given this a lot of thought."

"We have."

"Is this what you were discussing earlier?"

"Partly." He curls his hand around mine, taking me into the house and closing the door. "We need to talk to Lo," he calls out to the others, and they stop what they are doing, looking over at us. Galen's Adam's apple bobs in his throat, Theo smiles, and Caz bites down on his lip.

Saint leads me to the smaller of the two couches, sitting down beside me. The others sink onto the longer couch, sitting upright, looking anxious, and it has me on edge.

"What's going on?" My gaze skates between all of them. "You're making me nervous as fuck."

"Galen came up with a way to protect you from Sinner and his buddies," Saint starts explaining. "For reasons that will become obvious, we needed to discuss it among ourselves first to ensure we were all onboard."

"And we are," Caz blurts. "As long as you are."

"Okay. Now, I'm intrigued." My brows climb to my hairline.

Saint glances at Galen, and he nods, taking over the explanation. "The Sainthood is governed by a set of rules that have been in existence since the organization was started. Over the years, some of those rules have been amended, others have been added, but there are a few rules that are unchangeable. That no one would dare challenge." He wets his lips, and I smother a giggle. It's so weird seeing my super-confident guys looking so uncertain. I can't wait to hear this.

"Go on," I encourage.

"Women are regularly shared within The Sainthood," Theo says. "With one firm exception." He pauses for a nanosecond, and butterflies flood my chest, jumping around like crazy. My eyes widen as I sense where this is leading. Theo's eyes crinkle as he smiles. "Wives are strictly off-limits unless the husband agrees to share her with other members. It's a hard and fast rule. One that Sinner will have no choice but to abide by."

My heart careens around my chest, and blood rushes to my head. "Hang on here a second." I sit up straighter, eyeballing them one at a time, because I honestly can't believe they're suggesting this. "Are you saying we should get *married?*"

Saint laces his fingers in mine, flashing me a wide grin. "That's exactly what we're saying, princess. Marry one of us, and we can lay down the law with that bastard. Sinner won't be able to put a finger on you, and that's a fucking promise."

Chapter Ten
Galen

Shock splays across Lo's face as she stares at us like we've lost the plot. I get it. We're young, and it probably seems extreme. But, we've discussed it at length, and there are no other options that keep her safe. However, we won't force her into it if she really doesn't want to do it.

"Well, fuck," she says after a couple minutes of strained silence. "You've managed to shock me silent. That's a first. I feel like it deserves a medal or something." Her tinkling laughter betrays her nerves, and something has finally rattled the unshakeable Harlow Westbrook. I've never seen her look or sound anything less than confident. This has really thrown her.

My eyes meet Saint's, noting his concern. He's terrified she'll say no, and for more reasons than he'll ever admit.

"You're really serious about this?" Her eyes roam between us as she poses the question.

"We are," Saint affirms, tightening his grip on her hand.

"But only if you want to," Theo says, getting up and squeezing onto the couch beside her. He cups her face. "We love you, and we want to protect you."

Lo swivels so she's looking Theo right in the eye. I can almost hear my cousin's heart beating way too fast as fear takes hold of him.

When we talked about this, we agreed the decision on who she would marry would be Lo's. That we wouldn't influence her or disagree with her choice. But I know my cousin inside and out. He's more like my brother, and we've grown up practically joined at the hip. I know the way his mind works, and I know how desperately he craves love. We both do, but I've already resigned myself to the fact it won't be me. And I'm cool with that.

But Saint Lennox will be devastated if she doesn't pick him.

He won't show it, but I'll know.

Right now, he's looking at the way Lo and Theo are huddled together, touching intimately, their connection strong and unbreakable, forged when they were younger and consolidated when they reunited. Caz casts a glance at me, and I know he thinks it too—that she'll choose Theo.

He's the obvious choice, and he'll make a great husband.

"This is nuts." She chews on the corner of her lip, and I've never seen her so unsure. She doesn't know what to say, so who the fuck knows what's going through her mind.

"Is it?" Theo quirks a brow. "We've already decided we want you in our lives."

"Permanently," Saint adds, rubbing a hand up and down his thigh.

She looks back at him, and they stare at one another for a couple beats.

"We thought you wanted that too," Caz says.

"I do. You're my future." She's quick to reassure us, and there's no hint of uncertainty in that statement, so we all visibly relax. Sitting back, she tucks her hair behind her ears, tipping her chin up as she regains her usual composure. "If we do this, who will I marry?" Her gaze jumps between us.

"That's for you to decide," I say.

"You can't ask me to choose!" She looks horrified as she shakes her head. "Because I *can't* choose. I want you all."

"Legally, you can only marry one of us," Theo says. "But nothing will change outside that piece of paper," he adds. "Our relationship will continue as it has been."

She frowns. "I thought you said I couldn't be shared?" She scrunches up her nose. "I don't want to hide what we have. That's not what I'm about. What *we're* about."

"You won't have to hide anything," Saint says as she plants her hand on his thigh, stopping his jerky movements. "Your husband can decide to share you with his friends and make it clear you are off-limits to everyone else."

"It's such sexist bullshit." Her nostrils flare. "I should be the one deciding who I fuck."

"Are you really surprised?" Caz asks. "You've seen the way The Sainthood works. Women are possessions, playthings, nothing more."

"Yet Sinner needs women to help divert attention from the authorities. He's such a fucking hypocrite."

"He didn't write those rules," Saint says, not defending the asshole, just stating a fact.

"I'm surprised he hasn't changed it," she scoffs.

"He'll probably try at some point, but all rule changes have to go to a vote, and the majority of married members don't share their wives, so I doubt he'd succeed," I say.

"And there's no other way?" she asks.

Saint glares at her. "You make it sound like a fucking chore. Would marrying one of us really be so bad?"

Fuck. My heart hurts for my cousin. He's tied into knots over this, and I don't know if Lo even realizes.

"That's not what I meant." She kisses him softly. "Marriage is a big deal, and I don't want any of you to feel obligated. If we do this, it doesn't mean this has to be real."

Saint growls, narrowing his eyes. "Why the fuck wouldn't it be real?"

"Stop misconstruing my words!" She exhales heavily. "I don't want to be a burden, all right?" She yanks her hands from his, dropping her head, her chest heaving. "This whole situation makes me uncomfortable. I shouldn't need you guys to save me. I should be able to save myself. This makes me feel...weak and like I'm losing control."

"You're the strongest person we know, Lo," Saint says, his temper dialing down.

"And it's not weak to rely on the people who care about you," I say.

"We're a team," Caz adds.

"And there will be times when we need you to save us too," Saint says, softening his tone.

"Lo." Theo tilts her chin up, forcing her to look at him. "We have discussed this. We want to do this, not just because it keeps you safe but because *we love you*. It will be as real as any marriage—unless you're saying you don't want that or can't commit to that, and that's okay, because you *are* in control. You call the shots."

Saint opens his mouth to speak, and Caz kicks his foot, warning him to shut up, because we all know how stubborn he is when an idea lodges in his head. He wants this, because he's terrified of what his dad has planned for our girl, and he won't sleep easy at night until she's protected. But it's more than that. I saw his reaction when I first suggested it. He loves the idea of being married to Lo, and once that image took root in his brain, it grew branches.

He'll be devastated if he doesn't get to make her his.

"We can do this, and when everything is over, and you're safe, if you want a divorce, you can have it," Theo says, smoothing the worry lines in her brow with his thumbs.

Saint's nostrils flare, and his hands ball into fists at his sides. He glares at Theo, and I'm guessing he's seconds from punching him in the mouth for even daring to offer her a get-out-of-jail-free card. Caz kicks his foot again, shaking his head in warning.

Saint looks to me, and I try to reassure him with my eyes. To tell him to have faith in Lo. To believe she will do the right thing.

Silence engulfs the room, and it's excruciatingly painful as we watch Lo inwardly debate our proposal. She leans her head on Theo's shoulder, reaching out for Saint's hand at the same time. I can almost see the cogs turning in her head as I sit back, watching and waiting.

After a few minutes, she clears her throat and lifts her head. "I need some time to think about this."

"Of course." Theo is quick to agree. "You don't need to decide this second."

"But you do need to decide soon, because Sinner will recall us at any moment," Saint says.

Lo bobs her head and stands. "I'm going to take a walk."

We get up, and she kisses us, one by one, before grabbing her coat and boots and exiting the cabin.

"I need beer." Saint storms across the room, making a beeline for the refrigerator.

We sink back onto the couches, glancing at one another.

"I didn't think she'd be so shocked or so unsure," Caz says, placing his feet on the coffee table.

"It's rare to see Lo so shook up, but you've got to understand that marriage is a big deal to her," Theo says, accepting a beer from Saint as he reenters the space.

"Because of her parents," I surmise. Saint hands Caz a beer and places a bottle of water in my hand.

"Giana and Trey had this rare kind of love," Theo explains, as Saint reclaims his seat beside him. "My parent's marriage is a happy one, but they're not on that level. I used to watch Lo's parents when they were together. They were always holding hands or touching in some way, and when they looked at each other, you just knew no one or nothing around them existed. They lived and breathed for each other, and they doted on Lo. She was the center of their world."

"Yet Trey kept a ton of shit from Giana. He was coerced into taking another woman to his bed, and we've no idea what Giana was really up to, because it's clear she knows more than she let on." Saint swallows a mouthful of beer. "It doesn't sound like a fairy tale to me. We can give Lo so much more."

"I don't disagree," Theo says. "But Lo worshiped her parents, and I know she desired a marriage like they had because she told me that one time."

"You think that's what's going on in her head?" Saint asks, looking troubled. "That she wants that and she doesn't have it with us?"

"How do you know she doesn't?" I ask, tipping the cold liquid into my mouth. "I don't think we should second-guess what's going through her mind. And just because she told you that years ago, doesn't mean she still feels the same," I say, eyeballing Theo. "She's learned a lot about her parents since then, and she's older now."

"I didn't think this would be a big deal," Saint says. "She's so laid-back about everything." He looks miserable as sin, and for his sake, I hope Lo doesn't take too long to make up her mind.

"We also know she's smart and she thinks things through," Caz says, chugging his beer.

"No matter how we spin it, this *is* a big decision. A life-changing one," I add.

"And she's a girl," Caz supplies, stating the obvious. "We didn't stop to consider she's probably thought about this her whole life. A marriage contract isn't exactly romantic."

Fuck, none of us thought about that, and Caz is right. "Maybe we should have gone about this differently."

"We should've properly proposed. All of us," Theo agrees, nodding.

Saint drains his beer and stands, his eyes brimming with determination. "It's not too late to rectify that." He looks at Theo. "I need you with me." He points at me and Caz. "You two stay here and watch over the princess."

"Where are you going?" I ask.

He flashes me one of his supremely-annoying smug grins. "Ring shopping."

Theo grins, raising his hand for a knuckle touch. "Now you're talking."

"Come up with a wedding plan while we're gone," Saint adds, grabbing his wallet and keys from the coffee table. "I know we'll have to do this hush-hush, and in a rush, but that doesn't mean we can't make it romantic for our girl."

"What da fuck do we know about weddings?" Caz grumbles. "I wish I'd paid more attention when Giana was boring the shit out of us about her wedding."

I'd say that makes four of us.

"Google's your friend," Theo says, slapping his tablet into Caz's hands before the two assholes leave.

I nudge Caz in the elbow as I struggle to my feet. "You heard the man. Get your ass in gear, dude." I shuffle toward the door.

"Where are you going?"

"I need to talk to Lo."

"Galen." Caz censures me with a warning look.

"It's not what you think." I turn to face him. "I'm letting her know that her choice is a little easier."

Caz's eyes grow wide. "You're bowing out?" He steps toward me. "You don't have to do that. She's forgiven you, and you have every right to be considered as equally as we are."

I smile, slapping him on the shoulder. "Appreciate the support, but it's not that." I slip out of the house before he can quiz me further, following the tracking app we all now have installed on our phones, which leads me to Lo's location.

She's sitting in a pretty garden that's been created just inside the edge of the forest. It's a small circular shape with a covered wooden gazebo in the middle, occupying prime real estate. A couple of benches are sheltered underneath the gazebo, and our girl is sitting on one. Shrubs and flowerbeds surround the wooden structure on all sides, and I'm betting it's a gorgeous spot in the summer when all the flowers are in full bloom.

Lo looks up as I approach, her brow puckering. "Is everything okay? Has something happened?"

"Relax." I ease myself down beside her. "Nothing has happened. I want to talk to you."

She eyeballs me curiously. "Okay." She drags out the word, and I can tell she's still thoroughly confused.

"I'm not here to influence your decision, but I wanted to let you know it can't be me."

"Why not?" She pierces me with those gorgeous green eyes I dream about.

"I'm not eighteen till December. I can't legally marry without parental consent." Although Mom wouldn't stop me, I can't trust her with something this important.

"I just assumed you were the same age as us," Lo admits.

"Everyone does, and I don't bother correcting them."

"Why didn't you say anything inside?"

I shrug. "The others haven't realized, and I preferred to talk to you in private. No one believes it would be me anyway."

"Stop." She clasps my face in her hands. "Don't do that. I thought we had dealt with this." Her eyes probe mine. "You mean as much to me as the others."

"I know that." I offer her a reassuring smile.

"Do you?" She holds my face tighter. "Do you know how much I love you? Because I do, Galen." Her eyes blaze fiercely. "You haven't made it easy, but the heart knows. I fucking love you."

Emotion swells my chest and clogs my throat.

We move at the same time, our mouths colliding in a passionate kiss that confirms everything we're feeling. I close my eyes, winding my hands around the nape of her neck and angling my head as we kiss, amazed at the depth of the emotions swirling inside me.

I never thought I could feel this much for a girl. Until Harlow Westbrook swept into our lives, bowling us over with her sexy charm, sharp wit, smart intellect, and fierce loyalty. I hope she finds her way on to the same page as us, because I already know I'll never find another woman I love as much as this woman in my arms.

"Angel." I pant over her lips when we finally break apart. "I will never love anyone the way I love you."

We rest our foreheads together, still clinging to one another. "This is an impossible choice. One I don't want to make," she admits.

"Don't beat yourself up over it, baby." I brush my thumb along her plump lower lip. "We don't want that." I'm tempted to say it's only a piece of paper, but I don't want to denigrate the act to something so trivial. Not after our discussion inside.

It's clear from her torment that marriage is a big consideration for Lo, and I won't cheapen it.

She worries her bottom lip between her teeth, sighing as she drops her hands into her lap. "I hate this. It feels like a competition. It's like asking a mother to choose a favorite child." She averts her eyes. "I can't do it. I don't want to hurt any of you. This feels wrong." She looks back at me. "We'll find another way."

"There isn't time." Taking her hands, I lift them to my lips. "We'll be fine with whatever decision you make. You are still ours, Lo, and we're still yours. Marrying one of us doesn't change that."

I leave her to her thoughts, heading back inside the house.

"Thank fuck, you're back." Caz drags his hand through his hair. "This wedding shit is confusing as fuck."

I hang up my coat, smirking. "It seems Theo and I are the only ones not getting our panties in a bunch."

"That's 'cause Theo knows she'll choose him."

"It's not just that. He's confident in her feelings for him. He won't care if she doesn't choose him."

"What did you say to her?" he asks, gesturing me toward the kitchen table.

"I reminded her I'm only seventeen." Lo is the oldest, having turned eighteen in April. Caz and Theo turned eighteen in July, and Saint celebrated his birthday in early August. I'm the baby in the crew, but it's not something we ever dwell on, which is why I'm guessing it never even crossed the guys' minds.

"Holy shit. I'd totally forgotten that."

I shrug. "It's no biggie. At least it makes her choice a little easier."

We spend the next couple hours poring over websites, getting all the information we need on obtaining a marriage license and learning about everything else we might need to give our girl a special day. We can't organize anything until we talk to the others about where this should take place. Getting married in Lowell or Prestwick or any area where we're known is a big no-no, so city hall looks like the best option, but we need to speak to the guys and to Lo, to ensure they are happy with that, and then we can make more concrete plans.

The front door slams open, and I swivel in my chair, watching Saint storm into the house like a force of nature. "What's up?" I ask, sensing his dark mood.

"The asshole called me while we were in the jewelry store," he seethes. "He wants us back at the house tonight."

"Aw, fuck." Caz places his elbows on the table, resting his chin in his hands. "I don't want to leave."

"It sucks," Theo agrees. "But we knew it was coming."

"I thought we'd at least get until Sunday." He pouts.

"Where's Lo?" Saint asks, looking around.

"In the garden on the outskirts of the forest at the back," I explain.

"I'll get her. Start packing," Saint commands, slamming the door on his way back out.

"Did you get a ring?" I inquire.

"We got rings," Theo says, grinning. "An engagement ring and wedding band." He pulls two boxes from his inside pocket, quickly showing us the contents.

"Good choice." I squeeze his shoulder. "She'll love them." They're not traditional rings, but Lo's not a traditional bride. She's always marched to her own beat, and I'm glad the guys picked a ring that speaks to her personality.

"We got flowers and champagne too," he adds. "We hid them in the car."

We hurry upstairs to our rooms, packing our shit, and it's not long before the sounds of more footfalls thud on the stairs.

When I'm finished grabbing my things, I head to Lo's room to see if she needs any help.

"Need a hand?" I ask, leaning my hip against the door frame.

"Could you grab my toiletries from the bathroom?"

"Sure." I meander into her room, stopping to kiss her briefly.

She hands me a large zip-up bag with a purple leopard-print pattern. "Just dump everything in there."

I load up her toiletries and help her stuff the last of her clothes in her duffel bag, then I zip it up, ignoring her protests as I carry it out of the room. Saint comes out of his room at the same time, and he grabs both our bags, racing down the stairs.

We pile into the car as Lo activates the alarm and locks the front door. Saint helps her into the passenger seat while I tap out a message to Mom telling her I'll be over to see her tomorrow. I've been checking in daily with Mrs. Murphy, the housekeeper-slash-babysitter I hired to keep an eye on Mom, and I know she's gone off the rails again, because she disappeared for twenty-four hours. I wish I could say it's a shock, but the simple truth is, it's expected. I knew the stress of the explosion, and her daily hospital visits, would get to her and she'd turn to her usual crutch.

I feel like a selfish prick for saying this, but being here this week, away from dealing with Sinner's shit, and Mom's shit, has been a welcome relief. Sometimes, I just get so sick of my life.

I glance at the cabin as we drive off, wishing I could continue to hide from my responsibilities, but I've always known this was only a temporary reprieve from my fucked-up life. It's time to return to reality, and as I rest my head against the window, I wonder what kind of shitstorm awaits us back in Lowell.

Chapter Eleven
Harlow

Bile crawls up my throat as Saint turns the Land Rover into Mom's driveway, and I visibly cringe at the sight of a house I once loved. Sinner has ruined that for me too. Taken all the wonderful, happy moments I shared with my parents in that house and trampled all over them. I shouldn't dread returning home. But I do. I have no idea what lies in store for us behind those beautiful walls. Saint has been tight-lipped the whole journey home, and I don't know if it's because he's worried about what Sinner expects or he's salty because I haven't reached a decision.

Saint parks in the garage, and we slowly climb out of the car. No one speaks, and it's like the shadow of doom is hanging over us.

"Well, this shit is depressing," Caz says as he unloads our bags on the garage floor. "We should hit the curb." He flashes me a toothy grin, and my lips twitch.

"That's a new one for me," I admit. "But I'm guessing it means party?"

"Yep," he says, popping the P. He slings his arm around my

shoulders. "We should get fucked up. One last hoorah before shit rains down on us."

"I like the sound of that. I'm betting Ashley knows of a party."

"Find out," Saint says, "but don't make any concrete plans. We don't know what Sinner wants yet."

I tap out a message to Ashley Shaw and repocket my phone, following the guys into the house via the laundry room.

Theo heads to one of the drawers in the kitchen, pulling out a bunch of takeout menus. "Pizza?" he suggests, and we all nod. He makes the call while I wander through the lower level, seeking Mom. Saint trails behind me while Caz and Galen take our bags up to the bedrooms. I open and close all the doors downstairs, but there's no sign of life, which is odd, because Mom's car and Sinner's truck are in the garage.

"Have you made a decision?" Saint blurts as I poke my head in Dad's study.

I shake my head. "I've only had a few hours to think about it. You need to give me more time than that."

He shuffles awkwardly on his feet, running his hands back and forth across his shorn locks. "I'm trying to be patient, but it doesn't come naturally."

I smile, walking toward him. "Oh, I know that all too well, Saintly." I clasp his face in my hands, planting a hard kiss on his lips, before I rest my brow on his forehead. "I promise I won't take too long, but don't rush me. This decision is too important to rush."

He wraps his arms around me, pressing my head into his chest, and I lean against him, siphoning some of his warmth and his strength. "I don't mean to pressure you. I just can't help it sometimes."

I snort, and the sound is muffled against his chest. "I never want you to change," I supply when I feel him tensing against me. "I love you just the way you are."

Silence filters in the tiny gap between us, and I lift my head, peering up at him. Sliding my hands up to rest on his shoulders, I smile at the shocked expression on his face. I've never told Saint I love him, but he's the most arrogant of my guys, and I felt for sure he'd know it. However, there's always been a vulnerability with Saint, so it's not really surprising he doesn't believe it.

I wonder if anyone has ever told him he is loved?

Sinner sure as fuck doesn't have it in him, and he's never known his mother.

"I love you, Saint Lennox." My voice rings out loud and proud, and I stare deep in his eyes as I admit my truth. "I think I fell in love with you the instant our eyes connected that day at the warehouse."

"You love me?" he splutters, and the awestruck, hopeful look in his eyes hurts me as much as it overjoys me.

"Completely and utterly." I palm his face, bringing his mouth to mine. I kiss him softly, pouring everything I feel for him into every sweep of my lips, and his mouth moves tenderly against mine, in a way that isn't usual, sending my heart careening around my chest.

This guy. He's such a conundrum, but I wouldn't change a single thing about him.

He's perfect for me.

"For now and forever," I add over his lips. "To the ends of time."

"Lo." His tone is barely louder than a whisper and dripping with emotion. "I know I fell in love with you that day we first met because you've consumed my thoughts from that very first second." He threads his hands in my hair, gripping my neck, moving our faces even closer. "But I didn't realize it until recently because I've never known what love feels like. You've shown me that."

Tears sting the backs of my eyes, and my heart is so full it feels like it could burst.

"You own me, body, heart, and soul." His eyes flood with adoration. "I love you too, Harlow. Always have. Always will."

We move like magnets, clinging to one another as we kiss like we'll never get to do it again. Our hearts beat in sync as we drink from one another, our kissing growing more heated the longer it continues, and I could happily stay here in Saint's arms, letting his drugging kisses distract me, but I've got a decision to make, and I don't want to drag it out, because that's not fair to any of them.

Reluctantly, I break the kiss, resting my head on his chest, listening to his heart thump under my ear. "You make everything feel right, princess," Saint whispers. "And I'll be okay with whatever you decide." I'm not sure if he's trying to convince himself, or me, but, deep down, we both know that's a lie.

I head upstairs to search for Mom, but it's quiet up here too. They must have gone out without their cars. It's Saturday evening, so they're probably at dinner and planning on drinking themselves into oblivion, like usual. It's clear Sinner only called us back out of spite, so I message Ashley, telling her we'll meet her at the party later. One of the Lowell Academy jocks is throwing an open party, and it promises to be crazy. I could definitely use a little crazy right now.

I don't bother unpacking, depositing my bag on the floor in my closet, hoping we get to go to the barn sooner rather than later. Lately, being around this house makes my skin crawl. The barn instantly felt like home, and I'd much rather live there. I plug my earphones in, blasting Paramore, as I flop on my bed, trying to make sense of the mess in my head.

Theo calls me down when the pizza arrives, and we share a few beers as we eat. Conversation is muted, but the tension from the car is gone, thanks to my recent convo with Saint. We're clearing away the plates when Saint's cell pings. Pulling it out, he scowls, rubbing the back of his neck.

"What is it?" Galen asks, immediately on guard.

"It's Sinner. He's summoned us to the basement."

"The basement?" All the tiny hairs lift on my arms.

He's been here this whole time?

"What the fuck is he doing in our space?" The only time Sinner goes down there is to bark orders or grab the guys to do his bidding. *Is nowhere safe from ruination?* "That asshole puts me in an instant bad mood," I hiss, slamming dinnerware into the dishwasher. "I'm likely to punch him in his smug face the second I see him," I warn. I've lots of pent-up emotion that needs an outlet.

"Get in line," Saint drawls. "If he even looks funny at you, I'm liable to lay him out flat."

"Remember the end game," Theo cautions us all. "Everyone, calm the fuck down."

We make our way to the basement, opening the door and walking downstairs in single file. We're halfway down the stairs, before the room has come into view, when a whooshing sound tickles my eardrums, quickly followed by pain-filled screams. Acid churns in my gut, and I slam into Saint's back as he halts midstep. "Go back upstairs," he commands in a low voice, his eyes pleading with me to do what he says for once in my life.

He really should know better.

"He wanted us to see this; otherwise, he wouldn't have summoned all of us. Keep going." I push at his shoulders, ignoring the dread building inside me.

"Lo." Galen places his hand on my shoulder from behind.

"I know," I choke out as another anguished scream tears from Mom's mouth. "Go!" I shove at Saint. "We need to help her."

My legs almost go out from under me when we hit the basement floor and the disgusting scene is revealed. Panic races up my throat as I stare in horror at Mom.

Our couches have been pushed to the wall to make way for a new four-poster bed. But it's not an ordinary bed. Chains hang from the corners of the bed, holding up some kind of sex sling Mom is currently strapped to. It's made of sturdy black leather with stirrups and cut-out sections for easy access. She's completely naked, and Sinner fucks her pussy as she's suspended while his creepy buddy with the bald head and face ink pounds into her ass. Every time I've met that pervert, I feel sick to the pit of my stomach, so this has me enraged. Yanking Mom's head back, he grins at me, licking his lips as his gaze roams my body.

Another two guys kneel on the bed, one on each side, stroking their hard-ons as they grab at Mom, fondling her body and tugging at her tits. Pain punches me in the gut, and I grab the back of Saint's shirt to steady myself.

These images are enough to give me nightmares for years, but it's the angry, oozing lash marks across her chest, stomach, and legs that will ensure I never forget this sight.

Sinner glances over his shoulder, grinning like the sick lunatic he is, pumping his hips and thrusting into my mother as he raises the whip, bringing it down over her bleeding torso.

He is showing how truly sick and twisted he is. The curtain has fallen, and the window is wide-open. He's hiding nothing—not the true extent of his insanity, his inability to love, or his desire to hurt Mom, hurt me, hurt Saint. He really is a living, breathing monster. A creature of the night come to life from the pages of a horror story.

Mom's head lolls back as another gut-wrenching scream splits the air. Her voice is hoarse, her vocal cords as battered as her body. Anger whips through me, replacing the blood flowing through my veins, coating my eyes in a layer of sheer rage. I react on instinct, whipping my Strider out and lunging at Sinner before anyone can stop me. I jump up onto the bed in my boots, grabbing his head and yanking it back.

"Call your animals off," I growl, pressing the blade of my knife to his throat. "Or I'll gut you like the disgusting pig you are."

"You feel good pressed up against me," he says, pushing his ass back into me, as if I don't have a deadly weapon lined up against his skin. "Come join the party. You can replace my useless whore." His lips pull into a sneer as he looks over Mom's bruised and bloodied body before pulling his cock out of her.

The asshole sodomizing Mom thrusts his hips forward, eyeing me like I'm his next meal. "Get your filthy dick out of my mother or I'll cut it off and stuff it down your throat until you choke."

He smirks, thrusting harder into Mom, as if I'm no threat, and I'm so sick of assholes ignoring me and underestimating me.

In a lightning-fast move, I reach around, yank the dagger from my back pocket, and throw it at him, watching it embed in his shoulder with grim satisfaction. I could easily have stabbed him in the heart, and I was so fucking close to throwing caution to the wind, but there are too many lives at stake, and I need to be smart about this.

As much as I'd love to slaughter all of them, and hack them to pieces until they don't resemble anything close to human, all that will achieve is a life sentence behind bars, and sure death for my guys, so I rein my anger in, reminding myself their time will come. These bastards *are* going down.

The asshole staggers back, off the bed, stumbling over something, roaring as his fingers wrap around the dagger, and he pulls, hissing between his teeth as he yanks it from his body. Blood spurts from the wound as the dagger clangs to the ground.

Galen darts forward, retrieving it, grinning when he spots the angel emblem on the handle. Galen gave me a set of daggers as a peace offering a couple weeks ago, and I knew they would come in handy, so I've taken to carrying a few on me at all times.

The creep moves aside, nostrils flaring as he glares at me, and I spot the dead body at his feet for the first time. I've never seen the man before, but he looks young enough, no older than thirty if I had to guess. He's wearing The Sainthood leather cut, and his fingers are curled around a gun, for all the use it was to him. His glazed eyes stare vacantly into space, and dried blood surrounds the bullet hole between his eyebrows.

I think this must be the guy Saint hired to keep an eye on Mom. If Sinner figured out why he was here, that spells trouble for Saint, so I pray that secret died with him.

The other two perverts climb off the bed, standing back and waiting for Sinner's instruction as the dick with the face ink presses his hand to his shoulder, attempting to stem the flow of blood. The look he pins me with promises a world of retribution, but I'm not worried about him.

"Caz," I call out, keeping my knife pressed to Sinner's neck. "Get my mom down."

I expect her to protest, even if she is barely coherent, but she doesn't object. Her tired green eyes lift to mine, and all I see is relief and a world of pain in her gaze.

"I really wouldn't do that," Sinner coolly states as Caz

climbs on the bed. "You know the punishment for disobeying your president."

"This isn't official Sainthood business," Saint snaps from behind.

"It doesn't matter," Sinner replies, sounding far too calm for a man with a knife pressed to his jugular. I exert more pressure on the blade, feeling the moment it nicks his skin. He doesn't as much as flinch, and that irritates the fuck out of me.

"Leave the woman," the bald asshole hisses as Caz moves to untie Mom. "You heard your president."

"You know what I'm capable of," I tell Sinner, pressing my blade in farther. "And I don't need much encouragement to kill you. Continue pissing me off and see how that ends for you."

A dark chuckle rumbles from his chest. "I can't believe I had you pegged all wrong. You are truly magnificent, sweetheart. See how hard you make my dick."

"I'd rather not. I've no desire to be reacquainted with the pizza I just ate."

He chuckles again, and I hate that I'm entertaining him. I forcibly remind myself of all the reasons why I can't kill him, because I'm so close to doing it.

"Get Giana down," Saint says in a barely restrained voice, blatantly ignoring his father's instructions.

Theo helps Caz free Mom from the chains, and they lift her off the sling, carrying her over to the couch. Galen grabs the blue blanket from the chair, covering Mom with it.

"I don't know what you hoped this would achieve," Saint says, coming around so he's facing his father. "Or why you persist in pushing my buttons."

Theo comes up behind me, placing his hand on my arm and urging me to step back with his eyes. "Your mom needs you," he whispers, and that's about the only thing he could say to me at this moment.

Reluctantly, I remove my knife and jump down off the bed. Sinner climbs off the bed, smirking as he walks toward me.

Saint pulls me into his body, wrapping his arm around my waist, keeping me close while Theo stands on my other side, facing up to Sinner like he dares him to hurt me.

Sinner stops directly in front of me, completely naked, his hideous dick bobbing against his stomach. "I can't decide if you're incredibly smart or incredibly stupid," he says, clicking his fingers at one of his minions. The other three men, all members of the board alongside Sinner, are in the process of getting dressed. The shorter of the three steps forward, handing Sinner a lit cigarette.

Sinner lifts the cigarette to his mouth, drawing a long drag before blowing clouds of billowy smoke in my face. His blue eyes shimmer with mirth, and I can't figure out what angle he's playing here. "You've got balls, Harlow Westbrook," he says, leaning in closer. Saint jerks me back, and I'm grateful, because if that pervert's dick even glances off me, I'll slice it clean off his body.

"Be careful you don't push too far," he threatens, "because I haven't even started with you yet."

Chapter Twelve
Harlow

I text Ashley to let her know we won't make the party after all, double-checking she's still okay to attend the appointment with me in the morning. Caz carries Mom up to my room, gently laying her down on the bed. Galen hands me the first aid kit while Theo places a glass of water and pain pills on my bedside table and Saint retrieves her nightdress from the master suite. Galen leaves a towel and a bowl of tepid water beside me, squeezing my shoulder and kissing the top of my head.

"We're across the hall if you need us," Saint says, and I nod, swallowing thickly.

The guys move to Saint's bedroom while I attend to my mother's numerous wounds. I can barely breathe over the massive lump clogging my throat as I clean her up. Mom is conscious, but only just. She stares at the wall as I gently wash her wounds. Tears cling to my lashes, and I'm fighting to keep my stomach contents in as I apply antiseptic ointment to the raised wounds that pepper her upper body. I wish I could bathe her, but she's in too much pain.

Silent tears stream down her face as I bandage her up as best I can. I'm helping her into her nightdress when I spot the blood leaking from her back passage. I lose the fight with my composure, and a sob bursts from my mouth as I gently hold her to me.

I don't care what has gone down between us these past few weeks. Right now, all I care about is getting her away from that bastard. Her arms are limp as she clings to me, quietly sobbing into my chest. I want to yell at her, shake her until she sees sense, and demand to know what the fuck she thinks she's doing, insist that she tell me everything, but I can't accost her when she's so damaged, when her sanity is already in shreds.

I clean the blood from her ass, crying the entire time. Murderous rage mixes with helplessness as I change the sheets, stuffing the bloody ones in the trash. Mom dutifully takes the pain pills, and after tucking her in, I huddle under a blanket in the chair as I watch her fall asleep with a sharp ache in my heart.

"How is she?" Galen asks, quietly slipping into the room an hour later.

I shake my head, because I can't form words right now. Gently, he pulls me to my feet, enveloping me in a soft hug. "She'll be okay. She's tough like her daughter."

I close my eyes, inhaling his scent, praying for strength I'm not sure I have anymore. It's all becoming too much. First Dad. Then Sariah. Now this.

"I'm going to watch over her," Galen says, easing back a little.

"You don't have to do that. You're injured."

"So are you." He sweeps hair off my brow. "We're going to take it in turns." He places his lips on my mouth, kissing me like I'm a porcelain doll. "Theo is waiting for you in his bedroom. Go get some rest."

I kiss Mom on the forehead, making Galen promise they'll call me if she wakes or anything happens during the night. Saint and Caz are downstairs, he explains, keeping watch in case Sinner returns.

He left immediately after the showdown in the basement, and we're all on edge, waiting to see what he'll do next. There's no way he'll let me get away with pulling a knife on him or stabbing his second in command, but I don't regret it, and I'd do it again if it meant freeing Mom from being raped.

I knock on Theo's door before entering, finding him sitting up in bed, in a pair of sweatpants, with his tablet on his lap.

"How's Giana?" he asks, immediately putting his tablet aside and sitting up straighter, fixing troubled eyes on me.

"She's..." I burst out crying as I come unhinged. I've been so strong all week, not giving in to my turbulent emotion, fighting my grief, but I can't contain it anymore.

Theo jumps off the bed, bundling me into his arms, holding me as I cry against his naked chest. He runs his hand up and down my back, offering comforting words, encouraging me to let it all out.

"Sorry," I mumble sometime later when my tears have stopped. I swipe my fingers under my eyes, collecting the moisture there, before swiping at his damp chest.

"Nothing to be sorry for." He takes my hand, leading me to the bed, carefully placing me down against the headrest, before he joins me.

"The dead guy downstairs. Was he the guy Saint planted to watch Mom?"

Theo nods, confirming my suspicions. "He must've tried to intervene, and he paid for it with his life."

I hope that's how it went down, because I dread to think what Sinner would do if he knew Saint planted the guy in the house to watch over Mom. The fact Saint is still breathing suggests Sinner doesn't know, and I'm grateful for that small mercy. I hate that the guy died trying to protect Mom, and it's selfish to feel relief that the secret dies with him, but I won't pretend otherwise.

There is so much needless death in the world The Sainthood inhabits. Not that Sinner would see it like that. It's all part of the job, and he places no value on human life, making him the deadliest of enemies.

I rest my head on Theo's shoulder as his arm circles me. "Are we stupid to think we can win? That we can beat him at his own game? He's completely unpredictable, and that makes me nervous as hell."

"Sinner should never be underestimated," he agrees, smoothing a hand down my hair. "But neither should we." He tips my chin up so our eyes meet. "The key difference is we know he's a formidable enemy, whereas he thinks we're under his control and that we're not a threat. His arrogance will be his downfall."

"I hate feeling helpless. It feels like everything is crashing down around us."

He kisses my temple. "I understand why you feel like that, but we're not going to let things fall apart. We're making solid plans, and it will work."

"We need to get her away from him," I say. "I can't watch this any longer, and if we don't do something, he'll kill her."

"He won't, Lo." Theo caresses my cheeks with his thumbs. "He needs her to keep you in line. He won't kill her."

"He'll just beat her to within an inch of her life and let his buddies fuck her until she bleeds." A heavy weight settles on my chest, and pain ricochets through my skull. I squeeze my eyes shut, fighting the maelstrom blowing through my mind.

"We'll figure out a way to protect her." He kneads my

shoulders. "You're so tense, sweetheart. Let me run you a bath, and I have something else I think will help."

"Okay. Sure." Because I need something to distract me from taking my Glock and heading out into the night to hunt Sinner down.

Theo runs me a scented bath, helping me step into it before he walks away. I rest my head back against the ledge, closing my eyes, wondering how the fuck I'm supposed to choose one of my guys to marry, knowing it's got to happen, because there is zero doubt after what went down in the basement.

Even marriage won't protect me, at least not forever. Outwardly, Sinner can't lay a finger on me, and in the short-term, he'll have no choice but to negate his second initiation task; however, he'll look for any opportunity to corner me and take what he wants anyway.

We can't stay here after we're married, but how can I leave Mom alone with that monster?

The door creaks as Theo slips into the bathroom. He's shed his sweatpants, and he stands before me in his birthday suit, looking thoroughly fuckable and completely gorgeous. His hair is down, hanging around his face, and I long to run my fingers through it, to get lost in him. My libido wakes up, and I sit upright, leaving space at the end of the tub for my man to join me.

"Thought you could use this." He climbs into the tub, passing the lit blunt to me.

I rarely indulge, but I so need to get out of my head right now. "You know me well." I accept the blunt, pulling a few long drags, drawing the heady scent deep into my lungs.

We pass it back and forth in amicable silence, and it doesn't take long for me to feel the effects. Water sloshes as I crawl toward Theo, grinning as I straddle his lap.

"You feeling good, babe?" He runs his hands up my body, his fingers brushing against the underside of my breasts.

"I am, but you know what would make me feel really good?" I purr, leaning down to nip at his earlobe.

"My cock buried deep in your pussy?" His smile is knowing as his fingers tweak my nipples, and both buds harden at his sensual touch.

"Ding, ding, ding. Gold medal for the winner," I tease, as I lift my hips, grip his hard cock, and position myself over it.

Theo holds my face, kissing me with his lips and his tongue as I slide down over his shaft. We moan as my cunt grips his dick, and I smile as I run my fingers through his gorgeous hair. "Love you," I whisper, rubbing my nose against his.

"Love you too."

I ride him, slowly at first, keeping my hands on his shoulders to control my movements. The weed has removed the pain from my ribs, and I'm wondering why the fuck I didn't smoke earlier in the week. Theo grips my hips, helping me to move up and down on his throbbing length, while he face-plants my chest, licking and sucking my tits as I bounce on top of him. When we're both close, I get on all fours, and Theo slides inside me from behind. He thrusts inside me in one fast move but slowly eases back out so I feel every inch of him gripping my inner walls, and he does it over and over, driving me crazy with lust.

His fingers find my clit while he holds my hip with his other hand, and we orgasm together, moaning and writhing, like two people intimately acquainted with one another.

After, he lifts me out of the tepid bath, patting me dry and helping me into one of his T-shirts. We curl up in bed, and it doesn't take my overwrought brain long to fall asleep.

I wake up sometime in the middle of the night with my tongue stuck to the roof of my mouth, craving water. Careful not to wake Theo, I creep out from under the covers and tiptoe out of his room. I check on Mom first.

She's still fast asleep, and Caz is snoring in the chair, the blanket pooled by his feet on the floor. I check Saint's room and Galen's room, finding Galen passed out, but Saint's bed is empty, meaning he's still on guard duty downstairs.

I walk downstairs, finding him at the kitchen counter, pouring coffee down his throat in an attempt to keep awake.

"Hey."

He jumps, spilling coffee down the front of his shirt.

"Sorry. I didn't mean to startle you."

"What are you doing up?" His eyes trail the length of my bare legs.

"I woke up thirsty."

He slides off the stool, walking to the refrigerator and grabbing a bottle of water.

"Thanks." I kiss his lips quickly as I accept the water, hauling myself up onto the stool beside him.

"No sign of the bastard, I assume," I say, uncapping my water.

He shakes his head. "He's most likely crashing at HQ, but I didn't want to take any chances."

I glance at the clock. It's five a.m., and it's unlikely he'll return any time soon. Sinner likes to burn the midnight oil, and he rarely surfaces before midday. "You should go to bed. You look tired." I rub at the shadows under his eyes. "I'm going to watch over Mom for a while. I doubt I'll be able to go back to sleep, and I have some thinking to do."

"He's a sick bastard," he seethes, and a muscle pops in his jaw. "I'd like to say I'm surprised he'd do that to the woman he claims to love, but I've seen how he's treated his girlfriends over the years. He's a complete prick, and I doubt he's finished using Giana to get to you."

"Which is why I need to make my decision. There is no time to waste."

"There isn't," Saint agrees, sliding his cell to me. "I was going to show you this in the morning."

I read the text from Sinner confirming there will be a junior chapter meeting held next Friday evening. He's requested my presence, and that's all I need to know.

I hand him back his phone, sipping my water. "Can we pull it off on such short notice?"

"It'll be tight, but we'll make it happen. Sinner isn't the only one with useful contacts."

"Good." I climb down, tugging on his arm. "Come on. Bed for you."

I kiss Saint at his door, ignoring the pull to go inside. My pussy is such a greedy bitch.

Caz is grumpy when I wake him, refusing to trade guard duty with me, until I threaten to withhold sex, and he bolts like a racehorse let out of the gate.

I pull the covers up over Mom before settling in the chair to think. My head is clearer thanks to the weed and my talk with Saint earlier. Since the guys proposed the marriage idea to me yesterday morning, my emotions have veered all over the place, but I know what I should do now.

I pretty much ruled Theo and Caz out straightaway. On paper, Theo is the ideal husband, and we share an intense connection. He knows me inside and out, and his tender care of me tonight only cements that opinion.

But Theo is still confused over his sexuality, and there are feelings between him and Caz, which is something I don't want to get in the middle of. I don't want to tie either of them into marriage with me, because that could confuse things. I know they love me. That they will always be in my life, but I don't want to put restraints on either of them.

So, that left Galen and Saint, and that's been my biggest dilemma—which Lennox cousin to choose.

I could see myself marrying Galen because his pain speaks to mine and we lash out in the exact same way. Out of all my relationships, that is the one that has grown the most. Galen has opened himself up to me, and it's a beautiful thing. I've also seen the life he leads, and, arguably, he needs me more than the others.

But, so does Saint. He's never known love. He's never known anything but hate. I've watched him today, when he thinks I'm not looking, and I know he thinks he's hiding his feelings, but he can't hide from me anymore. He's been wearing his vulnerability on his sleeve all day.

I made the decision after our talk, but then all that shit went down, and I needed time to reflect on it, to make sure I'm sure.

And I am.

It's not because Galen graciously bowed out, making the decision easier, although I love him for telling me and trying to ease my pain. When it boils down to it, I would be making this choice even if Galen still had a horse in the race.

Saint is the most obvious choice—he's junior chapter leader, Sinner's son, and he carries the most clout—but that's not the reason either.

Out of all my guys, Saint would be the one most devastated if I didn't choose him. He would see it as a rejection, and it would gut him.

The others will understand and be fine with it. I'm confident about that, but Saint would carry that pain in his heart forever, and I cannot hurt him like that. I *won't* hurt him, because I love him too much to not give him this.

If I'm really honest with myself, it has always been Saint, because I fell in love with him first—at thirteen, during one of the worst moments in my life. The connection we forged that day never went away. For either of us.

I smile to myself as the angsty feeling in my chest disappears, replaced with a calm peace. Butterflies invade my chest, fluttering around, making me feel giddy. When the guys first suggested this, I thought they were all swinging from the cray-cray tree. But now it's clear they know me even better than I know myself, because this isn't a means to an end, this isn't a burden, and this is always the way it was meant to be.

And I'm excited.

I want to marry Saint, and screw anyone who says we're too young to know what's in our hearts, because they don't know what the fuck they're talking about. I used to want a marriage like my parents had, but it's become obvious their marriage wasn't the fantasy I built it up to be.

What I have with Saint—with all my guys—is as fucking real as it gets.

They would take a bullet for me, and I would take a bullet for them.

We don't sugarcoat shit, telling it straight, no matter how painful the truth is.

We fight as much as we fuck.

But when it comes down to it, we are there for one another with no questions asked.

Their love isn't all rainbows and unicorns. It's rough, it's tough, and sometimes it hurts, but I wouldn't have it any other way, because we're a team. I may be marrying Saint Lennox, but in my heart, I will be marrying all of them, and nothing or no one is ever going to tear us apart.

Especially not Neo "Sinner" Lennox.

Chapter Thirteen
Harlow

"Where are you going?" Caz asks, ambling into the kitchen, rubbing his tired eyes, as I snatch my jacket from the back of the chair.

"I've got a few errands to run." I'm deliberately vague, because I don't want them to know what I'm up to.

"I'll come with," he offers, stifling a yawn.

I shake my head, tweaking his nose. "Nope. This is something I need to do alone."

"Babe." He places his hands on my hips. "You know we don't want you going out by yourself. Especially after what went down yesterday. Sinner is a loose cannon. You shouldn't go out without one of us."

"I know how to take care of myself. I have my Glock and my knife, and I won't be entirely alone. I'm meeting Ashley."

"You are?" He quirks a brow. "I didn't think you two were that close."

"We're not, but she's helping me with something." I tweak his nose again. "Something important." I peck his lips superfast. "Something secret." I waggle my brows.

He sighs. "Saint won't like this."

"I'll probably be back before he even knows I'm gone." My tongue darts out, wetting my lips, and I love the instant hungry glaze that glints in Caz's eyes and how his gaze automatically lowers to my mouth. "Actually, let's meet at the barn. We need to talk."

"You mean…"

I kiss him quickly, smiling as I ease out of his hold. "I've made my decision." I swat his ass as I walk in the direction of the garage. "I'll text you when I'm done." Blowing him one final kiss, I leave the kitchen.

Sliding behind the wheel of Dad's Gran Turismo is comforting. It's a bit like returning to your own bed after weeks of sleeping in a hotel bed. I make a mental note to ask the guys about my Lexus. I've no clue what happened to it after the bomb. I know it's virtually indestructible, and the bomb didn't go off underneath my SUV, but I imagine the damage was still extensive. I don't know if it's salvageable or if I should be ordering a new custom one. The reasons Dad wanted me to drive it haven't changed, and it would give the guys peace of mind when I go off by myself.

The engine on the sports car hums beautifully when I power her up, and I settle back in my seat, cranking the music up high as I peel out of the garage, heading toward the city.

Ashley is waiting outside the studio when I arrive an hour later.

"Harlow." She leans in, hugging me. "It's good to see you out and about. You seemed in so much pain at the funeral."

"I'm okay. Still in one piece. I've a couple of minor cuts and scrapes, and there is some lingering bruising and soreness around my ribs, but I've endured worse."

"I was talking about emotional pain. How are you holding up?"

I shrug. "To be honest, I'm trying not to think about it. We have a lot on our plate, and we can't afford for me to fall apart." Pressure settles on my chest. "She's still the first thing on my mind every day though," I truthfully admit.

"I know no one can ever replace Sariah, but I meant what I said at the church. I'm here for you."

"I appreciate it, and thanks for setting up this appointment. Especially at such short notice, and on a Sunday too."

Her face lights up, and she loops her arm through mine. "I was glad to help. Michelle takes amazing pictures, and my family sends a lot of business her way, so she didn't mind doing this today."

We head into the studio, and Ashley introduces me to the photographer, leaving us to talk about my ideas while she goes to grab takeout coffee from the little coffee place down the road.

The photo shoot is fun, and I'm grinning like a loon, imagining the expression on the guys' faces when they see them, as we step out into the chilly November air a couple hours later.

Ashley and I grab a quick bite to eat at a Mexican diner before parting ways. I had thought of inviting her to come with me to the vintage designer store, but I dismissed the idea as fast. While she's given me no reason to distrust her, too much is riding on this strategy to let anyone else know what we're planning to do.

I step into the store, fluffing out my hair and removing my scarf as I wait for one of the assistants to approach me. I have shopped at this store before, so I'm hoping they'll have something that fits my vision. I know I could purchase something off-the-rack in one of the wedding stores, but I highly doubt a traditional wedding store will have the type of look I'm after, and we're tight on time because this will be a quick courthouse wedding.

The store manager, Maggie, recognizes me, rushing forward to greet me, hugging me like I'm a long-lost friend. I explain what I'm after, and she squeals, rubbing her hands in delight, while she dashes around the store, grabbing a few items.

A half hour later, I'm standing in front of the mirror in the changing area, fighting a massive grin.

"You look absolutely perfect," Maggie says, fluffing out the white layered tulle skirt. I fix the white lace leggings in place, admiring how shapely they make my legs look. "It's definitely got that whole Madonna eighties vibe. You're gorgeous."

"I love it." I hold out my arms, and she slips the short, white, fitted jacket over my arms. It complements the outfit, ensuring it doesn't come across as slutty. My midriff is on display, because the tight white crop top stops a few inches under my boobs, but the neckline is high, so it's not indecent. I opt for a pair of white high heels with a silver trim, and a sparkly silver clutch completes the look.

She packages up the clothing and boxes up the shoes and purse, and then I'm on my merry way.

I stop at a wedding store to pick up the silver tiara I ordered last night, because a queen can't get married without a crown, duh, and then I visit the jewelry store I found online, explaining the type of wedding band I'm after to the amused man behind the counter. The second he takes out the tray, I spot the perfect ring. It's a link wedding band in black tungsten, and there's enough room on the inside to add the inscription I want.

I'm worried he's having a coronary when I tell him I need four rings for my four grooms, and I wish I could record the moment because the guys would get such a kick out of the shocked look of horror on his face, but when I pass my platinum card over, he quickly gets over himself. I pay a premium to get a rush job on the engraving, and he promises to have all four rings for me to collect in a couple days.

I text Caz as I'm walking back to my car, arranging to meet them at the barn in an hour. Saint messages me a couple minutes later to confirm he has some guys coming to the house to watch over Mom while we're gone, and that eases a layer of stress off my shoulders. I need to talk to her later. To see if I can convince her to move someplace safe, and I'm waiting for Diesel to call me back.

I blast Paramore as I drive toward Prestwick, a deep contentment sinking bone-deep. My life might be a shitshow at the moment, but making this commitment to my guys feels incredibly right, and I have zero doubts.

I arrive before them, using the code to let myself in through the gate.

A blast of heat hits me the second I enter the barn, and my heart warms at Theo's thoughtfulness. I don't need proof to know he dialed in remotely to switch the heating on.

I'm remarkably calm as I kick off my shoes, grab a beer, and settle on the couch to wait for my guys.

Butterflies swoop into my chest as the rumble of an engine grows louder and then it cuts out, right outside.

"Honey, we're home!" Caz calls out, bursting through the door first, and I grin as I get to my feet, walking around the couch to greet the guys who are my everything.

I fling my arms around Caz, and he dips me down low as he slams his lips on mine, kissing me hard, making me dizzy with need.

"Dude, her ribs," Galen chastises him, and Caz pulls us upright, breaking our lip-lock.

"It's cool," I say as Galen plants his hands on my hips, lowering his head to kiss me.

"You okay?" he whispers over my lips, and I smile as I cup his gorgeous face.

"I'm more than good." I nuzzle my nose in his neck, inhaling his citrusy, woodsy scent

He nods, pecking my lips one final time before handing me to Theo.

Theo wraps his arms around me, hugging me to him, and his body heat seeps into mine, warming me all over. "Love you," he says in a low voice so only I can hear. "And I'm fine with whatever you've decided." His mouth slides against mine, and it's the softest, sweetest brushing of our lips, but it's everything.

Theo releases me, walking to the couches to join the others as Saint and I stare at one another. His eyes burrow into mine, and I know he wishes he could delve into my mind and find the truth. "Come here," he demands, and his deep, raw tone sends delightful shivers coursing down my spine. I step toward him, and he pulls me close, slanting his mouth over mine in a long, deep, slow, passionate kiss that is tinged with pain and fear.

He thinks I won't choose him. That he's not worthy.

My heart hurts. I grab his shirt, holding him closer, opening my mouth, and letting his tongue inside. I pour everything into this kiss, hoping he feels it and that it reassures him.

Conscious of the others, I break the kiss, because I don't want to prolong their agony. Taking Saint's hand, I drag him over to the couch. We sit down beside Galen, and Caz distributes beers.

"You know I'm not one for sugarcoating things," I start. "So, I won't beat around the bush." I let my gaze rake over each one of them. "I love you all. So fucking much. Choosing to marry only one of you was killing me until I realized I was overlooking the most important thing." I grab hold of Galen's and Saint's hands, fixing my gaze on Theo and Caz who are seated on the couch across from us. "I'm not just marrying one of you. I'm marrying *all* of you."

"What do you mean?" Caz asks, looking perplexed.

"I want a commitment ceremony with all of you, and it will be as binding as the legal marriage ceremony to me."

"What's a commitment ceremony?" Saint inquires.

I twist around so I'm facing him. "I researched it in the early hours this morning. It's what a lot of people do in polyamorous relationships. We commit our love in a ceremony that binds us together in our hearts." Nerves jangle in my chest. "It won't be legal, but I would view it in the same way. It's for us and only us."

I don't care whether society views our relationship as wrong, and I sure as fuck don't care that they wouldn't recognize my other three husbands. All I care about is us doing this together as a commitment of sharing our lives together. To me, doing this is more permanent than any marriage certificate because we are willingly choosing to commit ourselves to this relationship.

"I love it," Caz says. "And I don't need to think about it. I'm in."

"It's perfect," Galen adds, tucking my hair behind my ear. "I want to do it."

"I already know I'll love you till my dying days," Theo supplies. "And I want to commit to you."

Air whooshes out of my mouth in grateful relief, and I smile as I probe Saint's face. "What are your thoughts?"

"We're already committed as far as I'm concerned." He grips my chin. "But if this makes it more formal, then hell yeah. We're doing it."

The guys share grins, and my heart swells to bursting point. "Good, because I've already been talking with a lady who conducts these ceremonies, but I didn't set anything up, because I didn't want to presume anything."

"None of us have any doubts," Galen says. "You are it for us."

I'm choked with emotion, and my voice trembles as I speak. "And you are it for me."

"What about the legal wedding?" Saint asks.

"I would be happy to marry any of you. I hope you all know that." They bob their heads. "I've thought about it nonstop since you brought it up yesterday, and I have my reasons for the decision I've made. I'm not getting into it, unless any of you need to know." I don't want to hurt anyone or force Caz and Theo into discussing their feelings, when they've only just agreed to set those aside until Theo feels more ready to confront them, so I'd rather not elaborate on my decision, unless I have to.

"Just tell us," Saint says, squeezing my hand tighter.

Anticipation bleeds into the air, and I swallow over the lump in my throat as I twist around so I'm looking Saint directly in the face. Our knees brush, sending a jolt of electricity shooting up my leg.

"I want it to be you."

I peer deep into his eyes. Shock splays across his face, and he goes deathly still. He stares at me like he can't believe I just said that. I'm smiling as I clasp his face in my hands. "So, what do you say, Saintly? Wanna marry me?"

Chapter Fourteen
Harlow

His lips meld to mine as he scoops me onto his lap, kissing me frantically as pure, liquid emotion seeps from his lips to mine. "Really?" he asks, pressing his forehead to mine when he breaks the kiss.

"Really." I stare into his awestruck blue eyes. "I love you, and I want the world to know I'm yours." I lift my head from his, glancing over my shoulder at the others. "That I'm all of yours."

I inspect their faces for any hint of upset, finding none. In fact, I'd almost say they are relieved. These guys are as close as brothers, so they know what it would've done to Saint if I hadn't chosen him. They are happy I've made this decision, and another layer of stress lifts off my shoulders with that realization.

Theo clears his throat, his eyes popping wide and head nodding as he stares at Saint.

"Stand up," Saint says, all traces of disbelief gone from his tone. I let him pull me up as Theo, Galen, and Caz come around to stand beside Saint. I spot Theo subtly passing something to Saint behind their backs.

As one, they drop to their knees before me, and a gasp leaves my mouth.

"We did this all wrong yesterday," Galen says. "This is how it should've gone down."

Saint produces a little black box, popping the lid, and I can't stop the tears from flowing as I stare at the stunning ring. It's not a traditional engagement ring with one diamond but a row of five deep-blue stones, rimmed in tiny fine diamonds, set within a thick platinum band.

It couldn't be more perfect.

"Oh my God. I love it," I exclaim, wondering if they can hear how fast my heart is beating.

"I love you," Theo says, taking my hand. "From the first moment you entered my world, you breathed life into me. The way I feel about you is unparalleled, and I never want to experience what it's like to lose you again. I want to live my best life with you. Now and always." He kisses my knuckles before passing my hand to Caz.

"You blow my mind, babe," Caz says. "You're my every fantasy come to life and then some. Nothing has ever felt as right as holding you in my arms, and now I get to do that forever." He kisses my hand. "Love you."

"You've challenged me from the minute I met you, and you make me a better man," Galen says, clasping my hand. "Thank you for giving me a second chance, and I promise to prove I deserve it every day for the rest of my life. I love you."

Tears spill down my cheeks as unbridled emotion consumes me. Saint squeezes my hand, never taking his eyes off me as he brushes his lips against my knuckles. "I fell hard and fast the second our eyes met at thirteen, and there has only been you from that moment on. I don't know what it's like to love and be loved, but I promise to never stop fighting to give you what you deserve." He stands, and the others rise behind him. Saint removes the ring from the box, sliding it on my finger. "I love you, Harlow June Westbrook. *We* love you. Marry us?"

I grab them all into a group hug, and sobs wrack my chest as emotion literally oozes out of me. The guys look a little teary-eyed too, but they wouldn't be the legendary Saints if they didn't hold it together.

We laugh, kiss, and hug, and then the champagne is flowing, and they give me the biggest bunch of roses, and I know everything will be okay, because they've got my back and I've always got theirs.

"I think we should celebrate in style," Caz says a while later as we are lounging on the couches, finishing the champagne.

"What do you have in mind?" I ask.

"I think it's time we tested our new bed out, don't you?" Caz waggles his brows.

"An engagement fuck fest," Galen says, rubbing his hands. "I like the way you think, dude."

Caz rubs the bulge in his jeans. "I'm always thinking with my brain," he quips.

"I hate to rain on our parade," Saint says, tugging me in closer to him, his fingers running back and forth across the ring on my finger. "But we need to get back to Giana."

"Saintly's right. I need to get Mom to safety, so as much as I'm down for fucking your collective brains out, we'll have to take a rain check."

"Has Diesel called?" Saint asks.

"Not yet, but I can't wait for him. He could be on a new mission for all we know."

"Let's run through our options." Theo leans forward on his knees, setting his tablet aside. He was lodging an online application with city hall so Saint and I can get married on Thursday. Thankfully, you can get a license and get married the same day. I've messaged the lady I was talking to about the commitment ceremony to see if she can fit us in on the same day.

Other than that, I know nothing, because the guys want it to be a surprise. They are insisting on organizing everything, and I'm happy to let them work away. I've never had set ideas about my wedding day, and I trust the guys to plan it to perfection.

"Lo." Theo calls my name, dragging me out of my mind.

"Sorry. I got distracted. What were you saying?"

"Options for Giana."

"Okay, yeah. Well, the cabin is the obvious choice, but it's isolated, and it's too far from school. I don't like the thought of her being there by herself, and I don't want Sinner to discover that place."

"I agree," Saint says, running his finger across my ring again. "We need a safe place to escape to if the need arises. Sinner knows the location of all the safe houses The Sainthood uses, and your mom suspects he knows about this place, so we need to protect the cabin."

"We could always move her into my house, for the time being," Galen suggests.

"Sinner and his cronies are in and out of your house with their shipments all the time, and it's probably one of the first places he would look," I say. Besides, I'm not sure Mom would want to live in the same house as her former best friend, knowing she had an affair with her husband and got knocked up with his baby. A baby Alisha later aborted in favor of drug money.

"We could hire protection for her. Like, use a legit security firm," Caz suggests. "That might hold Sinner at bay for a couple days until we can find someplace else to stash her."

"That might work," Theo says. "But we're forgetting one very important thing. What if Giana doesn't want to go?"

"Then I'm done with her." A muscle clenches in my jaw. "I mean that. If she doesn't walk away now, I can't help her." If she has such little regard for her own life, I can't be a part of it anymore.

"Let's go talk to her." Saint stands, removing the car keys from his pocket and handing them to Galen. He only had one glass of champagne so he's the only one fit to drive.

Thankfully, Sinner's truck is absent when we arrive back at the house. Diesel messaged me en route, offering a better solution than Galen's house. He's on standby until I give him the go-ahead. I just need to convince Mom this is the right call to make.

The house is quiet when we step inside. Eerily so, and that frightens me. I race through the kitchen and out into the hall, slamming to a halt when I spot the four guys sitting on the floor, wearing Sainthood cuts, blowing cigarette clouds into the air as they smoke while staring at their phones.

"You can leave," Saint tells them, coming up behind me.

"Any problems?" Galen asks, coming up on my other side.

"She hasn't come downstairs, and no one has gone up," the

tall, dark-haired guy says, and I vaguely recognize him. I think he might go to our school.

"Thanks, man." Saint slaps him on the back.

"Anytime." He nods before looking at me. "We were sorry to hear about Sariah. Those bitches should burn in hell for what they did to her."

"Thanks. I'm pretty sure county jail is hell on Earth, so they'll get what's coming to them."

"Bank on it," Saint says, slinging his arm around my waist. "We've already put the word out." I squeeze Saint's waist in a show of gratitude, glad he's organized that. The case is coming before the court next month, and everyone knows they're going down. What Beth and the other two girls don't realize is The Sainthood has planned a "Welcome to Jail" party to end all parties.

Couldn't happen to more deserving recipients.

The guys filter out the front door, and I race up the stairs, eager to get to Mom.

My guys congregate in Saint's bedroom while I slip into my bedroom, where Mom is holed up. The curtains are still drawn, and it's dark as I pad over to the bed. "Mom." I sit down and switch on the lamp, biting back a hiss when I spot the bruised skin around her throat and her wrists and the raised lash marks on her upper chest. Her eyes bore into mine, confirming she wasn't sleeping. "It's after three."

"Is he here?" she croaks, and I don't miss the flare of panic that crosses her face.

"No. He left last night and hasn't been back."

"Good."

"But you know he will, and we need to make plans."

"I already have a plan." Her tone is neutral, and the expression on her face gives nothing away.

"Are you going to explain that?"

She shakes her head. "Nothing has changed in that regard. It's still safer if you don't know."

I sigh in exasperation. "You need to get out of here before he comes back."

Silence greets my statement, and I'm lining up arguments when she opens her mouth, shocking me. "I know."

I stare at her, examining her face to ensure she's not messing with me. "You mean that?"

She nods. "I thought I could do this, but I can't, and I'm adjusting my plan accordingly."

"No." I shake my head, tipping her chin up gently so she's looking me in the eye. "You aren't going to do anything else. You need to heal and rest and let us take care of him."

"I can't ask that of you. You're a child."

"I'm eighteen, Mom, and we both know I stopped being a child at thirteen."

"I never wanted this for you," she whispers. "I was supposed to protect you, and I've failed so badly."

"You don't need to worry," Saint says, and I jerk my head to the door. It's slightly ajar, and only his head is visible. "We're here to protect Harlow now."

I gesture him inside, and he closes the door after him.

"Do you promise to keep her safe, Saint?" Mom drills a hole in his skull.

"We do. You just focus on extracting yourself from Sinner's noose."

She sits up, clutching the covers around her chest, hissing and gritting her teeth. She lies back against the headrest. "We both know no one willingly walks away from Sinner Lennox."

"Which is why we have help," I supply.

"Help from who?"

"A good friend, Mom. Someone who knows how to hide a person and keep them safe."

"I won't leave the state, Harlow. I can't." She wets her chapped lips. "At least not yet."

I want to quiz her on that, but we're making great progress, and if we start arguing, she might change her mind. "Okay. I'll tell my friend that." I pause for a moment, licking my lips. "What do you want to do about the house?" I ask, because we'll be moving permanently to the barn tonight and I don't want to give Sinner free rein to do what he pleases here. Knowing him, he'd turn it into a drug house or a brothel.

"I want to sell it." She takes my hands. "I know you grew up here, but I can't bear to live in this house without your father. Especially now that bastard has tainted it by his very presence."

"I agree, Mom. You should sell it, and when all this has blown over, you should buy something new. Start afresh."

Saint has been tapping away on his cell while we're talking. "Theo has a guy on his way over to change all the locks, and if you like, he can get someone to install a high-tech security system with mounted cameras along the front wall and a new front gate that can only be accessed via a code. That way you can keep Sinner out until the house is sold."

"Ask Theo to set that up, please." She smiles at Saint. "He was always a resourceful young man. What is that?" Mom adds, noticing my ring, and I curse my lack of forethought. As much as I'd love to tell her I'm getting married, I can't. A, she'd probably freak, and B, I still don't trust her fully.

"A promise ring," I lie. "The guys just gave it to me."

She lifts my hand under the lamp, admiring the ring. "It's beautiful. You have good taste." She smiles at Saint, but it doesn't meet her eyes. She looks like she wants to say more, but her lips remain clamped shut.

"We should pack," Saint says, standing. "And get out of here as fast as we can."

I pull out my cell. "I'm on it." I tap out a message to Diesel as Saint leaves the room, telling him we're a go, asking that he house Mom somewhere within the state so she's close by.

I help Mom get dressed and packed, taking only essential clothing and personal belongings, while she retrieves some papers, cash, and her jewelry from the safe in her bedroom. By the time we finish, the guys have already packed up my stuff along with theirs and they are in the process of loading up the cars while a guy works on changing all the exterior locks.

Theo's boots thump off the tile floor in the hallway as he walks toward us, carrying a paper bag. He hands it to Mom. "Something to eat and drink, and there's some pain pills in there."

Tears pool in her eyes as she takes the offering. She kisses his cheek. "I'm sorry if I was less than welcoming when you first arrived."

"It's okay. I understood."

The screeching of tires outside has all of us turning our attention to the open front door. Adrenaline surges through my veins, and I withdraw my knife, ready to swing into action if that's Sinner or any of his perverted friends.

But it's a friendly face, one I'm not expecting.

"Lincoln?" Mom's brow puckers as she stares at my dad's former work colleague. "What are you doing here?" Mom's head whips around to me. "Is this the friend you were talking about?"

"Actually," Lincoln says, stepping inside the house. "My brother set this up, and you can trust him. Trust me." His face pales as he notices the marks and injuries clearly visible on Mom. "Jesus Christ, Giana." He drags a hand through his dark hair. "What has that bastard done to you?" Lincoln's anguished eyes meet mine briefly before flicking back to Mom. He takes her hands in his, drawing closer. "I'm so sorry I wasn't there for you. I promised Trey, and I didn't do enough."

"I'm not your responsibility," Mom says, squeezing his hands. "And you've nothing to apologize for. You're here now. That's all that counts."

He nods, releasing her hands and turning to me. "My brother said you were safe, but if anything changes, you know how to reach me."

"I'll be fine. Just look after Mom."

"I'll guard her with my life."

"I'd like a word with my daughter. Alone." Mom glances at the guys and Lincoln.

"I'll put your bags in the car and let you say your goodbyes, but don't take too long. We shouldn't delay." Lincoln swipes Mom's bags and exits the house with my guys in tow.

"I know we need to have a long talk, and I promise we'll do that soon. For now, I need you to promise me that you won't do anything reckless. Don't go after Sinner for this, Harlow, and stay out of his way. Let your boyfriends protect you."

It sounds so weird hearing Mom say boyfriends, as in plural, but I guess I'm lucky she's accepting of our unusual relationship. "I could say the same to you about Sinner. Whatever you are planning, don't do it. Trust us to deal with this. We *are* going to handle it." I hug her gently. "He's going to pay for what he did to all of us, Mom. He's not getting away with it."

Chapter Fifteen
Harlow

"What happened to my Lexus?" I ask the following morning as we exit the barn and climb into Saint's Land Rover, heading for school.

"There was extensive damage, but it wasn't totaled," Caz explains. "I dropped it into a buddy's garage, and they're working on it. We should be able to pick it up sometime next week."

I swivel in the passenger seat, turning around so I can blow him a kiss. "Thanks, babe."

Caz pokes his head through the gap between the two front seats, angling his head toward me. "I wish I had the time to work on it myself."

"You fix cars?"

He nods. "I used to work at the garage part-time after school, but my grades dropped, and Mom insisted I focus on school this year." He barks out a laugh. "Which is laughable, because it's made no fucking difference."

"I'd like to meet your mom," I say. "We should drop by sometime."

"She'd like that. She's always getting on my case because she hardly sees me these days."

"Then it's decided. We'll visit her soon."

He leans forward, pecking my lips. "I already know she'll love you."

I mess up his hair, and he pokes his tongue out at me before settling back in his seat.

"Have you heard from your dad?" Theo asks, lifting his head from his tablet and eyeballing Saint through the mirror.

"No." Saint's tone is clipped.

"Concerning," Galen murmurs.

"I know." Saint sighs. "He's got to know he's been locked out."

"And he'll know we helped with that." I turn up the heating in the car and snuggle into my warm sweater 'cause it's fucking cold today and my bones are chilled.

"He will, and he'll want blood," Galen adds.

"We stay away from him at all costs," Saint says. "We can attend to Sainthood business and use school as an excuse to avoid going near him."

"He won't buy it," Galen says.

"I don't fucking care!" Saint grips the steering wheel hard as we near the school, and it's obvious he's wound up tight, and ready to explode, so we drop the conversation—even though we all understand Sinner will be itching to take us down a few pegs for helping his fiancée dump his perverted ass.

Entering the familiar building without my bestie by my side is a heart-wrenching experience, only made bearable by the guys cocooning me on all sides. The crowd parts to let us pass, and a deathly hush descends.

"Fuck off," Saint snaps, glaring at everyone as we pass. "Go about your usual business. Now." It's clear he's not asking, and it's amazing how quickly everyone scurries off, at least pretending like they're not gawking at us.

A lump the size of a bus lodges in my throat as we approach my locker. Sariah's was directly across the hallway, and the sight of all the cards, gifts, and flowers adorning her locker almost undoes me. I stop, rooted to the spot, staring at her locker, while pain slices across my chest. I should probably be happy people cared enough to leave gifts and notes, but I'm mostly angry. The majority of these people ignored Sariah when she was a student here, and the hypocrisy astounds me.

"Lo." A familiar voice has me whipping my head around, and I close the distance to my locker. Sean is standing there with Emmett at his side, both towering over me.

"Hey." I grab Sean into a hug. "It's good to see you." I've sent him a few texts this past week, but I haven't had any response. Emmett told me he's struggling, big-time, and I'm concerned.

"This is all so fucking pointless." Sean shrugs, and Emmett shoots me worried eyes. "I hate it here without her."

My guys open their lockers, watching and listening, ready to step in if I need them.

"It sucks," I agree, because I'm already feeling her loss, so I can only imagine how awful it is for Sean. There is no doubt in my mind Sean and Sariah were in it for the long haul. They had a special kind of love that doesn't die overnight. It's going to take Sean a long time to get over her. If he ever will.

"It helps that you're here," he adds, attempting a smile that falls flat. "It helps me feel closer to her."

I hug him again. "I know what you mean." It's the same with Sean, although it also hurts, because I'm not used to seeing Sean without Sariah and it's a constant reminder that she's gone. But I can tell Sean needs the connection, and I want to be there for him.

"New ring?" Emmett blurts, his eyes widening when he notices the finger I'm wearing it on.

"Yeah." I slide the ring onto my middle finger, beseeching him to drop the subject with my eyes. Sean has just lost the love of his life. I don't want to rub my happiness in his face.

Emmett is no dumb jock, and he instantly gets it, switching the subject. "My sister asks me almost daily when you're dropping by."

"This week is hectic, but maybe next week?"

"Cool." Emmett's answering smile is wide, and Saint slams his locker shut with more force than necessary.

I roll my eyes. Some things will never change. "Careful, Saintly. Your crazy is showing."

He smacks my ass. Hard. And I glare at him. "Careful, princess. You know what happens when you push my buttons." He smirks, sliding his arm possessively around my shoulders. "And I know how much you love being punished." He eyeballs Emmett as he speaks. "Some might say you do it on purpose." He smacks me again, and I push him away, snarling. "Because you love when I spank your naughty ass."

Emmett's smile fades, replaced with a sour grimace. "I still can't believe you find that shit attractive." He shakes his head at me, and I shrug, because I won't apologize for who I am or what I enjoy. From the way he narrows his eyes at Saint, I know he'd love to throat punch him. I don't think those two will ever put their differences aside, no matter how much I beg them to stop acting like jealous idiots.

My cell pings with a message, and I'm grateful for the distraction. I pull it out, scowling as my ex's name pops up on the screen. *Great.* Just what I need. Darrow Knight riding my ass again. He's been notoriously quiet the past week, but he's aware of what happened, so I'm guessing that's the only reason he hasn't been pestering me for intel.

Guess my reprieve is over.

"I got one too," Galen whispers in my ear, glancing at my cell. "Is he asking you to meet?" I nod. "Same."

"Line it up for Wednesday," Saint says, eavesdropping on our conversation. "It's our only free night."

"I'll need to give him something," I remind them, wishing I'd had the forethought to take Dad's other files from the cabin. He has a bunch of work files—old cases he worked on for The Sainthood—that have proven useful before. The Arrows used the last file I gave them to get one of their guys out of jail. Throwing another couple Darrow's way might get him off my case, for a while.

"We'll think of something," Theo assures me, as the bell chimes, signaling we need to get to class.

The morning drags by, and I'm finding it hard to concentrate. At the start of senior year, I was determined to stick to my goal, to study hard and maintain a high GPA, so my Brown dream becomes a reality, but with everything hanging in the balance, I honestly don't care that much anymore. Surviving senior year alive is a more worthy goal, so it seems pointless wasting time in class when we could be plotting Sinner's downfall. Unless I totally flunk things, or my attendance falls below the minimum required, I'll graduate, and that's all that matters.

What we do after graduation is yet to be determined. But the world is our oyster. And Brown isn't the be-all and end-all.

We sit at our usual table in the cafeteria during lunch, but I toy with the food on my plate, having no appetite. The guys don't push it, understanding the pain I'm in, and I'm grateful they are leaving me to it. Sean barely talks, letting Emmett carry the conversation.

It's business as usual for the guys, and they're occupied

with a steady stream of idiots who approach the table, providing updates, placing orders, or putting requests in for ad hoc shit. Mostly, I tune them out, gnashing my teeth at a few bitches who are stupid enough to flirt with what belongs to me.

By the time the bell rings at the end of the day, I'm more than ready to get out of this hellhole.

The guys drop Theo and me at the barn, leaving to take care of some secret wedding mission, and I'm a lot less stressed stepping through the doors of our home than I was a half hour ago when leaving school. "Wow. You guys are really taking this seriously," I say, switching the Keurig on and making a fresh pot of coffee.

"We only get one shot to get this right," Theo says, coming up behind me and sliding his arms around my waist. "We want to make it special and memorable."

I twist around in his arms, weaving my fingers through his hair. "I already know it will be. You don't need to go to huge trouble on my account. Making you all mine is everything I need and want."

"Did you ever think about this? Back when we were dating?" Sweeping my hair aside, he places his lips on my neck.

"I did," I admit, arching my neck so he has more access. "Even though I knew it was silly, because I thought you weren't into me like that, I did visualize marrying you some day."

"Me too," he whispers, as his delectable mouth roams up and down my neck.

"You did?" I can't shield the disbelief from my tone.

He lifts his head, clasping my face. "My head was a mess back then. You know this. But you were still everything to me, Lo. I imagined marrying you. It might have confused me a little, but I still thought about it."

"You know, I never thought I'd say this, but I'm glad we

went through that pain." I grip his hips, pulling him flush to my body, and my core pulses as his hard length pushes against me.

"Because it's led us here," he whispers, gripping my ass cheeks in his large palms. "And I wouldn't change a single part of our history."

We move at the same time, our lips colliding in a hungry kiss that quickly becomes more. Our hips thrust against one another, and I need him to fill me in every place. "Fuck me," I whimper into his mouth. "Right here. Right now."

His eyes blaze with fierce need as he spins us around, pressing me down over the counter. "Does that hurt?" he asks, as his hands slide around to the band of my jeans and he pops the button.

"No," I lie, because the truth is my ribs are still fucking sore, but I've learned to live with the pain. "Just do it already. I need your cock inside me."

He pulls my jeans and panties down my legs and unbuttons my boots, tossing them aside. His hands glide up my legs, and liquid warmth floods my pussy, as my hips buck involuntarily against the side of the counter, needing friction, needing cock, needing Theo. The sound of clothing falling to the floor has me licking my lips and squirming with desire.

I cry out when his fingers push inside me, riding his hand as he pumps his digits into me. "Fuck, you are so wet."

"Don't sound surprised. You know what you do to me."

"I never take it for granted, beautiful." He leans over me, and his cock nudges against the crack in my ass.

"Take my ass," I hiss, moaning as his fingers stroke the perfect spot inside my pussy. I'm not sure if it's deliberate, but Theo has shied away from ass play since we reunited.

"Gladly, baby," he says, shoving his cock deep in my pussy. "Let me work up to that." He pounds into my cunt as he shoves his fingers into my mouth. "Suck." I do as I'm told, because the promise of what's to come has me feverish and on fire. Slowly, he works his fingers into my ass, one at a time, stretching me out, while his cock slides in and out of my cunt.

"Fuck, Theo. That feels so good." I push my ass back against his finger. "But I need your cock. Now, babe. Please."

He pulls his cock from my pussy, lining it up at my asshole, and slowly eases inside me. Using his other hand, he slides two fingers into my cunt.

"Oh my God, Theo." I push back against him when he's fully seated, and he holds his cock still as his fingers pump in and out of my pussy.

"I know, baby. You feel so good on my cock and my fingers." He loses control then, slamming in and out of my ass while his fingers work my cunt, and the pain in my ribs fades into the background as I let go, closing my eyes and savoring everything he's doing to me.

He circles my clit with his thumb as his fingers continue stroking the walls of my pussy, and I come apart on his hand as he rams into my ass, over and over, roaring as he comes, shooting his warm cum all over the cheeks of my ass.

We shower together afterward, and when we're clean, he carries me to the bed and takes me again, coming in my pussy this time. I drift to sleep in his arms with a big smile on my face.

Chapter Sixteen
Harlow

We meet Bryant Eccleston on Tuesday night in an abandoned house on the outskirts of Lowell, far from prying eyes. Bry is already inside when we arrive, talking in hushed tones on his cell. He cuts the call the second he sees us, sliding his cell into the back pocket of his jeans.

"Sup." He jerks his head in the guy's direction. "Lo," he adds, casting a quick glance over me. "I'm glad you're okay."

"No thanks to your fuck buddy," Saint snarls, folding his arms and staring at Bry. There is still no love lost there.

"One-time fuck buddy," Bry corrects him, adopting the same stance.

"Quit that shit." I push between them, dragging their arms down. I point between all of us. "Same team. Remember?"

Bry scrubs his hands down his face, looking more agitated than normal. "You're right." He shoves his hands in the front pockets of his jeans. "But feeling like I'm seconds from a dagger in the neck doesn't invoke confidence," he admits.

"Give us one good reason why we should trust you?" Galen asks.

"Because I haven't given you any reason not to," Bry snarls.

"Not good enough," Caz says.

Bry throws his hands in the air, sending me a frustrated look, pleading for help.

"Guys, knock it off. Bry is not our enemy. We're on the same page, so put your personal feelings aside and engage your brains." I level them all with a deadly look. I know we don't fully understand Bry's motives yet, and we are right to be cautious, but treating him like an archenemy is getting us nowhere. If they continue doing this, they'll push him firmly into Sinner's corner, and that won't benefit anyone.

"You said you have something for us," Saint says. "Let's hear it."

"I planted the cameras in Archer Quinn's office on Sunday, and it's already paying dividends."

"You should have led with that," Theo suggests.

"I would have if I could've gotten a word in edgewise!" Bry snaps.

"Focus!" I bark, glaring at all of them, because they're pissing me off now. "What have you discovered, Bry?"

"Diego is meeting the mole Saturday night. I have the exact time and location."

"A breakthrough at last. Thank fuck." Galen pushes strands of his messy dark hair out of his eyes. He hasn't been wearing it in his faux hawk lately, either because he's too lazy to style it, because we've been largely holed up alone, or he knows I love it wild and untamed.

"That's excellent, Bry." My smile is genuine, and his shoulders relax a smidgeon.

"Why is Diego meeting him and not Archer?" Saint asks.

"I'm guessing Diego has been the contact point all along.

Archer is the prez, so he's the most obvious choice, but maybe he knows Sinner is trying to find out the identity of the rat in his ranks, and he'd assume Archer or the VP is the one doing the meets. Diego is the sergeant at arms, someone Archer trusts, but this isn't his typical responsibility, so it's less likely he's being watched."

"Makes sense," Theo agrees.

"It doesn't matter anyway," Galen says. "Because we're about to find out who it is."

"And whether they know where that Leydon evidence is," I add, because that's the sole reason we want to find him.

"We need another favor," Saint says. His body language confirms he's still tense and on guard, and I need to do something about that later.

"What is it?" Bry coolly regards Saint.

"We need to distract Sinner, and a little payback should do the trick. Do you have details of the next Arrows shipment we can slip to him?"

"No, but I'll get them."

"Before Friday," Saint adds, and Bry nods, moving to leave.

"There's one more thing," I say, the thought just occurring to me. "Did you ever reach out to Taylor Tamlin?" It had been part of our plan before the bitch tried to kill us.

"I did, but we haven't met."

"You should," I say. "We need you to keep tabs on her."

Saint nods at me, instantly understanding where I'm going with this.

"I thought you had her handled." Bry's gaze jumps between Saint and me.

"We do, but I don't trust her to stick to it." I shrug. "Call it a hunch."

"Okay. I'll take one for the team." Bry waggles his brows, fighting a grin.

"Slap her around a bit while you're at it," I add, smirking. "And I hope you like the GI Jane look because I gave her a little homegrown haircut as a parting gift."

Bry chuckles. "I expect nothing less."

"She's lucky she's still fucking breathing," Caz says.

"I'll admit I was surprised," Bry says.

"She's small fry, and we've bigger balls to juggle," Galen says. "But Lo is right."

"As usual." I fix him with a smug look, and he flips me the bird. I laugh, and Bry surveys me curiously. "What?" I ask.

"It's not often I see you laughing like that. You should do it more."

Saint snarls, and I slam my lips against his as he opens his mouth to insult Bry, no doubt. I pull away when I feel him relaxing. "Behave," I whisper into his ear. "And I'll make it worth your while when we get home."

"Deal," he whispers back, sliding his hand under my sweater, placing it on my lower back.

"We done here?" Bry clips out, all good humor gone.

"Yeah. Thanks, Bry."

"I'll be in touch before Friday," he says before stalking off.

"I hoped by agreeing to marry you, you might ease up on the whole caveman routine, but, if anything, you're getting worse," I say, whipping my sweater up over my head.

Saint closes the door to the adjoining bedroom, lifting his shirt over his head as he moves toward me. "Don't you know me at all?" He flashes me a shit-eating grin while popping the button on my jeans.

"I do. That's the problem, because you're only going to get ten million times worse."

"You betcha, princess." His hand slides under my jeans and into my panties. "I also know how much my possessiveness turns you on, despite your protests." He slides two digits inside me, grinning as the proof coats his fingers.

I push him away, and he stumbles back. "You're an asshole." I shimmy my jeans down my legs, kicking them aside. "And I've changed my mind. I think I'll sleep with Galen tonight." I storm past him in my underwear, knowing there is no way in hell he'll let me leave.

He grabs my arm, pulling me back, plastering me to his front with my back to his bare chest. "I think you're testing me on purpose, princess."

Of course, I am, because he needs me to push his buttons. "Such petty behavior is beneath a *queen*." I emphasize the word so he knows exactly who he's dealing with.

"So is pretending to cockblock your king," he rasps, sliding his hand into my panties again. His fingers push into me roughly. "When we both know you're craving my dick."

I thrust my elbow back into his chest, forcing him to release me. "I never said I wasn't craving dick," I purr, turning around, facing the heated glare on his face. "But I have four dicks to choose from, and any one of them will do."

His arm darts out, and he grabs the nape of my neck in a firm grip. "Now you've done it." Pushing me to my knees, he keeps a tight hold of my neck while shoving his jeans down his legs, revealing he's going commando, as his long, hard cock springs free.

I look up at him, keeping a neutral expression on my face, pretending like my pussy isn't aching for his dick. "I'm not sucking you off," I lie.

"I'm not fucking asking." He forces my mouth open,

jamming his cock inside, and the second his velvety-soft skin hits the back of my throat, I give up the charade, wrapping my lips around his needy shaft, moaning as desire pools low in my belly.

"That's it, princess. Choke on my cock, like a good little girl."

I flip him the bird, and he laughs.

Asshole.

I work him over good, and it doesn't take long before he's shooting his salty cum down my throat. After, I let him fuck my pussy and my ass too, and by the time he falls asleep, he's completely stress free and I'm giving myself a silent pat on the back for taking such good care of my man.

"What the fuck is he doing here?" Galen hisses the following afternoon, as we skip the last class of the day, exiting the school building en route to my rendezvous with Darrow.

"Fuck." Saint curses under his breath, staring at Sinner. His father is sitting on the small wall in front of Saint's Land Rover, smoking a joint and flirting with two seniors who are on the cheerleading squad, both young enough to be his daughters.

He's a disgusting pig, and I'm glad Mom has finally come to her senses. I've been checking in with her daily, using one of my burner cells, and she seems okay. We don't know where she is, only that she's not too far away, and Lincoln is keeping her safe.

Saint clasps my hand, and we walk down the steps and along the path toward his father.

"Neo." Saint plants us in front of the asshole. "What do you want?"

"Now, now, son. Is that any way to greet the man who gave you life?" His amused grin is as fake as everything else about him.

A muscle flexes in Sinner's jaw as he stands, flicking the joint to the ground. He turns the full extent of his charm on the two girls fawning over him, holding out his cell. "Pop your digits in there, ladies, and I'll send you an invitation to my party." He drills me with a look. "I'll be celebrating finally freeing myself of the chains that have bound me for far too long."

Ice-cold dread drips down my spine. "You touch one hair on my mother's head, and I will kill you."

Saint yanks on my hand in warning.

The two girls look up from Sinner's cell, staring at me with their jaws trailing the ground.

"She was joking," Galen says, grabbing the cell out of their hands and steering them off to the side.

"Control your whore, or I'll do it for you," Sinner hisses.

"Harlow is not a whore. She's an initiate like us, and she deserves some goddamned respect." Saint visibly seethes as he glares at his dad, and I love how readily he jumps to defend me, but he needs to be careful too. Sinner is an unpredictable psycho, and he wouldn't think twice about hurting his own son. I plant my hand on Saint's lower back, urging him to hold it together.

"I'll treat your whore with respect when she's earned it. When she steps up to the plate and starts fucking acting like a member of our crew."

"Wow. Tell me how you really feel," I drawl, maintaining a calm façade while I'm seething on the inside.

"The next time you call her that, I will fucking kill you

myself." Saint's entire body shakes as he enters a lethal stare down with the sperm donor.

A deep chuckle rumbles from Sinner's chest, and he pins Saint with an amused grin. "This is like watching history repeat itself." He thumps Saint in the upper arm. "Take it from one who knows. Ditch her now, and save yourself the heartache."

"You wouldn't know heartache if it bit you in the ass," I blurt.

His good humor evaporates, and he darts forward, gripping my chin. "You know nothing about me. Nothing!" he roars, and it's clear I've hit a nerve.

Interesting.

Saint swats Sinner's arm away, pulling me into his side. "Was there a reason for your visit because we have someplace to be." He feigns disinterest, but he's a melting pot of rage waiting to combust.

"I'm here to remind you who you are." He pushes Saint's shoulders as Galen returns, injecting himself in between them.

"Leave him the fuck alone." Galen's fists clench into balls at his sides, and I know he's itching to flatten the asshole, because it's how I feel every time I'm in his company.

"You too," Sinner adds, poking Galen in the chest before trailing his gaze around all of us. "All of you. You are part of The Sainthood. Sworn to obey my command."

I snort, and that only enrages him further.

"You clearly have little regard for your lives or those of your loved ones." He loses his anger, flashing us a devilish grin that chills me to the bone. "It's time you remembered your duties." He steps up to me again, his lips tugging into a familiar smug grin that I hate so much. "I own you." He jabs his finger in my collarbone before eyeballing the others. "All of you, and you will obey or suffer the consequences."

Pushing Galen aside, he fixes his gaze upon his son. "You

are Saint Lennox. Junior chapter leader and my heir apparent. I know you conspired behind my back to take my fiancée away. I don't take kindly to loyalty being tested." His eyes burn with deep-seated rage. "I'm here to remind you of the importance of Friday night." His eyes flit to mine, and there's no disguising the lust in his eyes, but there is plenty of hatred too. My heart slams against my rib cage, and goose bumps sprout on my arms. "Do not stand in my way, or you'll be sorry. The last person who tried to take something precious from me didn't survive to tell the tale." He slaps Saint on the shoulder. "I'd hate for you to end up like your mother."

Chapter Seventeen
Harlow

"He's lying," Galen says as Saint drives us toward the biker bar Darrow favors.

"What if he's not?" Saint says, through gritted teeth, gripping the steering wheel so tight, his knuckles blanch white.

"He said it to do this very thing," Theo says. "Upset you. Distract you."

"Don't give him that power, man," Caz says.

"That's easier said than done." I run my hand along Saint's thigh. "What do you know of your mother?" I tentatively ask.

"Nothing." His bitter tone bounces off the walls of the Land Rover as he drives. I wait for him to elaborate, but he doesn't.

"Anytime we asked him as kids, he told us Saint's mother didn't want him. Said she was dead to him and was to be dead to us," Galen replies when Saint doesn't.

"Maybe he meant that literally," Caz says.

Brakes screech to a halt as Saint stops the car in the middle of the road. Car horns blare behind us, and more brakes screech as cars attempt to avoid crashing into us. Ordinarily, I'd rip Saint a new one for pulling this shit, but I say nothing because he's a hot mess right now.

Dagger-filled looks and angry fists are raised as the occupants of other cars pass by us, still honking their horns.

Some brave soul gets out of his car, stalking to Saint's window, pummeling his fists on the glass, shouting and demanding an explanation.

"Oh boy." Caz chuckles as Saint lowers the window, pointing a gun at the man's chest.

"You have three seconds to get back to your car before I put a bullet through your heart," Saint deadpans, his voice cold and cruel. "One, two—" The man races off with his tail between his legs, jumping into his truck and hightailing it out of there.

Saint shuts the window, tucking the gun back into the waistband of his jeans. "I don't want to talk about *my mother* or *my father* anymore." He spits out the words like it pains him to say it. "We have shit to do, and that asshole is not distracting me with lies. Whether she's alive or dead doesn't matter. She's always been dead to me, and I don't care." He starts up the car, speaking into the windshield. "So, unless you've got a death wish, drop the fucking subject."

We don't talk the rest of the journey, and I purposely focus on staring out of the passenger side window to stop myself from sneaking peeks at Saint. None of us buys the horseshit he's peddling, and I'm worried about him. We all know Sinner is capable of killing his mother, and it would explain her absence, but her running off when Saint was born stacks up too. By then, she would've realized who knocked her up. It's disgusting to think she left an innocent child with a monster, but it's not inconceivable to imagine her running. She would've known not to run when she was pregnant. Sinner would never have let her take off with his kid, so maybe it was her plan all along.

The only thing we know for sure is we'll never find out, and Sinner isn't above using whatever means necessary to control his son.

The guys wait at the abandoned store, like last time, and I take Saint's Land Rover, driving it to the sleazy biker bar and parking it outside.

I spot the back of Darrow's head the second I walk into the dive, making a beeline for the booth he's in, pressing down on my necklace to activate the recording device so the guys can listen in. Diesel gave Theo access to the cloud drive the recordings automatically copy to, and he synced it to an app on the guys' cell phones.

"You're late," Dar barks as I slide into the seat across from him.

"Bite me," I drawl.

"I wait for no one," he adds, his eyes dropping to my chest.

"I see you still have a healthy god complex." I lean back casually in the booth.

His tongue darts out, wetting his lips, as his eyes stay glued to my cleavage.

He's such a dog. "Eyes on my face, asshole."

He leers at me, running his finger around the rim of his half-empty glass. "I miss fucking your tight cunt," he admits, and I imagine the guys are restraining Saint right about now. "Tempest's no fun in bed."

"Not my problem, and not what we're here to discuss." I slide the lipstick across the table to him.

"What the fuck is this?" His brows knit together as he stares at it.

"It's a USB stick with a ton of my father's files on it." I had almost forgotten I'd copied those files as a backup a few months ago. I know this won't appease Darrow much, but it's the best we could come up with at short notice. "You'll be able to get more of your guys out of the joint."

"This isn't what we agreed." He drains his beer and slams the bottle down on the table, clicking his fingers at the bottle-blonde behind the counter. "We agreed you'd get me current intel on what The Sainthood is up to, and you've given me jack shit." Spittle flies from his mouth, and his nostrils flare.

I must have been temporarily brain-dead to ever find him attractive.

"I was in the fucking hospital, and I can't pull intel from my ass," I snap, my patience stretching thin. My fingers twitch with the ever-increasing need to put a bullet in his skull. I should've taken the opportunity when he kidnapped me, because he's a fucking nuisance, and he's getting on my last nerve. I unsheathe my knife, letting the feel of it in my palm ground me.

"This is piss-poor, and you know it." He grinds his teeth, and his eyes narrow to slits. The waitress plonks a fresh beer down on the table, and Darrow yanks her to him, slamming his mouth against hers and shoving his tongue in her mouth, all while keeping his eyes open and staring at me.

Anger burns red hot in his eyes at my lack of reaction. Abruptly, he pulls back, grabbing her wrist to keep her in place. "But you can make it up to me." Placing his gun on top of the table, he leers at me again, and I know what he's going to say before he says it. "Join me and Jazzie in the back room, and I won't put a bullet in your treacherous cunt."

I press the sharp edge of my knife to his balls under the table, grinning as his eyes widen in alarm, and his body stiffens. "I wouldn't fuck you if you were the last man on Earth and my pussy was about to shrivel up and die. Slide the gun over the table, and I won't push this knife into your balls and chop off your cock."

I press in a bit harder when he doesn't immediately move,

and he jerks against the seat, hissing through his teeth. "You are so dead, Lo."

"Brave words for a man with a knife pressed against his dick."

Blondie's eyes widen, and her lips twitch. Reaching across him, she takes the gun and hands it to me.

I nod my thanks. "At least someone still has a functioning brain."

"We're done, Lo," Darrow growls as I withdraw my knife, curling my gloved hand around the gun, pointing it at him. "You'd better watch your back."

I slip my Strider in my back pocket. "We're done because I say we're done, and if anyone needs to watch his back, it's you. The last person who tried to take me out didn't fare so well."

I slide out of the booth, keeping the gun trained on him. "And I need little incentive when it comes to your cheating ass." I glance at the gun in my hand. "This is the second weapon I have with your fingerprints on it." I lean down into his face, pinching his cheek. "There are more ways than violence or death to take down an enemy, and you'd do well to remember that."

I snatch the USB drive from the table. "I'll be holding on to this now." He can fuck off if he thinks I'm giving him anything.

He pushes Blondie away, clenching his fists on top of the table. "This isn't the last you've seen of me, Lo. You've made a grave mistake."

"I'm quaking in my boots." I throw back my head, laughing as I back away, keeping the gun trained on my ex. "Have a nice life, asshole," I say just before I exit, hurrying to the car and peeling out of there.

"He's going to make you his mission now," Theo says when the guys are back inside the car and Saint is situated behind the wheel again.

"Let him try," Saint snarls, thrusting the car forward.

Galen's cell pings, and he cracks up laughing. "Man, he's pathetic."

I look into the back seat, grinning. "Darrow is nothing if not predictable."

"You should meet with him," Theo says. "Hear what he's planning."

"It could be a trap," Saint suggests.

"Nah." Galen shakes his head, and waves of dark, silky hair fall into his eyes. He tosses them aside with a flip of his head. "He still thinks I want Lo dead. I can tell him I'm even more bloodthirsty now that I was almost killed in the explosion that was meant for her."

"Cold." Saint grins wickedly at his cousin.

"But perfect," Caz adds.

"Perfect would be his head on a spike," Saint snarls. "He's lucky he's still in one piece after the shit he said to you back there."

"I was so tempted to slice off his dick," I admit. "Like, I seriously had to talk myself off that ledge."

Caz chuckles. "You couldn't deprive us of that sight. When you chop his cock off, I want a front-row seat."

I lean back for a knuckle touch. "Deal, dude. Wouldn't want to deprive you of such quality entertainment."

I sneak out later that night to meet Ashley after the guys have gone to sleep. I'm planning on a quick snatch and grab so I'm back in the house before they notice I've left. It's why I asked Ashley to drive to Prestwick Forest to meet me.

I drive through the main entrance to the woods and pull into the parking lot, alongside Ashley's car, and kill my engine. "Girl, this place gives me the creeps at night," she says, exiting her car the same time I exit mine.

I shudder as I remember the time the guys dumped me in a pit filled with bones in the dead of night and left me to crawl out by myself. "You're preaching to the choir," I agree, opening the trunk of the Gran Turismo. Luckily, I emptied it out before coming here, because the four framed photos are big, and they barely fit.

"Those are seriously hot." Ashley grins, propping her hip against the side of her car as I close the trunk. "And I like that you didn't ask Michelle to cover up your scars or your injuries."

"I'm proud of my scars," I say. "And I never hide them. They remind me every day that I've faced off with monsters and come out stronger." I pull myself up on the hood of my car. "I did consider hiding the bruising on my ribs," I admit. "For about five seconds." I flash her a grin. "Because the sentiment is the same there. That bitch tried to take me out, but she failed. I'm still here, and what doesn't kill you makes you stronger."

"Amen, sister. I think they make the photos hotter, and I'm sure the guys will love them."

"I hope so, because I'm replacing the nude posters on their

walls with my own version." I've been planning it from the instant I stepped foot in their place.

Ashley tosses her long hair over one shoulder, grinning wildly. "I so want to be you when I grow up." I toss her a grin. "Why weren't we friends before? It was such a wasted opportunity."

"We're friends now."

"You should come to the party Friday night. I know my guys would love to hang out with your guys."

Ashley's house is a regular party scene because her rents are rarely home, always overseas on business. Friday party nights at Ashley Shaw's has been a Lowell Academy tradition for the past couple years now.

"We have this thing we gotta do Friday, but if it goes okay, we can drop by."

"Cool." She slides down the hood of her car, wiping her hands down the front of her jeans.

I'm a little less elegant getting off the hood of my car, but I manage.

She leans in, hugging me. "See you Friday."

"Thanks again, Ashley. I owe you big-time."

"It's nothing." She shrugs. "It's what friends do."

We leave at the same time, exiting the forest in different directions, and I'm sure it hasn't escaped her notice I'm not heading in the direction of Lowell.

Leaving the pictures in the trunk, I slip into the house, resetting the alarm.

"Where did you sneak off to?" Theo's voice is low as I tiptoe, in the dark, past the couch.

"Oh my fucking God!" I screech. "You almost gave me a coronary."

"Sorry." He gets up, coming around the couch, smiling as I rub a hand over my chest. "I didn't mean to startle you."

"And I didn't mean to disturb you."

"I get alerts anytime the alarm is activated or deactivated," he explains. "What were you up to?" he asks again, pulling me into his hips.

"I had something I needed to do."

His brows climb to his hairline. "In Prestwick Forest parking lot in the middle of the night?" he asks, confirming he checked the tracking app.

I tweak his nose. "I was picking up your wedding presents. I want it to be a complete surprise, so don't say anything to the others, please?"

"You didn't have to get us anything, but I'm sure we'll love it." He pulls his fingers along his lips in a zipping motion. "And these lips are sealed."

We part ways at the foot of the stairways, and I kiss him softly before he goes up one set of stairs and I take the other. We decided not to christen our new bed until after the wedding ceremonies tomorrow, so Saint is sleeping there while the others take the other three beds, and I move between them as the mood strikes me.

I can't resist tiptoeing to Saint's side, pressing a gentle kiss to his brow, as he lays spread-eagled across the big bed. Then I slip into the room I'm sharing with Galen tonight, shedding my clothes and climbing in beside him. I snuggle into his back, and he stirs, taking my hand, pulling it tight around his waist, and I love how he reaches for me, even in sleep.

Closing my eyes, I inhale his comforting scent, excited to be spending my last night as a single woman. By this time tomorrow, I'll be married to four of the most amazing, most gorgeous guys on the planet.

And I can't fucking wait.

Chapter Eighteen
Harlow

"Wait right here," I tell the guys the following day, as the limo pulls up to the curb outside the jewelry store in the city. The guys surprised me with breakfast that included champagne and strawberries, and after we packed our overnight bags, we drove to Prestwick Forest, where a shiny limousine with blacked-out windows awaited us.

I dash into the store and collect the engraved wedding bands before racing back outside with them safely tucked in my purse.

The driver takes us to the hotel next, and Theo checks us into the penthouse while we linger outside the elevator bank.

I walk around the plush penthouse in a daze. "Oh my God, you guys," I call out, standing at the foot of the bed with my mouth hanging open. "You've got to see this."

Caz dumps my bag on the floor as he steps into the master bedroom with a loopy grin on his face.

"Looks exactly like the picture on the hotel website," Galen says, walking into the room, followed by Theo and Saint.

"You knew about this?" I cast a glance over my shoulder.

"Yep." Saint flops down on one side of the mammoth four-poster bed.

"I couldn't believe I found a hotel with a bed large enough for all of us," Theo admits, coming up behind me and circling his arms around my waist.

"It was actually booked out for tonight," Galen explains, lying down with his hands tucked behind his head. "But our resident brainiac negotiated a deal with the couple who had reserved the place, getting them to relinquish it for tonight so it's all ours."

"Your smarts turn me on so much," I say, twisting my head around to kiss Theo. I rest my forehead against his. "Thank you." Emotion flows through my body, lighting me up from the inside out. "Thank you all. Today is already more than I expected."

"Nothing but the best for our girl." Caz stands in front of me, brushing a few stray strands of hair off my face. He leans down, kissing me, and heat rolls off Theo in waves from behind me.

"We have two hours before the city hall ceremony," Saint says, sitting up. "We'll get ready in the other bedroom so you have the master to yourself." Theo and Caz kiss me on both cheeks, smiling as they back out of the room.

Galen climbs off the bed, reeling me into his arms. "You okay?"

"Never better," I truthfully admit, suctioning my lips to his. I close my eyes, reveling in the taste of his fresh minty breath and the lingering hint of strawberry on his lips.

"Can't wait to marry you," he whispers, nipping at my earlobe after breaking our kiss. "Can't wait for our wedding night."

I groan, planting my hands on his hard chest. "Don't tease

the bride unless you want her to be a horny mess walking down the aisle."

A panty-melting grin graces his mouth. "That's just how I like my woman." He pecks my lips tenderly. "Enjoy your last few moments of singledom." With one final kiss, he walks out of the room, leaving me alone with Saint.

Saint takes his time getting off the bed, sauntering toward me casually, pinning me with that intense all-seeing gaze of his that always makes me feel like I'm stripped bare. His fingers sweep lightly across my face, and he tilts my chin up. "So fucking beautiful," he rasps, before claiming my lips in a slow, deep kiss that makes my toes curl. He grips the nape of my neck, forcing my eyes to his. "Any last-minute cold feet?"

"My feet are toasty warm." I grip his hips. "I want this, Saint. This is the happiest I've felt in a long time."

His shoulders relax, and I see the fear and panic he's working so hard to contain.

"Saint," I whisper, wrapping my arms around him. "I love you, and I'm going nowhere." My fingers trek up his sinful chest. "You're stuck with me now," I tease.

"That is music to my ears, princess." His teeth graze along the column of my neck as he palms my ass. "I can't wait to make you mine."

"Be gone with you then." I playfully shove him away. "I need to make myself presentable."

I take a nice, long soak in the pre-prepared tub with rose petals resting along the surface of the water, sipping from the glass of champagne left out for me, thanking my lucky stars for whoever or whatever led me to my Saints.

Although it's only been three months since they reappeared on the scene, it's as if I've known them longer. As if we've always been together. It's hard to imagine my life before they bulldozed their way into my heart, making it their home.

After I'm nicely relaxed, I dry off and sit in the nude at the dressing table, carefully applying my makeup. I leave my hair to dry naturally, applying a little bit of serum to tame any stray frizzy strands so it falls in soft cascading waves down my back. Then I get dressed, humming Paramore under my breath as I slip my feet into the stilettos, standing back to admire my appearance in the mirror. I have a little giggle to myself as I fix the diamante crown on my head and wrap the "boy toy" belt I found on eBay around my waist, imagining the guys' reactions.

"Babe." Caz knocks on the door, but he doesn't open it. "It's nearly time to leave. You almost ready?"

"I'm ready." Blood rushes to my head, and butterflies swoop into my belly. I knot my hands in an uncharacteristic surge of anxiety. Tugging at the layers of tulle on my skirt, I pull the tight crop top down, smoothing out any last-minute wrinkles. My tongue is almost glued to the roof of my dry mouth, as anxiety continues twisting knots in my stomach, and that fluttering feeling in my chest accelerates until I fear I'm about to have a coronary.

Get your shit together, Harlow.

I give myself a silent pep talk, breathing deeply until the panic has subsided and I'm more in control.

Drawing a brave breath, I march toward the door and swing it open, stepping confidently into the main room as my composure returns.

Four pairs of heated eyes dart to mine, and time stands still. I stop breathing, sucking in a gasp as I drink in the sight of my gorgeous guys.

Caz is wearing a white button-down shirt with dark jeans, both items hugging his muscular body in all the right places. His eyebrow piercing and lip ring are in, and his dark hair is styled back from his face. His warm brown eyes glint with heat as his gaze rakes over me, and he smiles in appreciation.

Theo is wearing gray skinny jeans, a rocker T-shirt, and a fitted black jacket with a patterned trim. Bunches of bangles and leather ties adorn his wrists. His hair is freshly washed, hanging loose around his face, and my fingers twitch with a craving to touch the silky strands. Theo gulps, his Adam's apple bobbing in his throat as he drinks his fill of me. He blows me a kiss, mouthing I love you, and my heart speeds up.

My eyes flit to Galen, and I smile at my dark prince. He's wearing a tight-fitting black shirt with the sleeves rolled up to his elbows, showcasing the ink on his arms. The top few buttons are undone, highlighting his toned chest and the colorful ink running up one side of his neck. Black fitted pants and new black boots complete his sexy look. His hair is artfully styled in a mess of tumbles on top of his head, and his green eyes radiate happiness as he stares at me in awe.

Saint steps forward, and I suck in another gasp. Our eyes connect, and I stop breathing again. He is the epitome of sex on a stick in his fitted black suit with black button-down shirt. Unlike Galen, his shirt is buttoned to the top, hiding the ink on his chest.

He closes the gap between us, standing directly in front of me. "Princess." His voice is all choked up, and it inflames the messy ball of emotion churning in my gut. Lifting his hand, he gently touches my face, tipping my chin up. His tattooed fingers lightly hold me in place. Adoration and something much deeper swim in the depths of his beautiful blue eyes as he stares at me. "You are breathtaking and we're the luckiest bastards alive." He takes my hand, lifting it to his mouth, and kissing across my knuckles.

"Wow." Caz steps forward and Saint passes my hand to his, stepping aside. "You look so fucking hot. I want to live inside you and never resurface for air."

I giggle, peering into his fiery brown eyes as he too kisses the back of my hand. "Thanks. I think."

Theo is up next, and he can't contain the ginormous grin lighting up his face. "Madonna's got nothing on Harlow Westbrook." He presses a feather-soft kiss to my cheek, careful not to smudge my makeup. "You're stunning, babe."

I'm fighting tears by this point, and we haven't even gotten to the ceremony yet.

"You're a knockout, angel," Galen agrees, threading his fingers in mine. "And you couldn't be any more perfect."

Saint hands me a simple bouquet of white roses, the short stems securely wrapped in white ribbon, and I almost lose it. "Stop it!" I smile through my tears. "You're going to ruin my makeup." I laugh to deflect the potent emotion consuming me. "And you are all so handsome and so fucking hot. If anyone's lucky, it's most definitely me."

We snap a few pics, including a group selfie, before we head out. We guzzle some more champagne in the limo en route to city hall, and I'm grateful when Theo passes me a bottle of water, because I'm feeling a little tipsy, and I want to be fully coherent when I say my vows.

The justice of the peace we booked is waiting for us when we reach the designated room in city hall, and he wastes no time getting started. I hold Saint's hands as we face one another with the guys standing close behind us.

Much of the ceremony is a blur because I'm transfixed by the man unraveling before my eyes. I've never seen so much emotion on Saint's face before, and to know it's all for me is mind-fucking-blowing.

He stumbles over his vows, and tears well in my eyes as I watch my brave, broken, sexy boy commit himself to me. My vows ring out confident and clear, and I keep my eyes on Saint, as I recite the words, until the very end when I purposely lock eyes with Caz, Theo, and Galen too. We exchange rings, and I get tingles sliding the black band on Saint's finger, knowing he's mine for life.

Saint kisses the shit out of me when the officiant confirms we are husband and wife, and I'm barely breathing when I finally come up for air.

The poor officiant almost keels over in shock when I kiss each of my guys in turn, and I'm waylaid as a fit of giggles accosts me. I double over laughing, because the look on his face is priceless, and I'm betting this is one wedding he won't forget in a hurry.

Saint clutches our wedding certificate in one hand, and me in the other, as we make our way out of the building with matching wide smiles.

We pose on the steps for some official photos, and then Theo gives the photographer and our driver the address for the commitment ceremony, and we get back in the limo. I cannot believe they went to such lengths to ensure today was special, and it only makes me love them more.

"Ready to get married again, wifey," Caz teases, as we pile out of the limo at the small private building where our group union is being celebrated.

"You betcha," I say, looping my arm through his and letting him lead the way.

Tamara, the female celebrant, greets us when we arrive, ushering us into a cozy waiting room filled with colorful couches and an assortment of beanbags. She runs through the ceremony with us, explaining a few things, before stepping into the room next door, giving us a few moments alone.

Saint and Galen are on either side of me, and I fling my arms around them, urging the other two to join us with my eyes. We stand in a circle, with our arms locked around one another, and no words are spoken, because none are needed.

Emotion is thick in the air and in their eyes, as my gaze meets theirs, one at a time. My heart pounds as the magnitude of what we are about to do truly sinks in.

This is it.

The moment we bond ourselves together for life, because there's no doubt we're in this forever.

The strains of my favorite Paramore song waft from under the door, and we break apart with matching smiles. Saint and I slip our wedding bands off, adding them to the box Theo holds open with the other three bands. Then Saint opens the double doors to the main room, and one by one, my handsome guys walk up the aisle, carpeted in a purple-and-gold-patterned rug. The quaint little room is adorned with large, vibrant prints on the wall, an abundance of floral arrangements, and cute little wooden chairs decorated with white ribbons.

I have no nerves as I follow last, singing along with Hayley Williams, clutching my bouquet in my hands, grinning as my guys watch me walk toward them with various adoring awestruck looks.

We hold hands in a circle as Tamara conducts the ceremony, and this time, I hear every beautiful word. My smile is so wide it threatens to split my face, and my heart is so full I half-expect it to burst from my chest.

She speaks of a commitment of the heart and the soul and how love transcends all. One by one, we speak the vows we each wrote, and I can't hold my tears at bay any longer. I have to repeatedly pause when reciting my vows, overwhelmed with the love pouring into me from my four men.

"When I was young, I aspired to a love like my parents had," I say, smiling at all of them. "I wanted to find that one person who owned half of my soul and bond myself to him for life. After I was kidnapped, I lost the part of my soul that believed in good things and I struggled to hold on to the notion that I deserved love. I couldn't believe love was strong enough to mend the splinters in my heart and the damage to my psyche." I smile through my tears at Theo. "You helped to restore my hope, but when we ended, I fell into a deeper well, and I did what I needed to, to survive. I shut off my heart to protect myself from ever feeling heartbreak again, and I closed myself completely to the notion of love."

My chest heaves as I stop to draw a breath. "And it worked for a long time. I existed by numbing myself to all feeling, but I wasn't really living. I never thought I'd find anyone worthy enough to crack through the shell I'd erected around my heart. Until I met all of you."

My lower lip wobbles, and tears spill down my cheeks. "Just look at how far I've come," I add spontaneously, laughing through my tears.

Saint lifts his hand, brushing my tears away.

Tamara smiles warmly, encouraging me to go on.

"I didn't even cry at my father's funeral," I admit, my tears giving way to overwhelming sadness. "And I loved him so damn much, but that's how closed off I was." I let my gaze linger on each one of them in turn. "When all that stuff came to light about my dad, and I realized my parents' marriage wasn't what I'd thought it was, I would've convinced myself love didn't exist, if I didn't have you. Every day I struggled to accept what I now knew of the past, you were there, showing me what true love looks like and feels like."

I lift my shoulders confidently, and the swell of love in my heart for these guys is irrefutable and infinite. "Love isn't hearts and flowers or unicorns and rainbows. It's messy. It's real. It's raw. It's flawed. It hurts as much as it heals. But true love is *life*, because that's what you've all breathed into me. I'm finally living because your love has broken through my walls, and you've reached deep inside me, reminding me who

I am, demonstrating that love does exist and that I am worthy of it."

I stop again, and my chest heaves with the weight of the love I feel for them. "I love you all now and for the rest of my life. You are the missing pieces of my soul I didn't realize I was searching for. Now, I feel whole." A serene calmness washes over me as the words resonate deep in my heart and soul.

I look to my left, at Theo, and we break our handhold so he can retrieve the box with our rings. I remove Theo's first. "I thought of engraving your rings with a different message for each one of you, but I changed my mind. I love you all equally, even though what we share is uniquely different, because you all love and support me in different ways. But the sentiment is the same. I didn't believe love existed for me—until I found you." I let my gaze roam between them. "You are the only exception." There's a reason I've been hooked on this particular Paramore song for weeks. The words speak to my very soul, and there was no other fitting phrase to engrave on their rings.

I slide the bands on each of their fingers, fighting a fresh bout of emotion. "I want you to wear those words on your fingers and imprint them into your hearts forever more, because you are the only ones who were ever worthy of my heart, and you are the only ones who will ever own it."

Chapter Nineteen
Harlow

We're all giddy, and maybe a little drunk, as we leave the restaurant, spilling out into the dark, chilly nighttime air. Caz and I are walking ahead of the others. "Fuck, my balls are icing up," Caz moans, wrapping his arms around his chest as we walk down the sidewalk toward the limo.

"Want me to warm them up, baby?" I purr, grinding my body up against his.

I shriek when he scoops me up into his arms, running toward the car. "Now you're talking."

The driver opens the door, and Caz slides me inside, slapping my ass as I scoot over in the seat. He clambers in behind me, and my fingers pop the buttons on his jeans, as I lick my lips in anticipation.

The guys have given me a truly memorable day. After the commitment celebration, we moved to a steak restaurant, where Theo had reserved a table in a quiet private nook. We dined on mouthwatering steaks and drank the finest champagne—courtesy of our new fake passports—and conversation was lively, as we took some time out to just enjoy ourselves. All the shit waiting in the wings will still be there when we return to Lowell tomorrow, and we made a deal not to talk about anything Sainthood related today. So, we laughed and kissed and touched, and I never want this day to end.

Caz groans as my fingers wrap around his hard length. Thank fuck, we have the privacy screen up.

Saint pops an eyebrow when he crawls into the limo, plonking his sexy ass in the seat across from us. "Starting the party without us, my queen?" he asks, tsking while his eyes drop to where I'm stroking Caz.

"What happened to princess?" I inquire, pumping Caz faster as he nips and sucks at my neck.

Galen and Theo get in the car, shutting the door behind them, and the limo pulls away from the curb.

"Our wife has never been a princess," Saint says, and my heart blossoms in my chest. I will never tire of hearing that word leave their mouths. "She's always been a queen."

"Damn fucking straight." I know Saint only coined the princess nickname to piss me off, and somehow, it stuck. It had grown on me, but queen has a much nicer ring to it.

I tug at Caz's jeans, and he lifts his hips, letting me pull the jeans down so I have greater access. His cock stands proudly between his spread thighs, and I notice the way Theo's eye's latch onto Caz's dick like heat-seeking missiles. I really hope Theo can find a way to come to terms with his feelings and act on his attraction to Caz, because the sexual chemistry is building by the day.

Saint glances at Theo before his eyes land on mine. *He knows.* He's got to. There's no way he and Galen don't feel the additional sexual charge in the air.

Galen's groans draw my attention away from Saint, and I squirm in my seat as I watch him pull his monster cock from his pants, stroking himself in measured strokes. I reposition myself so I'm kneeling between both of them. Lowering my lips over Galen's shaft, I continue pumping Caz. They throw their heads back, and widen their thighs, grinning conspiratorially as I work them over at the same time. I glance over my shoulder at Saint and Theo. Both are watching with matching bulges in the crotches of their pants and dark, dilated pupils.

I alternate between Galen and Caz, switching between my hand and my mouth, focusing on Caz when he thrusts his hips forward and shoots down my throat with a loud "fuck." Then I give my sole attention to Galen, swallowing his big cock until it hits the back of my mouth, sliding up and down his length while my fingers circle his base, pumping him fast. He explodes in my mouth just as we reach the hotel in a master feat of perfect timing.

The guys zip themselves up, winking at me as the driver opens the door.

We rush into the hotel, eager to get to the penthouse and properly celebrate our marriage. When the elevator arrives, Galen ushers me inside while Saint places his arm across the door, stopping anyone else from entering. The older couple, who were waiting for an elevator alongside us, stare down their noses at Saint as he blocks them from joining us.

"That was rude," I say the instant the doors slide shut.

"Do I look like I give a fuck?" Saint says, dropping to his knees in front of me.

"What are—" I shriek, cutting myself off, when he lifts the copious tulle layers and shoves his head up my skirt.

Saint's hands part my thighs, nudging them aside, as Theo slides behind me, wrapping his arm around my waist. "Relax and enjoy it, our queen." His fingers move up over my exposed midriff, pushing under the hem of my crop top and up over my lacy bra. He tweaks my nipple between his fingers as Saint moves my matching lace panties aside, plunging two fingers inside me. I shriek again, and my head drops back on Theo's shoulder. He continues toying with my breast as Saint pumps his fingers in and out of my pussy.

"Our wife is dripping," Saint exclaims, removing his hand from under my skirt and shoving his fingers in his mouth. "Mmm." He glances at the digital floor counter, smirking as he licks his fingers clean.

"That is so fucking hot," I rasp.

Saint stands. "You taste like a sin I want to indulge in over and over and over again." He roughly grabs my other breast, kneading it through my top.

The elevator pings, and Galen and Caz step out into our penthouse, already pulling their shirts up and over their heads. Theo sweeps me up into his arms, carrying me into the master bedroom while Saint trails us.

Theo places me on my feet by the bed, kissing me softly. Caz kicks off his jeans and boxers, standing buck-ass naked. His cock is already hard again, and I smile. My guys are like Energizer bunnies, with incredible stamina, and they are always ready to go.

The guys dispose of their clothing in record time, and then they descend on me like vultures, stripping me out of my wedding outfit as if it's a team exercise.

I lean back against Galen as Theo slides my panties down my legs, leaving me standing there in just my stilettos.

"Heels on or off?" Saint asks his best friends.

"On" is the unanimous verdict, and I don't protest as Saint throws me down on the bed. He climbs up one side while Theo climbs up the other.

"Ready to be fucked, my queen?" Saint asks, crawling between my thighs.

"Hell yeah."

Saint dips his head to the apex of my thighs and feasts on me, using his fingers and his tongue to work me into a sweat while Theo aligns my mouth to his for a sensual kiss that sends shivers coursing through me. Galen and Caz sit on my vacant side, and their hands freely roam my body, fondling my breasts and running over my flat stomach and the raised scars on my arms and upper torso.

"Time to come for us, Lo." Saint pinches my clit, and I damn near come out of my skin. I scream, bucking and writhing as his tongue laps at my essence. Saint is so good at that, and I could happily spend every waking minute letting him eat me out. My body spasms and jerks as my climax whips through me, rendering my limbs to Jell-O.

I don't have time to recover before Saint penetrates me, slamming into me forcefully, gripping my hips as he fucks me hard and fast. The others continue kissing and touching me while Saint lays siege to my body. Then he flips me around, until I'm riding him, and Theo moves up behind me. Caz tosses him some lube, and I watch as their eyes connect, and something passes between them. Electricity crackles in the air, and I want to yell at them to just screw already, but it can't be rushed, and they need to go at their own pace.

Theo peppers kisses along my neck and down my spine while he applies lube to his fingers before pushing them in my ass. I moan, pressing down hard on Saint's cock as the feeling of fullness consumes me. Caz slowly strokes his dick as he watches Theo coat his cock with lube while he continues to finger fuck my ass with his free hand. Caz licks his lips, his gaze moving between me and Theo, and without looking behind, I know Theo is watching him too, well aware he's turning one of his best friends on.

Theo throws the lube on the bed, and his hand moves around my front, as he presses up against my back. His fingers find my clit, and he gently teases it while Saint shoves his cock inside me with increasing speed. Caz groans, and his hips lift off the bed, his cock hard, the veins pulsing and straining on each side of his shaft. Theo moans, and I angle my arm back, looping it around his neck. I twist my head around to look at him, and his eyes are locked on where Caz's fingers are wrapped around his cock.

The heat in Theo's eyes causes a flood of warmth to gush from my pussy, and I clench and unclench around Saint's cock, as liquid lust consumes me. Saint curses, ramming me down harder on top of him, as I pull Theo's head toward me. Theo's lips press against mine, and he holds my waist steady as he eases into my ass while our lips collide in a smoking-hot kiss that undoes me.

I growl into his mouth, and my body is no longer my own. I'm a riot of sensation. A mass of cells remaking themselves with every thrust and every touch. I transcend my body, existing in a realm where there is only unending pleasure and the men who know how to work my body into a frenzy with their skillful touches.

Chapter Twenty
Harlow

Saint clasps my hips tight, taking control from below, slamming me up and down on his shaft while Theo ruts in and out of my ass while making love to my mouth. Heat sears into my skin where Caz drills a hole in my body with his dark gaze, and I feel the intensity of Galen's attention too. It's almost too much, yet not enough too, because I'm a greedy bitch and I want more.

I will always want more.

My eyes pop wide when fingers touch my clit, and I break my lip-lock with Theo, lowering my gaze to where Galen is rubbing two fingers back and forth across my sensitive bundle of nerves. He stretches forward, and our lips meld together in a searing-hot kiss. Lust is thick and heavy in my belly, and I clench around Saint, hugging his cock tight.

"Fuck. That's it, my queen," Saint says through gritted teeth. "Squeeze my cock just like that."

Galen's lips roam my body as his fingers stroke his length, and I'm dying to taste him again. Caz is lying on his side on the bed, fisting his cock and staring at where my tits are jiggling as I bounce up and down on top of Saint. He shoots me a flirty wink, and I poke my tongue out at him.

Saint roars, and that's the only warning I get before his warm cum spills inside me. I feel it embedding deep, and it's so fucking hot.

Galen's mouth moves to my neck, and he pushes my hair aside, kissing that sensitive spot just under my ear as Saint pulses inside me, emptying every last drop into me.

I drape myself over Saint's chest, kissing him deeply. "I love you," I murmur into his ear.

He pulls my mouth back to his, biting down on my lip and drawing blood. "I fucking love you so much."

Theo stops thrusting, holding my hips and keeping me steady as Saint slides out of me with a slick pop. Caz waggles his brows as he occupies the empty space, grabbing the base of his cock, stretching his skin tight while holding it out for me. Theo slips out of my ass, positioning me over Caz, situating me on his erection.

"That feels so damn good," I purr, gently rocking up and down as I adjust to the feel of him. Theo flattens my body onto Caz, lifting my ass a little. I tug Caz's lower lip into my mouth, sucking hard. His cock jerks inside me, and I cry out as Theo pushes into my ass again. Straightening up a little, I slam up and down on Caz's cock while Theo fucks my ass. Theo's fingers move low on my belly, and he plays with my clit while Caz squeezes my tits.

They thrust in perfect synchronization, and our bodies move beautifully together. I take turns kissing them, and I'm aware of the heated looks we're all sharing.

"Fuck." Caz moans, thrusting his hips up. "I can fucking feel you sliding inside her, man."

"I know," Theo says, his voice heavy with desire. "I can feel you too." Their eyes lock, and my breath stalls in anticipation as

I watch them stare at one another, the attraction potent and pulsing in the air. Caz's hands drop lower on my body, and I take one of them, moving it down to where Theo's fingers still brush against my clit. Their fingers entwine, and they take turns rubbing my clit while rocking into me and eye-fucking one another.

It's one of the most erotic moments of my life, and I can't wait for Theo's walls to drop, for him to let Caz in—pun intended—because I know it's going to be epically dirty, and I'm already visualizing the dynamics, so aroused at the thought of them fucking one another.

I continue riding Caz while Theo pounds harder and faster into my butt. Galen is jerking himself off on the bed, and I gesture him forward with my fingers. Saint is sprawled out, naked, in a chair, swigging from a bottle of bourbon, observing and taking it all in.

He didn't miss what just went down with Caz and Theo, and I'd love to burrow inside his brain, to know what he's thinking. He doesn't look upset or disgusted or alarmed, but Saint is a master at masking his true feelings, so who knows? I blow him a kiss, and he grins, seductively licking the rim of his glass, making me laugh.

Galen crawls toward me, and the lust-drenched look in his eyes sends delicious tremors of anticipation zipping all over me. I love the way Galen fucks me. Taking what he wants without apology and drilling his big dick inside me like he wishes he could properly impale me. Seriously, I can't ever get enough.

"Stand at the side of the bed," I tell him. "I want you to fuck my mouth."

He gets into position, fisting his hand in my hair, tugging my head back. My body arches with the movement, and Theo grips one hip as Caz holds on to the other, ensuring they are at the right angle to continue fucking me. Opening my mouth wide, I let Galen in, giving myself over to pure sensation again, ignoring everything but the way the three of them are taking me.

The only sounds in the room are skin slapping skin, a chorus of moans and groans, and the occasional expletive.

Theo shouts my name as he comes in my ass, his cock thrusting deep as he spills inside me. I feel his cum dripping down the backs of my thighs, and the instant Galen rubs my clit, I burst apart in a harmony of sensual beats.

"Let's switch," Caz says, lifting me off his dick while Theo climbs off the bed. Their arms brush in the exchange, and I watch with bated breath as their eyes meet, and time seems to stand still. They stare at one another, chests heaving, skin glistening with sweat, as the scent of sex swirls through the air. Galen comes around the other side of the bed, climbing up and positioning himself underneath me, watching Theo's and Caz's intense sexually charged stare-down.

Galen looks at me, and I see the acknowledgment there too.

It's clear now that Galen and Saint are obviously aware of the attraction building between their two other friends. But they're guys, and I doubt either of them will discuss it unless someone else broaches the subject. As much as I'd love to know their thoughts, I promised myself, and Theo, that I wouldn't interfere, and I'm sticking to my guns.

Galen pulls me down over his cock as Theo breaks his eye lock with Caz, shooting him a shy smile as he grabs a beer from the bucket on the bedside table and walks over to where Saint is sitting, flopping into the chair beside him.

Galen moves inside me, reclaiming my attention, and I lean down, kissing him hard. My walls hug his thick, long length, and I scream as he thrusts up into me, hitting my cervix. Caz climbs back on the bed, behind me, nibbling at the skin on my shoulders, dragging his fingers reverentially down along the ink on my back as he coats his cock in the cum Theo left behind. It's so fucking hot, and liquid heat gushes from my pussy, causing Galen to curse.

I look over my shoulder, and Theo is rooted to the spot, watching Caz slide his cock up and down the seam of my ass. Caz swirls his fingers around the salty cum covering my asshole, and in a deliberate move, he turns his head to Theo while shoving his fingers into his mouth.

I shatter on top of Galen's cock, coming explosively, so turned on by Caz's dirty attempts at seduction that I'm no longer in any control of my body.

"Fuck her," Theo demands, his voice deep and gritty. "Fuck our queen deep and hard."

I'm reading between the lines, and I'm guessing Caz is too as he slams into my ass without warning, and I scream. He owns my ass, pounding into me hard, and I wonder if he's imagining I'm Theo.

Looping my arm back around his neck, I pull his head to mine, pressing my lips to his ear, and whisper, "Imagine I'm him. Fuck my ass as if you're fucking his ass. I want to know what that feels like."

Caz loses control, slamming in and out of me, his breath oozing out in exaggerated spurts. "You know what I'm imagining, queenie," he grunts in my ear. "I'm imagining fucking him while he's fucking you."

"Oh God." I moan, and I'm so close to the ledge again. Galen's hands are all over my body, tweaking my nipples and rubbing my clit, and I'm like a live wire, thrashing and jerking around on top of his cock while my other husband claims my ass.

"And him fucking me while I'm fucking you," Caz adds, roughly grabbing both my tits, pushing Galen's fingers aside. I'm lifted off Galen's cock until only the tip is inside me as Caz plasters his chest to my back, keeping me upright while he rocks his hips and his cock in and out of my ass.

He roars, bucking his hips and squeezing my tits as he comes, spilling his seed into my ass.

Is it gross to want to shove my fingers into my puckered hole, to swipe my fingers in their joint cum and paint every inch of my skin in it?

"The thought of having you both at once turns me on so much," Caz admits into my ear.

"Trust me, I know."

A broad smile crosses his face, and he kisses me one final time before dropping flat on the floor, placing a hand over his stomach, with his chest heaving as he attempts to come down from his sexual high.

"Now you're all mine," Galen leers, hauling me down to him for a punishing kiss.

"Now you've got me, what are you going to do with me?" I challenge when our lips pull apart.

He pinches my nipples, twisting and turning them, and a jolt of pleasure darts to my core. "I always know what I want, Lo." He whacks my ass. "On all fours, angel."

I obey his command, licking my lips as he lines up behind me, sliding his cock up and down my slit and in between the cracks of my ass.

"You're so fucking hot, angel," he says, thrusting inside my cunt in one expert move.

I move, pushing my ass back into him as he pummels my pussy from behind. His fingers dig into my hips, in a way I know will leave bruises, but I welcome them.

I want my guys' fingerprints all over me and their cum filling my body.

Always.

I will never get enough.

Chapter Twenty-One
Harlow

"Yesterday was officially the best day of my life," I admit as we leave the hotel the following morning. We're all tired, existing on only a few hours of sleep, because we stayed up most of the night fucking. My body is aching and worn-out, but I wouldn't have it any other way. I know, every time I move today, my exhausted limbs will remind me of the many ways my guys proved their love last night.

Saint arranged for someone to drop the Land Rover at the hotel so we could go straight to school. As much as I want to stay in bed with my new husbands all day, missing two days of school might reach Sinner's ears, and we don't wish to ruin the surprise before tonight's meeting, because there's no fun in that.

I cannot wait to see him go postal when he finds out we've thwarted his perverted plan.

"Today sucks," Caz says. "I'd much rather be balls deep inside you than listening to Batshit Branning boring me to tears."

"We have every other night, babe," I say, leaning back to mess up his hair.

"And we still have to christen our bed," Galen reminds us.

"Thank you for yesterday and last night," I say, beaming at all of them as my fingers move over the console, finding Saint's hand. His fingers thread through mine, and he squeezes. "It was the best wedding day and night I could have asked for."

"We're glad you enjoyed it," Theo says, "even if someone did ruin the wedding cake." He drills a look at Saint through the mirror.

Saint flashes him one of his signature smiles. "I wouldn't say smearing wedding cake all over our bride's naked body, and then licking her clean, was a waste."

"That should be a new tradition," Caz agrees. His lips twitch. "A nicer version of the wedding brownie."

I burst out laughing, glancing at my watch. "I think that's a new record for you." Caz decided to choose a wedding-themed word of the day today, and we had great fun reading through the options on the urban dictionary after we came out of the shower.

"That is seriously disgusting," Theo admits, wrinkling his nose. "I'm down for most things, but poop play is definitely not something I'll ever understand, let alone try."

"Poop fetishes seem strange to me," I agree. "And I'll never go there, but to each their own." I shrug. If that gets your rocks off, so be it. I'll never kink shame.

"Rings in here," Theo says, popping open the lid of the box, as Saint pulls into the parking lot at the school. We need to keep our marriage a secret until after the meeting, so we all place our wedding bands in the box, entrusting them to Theo's care. I reposition my engagement ring on my middle finger before getting out of the car. Saint weaves his fingers through mine, and we walk into the school building, ready to face whatever this day throws at us.

"You need to wait here," I instruct when we reach the barn after the longest fucking day of my life. Today snailed by—like every time I looked at my watch, it seemed as if time had stood still, but I shouldn't be surprised. When I'm anticipating something, the day usually crawls by, yet when I'm dreading something, the day flies by so fast it's as if time fast forwarded. "And turn around," I add, heading toward my Gran Turismo. "I'll be a few minutes, and no peeking." Caz's head pivots a little, and I stomp over to him, placing my hands on my hips as I stand before all of them. "I went to a lot of trouble for these wedding gifts, and you're not going to ruin them by spoiling the surprise." I jab my finger in Caz's direction. "Behave or no sex for the rest of the year." He opens his mouth to protest, clamping his lips shut when he sees the glare on my face. "Theo, keep them in line, or I swear I'll give all your pubes a trim."

Galen's lips twitch, and warning drips from every pore in Saint's body. "Itchy pubes are no joke," I tell Galen, smothering a snort of hilarity and ignoring the dark glare coming from his cousin. "Ask Saintly. He can tell you all about it." Figure that will distract them long enough for me to get inside and get the pictures up on the wall.

I leave Saint steaming, attempting to ignore telling them the story, while I lug the frames inside, one at a time.

Ten minutes later, I have them up on the walls, and I stand back to admire them. Damn. They are seriously hot, if I do say so myself. Pushing strands of damp hair back from my brow, I open the front door and call them inside.

"Thanks for that," Saint drawls, pursing his lips as he strolls past me.

I shrug, failing to hide my grin. "You can always punish me later." I tug on his arm. "Wait a sec. I want to show you together."

Theo and Caz stand beside Saint while Galen takes up the rear.

I usher them forward, stopping in front of the framed nudes of me now hanging on the wall. "Ta-da." I stretch my arms out, turning around so I can see the expressions on their faces.

"Holy fucking shit!" Galen exclaims, stepping in closer. He runs his fingers over the glass in the place where his name is printed in mock graffiti.

"I got one for each of you," I explain. "That's why the poses are different, and I wrote a personal message for each of you." It's not lengthy as I didn't want to detract from the sexy photo, but I wanted to individualize them.

"The photographer better have been a woman," Saint growls, his gaze skimming across all four photographs.

I roll my eyes. He's utterly predictable, but it's reassuring in a way. "I didn't want you up on a murder charge, so, yes, it was a woman."

"These are beautiful, Lo." Theo pulls me under his arm, pressing a kiss to my temple.

"They're perfect," Saint agrees. "You look like a fucking queen."

Warmth blooms on my cheeks. "Well, I couldn't look at those Godawful tacky posters with their airbrushed bodies and plastic tits any longer."

"Massive improvement," Caz says, pecking my lips.

"Thanks, queenie. I love mine." His eyes glint mischievously. "Now I have something to jerk off to when you're not around."

"That's an added bonus," I agree, smirking. "Just try not to get cum on the glass."

"We'll have to cover them if Granddad is dropping by," Saint says. "Unless you're happy for me to slice his head off his shoulders."

I'm tempted to argue, just to push his buttons, but I think better of it. These photos remind me of the best day of my life, and they are for my guys' eyes only.

It doesn't matter that Diesel has seen me naked.

These are not for his viewing.

"I'll get something we can throw over them for when he visits," I agree.

We shower and get changed, preparing to leave for the meeting at Sainthood HQ. The guys are wearing their leather cuts over black shirts and black jeans. I dress in black skinny jeans and my scuffed boots with a tight black and red T-shirt on top. I zip up my black hoodie and tie my hair into a high ponytail. We all tuck our guns in our jeans, and I strap my knife to the outside of my thigh.

"Don't forget this," Theo says, approaching me with the necklace Diesel gave me. He fastens it around my neck.

"Thanks. You still have the recording of my initiation meeting safe and close at hand, right?"

He nods. "I've backed it up to a couple places, and I have a password-protected file on my phone. When we need it, I can pull it up in seconds."

"Good." I exhale heavily. Sinner will lose his mind when he realizes we have incriminating evidence on him and the board. Especially when the commissioner gets "taken down." That recording proves they set it for me as a task and that the motive behind his assassination came from them. We're holding this in reserve to pull out when we need it.

"Okay." Saint stands in front of us, folding his arms. "These meetings are usually a shitshow," he explains. "An opportunity for Sinner to lord his power over us. I'm not going to tell you what to do, only stay sharp and be smart. Let's not antagonize him in front of other junior chapter members because he won't take kindly to that."

"We need to pick our battles." I tug the zipper of my hoodie up under my chin. "I got it."

Theo distributes our wedding bands, and we put them on, agreeing to keep our hands under the table during the meeting so we don't tip him off early.

I let Galen take shotgun, and I jump in the back, sitting in between Theo and Caz. Galen blasts rock music, and we don't talk as Saint drives us to Prestwick for the meeting.

He pulls into the parking lot, gliding into a vacant parking space, alongside a truck and a couple of motorcycles.

"Watch your backs," Saint warns as we get out. He rounds the hood, taking my hand, and we walk into the devil's lair.

Chapter Twenty-Two
Harlow

The lower level of the building is a lot like The Bulls warehouse we torched. A narrow hallway opens out into a large space. Stools are lined up under the counter of a bar that resides on one side with a myriad of couches, tables, and chairs on the other.

Several men in leather cuts are dispersed across the room, many with scantily clad young girls sprawled across their lap.

Club paraphernalia lines the walls alongside the entrance to the small kitchen. Facing the bar are two pool tables, and a bunch of older members lifts their heads from their game, nodding at Saint and the guys. A couple eye me with blatant interest, and Saint gnashes his teeth at them.

"This one's possessive," a guy with a shock of thick red hair says. "But not for long, according to my intel." He licks his lips, letting his gaze freely roam my body.

Saint tilts his head to the side, and Caz grabs the man, shoving him into the wall before thrusting his fist in his face. The guy slumps to the ground, out cold, and an icy chill infiltrates the room. Eyeballs are glued to my back, and nervous adrenaline prickles underneath the surface of my skin.

The guy's friends simmer and seethe, but they say nothing.

The dynamics within The Sainthood are fascinating to me. That the guys get away with this, purely because Saint and Galen are in positions of leadership within the junior chapter, and they are related to the current president, is unbelievable.

"The bedrooms are back there," Saint explains, pulling me away from the pool tables and pointing to the corridor on the left. "And these are the stairs to the upper levels that house the office and meeting rooms."

We trek up the stairs after a couple of younger members, and Saint leads me along the hallway, past a few closed wooden doors, and through the double doors at the very end. I press on the necklace to automate the recording software as we walk across the worn hardwood floor.

All conversation mutes, and every person in the room looks at us. About fifteen guys are sitting around the rectangular wooden table in the center of the room, and they nod their heads in acknowledgment.

"Gentlemen." Saint steers me to the end of the table, pulling out the chair on the left side for me. "This is Harlow Westbrook."

I jerk my head up, offering a tight smile as I glance at the guys around the table. "Sup."

A chorus of greetings whips around the table from all but a couple of guys, who sit near the end, eyeing me warily. And I get it. Most probably don't want women in the organization; however, they've no choice but to suck it up, because it's the president's order.

A few more bodies filter into the room as Saint sits down beside me, at the end of the table, and Galen takes the seat across from me. Theo slides in next to me with Caz claiming the seat beside Galen.

Footsteps thud across the room, claiming my attention, and I smile as Bry walks toward us.

"Hey." He nods at the guys. "Lo."

"Bry."

He sits in the empty chair beside Theo, surreptitiously handing him a folded note. Theo passes it to me, and I slip it into Saint's waiting palm. Saint dips his head, reading the details of The Arrows next shipment. He jerks his head at Bry, in a barely there acknowledgment, and I kick him in the shin. Saint narrows his eyes at me, and I pin him with a look that tells him not to fuck around. Bry has come through for us, and this hostile shit ends now. He needs to start treating him with more respect.

"Thanks, man," Saint says, and he almost sounds sincere.

I'm about to kick him again when the doors burst open, heralding Satan's arrival.

"Welcome, my little cherubs," Sinner says, stalking into the room with the bald creep I hate. He's rubbing at his shoulder, and it gives me immense pleasure to know I inflicted pain. Sinner occupies the seat at the head of the table, and the creep sits on his right-hand side. "I see we have our new female initiate with us today," Sinner adds, smiling like the cat that got the cream when his eyes land on me.

It hasn't escaped my notice I'm the only female here, confirming what I've suspected all along—Sinner's "we're letting women into the ranks" statement is a load of bull. It was a ploy to trap me, to control me, and nothing more.

The creep's mouth curls in a sneer, and he levels me with a look suffused with venom, making an obscene gesture with his fingers, which I ignore, despite the distaste flooding my mouth.

Another man enters the room, sitting down on Sinner's

other side. I recognize the scraggly beard and disinterested scowl from the initiation meeting. He's another board member and another asshole probably salivating at the prospect of raping me.

I can't wait until they find out they can't touch me.

"Everyone welcome Harlow Westbrook," Sinner says. Fists pound on top of the table in some weird supposedly manly ritual.

I barely avoid an eye roll.

"Let's get down to business," Sinner says. "I'd like to wrap this meeting up earlier than usual." A nasty shudder works its way through me when he fixes me with a loaded look. "Because I've an important engagement after this."

Saint clenches his fists on top of his thighs, and I reach over, uncurling his fingers.

Sinner concentrates on business, talking about shipments due in and some new clients. He mentions plans to attack The Arrows, warning junior members to be extra vigilant, but he's deliberately hazy on the details. Then Saint gives a roundup of distributions for the next week, and he confirms the supply pipeline is up and running in Lowell Academy.

Sinner resumes talking when Saint has finished his update. "Some of you may be aware that we're diversifying our business interests, and I want to bring everyone up to speed. Smart businessmen know that spreading risk across various entities is a shrewd strategy, and we're no different. Developing different income streams is a smart play, and it's been our main focus this past year, but we need to do more to protect our interests and safeguard the future of this club. If one of our income revenues is hit, we want to ensure we're not crippled because we have other income to fall back on. That is why the board has taken the decision to enter the sex trafficking trade."

Deathly silence greets his statement, initially, and then a

few guys shift uneasily in their seats. Some wary expressions are traded around the table. It's clear this is news to a lot of junior members.

The hesitant reaction greatly displeases Sinner. He slams his fist down on the tabletop, and a few guys jump. Sinner leans forward, glaring at everyone seated around the table. "This is a good thing for The Sainthood." He slams his fist down again. "A *great* thing, and we expect every member to fully support our initiative."

I clamp a hand over my mouth to stop the snort dying to break free. Sinner's as delusional as ever. Saint squeezes my hand under the table in warning, but I've got this. I'm bottling up all my frustration to unleash on him after we make our big revelation.

Sinner straightens up, running his hands through his hair. His features even out, and he smiles, leaning back in his chair, as if he didn't just throw a hissy fit like a toddler. He lets his gaze roam the table. "An opportunity opened up, and we jumped at the chance to expand our business interests. Right now, we're testing the waters. We suffered a minor setback recently, but a new shipment will be arriving in a couple of weeks, and we expect demand to grow from there."

"How will this impact us?" a guy with multiple facial piercings asks.

"It won't impact you in the short-term," Sinner says. "But when you become full members, you'll be expected to help with deliveries." A revolting smile slips over his mouth. "You'll get an opportunity to sample the goods, so it's far from a thankless task. Although no one is permitted to hurt the merchandise. Clients want them young, innocent, and unmarked." Sinner licks his lips, leaning back in his chair, as he stares straight at me, daring me to challenge him.

I bite down hard on the inside of my cheek to stop myself from throwing my knife into his cold, cruel heart.

The meeting ends then, and chairs scrape as junior members exit the room. Bry stands, ready to leave. "Stay there," Saint commands, eyeing Bry.

Bry reclaims his seat without question, and we share a look. I straighten my shoulders and hold my head up, preparing for the showdown. The other three board members come into the room, blatantly leering at me, and my skin crawls. I gulp over the bile gathering at the back of my throat and grip Saint's hand harder.

"You can leave," Sinner says, peering into Saint's eyes. "We have some chores for your whore to attend to."

"Or they can watch," Baldy says. "Might pick up a few tips."

I snort, unable to hold stuff inside any longer. "Trust me, my guys need no instruction on how to please a woman. They score an A-plus every time." I let my full derision show on my face as I look Baldy over from head to toe. "Yeah, there's definitely nothing they could learn from you. Unless you want to teach them how to be a spineless ugly fuck who rapes women to get his rocks off."

His chair falls to the floor as he jumps up. "You need to be taught a lesson. Cunt." He spits on the floor, and I lean back in my chair, grinning. Bry is looking at me like I have a death wish, and I suppose that's how it must look.

"She *will* be taught a valuable lesson," Sinner says, and his clinical tone raises goose bumps on my arms. "Get the fuck out," he adds, jabbing his finger at Saint. "Lessons start now. You can update me on our other business after we've disciplined your whore." A laugh rumbles from his chest, and the others join him.

Saint whips his gun out, pointing it at his father. The board members laugh again, peering at Saint like he's a naughty toddler who needs to be put in time-out. "I warned you not to call Harlow that," Saint grits out, raising his gun and pointing it straight at Sinner's skull.

Sinner stands, walking toward us. "And I told you, you have no say in this matter. Unless you want your whore to fail initiation, and you know what happens to recruits who don't pass."

"You're not laying a finger on her," Saint says, brandishing his gun at all the men. "None of you are."

Sinner grits his teeth as he comes around behind me, placing his hands on my shoulders. "I've got my hands on her now. What're you going to do about that, huh?" He's baiting his son on purpose, and I almost wish Saint would pull the trigger even though I know it'd end in a bloodbath and not all of us would get out alive.

Saint stands, keeping his gun trained on his dad while he pulls the paper from his back pocket. He thrusts it at his father. "Invoke my right as Harlow's husband," Saint hisses.

Sinner grabs the marriage certificate from his son's hand, his nostrils flaring as he reads over it.

"Now, take your filthy paws off my wife because the only men I'll be sharing her with are Galen, Caz, and Theo, and the rest of you perverts can go fuck yourselves. Literally."

Chapter Twenty-Three
Harlow

"Y̲ou've done it now, boy." Sinner crumples the certificate in his hand, tossing it on the floor. "You... you..." He shoves at Saint's shoulders, and Saint stumbles a little, grabbing the back of the chair with his free hand to steady himself. "You dare to overrule me? To deny me my right to fuck her? It's a fucking initiation task!" he yells, spittle flying from his mouth.

"You'll pay for this, Saint. You put that fucking whore ahead of your own flesh and blood!" Sinner thumps his fisted hand over his heart. "After all I've done for you? You ungrateful little shit." A muscle pops in his jaw as he visibly seethes. "I thought you were smarter than this. Is her pussy that fucking magical she nuked your brain cells?" He shakes his head, really on a roll now. "You let that cunt trick you into marriage, and now everything's fucked!" he screeches, his eyes almost bugging out of his head. "You've fucked everything up!"

He shoves Saint again, and I'm two seconds away from losing my shit. If he puts his hands on him again, I will not be accountable for my actions.

Galen and Caz get up, standing behind Saint. They're clearly sharing my thoughts, and they're primed and ready to go into battle.

Theo and I rise together, and I inch closer to Saint so we're presenting a united front. We're a solid fucking team, and it's about time Sinner realized we're no pushovers.

"It's true?" Baldy asks, coming toward us.

"Yes," Sinner barks. "They're married."

Shock splays across Bry's face as our eyes meet. He's still sitting, but he's alert and ready to intervene if necessary. I'd like to think he'd intervene on our behalf, but I honestly don't know how strong his allegiance is to Sinner and whether he'd stand with him or against him. I haven't forgotten how he insinuated he was keeping something from us during a previous conversation he and I shared, and while I trust my gut, and my gut says Bry is an ally, I can't ignore the fact he is hiding something from us.

"Then it's decided," a man with sandy-brown hair says. "Your son has spoken, and that's that."

"You think I don't know that!" Sinner roars.

"It's one of our most sacred rules," Scraggly Beard adds. "As much as this is disappointing, we can't dishonor tradition."

I glare at the prick. *Gee, sorry you don't get to gang-rape me after all.*

"Don't throw the rulebook at me!" Sinner yells, picking up a chair and throwing it at his colleague. "I know the fucking rules!" he roars, as the man ducks down, and the chair crashes into the wall behind him, instantly breaking apart. Sinner lifts another chair, flinging it across the room this time. It flies through the window, shattering the glass, sending shards raining down on the floor.

"Holy shit," Caz whispers under his breath, pinning troubled eyes on Saint.

Sinner is self-destructing before our eyes, and it's terrifyingly fascinating to watch.

Sinner grabs fistfuls of his hair, pacing the room, his boots crunching on glass underfoot. The other board members eye him warily, and he looks truly psychotic pacing the floor, yanking on his hair, and muttering to himself.

Outside, shouts and raised voices can be heard, and I hope the chair landed on solid ground without injuring anyone.

Sinner slams to a halt, narrowing his eyes and jerking his head in our direction. Then he flies across the room, making a beeline for Saint with clear murder in his eyes. I unsheathe my knife, stepping in front of Saint at the last minute.

I point the sharp edge of my blade at Sinner's chest, right where his heart is. "Move one more millimeter and you'll impale yourself on my knife," I warn. "No one threatens my husband. Especially not you." Our eyes meet with a mutual expression of hatred. His dark pupils shine with loathing, and I imagine mine are the same. "Back the fuck up, asshole."

Saint's hand lands on my hip, and he applies a little pressure, but I don't need his subtle warning. As much as I want to drive my knife straight through Sinner's heart, I won't do it, because I refuse to throw my life away on his.

I want vengeance. I want justice for my father. And that means Sinner behind bars. Death would be far too easy for a monster like him.

"Sinner." Baldy moves cautiously toward his president. "Step back." His beady eyes move to mine. "You won't get away with disrespecting the president like this. We have rules for a reason."

"Fuck your rules. You want me to take out the commissioner, then we'll play this our way, or you can find yourself another assassin."

Sinner starts pacing again, mumbling to himself as he pulls strands out of his hair, and his crazy is really showing now.

Tension is like invisible fog in the room as we all wait to see what he does next.

I'm expecting more chair throwing, more yelling, and more attempts to hurt my husband, but he surprises us all.

He stops pacing, rooting himself to the spot and lowering his head so his hair shields his face. A few tense beats pass, and when he lifts his head, he's smiling.

Like legit smiling.

What the actual fuck?

Saint cocks his head to the side, scrutinizing his dad's face while the rest of us trade guarded, puzzled looks.

"You know what, son?" He walks toward us, wearing the same lopsided smile. "It's okay." He slaps Saint on the shoulder. "This is a good thing."

My eyes narrow suspiciously, and Saint pulls me in closer to his side. "It is?" Suspicion laces his tone.

"Of course!" Sinner's eyes light up. "Giana would never take me back if I'd fucked her daughter." He squeezes Saint's shoulder. "You did me a favor, son. I owe you." He winks at me, and my insides turn in on themselves. "Harlow's a fine piece of ass, plus she's got lady balls. You did good, boy."

My mouth hangs open. *What is going on here? Is this an act, or he's truly this insane?*

"Welcome to the family, sweetheart." He yanks me into a hug before anyone can stop him.

"Get the fuck away from me," I snap as strong arms pull me back.

"No touching means no fucking touching," Saint grits out, wrapping his arms around me as I lean back against him.

Sinner raises his palms. "I meant no harm. Scout's honor.

Harlow is my daughter-in-law. I would never harm a hair on her head."

An incredulous laugh bursts from my chest. "Sorry, did I miss something here? Did someone perform a lobotomy on your brain, and we missed it?"

"Now, now, Harlow. There's no reason to be mean." He loses the grin, and a familiar cold glint reappears in his eyes. "I'm trying to mend bridges here. You could be a little more gracious."

I stare at him, truly at a loss for words.

I've called Sinner a psycho before, but this is the first time where I genuinely believe he is psychotic, in the clinical sense, because this behavior is in no way normal. That's what makes him so scary. He is completely unpredictable with a manic violent streak and no empathy or no moral code.

Suddenly, pushing his buttons doesn't seem like such a smart move, so I decide to play along. "You're right," I lie. "And I hate arguing. We should try to get along. It'll be easier now that you're no longer trying to rape me," I add, because sometimes I just can't stop myself. Not that I really believe he will stop. He'll just adjust his plans. But, for now, we've bought some time.

"Rape." He rolls his eyes, like the very idea is unconscionable. "Please, Harlow. We both know you would've been begging for my cock."

"No, Neo. I really wouldn't."

"Can we move this along," Scraggly Beard says. "I need to wet my dick in one of the hoodrats."

"Show some respect!" Sinner barks, returning to his seat. "And we still have some business to discuss." He plonks into his seat at the head of the table, waving his hands at us. "Sit!" he demands.

We return to our seats, keeping our hands on top of the

table this time. Bry's eyes fixate on the identical wedding bands on my guys' fingers, and he's still wearing a hint of shock on his face.

"Where are you with finding the bastard responsible for trying to kill you?" he asks, as if he didn't just have a meltdown.

"We're handling it. It's not gang connected. It was retaliation for a kill at the warehouse," Saint explains. "It's personal and we will deal with it."

"I want the specifics," Sinner says, drumming his fingers on the table.

"When we have all the facts, I'll share them with you," Saint lies.

"See that you do."

"We have some intel," Saint adds, extracting the piece of paper Bry handed him. Saint passes it to Theo. "Courtesy of Bryant. The Arrows have a big drugs shipment arriving next week via a new secret route."

"They're expecting us to hit back," Sinner says.

"Yes, and they're going to a lot of trouble to avoid an attack," Saint says. "I say we grab a few reliable men, let them shadow the truck to their warehouse, and then we plan a full-scale attack."

Bry jerks upright in his seat, pinning Saint with a dark look.

Saint ignores him, continuing to outline his plan. "The Arrows won't suspect anything. They'll expect their new route has worked, and when they least expect it, we'll swoop in. Steal their cargo and set fire to their warehouse. Cut them off at the knees."

Silence greets his suggestion, and the only sound in the room is the steady tick-tock of the clock on the wall.

"I like it," Sinner says, a minute later, looking at the other board members. They nod in agreement. "Email me the details."

"Already done," Theo says, explaining why he was tapping away on his cell phone the past few minutes.

"Good. All that leaves then is the matter of your initiation, Harlow." He attempts a sugary smile, but it's all wrong.

"I've been giving that some thought," Galen says, injecting himself in to the conversation. "Each initiate is given three tasks, but most of those are equal in status. Lo has already brokered the deal with Lowell Academy, her second task is null and void—"

"Which is why I broached the subject," Sinner replies, cutting his nephew off mid-sentence. He levels Galen with a withering look that confirms he doesn't appreciate his interference. "We need to agree on a replacement task."

"That's the thing," Galen continues, undeterred. "I don't believe we do. Your third task is a big ask."

"A fucking monster ask," Saint agrees.

"So, we think there is no need for a replacement task. Assassinating the commissioner is worthy of two tasks, and when Lo accomplishes it, she will be deemed to have successfully concluded initiation."

"Are you asking or telling me?" Sinner coolly replies.

"Asking, of course." Galen smiles politely at his uncle, disguising the fact he'd love to riddle him with bullets.

"We've seen your great capacity for compromise tonight," Theo says, feeding the arrogant beast. "We're merely asking for an extension of that concession."

"She's not getting out of this one." Sinner points his finger at Saint.

"No one is asking that," I say. "I'm prepared to carry out your wishes where the commissioner is concerned. I understand the seriousness of it."

"Very well." Sinner stands. "But it's got to happen soon. I'll contact you next week with the arrangements."

The meeting disbands, and the other board members disappear through the door. I marginally relax.

"I am glad we could resolve our differences, Harlow," Sinner says, coming up alongside me. "It will help with Giana."

"You do know she wants nothing more to do with you?" I say. "And that's all on you."

"I can be very persuasive when I need to be." He flashes me a shit-eating grin, and I want to slash it to pieces with my knife.

All the blood drains from my face. "Leave her alone, Neo."

"Can't do that, sweetheart. I miss her. Need her. And she needs me too."

Yeah, no she doesn't.

He pats my arm, and I jerk back out of his reach. "I highly doubt that."

He grins, and his usual devious expression is firmly planted on his face.

Goose bumps prickle on my arms, and I sit up straighter in my chair.

"That's where you're wrong, daughter-in-law. If she doesn't miss me, doesn't need me, why did she agree to have dinner with me tomorrow night?"

Chapter Twenty-Four

Harlow

"He's lying," I say after Sinner has exited the room, leaving us alone with Bry. We're standing at the end of the table, reeling from that little bomb Sinner just dropped. "She wouldn't go back. Not after he did that to her." I power on my burner cell and dial Mom's number, chewing on my lip in agitation as I listen to the ringtone. It rings out, so I call again, but she doesn't pick up, and I'm not feeling the warm fuzzies.

"What the fuck was that back there?" Bry blurts, glaring at Saint.

"I improvised," Saint drawls, returning his glare. "And what difference does it make? You're one of us now."

"Or are you?" Galen asks, plucking the cell phone from my fingers and ending my fourth unanswered call.

"Don't start with this bullshit again," Bry hisses, running a hand back and forth across the top of his cropped hair. "I think I've more than proven myself at this point."

"So, you shouldn't care if we blow The Arrows supply

warehouse to kingdom come then," Caz says, smoothing my furrowed brow with his thumbs.

"I care because they'll fucking know they have a mole and they'll come after me and my family."

"We'll protect your family," Saint says. "Unless that's not what you're really worried about."

Bry pushes himself all up in Saint's face. "Say what you fucking mean, asshole."

Saint shoves him back a couple steps. "Get the fuck out of my face."

Bry reclaims the space, pushing his chest against Saint's. "We're supposed to be a team," he says through gritted teeth. "We should've discussed it first."

"Improvisation means spontaneous, asshole," Saint retorts, pushing him back again.

"I know what the word means!" Bry hisses, and his fists clench at his side, his biceps rippling as he prepares to let his fists fly.

I slide in between them. "That is enough." I eyeball them, warning them to back the fuck down. I drill a hole in Bry's face. "Saint is our leader, and we don't get to question his decisions or his motivations. We will protect your family, but if there's more to this, you need to tell us right now."

"Like you told me your plans to get married?"

"That's got nothing to do with this, Bry."

"The hell it doesn't." He steps back, rubbing his temples. "You say we're a team, but we're not. I'm still on the outskirts. I'm always on the fucking outskirts, and I'm sick of it." He throws his hands in the air. "Fuck this. I'm out of here." He stomps off before I can stop him, leaving me wondering what the hell just went down.

"What the fuck is his problem?" Caz asks.

"I don't know, but I still don't trust him," Saint says.

"He's hiding something," Galen agrees.

"He more or less admitted that to me one time," I remind them.

"We should go." Theo threads his fingers in mine, casting a none too subtle glance at the camera mounted in the corner of the room.

We walk silently out of the room and out of the building, and no one speaks until we're back in the car. I sit in the back, in between Theo and Caz again, and Theo kneads my tense shoulders. "If Giana's not picking up, call Diesel. See if he can find out what's going on," he suggests.

"I already sent him a text," I confirm. "Because he didn't answer my call either." I stare at Saint through the mirror. "Please tell me she isn't this stupid."

Saint shoots me a sympathetic look. "Their relationship has always been fucked up. Maybe Dad said it to piss you off, or maybe it's true. You need to prepare yourself for that."

"She's dead to me if she takes him back. I mean that. I'm done with her if she has such little self-preservation."

"Let's just wait until we have the facts," Theo coaxes, pressing a kiss to my cheek as he continues massaging my shoulders, while Caz holds my hand in his warm, large palm, offering me silent support.

We ditch Ashley's party, heading straight back to the barn, because we're no longer in the mood. Instead, we settle in front of the fire, attempting to watch a movie as we drink some beers. But I can't stop my brain from working overtime, and I need to be doing something to distract me. "I'm going to work out for a while," I say, putting my beer bottle down.

"Is that wise?" Theo asks. "You're still healing."

I wish I could indulge in some vigorous kickboxing, as I really need to hit something, but Theo is right. My ribs are still sore, and it'd only risk further injury.

One of the first things Diesel taught me as a kid is that you're no use to anyone, least of all yourself, if you're not in prime physical condition. I've been slacking these past couple months. There's been little downtime to work out in our home gym or to attend my usual weekly kickboxing class, and I'm feeling the effects. As soon as my ribs are healed, I'm getting in better shape. Although I've zero desire to return to my kickboxing classes now that my bestie is gone. I met Sariah there, and I can't go back without her. All it would do is serve to highlight her loss, and I'm struggling as it is.

I'll have to make do with our home gym and joining the guys on runs. And maybe I can convince Diesel to train with me again.

"I'll just do some light running," I reassure Theo, because I can manage that much. Hopefully, it will help to burn off some of this restless frustration.

"I'll come with," Galen supplies. "I need to rebuild my stamina and my strength."

We change into training clothes, making our way outside to the smaller structure that houses the gym and recreational area. We run amicably side by side on treadmills, and I stare into the woods beyond the wide windows as I push my limbs faster, not really seeing the forest, because my brain refuses to switch off. I run until sweat plasters strands of hair to my brow and trickles down my spine and my legs feel like they might go out from under me.

"Here," Galen says, leaning over the arm of my treadmill, holding out a bottle of water to me. I didn't even realize he had stopped running. He uses his training top to wipe sweat from his face, tossing it on the floor before guzzling water. I watch his throat work, and it's hot as fuck. Desire coils in my belly, and I switch off my treadmill, leaning back against it as I quench my thirst, never taking my eyes off my sexy husband.

"You keep looking at me like that and I'll be balls deep inside you before you can blink."

I lick my lips, recapping my water bottle and sliding it into the cup holder. "Is that a promise?" I arch a brow, pushing damp strands of hair off my face.

Galen's dark chuckle reverberates through me, and a delicious shiver ghosts over my skin. "Damn fucking straight." He grabs me off the machine, throwing me over his shoulder.

I admire his tight ass from this angle as he strides across the space before setting me down and pushing me up against the wall. His lips descend on mine, and he plunges his tongue into my mouth while his hips pin me to the wall. The feel of his big erection pressing against my pussy through my thin yoga pants turns me frenzied, and I claw at his back while I wrap one leg around his waist, thrusting my core against his cock.

He growls into my mouth before ripping my pants and panties away. Shoving his shorts to his ankles, he lifts my other leg until I'm snugly wrapped around his waist, at the perfect angle, and he pushes inside me in one hard move.

We fuck like savages against the wall, clawing, biting, and bruising one another, and I can't get enough.

This. This is what I needed to distract me.

"Harder, my dark prince," I rasp, biting his lower lip and drawing blood. "Deeper. Rougher." I cry out as he slams into me with force, but it's still not enough. "More," I demand, digging my nails into his shoulders as his lips fasten on my neck and he sucks hard.

Galen pushes me on all fours on the floor, entering me from behind in one swift thrust, and I scream as he pushes in so deep I see stars.

"Yes." I whimper as he drapes himself over me, pounding his cock inside me while he squeezes and tweaks my nipples. When his hands move lower and he viciously rubs my clit, I explode around him, gripping his cock tight as he spills his seed inside me.

"Fuck." Galen pulls out, flopping flat on the floor, pulling me into his side. His chest heaves, and air gushes from his lungs in exaggerated spurts. "I always feel like I've just gone ten rounds in the ring with Mike Tyson after we fuck."

"Is that a bad thing?" I ask, genuinely curious, because I've always felt he gets off on the pain the same way I do.

"Fuck no." His tongue darts out, licking a spot of blood on my lip. "Never. Sex with you is literally out of this world."

"I love fucking you," I admit. "I love fucking all of you."

"We've noticed." He smirks, and I tweak his nipple.

I make swirly patterns on his stomach with my finger while contemplating my next words. I promised Theo I wouldn't interfere, but that was before I realized Saint and Galen are aware of the attraction between him and Caz. Now, I'm curious. "I know you've noticed about Caz and Theo," I admit, wanting to see what he says. "Why haven't you or Saint said anything?"

He tightens his arm around me, pressing a kiss into my hair. "It's not our business, and we're not exactly the touchy-feely type."

"It doesn't bother you?" I ask, propping up on one elbow so I'm looking into his face.

"Nope. It might change the dynamic, but we'll deal with it if that happens."

Warmth spreads across my chest, and I rest my head on his arm, kissing the underside of his prickly jawline. "I love how you guys support each other, no matter what. It's beautiful to behold."

"If we don't have each other's backs, we've got nothing. We realized that a long time ago." He toys with my hair as my lips trail up and down his neck, sending a rake of shivers firing in all directions.

"I promised I wouldn't interfere, but I think it would help Theo to know you and Saint support him."

"I'll see what Saintly says," Galen promises, cupping my face and forcing my chin up. "You make everything better, angel. I hope you know that."

"I feel the same way about you guys." I peer into his loving green eyes. "You're my only family now."

I'm not sure what he sees in my face, but he kisses me softly, pulling me in closer to his sexy body. "Don't write your mom off yet. We don't know anything other than Sinner is completely fucked in the head."

"I know she's avoiding me. I've called her a ton of times now, and she hasn't called me back."

"I know what it's like to think the worst, but Giana isn't like my mom."

"How is Alisha?" I ask. "Have you heard from her since your last visit?" Galen dropped in to see her the day after we returned from the cabin, but he was fairly tight-lipped afterward.

"She's not good." He sighs, nuzzling his nose in my neck. "And I'm running out of patience." He buries his face in my neck, exhaling heavily.

I run my hand up and down his arm, my fingers lingering on the defined contours of his upper arms. "No one would blame you for that or fault you for all the ways you have loved and cared for her."

"I told Mrs. Murphy I'd come for dinner on Sunday, but I'm dreading it, because I never know what state I'll find her in."

"I'll come with," I offer. "If you like."

He lifts his head, staring into my face. "You don't have to."

"I want to." I make a note to message the gardener to see if he can get the maze finished by then.

"Okay." He visibly relaxes.

"You should ask me more." I sit up as a cool breeze whips across my skin. "We're a team in every part of our lives, and I want to be there for you."

"I'm not very good at asking for help," he admits, wincing a little when he sits upright.

I stand, extending my hand to help him up. "I've noticed." I grin as I pull him to his feet. "But get used to it. Because you're stuck with me now."

Chapter Twenty-Five

Harlow

Mom finally returns my call the following morning, and we have an epic argument over the phone when she admits she *is* meeting Sinner for dinner tonight. "Do you have a fucking death wish, Mom?" I hiss.

Behind me, the guys are silently setting the table for breakfast, sharing troubled looks as I screech down the phone.

"He's truly apologetic, and I at least owe him the opportunity to have his say."

"Are you insane?" I yell. "You owe him nothing. He tied you up and raped you with his buddies. In what universe is that okay?"

"I'm not saying it's okay. I just want to hear him out."

"Have you considered it could be a trap?" I pace the floor, so enraged I could scream. "Do you know how many times he's threatened your life?" She doesn't, because I've never admitted it fully, but I'm done holding back.

Mom was safe.

Hidden with protection someplace where he couldn't hurt her and he couldn't use her against me anymore.

If she goes back, she will undo everything. "He could kill you, Mom!"

"He won't get the chance," she snaps, as if she can outwit him. "We are meeting in a public place for a reason. I'm not as naïve as you seem to think I am."

"I can't support this. I won't."

"I'm not asking you to."

"Good, because I won't be there if you choose to throw your life away by getting back with that fucking psycho, and he *is* a psycho, Mom. That's why he's so dangerous."

"I know how to handle Sinner."

No, she doesn't, or she wouldn't have ended up tied to a sex sling in our basement, abused, bruised, and bleeding.

"You know what, Mom. I can't do this anymore. Do what you like. It's clear my opinion counts for nothing." I hang up before she can reply, throwing the burner cell at the wall as I scream in sheer frustration.

I drop to my knees, burying my face in my hands.

"Hey." Theo's voice is soft as he kneels beside me, scooping me into his arms. "We'll follow her. Keep an eye on her and make sure she's safe."

"How?" I ask, looking into his eyes. They are more brown than green today, and I can see the little amber ring around the edge from this proximity.

"Diesel placed a tracker on her new cell phone. We can go there and watch to ensure he doesn't hurt her."

"We can't." I shake my head. "The mole is meeting The Arrows tonight. We've got to be there. We might not get another chance."

"We could always split up," Caz suggests as he walks by carrying a pot of coffee.

"We could," Saint says. "But separating makes me nervous. It's better if we stick together. We could ask Diesel or his brother to follow your mom, and I could send a couple guys as well?"

"Let me check with Diesel," I say, climbing to my feet. I run to the bedroom, grabbing a new burner cell from my stash, and call my trainer-slash-friend. This time, he answers straightaway.

"You okay?" he asks, and his tone is a little off.

"Yes. I'm just worried about Mom."

"I heard." He sighs.

"She can't meet him, Diesel. He's too unpredictable."

"It's too late. She's already left the place she was staying at with Lincoln."

"For fuck's sake. Ugh." I press my forehead against the wall. "Couldn't you stop her?" I lean over the railing, noticing the guys sitting down, so I walk out of the bedroom and down the stairs with the phone pressed to my ear.

"She's not a prisoner, Lo. I went over there last night when I got your message, and I tried talking to her, but she refused to listen. She's not thinking clearly right now, but neither I nor Lincoln could get through to her."

"I'm worried about her. Plus this could fuck everything up. He'll use her against me again. This is only going to make everything ten times harder."

"I know." His tired sigh trickles down the line.

I slide onto a seat beside Saint, and his hand automatically goes to my thigh. "We have that mole meeting tonight, so we can't shadow Mom. Could you or Lincoln watch her?" Theo loads my plate with food as I talk.

"It's already arranged with Lincoln. I have somewhere I must be, but I'm on standby if I'm needed."

"Saint said he could send a couple guys with Lincoln if you like."

"I've got it handled." His tone is sharper than usual, and it throws me for a second.

Awkward silence pervades.

"What is it?" I ask, and Saint lifts his eyes to mine, his brow puckering as he listens to one side of the conversation.

"Were you even going to tell me?" Diesel asks, softening his tone this time.

I open my mouth to ask what when it clicks. Shit. I should've known he'd find out. "Of course. But I was hoping to tell you face to face."

"I know things are desperate, but we could've found another way."

"Diesel, I didn't marry them solely to get Sinner off my back." Saint squeezes my thigh. "I love them. They're my future." It's as simple as that. My eyes meet Theo's across the table, and he smiles.

"You're so young," Diesel says after a few tense, silent beats. "Too young to make that call now."

"You don't get to decide that for me, and I may be young, but I know what I feel in my heart is forever." He sighs, and I know this has hurt him, because he still has feelings for me. "This is why I wanted to talk to you in person," I say.

"I'm sorry, Lo. I'm being unfair. I know you love them and they love you. I've seen it. It's just... You've been through so much, and it seems like an extreme solution, but I also know how mature you are for your age, and I know they've had to grow up fast too. I might not fully understand it, but I accept it. As long as you're happy."

"I am happy. Now all that's left is to deal with Sinner. We need to stop The Sainthood before more women get hurt."

The guys have drug deliveries to coordinate, so we separate after lunch with Galen, Saint, and Caz heading to take care of business while Theo comes with me to visit Emmett's little sister.

I'm pleasantly surprised when Sean opens the door to Emmett's house. "I didn't know you'd be here," I say, accepting his hug.

"We had practice earlier, and when Emmett mentioned you were dropping by, I decided to come too." He steps aside, letting us enter.

"Hey." Emmett rushes toward the door, pulling a sweater over his bare chest. His hair is damp, and little beads of water cling to his cheeks, confirming he's not long out of the shower. "Thanks for coming. Lynn is so excited to meet you."

"Are your parents here?" Theo asks, as we follow Emmett and Sean through the large entryway into a massive open-plan kitchen and dining room.

"They're out of town for the weekend. It's just us," Emmett confirms, leading me over to the large wooden table where his sister is at.

Lynn is sitting in a comfy recliner chair with a blanket draped over her lap. Her dark hair is wispy and close to her head, confirming the growth is new. Emmett said the new drug she's taking is helping, and her leukemia is in remission, but she's clearly been through a lot. Her big brown eyes are exactly like her older brother's, and they are bright with excitement as we approach. Her cheeks pinken when she spots Theo at my side, and she dips her chin shyly.

She's got good taste. I like her already.

"Harlow, this is my sister Lynn."

I take the seat beside her, smiling. "Hey, Lynn. It's nice to finally meet you. Emmett talks about you all the time."

"You too," she says in a quiet voice. Her eyelashes flutter as she glances at Theo, and her cheeks redden some more. Someone definitely has a little crush, and I wholeheartedly approve. Sean looks at Lynn with an amused expression while Emmett's face is as dark as thunder.

I smother my laughter, focusing on the sick little girl. "Emmett tells me you're interested in kickboxing."

She nods repeatedly, and her eyes pop wide. "I brought something you might like." I hand her my cell with the video of Sariah and me performing at the annual state kickboxing event two years ago. I look over at Sean. "Sar is in the video," I warn, because I don't know if it will upset him. He moves his seat closer, looking over Lynn's shoulder as they watch the recording together.

We spend a pleasant couple of hours at Emmett's house, and I didn't realize how much I needed this visit. It helps to do something normal. To spend time with people I care about, who have no agenda or ulterior motive.

Sean and I also talk properly for the first time, and though it's upsetting for both of us, it helps to discuss our feelings and how much we're missing Sariah.

I feel a little lighter as we leave although I'm sure it won't last long.

We meet the guys at a local Thai place for dinner before heading back to the barn to get ready for our recon mission. The guys load the truck with weapons and a bunch of surveillance equipment, and then we set out, following the coordinates Bry sent us. He's meeting us on the outskirts of Fenton, a couple miles from the meeting place.

"Isn't it risky them meeting in Fenton?" I ask, quickly removing my dirty boots from the dash when Saint growls at me. He's as anal as ever about this car, and no matter what we have going down, he always makes time to look after it. It's so clean I could eat my dinner off the floor.

"Meeting anywhere around Lowell or Prestwick is riskier, so I guess that's why they chose this location," Saint says.

"I hope The Bulls aren't facilitating it," Galen pipes up from the back seat.

"They're dead men if they are," Saint adds.

Saint blares music while we drive, muting conversation, and my mind wanders to my mother's date. I'm ready to wash my hands of her. Truly, I am, but I'm still sick to my stomach at the thought of her being anywhere near that sick bastard.

We turn into the entrance of Fenton Forest a few minutes later, and Saint cuts the music as we pull up alongside Bry's black Chevy Silverado pickup. Saint lowers the window, resting his elbow on the door.

Bry steps closer, and he's similarly dressed to us in his black cargo pants, black boots, and black hoodie. He's wearing a black skullcap on his head, and the bulge of his gun belt is obvious under his hoodie.

"What's the update?" Saint asks in a barely civil tone.

"The meeting is still going ahead as scheduled, which gives us an hour to get into position."

"We'll tail you," Saint says, and Bry nods, sparing a quick glance at me before he hops back into his truck.

We follow behind him, along an old, bumpy road that winds around the perimeter of the forest.

"You see anything?" Saint asks, looking in the mirror at Theo.

"The coast is clear so far," Theo says, without lifting his eyes from his tablet. "I don't see any evidence of an ambush or anyone following us."

"You can tell that?" I ask, swiveling a little in my seat so I can see his face.

"This new software Diesel hooked me up with is the shit." He looks up at me, and excitement lights up his eyes. "And he's promised to get me some other stuff that is way cool. It pays to have contacts in the right places."

Caz snorts. "Careful you don't cream your pants."

Theo elbows him. "Don't pretend like tinkering underneath a car doesn't get your rocks off." He shrugs, smiling. "It's good to have a passion."

"Yeah, dude. It is." Caz drills him with a heated look, and my eyes meet Galen's in understanding.

It's dark in the car, so I can't be sure, but I think Theo's blushing.

I turn back around in my seat, leaving them to their moment. Saint spares a quick look at me, and I grin at him. I love that the tension between the guys is giving way to something else, and I love that we're doing something. It feels like I've spent months sitting on my butt, and I'm itching for some action. Itching to put our plan into motion and take those assholes down.

"I really hope we get some answers tonight," I admit, as Saint pushes the Land Rover up an incline.

"We better, because I'm ready to end this," Saint says, articulating my thoughts.

"We've got to stop him before this new truckload of girls arrives in Lowell," Galen adds. "If other members get a taste for this business, it might not cease when Sinner goes down."

"It will," I say, turning around to look at him. "Diesel will make sure of it." The only reason VERO—the covert organization he works for—hasn't shut it down is because they want to give Sinner enough rope to hang himself. Plus, they are trusting in Diesel, in *us*, to help nail his ass to the wall.

We drive higher and higher up the mountain, passing an isolated house plunged in darkness, before the road levels out. Bry parks behind a one-level structure made of corrugated iron, and we pull up beside him.

We congregate between both vehicles, and I lean back against the hood as I scan our surroundings. You can see so much from this height, and familiar sprawling towns are spread out below us on one side, lights twinkling for miles. On the other side is the less well-known part of Fenton Forest, where the meeting is taking place.

"Is that it?" I ask, pointing at the small derelict wooden structure in the near distance, at ground level. The property has clearly seen better days, and it's obviously uninhabitable. Half the roof is missing, and the back part of the structure has been torn down. The front door is missing, and all the windows are boarded up. It's surrounded by thick trees on all sides, and the only access point is the dirt track leading from the front section of the woods.

"Yep. I did a little digging, and it's an old cabin that's been in Diego's family for generations. Very few people know about it."

"We should set up," Theo says, opening the trunk. "We need to be in position before they arrive."

"I spotted that little hilly section there when I was staking out the place a couple days ago." Bry points at a raised section at the front of the mountain. "It's deep enough to conceal us, but we'll still have a good vantage point."

"It's perfect," Saint agrees.

We won't be seen up here, but we are close enough that we should be able to make out the identity of the mole with the use of the binoculars Theo procured for us.

Galen and I sit on top of the hilly ledge with Bry while the others unload two boxes.

"Has Darrow said anything to you?" I ask, purely to make conversation because the tension in the air is brutal.

"Nothing. He's keeping me at arm's length. We barely even talk these days," Bry admits.

"That's odd," Galen says. "Do you think he suspects you?"

Bry shrugs. "I honestly don't know." He leans forward on

his elbows. "But I've been thinking about what went down last night, and it's time I made my move. Sinner must know my position is compromised if The Arrows warehouse is taken out, so there isn't anything more I can do. That will neuter the bastards, and while they'll retaliate, it won't be immediate because they won't have enough firepower to come back at you."

"He's expecting you to hand him the rat. What do you plan to do there?" I inquire, remembering Bry's initiation tasks.

He shrugs. "I guess it depends on who he is and how forthcoming he is with us."

"We offer him up to Sinner on a platter if he refuses to play with us, and if he does, we'll need to find a scapegoat to offer in his place," I suggest.

"You're all in now?" Saint asks, dropping one of the boxes on the ground.

"I am."

"That's good," I say, when no one else speaks. We have to give Bry the benefit of the doubt at this stage.

"I expect the bullshit to end." Bry drills Saint with a loaded look. "I'm one of you. Period."

"You need to switch schools," Caz says, dumping the second box.

"I know," Bry agrees. "My parents won't approve, but I'll smooth things over."

We help Theo unpack the boxes, and then we get in position. Theo adjusts the coordinates of the infrared surveillance software so it's fixed on the meeting point down below, testing that the recording mechanism works. Satisfied, he hands us a set of binoculars each before Caz helps him to prop up a large stabilized binocular on a stand.

I set my AR-15 on its stand and set it off to the side. No one expects I'll need it, but we felt it was best to come prepared, in case this is an ambush and we come under fire.

I switch on my burner cell, to check for updates from Diesel, and my heart rate kicks off when I see the urgent text, asking me to call him ASAP. Something must be wrong, and fear creeps into my veins at the thought something has happened to Mom. My finger is hovering over the call button when Theo speaks up. "We have movement. I see vehicles approaching. Be on guard."

I could step away to call Diesel, but if Diego or the mole are using any tracking software they might pick up on the signal. Theo has gone to huge lengths to mask the software he's using so there's no trace if they are smart enough to run any checks, and I can't blow this operation, because it's too important. It's too risky to return Diesel's call right now, so I power off the phone and repocket it.

"Will we be able to hear them from up here?" I whisper as we watch a car and a truck pull up in front of the dilapidated old cabin.

"No. I didn't want to risk using a drone in case they spotted it, and the only other way it could've worked was if I planted a recording device somewhere in the vicinity of the meeting place. While it's unlikely they have any cameras on the place, I didn't think it was a risk we should take."

"We don't need to hear them anyway," Saint says. "We only need to confirm the identity of the rat. Then we'll follow him, take him when he's not watching, and interrogate him."

I nod, because it's a solid plan.

We're deathly quiet as we watch two figures climb out of the vehicles. I squint through the binoculars, but it's so dark down there I can't distinguish the features of the people meeting.

"I can't see shit," Caz says, adjusting the lens on his binoculars.

"Hang on a second," Theo says, moving to the larger binoculars set up on the stand.

I move my binoculars from the first figure to the second, and while I can't see the features, something else becomes apparent. "Is that—"

"Holy shit," Theo hisses. He jerks his head back. "You need to see this, Lo."

I scoot over, pressing my eyes to the lens, and all the blood drains from my face.

"What is it?" Saint asks, impatience evident in his tone.

"Mom," I whisper, taking another look in case my eyes are deceiving me. I sit back on my heels, staring at Theo in shock.

"You don't mean..." Galen says, his voice trailing off.

"It's Mom," I say, finding my voice. I stare at Saint in horror as a million different thoughts swirl through my mind. "Giana is the mole. She's the one who's been selling The Sainthood out."

Chapter Twenty-Six
Harlow

"This is so fucked up," Caz says as Theo places his eyes back on the large binoculars.

"And dangerous," I add, as my brain struggles to comprehend the revelation. "What the fuck was she thinking?" I climb to my feet and stalk off toward the cars. My chest tightens, and panic has a vise grip on my heart. My breath oozes out in strangled spurts, and I can't breathe, can't think, over the sheer terror racing through my body, replacing the blood flowing through my veins.

If Sinner finds out about this...

"Breathe, my queen." Saint places his hands on my shoulders, peering intently into my eyes, concern etched upon his face. "Nice and slow. In and out." He breathes with me until the panic subsides and my breathing levels out.

"What the fuck has she done, Saint?" Tears stab the backs of my eyes. "It's a suicide mission. He will slaughter her when he finds out, and he *will* find out, because if we could uncover the truth, so can he."

"I know."

I appreciate that he doesn't baby me, giving it to me straight. Mom is in even graver danger than I thought.

Saint pulls me into his warm body, and I go willingly, resting my head on his chest and banding my arms around his waist. The steady, strong beat of his heart under my ear is comforting.

"She has to leave. Get out of the country. Go into hiding." My words are muffled against his hoodie.

"We'll convince her," Saint says.

I lift my head, shucking out of his embrace. "She's going to go back to him. That's what this dinner is about. She's not finished whatever she's planning to do. She won't agree." I bite down on my lip hard, drawing blood. "I can't believe my dad thought she was ignorant to everything. That's clearly not the case."

"No. Giana knows a lot more than she's let on," Saint agrees, rubbing his thumb up and down the side of my neck. "And we'll fucking kidnap her and force her to leave if we have to."

I nod, because Mom is getting the fuck off US soil whether she likes it or not.

Footsteps approach, and we turn around. "You need to see this," Bry says, lifting one shoulder.

We run to the others, dropping to the ground and getting into position. "What's going on?" I ask.

Caz hands me my binoculars. "I fixed them so you should be able to see."

"They're arguing about something," Theo explains as I lift the binoculars to my eyes.

Mom is pacing the ground in front of Diego, and from the speed her lips are moving and the agitation in her limbs, I can tell she's shouting at him. She waves her hands animatedly in the air, before grabbing his arm. Her eyes widen as she talks.

He shakes his head, removing her grip and backing away. Diego says something else, and Mom shakes her head, reaching for him again, imploring with her eyes. Whatever she wants, he's not agreeing to. He flings up his hands, shaking his head sadly as he steps back.

Mom's shoulders lift, and she juts her lip out. Her eyes blaze with a ferocity I've rarely seen. She says something else, and it's a parting shot before she strides to her car, gets in, and peels out of there, tires screeching as she leaves little dust clouds in her wake. Diego stares at the departing car, shaking his head as he pulls out his cell and places a call.

"We need to go after her." I jump up. "She must be going to meet Sinner now."

Caz and Theo are already dismantling the large binoculars and the stand.

"What do you think that was about?" Bry asks as Saint and Galen start packing up one of the boxes.

"She's planning something, and my guess is she asked The Arrows for help and they've said no." I rub a tense spot between my brows. "Or maybe they want her to lay low for a bit, and she's fed up waiting." I sigh. "I don't know, and we won't until we confront her."

"We should go now before we lose her," Bry suggests. "The others can follow us."

I nod. "We're going to trail her," I call out, backing away. "You have her coordinates. Follow us."

"Lo, wait." Saint stops what he's doing, straightening up. "I'd prefer if you stayed with us."

I don't have time for his bullshit right now. "I'm going with Bry. I'll see you there."

I walk off with Bry in the direction of his Chevy, ignoring the slew of expletives peppering the air behind me.

"He really doesn't like me." Bry chuckles.

"Don't pretend like it's not mutual," I drawl, eyeballing Bry as he opens the passenger door for me.

"He needs to get over himself," Bry says.

I wait for him to slide behind the wheel before I reply. "Saint doesn't trust easily, and if you grew up with Sinner and no mother, you'd understand." The reality is, it goes beyond trust. Saint doesn't *like* many people I've come to realize. He would be perfectly happy living on an island with only me and the guys.

"I grew up without my birth parents, and I'm not a raging asshole," Bry admits.

"You're adopted?"

Bry nods.

"I didn't know that," I admit.

He shrugs as he turns the key. The engine rumbles, purring steadily, as Bry reverses from his spot. "I was adopted when I was a baby. My parents are the only parents I've ever known, and they've never treated me any differently to my two brothers. Most times, I actually forget I'm adopted."

I could've sworn he said he had three brothers before, but I was obviously mistaken. "They sound like good people."

"They are." He swings the truck around.

"Then you're luckier than Saint. He had a shit upbringing. Don't be so hard on him. I think if you both let your barriers down, you'd find you have a lot in common."

Bry snorts. "I doubt that. But I'm sorry for whatever he's endured. Sinner is a sick bastard, and I can't imagine growing up with him as a dad." Bry moves the truck forward as Caz comes running toward us, slamming his hands down on the hood.

Bry jerks the truck to a halt, scowling in annoyance when Caz rounds the hood, climbing into the back seat.

I roll my eyes. "Seriously?"

Caz grins, popping his head through the console to smack a kiss on my cheek. "Don't act surprised, queenie. You know what he's like."

"Queenie?" Bry's tone is suffused with amusement.

"My status has been upgraded from princess, thanks to our marriage." I smirk. "Or that's the official line. Truth is, I've always been a motherfucking queen, and they know it."

Bry throws back his head, laughing as we start our decline.

"You've always been queen of my cock," Caz supplies, grinning as he sits back, spreads his thighs, and places his hand over his crotch.

"Thanks for stating the obvious," Bry deadpans as we jolt up and down over bumpy terrain.

"I get it," Caz replies. "I'd be a jealous prick too if I lost my chance with the only girl who matters."

"Caz." I glare at him through the mirror. "Zip it."

"It would never have happened," Bry says, eyeing Caz briefly through the mirror. "I've made my peace with that, and I'm glad Lo is in my life as a friend. Doesn't mean I want to hear the deets of your sexual exploits, so keep that shit to yourself."

"I only said she was queen of my cock," Caz adds. "It's not like I told you about the time she—"

I swivel in my chair, the leather squelching in the process, pinning Caz with a lethal look. "Say one more word and I will follow through on my cockblocking threat. Don't fucking push me."

Caz grins, and I flip him the bird. Asshole was winding me up. At least it distracted me from worrying about Mom.

We make it onto the road in time, spotting Mom's car in the distance. Bry keeps pace with her, staying far enough back that she doesn't suspect she's being followed. It helps that she doesn't know or recognize Bry's truck.

"Switch your phone on," Caz says, lifting his head from his cell. "Saint's been trying to reach you."

I power up my cell, spotting the missed calls from Saint and Diesel. I return Saint's call first.

"You okay?" are the first words out of his mouth when the call connects.

I roll my eyes and count to ten in my head. "I'm fine." My tone is clipped. "What is it?"

"Granddad called me when he couldn't get you to let us know your mom left her cell with the tracker behind at the house. She also figured out Lincoln was tailing her, and she managed to ditch him."

I'm glad we left when we did, or we would've lost her. "I don't have a good feeling about this," I admit as the tiny hairs lift on the back of my neck. "She wanted to ensure no one knew where she was. Why?"

"I don't know, but we'll find out soon enough. You should answer the pervert. He's worried about you."

"I'll text him. See you soon." I end the call and type out a brief message to Diesel letting him know I'm okay and I'll call him later. Then I power off the cell and repocket it.

We trail Mom to the center of Lowell, watching as she parks in the main parking garage in town and hops out with her car keys dangling from her fingers and one hand firmly holding the strap of her bag. Bry kills the engine, and we exit the truck where Bry parked it at the curb across the road, following Mom from a safe distance.

She strides with confidence toward one of the most popular Italian restaurants in the square. We hang back behind the giant water feature in the center of the square, watching surreptitiously as she enters the restaurant and is led to a table at the front by the window. We have a front-row seat as Sinner stands to greet her, clasping her cheeks in his large palms and kissing her on the lips.

Rage swirls in my gut, and my fingers itch to pull out my gun and riddle his body with bullets through the glass.

Caz maneuvers behind me, linking his pinkie with mine, and it helps to calm me down.

We watch as Mom sits down across from the bastard, setting her purse in her lap. A waitress pours red wine in her glass, and she takes a large gulp as Sinner leans across the table, talking to her while she drinks.

"I wish we could hear what they're saying," I mutter, growing more and more uneasy. Something is off, and pressure weighs on my chest, mixing with the knotted balls in my stomach, accelerating my anxiety to epic levels.

I'm furious at Mom—for a lot of things—but she's the only parent I have left, and I don't want anything to happen to her.

The longer they sit across from one another, the more the bad feeling grows in my gut, until I'm wound so tight, I'm in danger of snapping.

Caz senses my mood, wrapping his hand around mine and squeezing.

Mom doesn't even look at the menu, allowing Sinner to order for her when the waitress reappears. By the way she's knocking back wine and clutching her purse tight, I can tell she's on edge, and that's not helping my anxiety.

I jerk my head around at the sound of approaching footfalls, my anxiety dipping a little when I see the cavalry coming toward us.

"What's going on?" Saint asks, shoving Bry out of the way so he can flank me on my other side. Bry snarls, gnashing his teeth. Saint ignores him, focusing on me.

"They've just ordered," I explain, keeping my eyes on their table. "And now your dad is trying to take her hand across the table, but she's having none of it." If I wasn't so anxious, that'd raise a smile.

Sinner's loving look fades as he yanks his hand back, narrowing his eyes at Mom. She smiles, loosening the death hold on her purse and setting her wineglass down. Sinner's nostrils flare as she speaks, and it's clear he doesn't like what she's saying.

I watch, in horror, as she unzips her purse, removing a gun. My heart slams behind my rib cage, and panic lurches up my throat when she stands, pointing the gun at his face.

In the middle of a packed restaurant on a busy Saturday night.

With tons of innocent bystanders and witnesses around.

"Fuck." Galen drags a hand through his hair. "What the hell is she doing?"

"I think that's obvious," Theo murmurs.

It's clear Mom has reached a breaking point. That the gang rape has messed her up more than I thought. Tightness spreads across my chest, and I watch the scene unfold as if I'm not here. I'm floating on a cloud overhead, watching Mom walk around the table and press the gun into Sinner's forehead. His palms are raised, and he actually looks scared. Mom's mouth flies as she shouts at him.

Loud screams reach our ears through the open doorway as the diners surrounding their table notice what's going on. Some stand, and others run toward the door, knocking chairs over in their haste to get away. Others stay rooted to their chairs, staring in shocked horror at the crazy woman pointing a gun at her male companion.

I snap out of the haze I'm in, nudging the guys out of my way, as I take off running toward the restaurant.

Chapter Twenty-Seven
Harlow

I shove past people fleeing the restaurant, most of them either crying or screaming, pushing them aside as I race inside. "Mom! Don't!" I yell to be heard over the noise.

Her head whips around to mine, and Sinner makes a grab for the gun while she's distracted. The gun veers wildly around, and a shot goes off. The screaming accelerates, and several diners dive to the floor, covering their heads with their hands. My breath stutters in my chest, and my eyes widen in horror as the bullet whizzes through the packed restaurant.

"Shit." Saint reaches my side, his eyes darting wildly around the room as more diners scream and shout, making a beeline for the exit. The bullet lodges in the back of the bar, narrowly missing the bartender, and he ducks down as he scurries away while bottles shatter over his head, raining alcohol and shards of glass everywhere. "Theo!" Saint roars as the others emerge from the crowds swarming out the door.

"We've got this," Galen shouts.

Mom turns back to her fiancé, pinning him with eyes loaded with venom, as they grapple for control of the gun. Her fingers are curled tightly around the weapon, and I'd challenge any man to pry it away from her. "Take your hand off. Now." She wets her lips. "There's no need for anyone else to get hurt."

"Mom." I sidle up beside her. "What the fuck are you doing?" I hiss.

"What I should have done months ago." A dry laugh bursts from her lips. "What I should've done *years* ago." She presses the muzzle of the gun to his cheek, and a clicking sound rings out as she readies the gun.

"Stop!" I gently clasp her arm. "You can't do this."

"It needs to end, Harlow!" she screeches. Her hand shakes a little, and she exudes nervous energy by the bucketful. Sinner looks up at me, pleading for my help. Little beads of sweat dampen his brow, and his Adam's apple jumps in his throat. In this moment, he's genuinely scared of her and terrified she's going to do it. I wish to fuck I could let her, but I can't.

"I know, Mom. But not like this." I lower my voice, speaking softly to her as if she's a child.

"This is the only way." She sniffs. "Keep your hands up in the air where I can see them!" she shouts, pressing the gun to his temple. I drop my eyes to where Sinner's hand is going for the gun in his pocket. He's an idiot if he thinks he'd get away with shooting her before she gets there first.

"Do it," Saint says, leveling his dad with a stern look.

"Let's talk about this, sweetheart," Sinner says, raising his palms, as commotion rains around us.

Saint grabs his dad's gun from his pocket, not trusting he won't try it again.

"There is nothing to talk about, you sick bastard." She shoves the gun harder into his temple, and he winces. "You think you own me. That you can manipulate me and my daughter, well, that ends now. You are scum of the Earth, Neo. There isn't another living soul on this planet I hate more than I hate you." Her eyes burn with loathing. "I despise you and every-thing you stand for. You—"

Sirens blare in the distance, distracting us all and cutting Mom off midsentence.

"We need to get out of here now, Lo," Saint says in a low tone only I can hear.

"Mom." I press my mouth to her ear, saying the only words that stand any chance of getting through to her. "If you do this, like this, I will lose you too. Please don't do that to me. To Dad. He made me promise to keep you safe."

Her tortured eyes meet mine. "I have to, Harlow. He won't stop."

"We have a plan," I whisper. "He *will* be stopped. I need you to trust me on that."

The sirens grow louder as Theo, Caz, and Galen come racing across the now empty restaurant toward us.

I watch the cogs churning in her mind, spotting the instant she makes her decision. "You can thank my daughter for saving your life," she barks before slamming the gun to the side of Sinner's head with force, knocking him out cold.

"Go with Bry," Saint instructs, taking the gun from Mom's hand. "Go to the cabin. Galen, you go with them."

"Come on, Giana." Galen slides his arm around Mom's shoulder. She's virtually comatose; standing mute and rigid, and I'm guessing she's in numbed shock as the adrenaline wears off.

"Theo, pull the car right up out front," Saint instructs, and Theo races out the door without waiting. Caz grunts as he lifts Sinner's unconscious form, slinging him over his shoulder, while Saint strides to where the manager is cowering inside the door, fingers clutched around his phone. "I'll deal with him. Get the fuck out of here now," Saint roars over his shoulder.

Galen scoops Giana up, his face contorting in pain, but he doesn't complain as we run out the door.

Bry stayed outside, and it was a smart move because there are a few diners lingering outside, recording on their cell phones. We need to keep his identity protected, and if anyone had caught him inside the restaurant with us, his cover would be blown. "Bry's gone for the car," I tell Galen, pointing at his retreating form in the distance. "Follow him while I deal with this."

Galen doesn't argue, taking off in the direction Bry has gone, while I whip my gun from the waistband of my jeans. I point it at the nearest couple. "I don't want to hurt anyone, but I will if you don't cooperate," I shout, angling my gun so it's roaming the people still here. A guy tries to slip behind the water fountain, and I pop off a warning shot. It embeds in the side of the basin, cracking the stone, sending water gushing over the edge onto the ground. The guy's cell drops to the floor, smashing into pieces, as he falls to his knees, cowering and whimpering.

"Hand me your cells. Now!" I add when they're too slow to move. The sirens are growing closer, and time is running out. "Put them in my pocket," I shout as they approach me. "You!" I glare at the guy still crouched on the ground. "Pick up those pieces and hand them to me." I know enough to not leave his shattered cell phone on the ground.

I lower my gun when I have all the phones in my possession. "You didn't see anything tonight." I drill them with a look. "We have your cells which means we know everything about you. You breathe one word about what you witnessed tonight, and we will come for you and your family." A woman sobs, clinging to her husband, but I've no time to feel remorse. "Do you fucking understand?" I roar as Galen shouts at me in the distance.

They nod vigorously. "Then what the fuck are you still doing here?" I yell. "Go. Now!"

I sprint away as the sirens blare loudly, confirming the police are almost here. I race toward the curb where Bry has the car idling, sliding into the back seat. Bry floors it out of here, taking a left up a side street, just as police enter the square from the opposite direction.

No one speaks as Bry maneuvers his way out of Lowell using alleyways and back roads. Mom has her head pressed against the window, and her eyes are closed. She's clutching her purse to her stomach, and her limbs are stiff, betraying her emotions.

I have so much I want to say, yet I don't even know where to start. And having this conversation in a car, when we're fleeing to safety isn't wise, so I keep my lips closed, waiting until we reach the cabin to interrogate her.

I hate that we're placing our safe haven at risk by going there, but there isn't any other option. Saint knows that, and it's why he suggested it. I tap out a message to Diesel, letting him know what's happened and asking him to meet us there. We need to get Mom out of the country tonight, because Sinner will want her dead for this.

I only start relaxing when we move onto the highway and Bry steps on it, putting as much distance between us and the carnage we left behind. I punch coordinates into the GPS app on my cell and pass it to Bry, poking my head through the gap in the front seats. "This is where we're headed." He drops my cell into his cup holder, nodding.

"You took care of shit in the restaurant?" I ask Galen.

He turns to face me. "It's handled. Theo wiped the camera feed inside, and I've no doubt he's wiping the cameras in the square as we speak. Caz retrieved the bullet from the bar, and

Saint will dispose of the gun, as well as ensure the manager doesn't speak to the cops."

"I got the cells from the idiots outside, but there were a ton of witnesses. Someone is bound to have recognized Sinner."

"Sinner will deal with that," Galen says. "He has a bunch of cops on payroll. He'll make it go away because he looks weak if word gets out."

Mom nods off at some point on the journey, and I take the opportunity to grab a little shut-eye myself.

"Lo." Someone shakes my shoulders. "We're here." I blink my eyes open, stifling a yawn as I stare into Galen's piercing green eyes. He presses his lips to mine briefly. "You hanging in there?"

I nod, looking around me. The truck is parked at the front door to the cabin, and it's open. "Where are Mom and Bry?"

"They're inside. Theo sent me the codes because I didn't want to wake you until I had to."

"And the others?"

"They're en route. About an hour behind us. They dumped Sinner at his place first."

"Is Diesel here yet?"

Galen shakes his head, holding my waist and helping me down from the truck. He slams the door shut, and I slide my arms around his neck. "Did tonight really happen, or did I dream Mom pulled a gun on Sinner in a crowded restaurant?"

"I wish it was a figment of our imagination too." He winds his hands into my hair. "Sinner will go nuts, Lo. Your mom needs to get overseas ASAP."

"I know. Why do you think I called Diesel? He's the only one who can make her disappear fast."

"Sinner won't be happy with us either," Galen adds.

"He can eat shit," I snap. "He's the reason for this, and I know he's a psycho, but even he's got to accept we would not let him harm my mother. We'll just have to make sure he's distracted taking down The Arrows and the commissioner. Hopefully, he'll have cooled off a bit by then."

Galen doesn't look convinced, and neither am I. But we will worry about that another day.

"Come on." I let my arms drop to my sides, linking his hand in mine. "Let's get inside."

Mom is asleep on the couch, draped in a blanket. Bry is in the kitchen, making coffee. "Nice place," he says, looking over his shoulder as we enter the space.

"This cabin has been in my dad's family for generations. The men used it for hunting weekends, and the past few years, I came here every month with my dad to meet my trainer." I figure there's not much point concealing the truth from him now.

"No one knows about this place," Galen adds, coming up behind me. "We expect you to keep its whereabouts to yourself."

"I won't tell anyone," Bry promises, handing me a mug of steaming hot coffee. He eyeballs Galen as he passes him a coffee. "You have my word."

Galen nods. "Good."

We sit at the table in silence, drinking coffee while waiting for the others to arrive.

Diesel shows up next with his brother Lincoln in tow. "Hey." Diesel gives me a quick hug at the door.

"Thanks for coming so fast."

"We're worried about Giana," Lincoln says, squeezing my hand as he goes past me.

"He's pissed," Diesel says, lowering his voice. "And he feels responsible, because he let her get away."

"I didn't pick my stubborn streak off the ground," I admit.

"She wanted to do this, and there's nothing he could've done to stop it."

"Thank fuck, *you* did." Diesel closes the door and we walk inside.

"It was a team effort."

"I'm aware. I've been speaking with Theo. You guys did good." As we enter the kitchen, he squeezes my shoulders before coming to a dead stop. "Who the fuck are you?" His sharp tone is directed at Bry.

"This is Bryant Eccleston. He's a friend and fellow initiate." I drag Diesel over to the table. "Bry, this is my trainer and good friend, Diesel."

Bry jerks his head in greeting, and the two men eye one another. Over Diesel's shoulder, I spot Lincoln kneeling in front of Mom, checking her over for injuries. She's still asleep, but she won't be for much longer, because as soon as the guys get here, I'm waking her up and demanding answers.

Chapter Twenty-Eight
Harlow

Galen and I stand in front of the house as Saint's Land Rover comes toward us. "I hope we haven't made a mistake trusting Bryant," Galen says.

"It's not like we had much choice," I admit, folding my arms around myself to ward off the strong minty breeze blowing from the surrounding forest.

Saint pulls the car in behind Diesel's Land Rover, killing the engine. "I'm changing my car," Saint growls as he climbs out. He eyes Diesel's almost identical Land Rover with an evil lens, as if he'd like to set fire to it.

"Same taste in wheels. Same taste in women," Caz says, grinning as he shuts the car door. "I think you and Granddad were separated at birth." He slaps Saint on the back, chuckling.

"Fuck off," Saint snaps. "Unless you'd like to wear your insides on the outside." He flashes him a manic grin.

"The truth hurts, bruh. You two have more in common, and you know it." Caz grins right back, stopping to kiss my hair before he wanders into the house.

"Did anyone follow you?" Galen asks, earning a scathing look from Saint.

"Do we look like fucking amateurs to you?" His nostrils flare. "Of course, no one followed us! Sinner was still out for the count when we tossed his psychotic ass on his bed."

"He'll be thirsty for our blood tomorrow though," Theo says, pressing a feather-soft kiss on my cheek before he walks inside.

Saint's hands ball up at his side, and from his rigid stance, bad mood, and the rage that vibrates from his every cell, I can tell he is pissed as fuck. "He can fucking try. I'll—"

I crush my lips to his, pushing my tongue inside his mouth, sucking some of the aggression from his psyche as we devour one another. He grabs my ass, pulling me in flush to his body, as our lips assault one another in a melting pot of need and anger. When we pull back, both panting, Galen is nowhere in sight. I trace my hands up Saint's impressive chest, over his shoulders, linking them behind his neck. "Better, babe?"

"I want to fuck you so bad right now," he admits, squeezing my ass cheeks. He grazes his nose along the column of my neck. "*That* would make me better."

"I'll let you angry fuck me later," I promise, closing my eyes momentarily, enjoying the feel of his hands on me.

He bands his arms around me, cradling me protectively to his chest. "Just when I think we're getting a handle on things, your mom has to go and fuck everything up."

I exhale heavily. "Yep. Giana has royally screwed us, but it was almost worth it to see Sinner shitting his pants."

Saint's chest rumbles with silent laughter. "That was an Oscar-worthy moment for sure." He nips at my ear, before letting me go. "Let's get some answers." He threads his fingers through mine, leading me into the house.

Mom is sitting up on the couch, and everyone has moved

into the living room. "It's peppermint," Theo says, handing Mom a mug. "It's the only tea I could find." Steam billows from the top of her mug, and she buries her nose in the scented clouds.

"Thank you, Theo."

Galen thrusts a beer in my hand. "Figured you might need this." He distributes beer while Bry sets a tray with the coffee pot, some cups, and cookies down on the coffee table. Everyone helps themselves to either beer or coffee and Mom sips her tea while we get settled.

Saint pulls me down on his lap in the chair.

"You need to give me some answers," I say, staring at Mom. She cradles the mug in her hands, sitting back in the couch as she nods. "What do you know, and how long have you known?" I ask.

She clears her throat and wets her lips. "I know Trey tried to keep me protected, but I grew up in this world. He always seemed to forget that." Her eyes well with tears. "I loved your father so very much, Harlow. Out of everything these past few months, that has hurt the most. To pretend like I'm not still devastated over his loss. To act like every single touch from Sinner didn't feel like a betrayal. To have you think I could ever replace the love of my life so easily."

"Why did you do it, Mom? What were you hoping to achieve?" I sit upright on Saint's lap, and every muscle in my body is wound as tight as a ball of yarn. Saint runs his hand up and down my spine in a soothing gesture, but nothing can erase the tension winding inside every part of me.

"I wanted to keep you safe, and I wanted to avenge Trey's murder. I wanted that bastard to pay." A muscle clenches in her jaw, and she visibly trembles.

"How the fuck was welcoming that man into our home keeping me safe?" Disbelief meanders through my tone.

"Because keeping your enemies close is always a smart strategy. One that bastard taught me. And I knew he would come for me, so I decided to preempt it, because I wanted to be the one in control." Mom puts her cup down, patting the space beside her. "Please come sit with me."

Reluctantly, I slide off Saint's lap. Theo gets up from the couch, making room for Galen to slide across, leaving a space empty beside Mom. I sit down, and Theo settles on the floor, between my knees, with his back against the couch. Galen laces his fingers in mine as my other hand rests on Theo's shoulder, my fingers toying with his hair.

"Honey." Mom peers deep into my eyes. "There is one thing I didn't know before I put my plan into place, and it's important you understand this, because I would *never* have let Sinner into our home if I'd known he was the one behind your kidnapping." Her eyes blaze with unrestrained fury. "I've always believed David Jennings was behind that because The Sainthood didn't hurt children. Not as long as I'd been a part of that world. Jennings made no secret of his desire to take my business right out from under my nose, and he was a dirty player. We were engaged in an all-out war, and I was sickened when you were taken. I instantly knew he was involved, and when the police found evidence confirming it, I didn't doubt it."

Jennings was a competitor and business rival of Mom's, so I understand why she'd believe the story The Sainthood concocted to hide behind. Truth is, that man is innocent, and he's still rotting behind bars. His family were forced to flee town, and the judge ruled he had to issue a substantial compensation, so he lost everything. That's something that needs to be put right, but it'll have to wait, because dealing with Sinner is our main priority.

She pauses to draw a breath. "I'm so mad at your father for

concealing that truth from me. I'd known for some time that Sinner was blackmailing Trey into helping them avoid jail for their crimes. I knew he was holding me over him, but I had no idea it was as bad as it was. I got an inkling there was more to it when I found out Sinner had forced Trey into an affair with Alisha, but still, your father downplayed it. I knew then Sinner was holding more over his head, and I pleaded with Trey to tell me, but he made me promise to drop it. He told me it was the best way of keeping you safe, and I believed him." She lowers her eyes to her lap, and you could hear a pin drop in the room.

Everyone is quiet, listening attentively, waiting for her to admit it all.

"How did you discover the truth?" I ask.

She lifts her chin. "Sinner told me a few weeks ago. That bastard took great delight in telling me how he was the one to mark your skin and how he imagined it was me the entire time." Her voice cracks. "I'm so sorry, honey. I swear I didn't know. He told me he'd do worse to you now unless I did whatever he wanted. It was then I knew how badly I'd fucked up. How I'd put you in even more danger, but I couldn't see any way out." She breaks down as sobs rip from her chest. Theo grasps my hand, rubbing soothing circles on my skin as I stare off into space.

"He's been playing us against one another," I calmly admit. "Threatening to hurt you if I didn't cooperate and vice versa."

"Why didn't you tell Lo?" Saint asks. "If we'd known what you were planning, we could've been working together instead of giving that asshole further ammunition to hurt you both."

"I couldn't tell Harlow, because I knew she'd never approve of my plan, and I needed her reactions to be natural." She turns to face me again. "I didn't know you knew him. I understood that allowing any man into the house so soon after your father's passing would infuriate you. I needed Sinner to see that. To know you were clueless. That you were lashing out as you would with any man who threatened to take your dad's place."

"You think I couldn't have acted that part?" I inquire, wondering if Mom knows me at all. "If you'd told me the truth, I would've put on a good show. He'd never have known." I shake my head, because this is all so futile. I kept her out of my plans first out of loyalty to Dad and our joint desire to protect Mom and then because I lost all faith in her. She kept me out of her plans to protect me, but all we've done is compound the situation and make it worse.

"I thought I was doing the right thing." She visibly swallows. "And it hasn't all been bad." A small smile graces her lips, as she rakes her gaze over my husbands. "You found love, and you have good men protecting you now."

"Mom. You're not distracting me with that. Not until I know everything."

She drops her eyes to my hand, the one intertwined with Theo's hand, her gaze fixating on the rings on my finger. "I'm not trying to distract you. Merely stating the truth. And we will be discussing your marriage after this conversation."

"What was your plan?" I ask, deliberately ignoring her statement. She doesn't get to switch the Mom card on and off as it pleases her, even if there was a reason behind her behavior. It's going to take some time before Mom and I can put all this behind us, if we even can.

"Initially, when Trey died, I didn't suspect anything because I was heartbroken. However, when the shock wore off, and I had time to think about it, I knew it was no accident." She thumps her hand over her chest. "I knew in my heart that Sinner had something to do with it. It was something I'd always feared. I started going through your father's things, trying to find something to confirm my suspicions. I found a bunch of stuff hidden in the attic, and among the papers was an informant contract your father signed with the FBI. I reached out to the agent in charge, and he told me that Trey was helping them to take Sinner down. I knew what I had to do then."

She tucks hair behind her ears. "I offered to take over. Said I would help them to continue Trey's work if they promised you'd be looked after in the event anything happened to me."

"What?" I splutter, unsure if my ears heard this correctly. *Mom* has been working with the FBI? What the actual fuck.

"It's all been for you, Harlow. Everything I have done has been about keeping you safe."

Chapter Twenty-Nine
Harlow

"You're working with the FBI?" Diesel asks, looking concerned, while my brain continues to spin over Mom's revelations.

"Yes. But I doubt they'll want anything to do with me after tonight."

"What about The Arrows?" I ask before we get into that. "Where do they fit into things?"

"Diego Santana is an FBI informant too."

"What the fuck?" Bry blurts, his mouth opening in shock. "Why would he do that?"

Mom shrugs. "I'm not privy to all the inner workings of gangland politics, and I didn't care enough to ask. We've been working together, trying to pit one crew against the other, hoping it would distract Archer Quinn and Sinner long enough for the FBI to make enough of a case against both organizations."

"What happened tonight? We saw you arguing with Diego," I say.

"How did you know about that meeting?" Mom asks.

"Bry installed a camera in Archer's office, and we gleaned the details from that."

"You need to remove that, son." Mom drills him with a look. "If Archer discovers it, it could put Diego and the whole case in jeopardy."

"I think that's a moot point after tonight. Your actions have thrown everything into jeopardy," I say. "What were you thinking?"

"That I'd had enough, Harlow." Her shoulders slump in defeat. "Something broke inside me that day in the basement," she quietly admits. "I realized that I'd never be able to beat him. It doesn't matter if I have the FBI on my side. Sinner is too smart. I stupidly thought he still loved me. That I could manipulate him into walking into a trap, but he doesn't love me. He hates me. And he hates you. And the only way it will stop is if he's dead."

"You asked Diego to help and he said no," I surmise.

She bobs her head. "He told me not to do it. To stick with the plan. My FBI handler wants me to return to Sinner. He said it's the only way, and that's what Diego reiterated. I hadn't planned on doing what I did in the restaurant, but I just flipped. I can't do this anymore. I can't pretend, and I'm... scared. For me. For you. I just wanted it over."

"Trey would not want you languishing in a jail cell for the rest of your life," Lincoln says.

"My brother is right," Diesel adds. "I'm glad they stopped you from making an even bigger mistake."

"I've messed everything up. I'm sorry, honey." Mom's eyes fill with tears. "I only wanted to protect you and to make that bastard pay for what he did to your father."

I wrangle my hands from Galen and Theo, taking Mom's hands in mine. "It's okay, Mom. We'll figure out a way to make this work, but you've got to leave. Tonight. I can't do this unless I know you're safe."

She shakes her head. "I'm not leaving you to face this alone."

"Harlow is right, Giana." Lincoln sits forward on his elbows. "Sinner will only continue to play you both. If you are hidden away, he can't use you to threaten Lo. It will make things easier for her."

"What do you think?" Mom tips her chin up, leveling her gaze on Diesel. "From what Lincoln's told me, Trey trusted you completely." She glances at me with a wry smile. "He'd never have entrusted our daughter's safety to you otherwise." I guess Lincoln has filled in some of the other gaps for Mom.

"I agree that moving you overseas is the best option. I've already made plans, and we can stash you at one of our safe houses in Europe. Lincoln has already agreed to go with you, and I'll have a team guarding you both."

"What about my daughter?"

"Lo can take care of herself," Diesel confirms. "She has the guys, and I'm here for her too. We'll ensure she's safe. I promise."

She eyeballs me, scrutinizing my face, as if committing it to memory. "Okay. If you're sure it's the right thing to do."

Air whooshes out of my mouth in grateful relief. "It is, Mom."

She pulls me into a hug, and I don't resist, sinking against her, wondering when we last hugged with such genuine affection. I've missed her. More than I've cared to admit to myself. She's gone about everything all wrong, but she acted out of love. She sacrificed herself for me and my dad, and that's all that matters. Any lingering hate in my heart disappears.

"One more thing." I shuck out of her hold. "Do you have

the evidence proving Sinner and The Sainthood murdered Daphne Leydon?" I suspect I already know the answer.

She shakes her head. "If I'd found it, I would have already entrusted it to the FBI. I have no idea where it is or who has it."

Like I thought. Well, damn it all to hell. We were really hoping the mole had some intel.

"We should go now." Lincoln stands. "I have your bag from the house in the car, and we can get whatever else you need when we're abroad."

"Take Giana to the car," Diesel says. "I need a word with Lo and the guys."

"I need to use the bathroom," Mom says, and I tell her where it is. Lincoln goes with her, and I purse my lips, watching him place his hand on her lower back as he leads her to the downstairs bathroom. He's awfully protective, and I've noticed how he hasn't taken his eyes off Mom the entire time we've been here.

Is it guilt? Responsibility? Or am I right in suspecting it's more?

"What's up?" Saint asks, yanking me out of my head and back into the moment.

"I'm wondering why the FBI didn't tell me about this agreement with Giana. It makes me nervous. I helped broker the deal with Trey, so why would they keep this a secret from me? It makes no sense."

"Would this have anything to do with those Homeland files?" I ask.

"I doubt it, but at this point, who the fuck knows." Diesel rubs the back of his neck. "And we've still got that DEA asshole threatening us."

Out of the corner of my eye, I spy Bry stiffening.

"I thought you were going to fix that?" Saint huffs out, kicking his feet up on the coffee table.

"I met him earlier, and his assholishness hasn't dialed down. He's still refusing to play ball, and I'm all out of patience."

"I say we grab him, force him to tell us, and if he won't cooperate, we put a bullet in his skull," Galen suggests.

"He's a loose end we need to tie up," Diesel agrees, as Mom and Lincoln return. "I'll call you later to set that up."

"Walk me out?" Mom asks, and I trail her outside.

"Are we going to be okay?" she asks as Lincoln climbs into the passenger seat of Diesel's Land Rover.

"I don't know, but I hope so. It's what I want." Which is a huge step forward for me.

"I never meant for it to happen like this. Please say you believe me."

"I do. I believe you."

"I don't deserve your graciousness, but I'm thankful for it." She sweeps hair off my face. "Trey would be so proud if he could see you now, Harlow. He loved you so much. I adored the close bond you two shared. Seeing him with you always made me love him even more." Her lips twitch. "Although, I'm not sure what he'd say about your four new husbands."

"I'm sure he'd want to kick their asses, but once he saw how good they are to me, he'd be onboard."

"They *are* good to you, and I trust them to make you happy and to look after you."

"You're not mad?" I tilt my head to the side, wondering if she's being truthful or she just doesn't want to leave on a sour note.

"I'm not going to criticize your decision, because you know when you know. You should never deny your heart."

"I love them, and I know what I want."

She reels me into a hug. "If there's anything good to come from this sorry state of affairs, it's that you have found your future. I look forward to getting to know them better when this is all over and done with."

"Thanks, Mom."

"Giana, we need to go," Diesel reiterates, coming up behind her.

"Be safe, honey. You are everything to me." She kisses my forehead. "I'm so proud of the young woman you've become, and I love you so very much."

"I love you too, Mom. I might not approve of how you went about things, but I know you did it for me and for Dad."

She hugs me one final time before getting into the car.

"Don't worry. She's in good hands," Diesel reassures me. "We'll take care of her."

"Thank you for this."

"No thanks are necessary." He jangles his keys in his hands. "I'll call later, and we can talk about the DEA agent, but I also wanted to let you know my boss has approved the plan for the commissioner."

"He has? I honestly didn't think he'd go for it."

"He understands it's our best chance of getting to the bottom of this. Whoever has that evidence hasn't come forward so far, and he believes this might be the push they need to come clean."

"I hope he's right. And he's seriously okay working with us on this?" I expected him to balk at the notion of trusting an eighteen-year-old sharpshooter and the offspring of the man he wants to take down.

"He trusts my judgment, and giving him those files went a long way toward securing his loyalty. He was delighted to get them back. The head of Homeland Security is a friend of his."

"Well, that's good. I suppose."

"It is. There's no way you could've pulled this off without VERO's help. My boss is going to speak to the commissioner this week. Let me know when Sinner has put the plan in motion."

"Will do."

He opens his arms, and I hug him briefly. "Mind yourself."

"You too," I tell him, waving them off before retreating inside the cabin.

I lean back against the closed door, rubbing my tired eyes. It's been a long, exhausting day.

"Lo?" Saint calls out.

"I'm coming." I push off the door.

"Not yet you aren't," Caz retorts with a chuckle.

"Have I ever told you I love your one-track mind?" I quip, stepping into the living room.

"A time or ten," he replies, swatting my butt as I pass.

"We need to talk," Bry says, and I pick up a thread of anxiety in his tone. He's standing against the wall with his legs slightly spread and his arms folded across his torso. His face is stretched tight, highlighting the prominent scar that runs from the corner of his eye into his hairline.

"So, you've said," Galen drawls, eyeing him suspiciously.

"What has you on edge?" I ask, plopping down on the couch alongside Theo.

"It's about this DEA agent."

"What about him?" Saint asks, sitting up straighter and outright glaring at Bry.

"How is he involved? I don't get why he's a threat," Bry asks.

"He has a video of me killing Luke McKenzie, and he's threatening to use it to take me down," I say.

"Not just you," Theo adds. "You weren't the target. We were."

Bry gulps hard, and a host of emotions flits across his face.

"Spit it out, Bry. What don't we know?" I ask.

"If I got the video, would you lay off him?"

Saint opens his mouth to speak, but I silence him with a look. I stand, walking over to Bry.

"How would you be able to get that video? And why do you care?"

He drags his hand back and forth across the top of his head, and his tongue darts out, wetting his lips.

"Bry." I'm pretty much all out of patience by now.

"Because he's my brother. That's why."

Chapter Thirty

Caz

"I knew you lied to me before," Lo says, fixing Bryant with a wary expression. "You told me during training that you had three brothers, yet earlier, you said you had two."

"I wasn't lying when I said I have two adopted brothers. That's the truth. But, Howie—the DEA agent—he's my biological brother."

"Start explaining," Saint snaps, and I can tell by his tone he's ready to rip Bryant Eccleston in two.

"I was adopted when I was a baby after my mom committed suicide. My father died from cancer while my mom was pregnant with me, and after she lost my older sister a few months before I was born, she lost the will to live." He shrugs. "Or so Howie tells me."

"Why didn't your brother assume guardianship?" Theo asks.

"He was in his early twenties and not capable of minding a baby."

"Wow. That's a big age gap," Lo says.

"I was a surprise or a mistake." Bryant shrugs casually as if it's no biggie.

"That's no excuse for your brother not stepping up." Galen's tone is scathing, but I'm not surprised. He was brother, mother, *and* father to his little sister before she died, because his parents bailed, and he didn't hesitate to be there for her even though he was only a kid himself.

"He'd just enlisted in the military, and he ended up overseas for years," Bryant explains in a defensive tone. "I didn't realize I had another brother until two years ago when Howie found me."

"What does he have against The Sainthood? What is he after?" Galen asks.

Bryant walks over to the couch, sitting down on the arm. "What does everyone want?" He arches a brow.

"His beef is with Sinner," Lo surmises, and Bryant nods.

"Why is he holding that recording over our heads then? That's got nothing to do with Sinner other than it'd bring heat on the organization if it got out," Saint says.

"I don't know. He told me nothing about that recording, but I'll find out. I promise."

"I want you to set up a meeting," Saint adds. "For tomorrow or Monday. This can't wait."

"Consider it done," Bryant says, bobbing his head.

"Your brother wanted you to get close to The Sainthood to help him. That's why you switched allegiances," I suggest.

"Yeah. I couldn't give a fuck about either crew, to be honest."

"Why does your brother hate Sinner? What did he do to him?" Lo asks.

Bryant's eyes darken. "Sinner killed our sister." A muscle pops in his jaw.

Heavy silence lingers in the air like fog. It's no surprise

Sinner has picked up so many enemies or that they're gunning for him now. It was only a matter of time before someone made him pay.

"I'm so sorry," Lo says. "Do you know why?"

"She was a hoodrat. Sinner took a shine to her. Got her addicted to drugs, and it all went to shit then. She fell apart, and Sinner wanted her gone. Howie thinks Sinner was worried she might blurt something, because she'd been around him enough to be privy to a ton of shit that had gone down. So, he silenced her."

Saint shifts uncomfortably on his seat, and his lips pull into a grimace as he lowers his gaze to the floor. Lo looks at Galen, and they share a silent communication. Theo sits up straighter, scrubbing a hand over his jaw. "If this happened eighteen years ago, why is your brother only seeking vengeance now?"

"At first, it was because he was overseas for years with the military, and he buried himself in work to forget his pain. I'm not sure when that changed. When he decided he wanted revenge, but at some point, he hired a couple guys to go after Sinner, but both of them failed. He realized he'd have to take care of it himself and that he needed to be smarter about it. He wanted justice for our sister, and killing Sinner, without him admitting to the crime, wouldn't avenge Jess's murder. So, he came home and got a job with the DEA. He's building contacts and utilizing the resources at his disposal to find anything he can to use as leverage to force Sinner into admitting the truth."

"If he thinks that recording is leverage, he's sorely mistaken," Lo pipes up. "Sinner doesn't give a fuck about me. He'd probably thank your brother for getting me off his back."

"And there's little love lost between me and my father," Saint grits out. "If your brother releases that tape, Sinner will make us take the fall. He'll say we acted independently of The Sainthood."

"Maybe Howie thought it might work because Lo is Giana's daughter," Bryant suggests.

"It still doesn't explain why he didn't tell you about it," I add.

"We need to talk to him. Face to face," Saint says. "It's the only way we'll get answers."

"I'll set it up," Bryant says. "Howie is very...dogmatic, but when he learns we share the same goal, that we all want to see Sinner punished for his crimes, I think we can find a way to work together."

"This could end up being a good thing," Lo says, looking deep in thought. "We already have VERO and the FBI onboard, and Diesel said the head of Homeland Security will be thrilled to get those files back. If we can get the DEA on our side too, and we all work together, we've got to find that evidence."

"One would think so," Saint says, lifting his chin. "But I've learned to never underestimate my father. That's something none of us should ever forget."

We leave the cabin at eleven a.m. the following morning to make the journey back to Prestwick. Galen is expected at his mom's house for dinner, and Lo has roped all of us into attending because she has a surprise for Galen, and she wants everyone there to see his reaction.

She hired a landscaping company to tidy up the gardens and restore the maze to its former glory, and they have been working around the clock this week to get it finished for today. Lo even spoke to Mrs. Murphy, Alisha's babysitter-slash-housekeeper, making her promise not to breathe a word to Galen. She also enlisted her help in keeping him away from the house this week.

I know that maze is important to Galen and Lo, and I can't wait to see my buddy's face light up when he realizes what she's done.

We pull up to the monstrosity that's been in Galen's family for generations a couple hours later, and a nasty shiver works its way through me as I glance at the house. Thick ivy crawls up the front façade of the old two-story gray-bricked house, adding to the overall creep factor of the place. This house always gives me a mad case of the heebie-jeebies, and I generally avoid spending much time here.

I help Lo out of the back seat and stretch my arms up over my head, loosening my taut muscles while fighting a yawn.

Mrs. Murphy opens the door with a flourish and a warm, inviting smile. "I'm so glad you could all make it. Your mom is delighted," she tells Galen, stepping aside to let him in.

"I doubt that," Saint mutters under his breath. "If Alisha is sober, I'll eat my dick."

"Do you always have to think the worst of her?" Theo asks, placing his hand on Lo's back as we step inside the mausoleum.

"I'm not a total prick," Saint says, lowering his voice and stepping back as Lo walks up beside Galen, holding his hand as they talk with Mrs. Murphy. "I know my dad and my uncle fucked up Alisha's life," Saint continues, "but there comes a point when a person has to take responsibility for their own actions."

I'm more in agreement with Saint than Theo on this topic, because I can relate. For so long, I blamed my deadbeat father for my mother's actions. Yes, she's downtrodden, because he treats her like shit, but she has choices. There are *always* choices. And she chooses to stay with that piece of shit. That realization hurt, because it means there's nothing I can do to change the situation. I've tried so hard to help her. Offering her my savings so she could take Jake and Nelia away from that bastard, but she refuses to leave him.

That's when I decided I was done. I still visit weekly, when Dad's not there, but it's mainly for my brother and sister, to ensure they are okay and they have everything they need.

So, I agree with Saint. There comes a time in everyone's life when they must stand up and be counted—it's what separates the strong from the weak.

"Alisha has chosen to check out on life instead of being there for her son," Saint says, as I rejoin the conversation. "I can't forgive her for that, and I won't fucking apologize for calling her out for the junkie whore she is."

Harsh, but true.

I trail Theo and Saint as they follow Galen, Lo, and Mrs. Murphy along the dark, grim hallway. Cobwebs cling to the ornate cornices, and another shudder whips through me. The ghosts of Galen's ancestors breathe heavily on my neck as I force one foot in front of the other, and the urge to run screaming from the house accelerates with every step.

I'm already on a countdown to when we get to leave.

Needing a distraction, I focus on how fuckable Theo's butt looks in the tight, ripped jeans he's wearing today. The denim molds itself to his shapely ass, and my fingers itch with a craving to touch him.

There has always been this lingering attraction between us, but I've largely ignored it, because Theo always gave off "don't touch me" vibes, so it never seemed like a possibility.

Until recently.

The air is shifting now Lo is in our lives. Maybe because she's softening our rough edges. Or we're all more openly sexual, because we have sex on tap and Lo's refreshing attitude means we can be ourselves around her. Or, perhaps Theo is finally coming around to the idea there could be an "us." Whatever it is, I cannot get the idea of touching him and fucking him out of my head, and it's becoming a problem, because I get hard just looking at him these days.

I've lost count of the times I've jerked off in the shower to images of the three of us screwing our brains out.

The visuals resurge to the forefront of my mind, and I indulge them.

Anything to avoid thinking of creepy-crawlies and soulless ghosts swirling around me as I walk the oppressive hallways of this dark, depressive mansion.

I let my mind go there, imagining I'm fucking Theo while he fucks our girl. Then we'd switch, and I'd take him into my ass while I pound Lo. Sweat dots the back of my neck, and my dick swells painfully behind the zipper of my jeans as I give in to my deepest desires, wishing I knew how to make them a reality.

Chapter Thirty-One

Caz

I return to the land of the living when I'm shoved forcibly against the wall and a warm, tight body presses up against me. "What were you just thinking?" Lo purrs in that sultry, seductive voice I love so much. Her arms creep around my neck, and she thrusts her gorgeous tits against my chest.

My cock throbs with visceral need, and I rock my hips against her. I glance around, but the others have disappeared into the dining room up ahead. "You don't want to know," I croak, urging the beast in my boxers to calm the fuck down.

"Wouldn't have asked if I didn't want to know." She slides her hand between our bodies, rubbing my dick through my jeans.

A groan rumbles from the back of my throat. "I was imagining Theo fucking me while I fucked you," I truthfully admit, because I'm not ashamed of my thoughts.

"I dream about that too." Her pupils dilate, and precum seeps from the crown of my cock.

I slam my head back against the wall. "Fuck. Kill me now."

"I've a better idea." The wicked glint in her eyes tells me all I need to know.

"We can't. Dinner's about to be served."

She palms my dick, giving it a firm squeeze. "Are you doubting my talents? You think I can't get you off in a matter of minutes?"

I grab her wrist, tugging her past the open doorway toward the bathroom at the end of the hallway. "You know I love a challenge, and you've just set one." I pull her into the bathroom and lock the door, shoving her to her knees as I unzip my jeans, pushing them and my boxers down my legs.

Her tongue darts out, and she licks my balls. A primitive moan crawls up my throat, and my dick pulses when she rubs her finger against my taint, teasing my asshole.

"Get ready, babe. I'm about to blow your mind," she promises.

Lo takes my cock into her mouth the same time one finger slides into my ass. She sucks me hard, pumping her finger in and out of my ass, while her free hand alternates between cupping my balls and holding the base of my shaft in her tight grip.

My eyes roll back in my head as I give myself over to sensation. Grabbing the back of her head, I hold her in place as I fuck her mouth raw. A familiar tingle starts at the base of my spine, and my balls tighten. I bite down on my lip to contain my roar as my orgasm rockets through me. I spill deep into her mouth, my cock pulsing as I release every single drop down her throat.

When she pulls her finger from my ass, I lift her up by the shoulders and make love to her mouth, savoring the taste of me on her lips. "God, I fucking love you," I rasp over her mouth. "I must've done something right in this life to deserve someone like you."

"Ditto, babe." She pecks my lips softly, smiling as she eases out of my hold to wash her hands. I yank up my jeans and boxers, fixing myself into place, as Lo smooths out her hair and reapplies gloss to her lips.

We exit the bathroom with matching grins, walking into the dining room hand in hand. Four pairs of eyes swing our direction. "Harlow! Caz!" Alisha slurs, lifting a glass filled to the brim with clear liquid I know isn't water. "How lovely to see you." Her gaze drops to our conjoined hands, and she frowns, turning to her son. "Baby, why is your wife holding hands with your friend?"

Saint rolls his eyes to the ceiling while Theo stares at Lo and me, his cheeks flushing. I'm quite partial to that look on him, and my cock stirs in my jeans again.

If we don't fuck soon, I'm likely to explode.

Galen sighs. "Mom, I just told you. Harlow is married to all of us."

Alisha wrinkles her nose in distaste, and my anger rises. For once, couldn't she put aside her own selfish thoughts and think of her son? "I didn't think that was possible."

"Well, it is." Galen's tone is snippy as he stands, holding out the chair beside him for Lo. She kisses him briefly, before sitting beside him, and I drop into the chair on his other side.

Mrs. Murphy carries plates loaded with food into the room, and we tuck in. She leaves some extras in bowls in the middle of the table, along with two large pitchers of water, before excusing herself, pulling the heavy, ornate doors closed behind her.

No one is speaking—we're too busy eating our body weight in pot roast—but it's not awkward.

Until Alisha decides to put her big foot in it.

"It's strange to think if I hadn't aborted Trey's baby you and your wife would share a sibling, isn't it?" she says to Galen, grinning like she's just told a joke.

All the blood drains from Lo's face, and she shoves her plate away, knotting her hands in her lap.

"Mom." Galen's silverware clangs off the table as he drops it, thumping his fist on the table. "Why would you even bring that up?" he says, through gritted teeth, snagging Lo's hand under the table.

"I don't know, I just..." She shrugs, shooting a timid smile in Lo's direction. Lo glares at her with murderous intent, and Alisha gulps. "It just popped into my head," she blurts. "Ugh." She slams her glass down, pressing her palms into her head. "I'm bad. Bad. Bad." She slaps her cheeks, fisting her hands, and hitting herself in the face. She accidentally elbows her glass, and it crashes on top of the table, shattering and spilling vodka everywhere.

Lo reacts fast, jumping to her feet before vodka pours all over her.

"I'll get Mrs. Murphy," Theo says while Galen stands, going to his mom and prying her hands from her face. Her nails are unkempt, and she's torn her frail skin. Little beads of blood seep from a small tear on her cheek.

"Mom, stop." Galen holds her wrists down in front of her, as Saint slips out of the room.

"I'm sorry!" she whimpers, letting her head drop forward on his chest. "I know I mess everything up, but I'm not all bad. I've done good things." She lifts her chin, peeking up at her son with a pleading expression.

I don't know how the fuck Galen has put up with this for years. He deserves the Nobel fucking Peace Prize for his efforts.

Galen releases her hands as Saint steps back into the room. "Good things for you," Alisha adds, cupping Galen's face. "My baby. My precious boy. I won't let anyone hurt you."

What a fucking joke.

This is going to sound cold, but, honestly, the best thing Alisha Lennox could do for her son is die and release him from the burden of caring for her.

She hiccups, and Galen's pained eyes meet Saint's over his mom's shoulder. Saint sets the first aid box down on the table, and I bundle Lo in my arms as we watch Galen attend to the cut on her face.

Mrs. Murphy arrives to clean up the mess on the table, her sad gaze roaming over Alisha as she sobs into Galen's shirt.

"I'll get her to bed," Mrs. Murphy says. "You finish your dinner." She coaxes Alisha from Galen's arms, and his shoulders slump as she's led out of the room.

"You should eat," Galen says in a deadpan voice. "I've lost my appetite."

"I think we all have," Lo says, leaving my embrace and going to Galen. She snakes her arms around him, holding him tight.

"Let's just leave." Galen sounds dejected, and I don't blame him. No matter how often Alisha embarrasses him like this, it never gets any easier even when he knows we understand.

"Lo has something to show you first," Saint says, clamping his hand on his cousin's shoulder. "Something that'll cheer you up."

We head outside, letting Lo and Galen walk ahead of us.

"She's getting worse," Saint says under his breath as we walk.

"She looks awful," I admit, because every time I see her, she appears to be thinner and paler.

"We need to get her into rehab," Theo suggests.

"It's a waste of money," Saint says. "Money Galen doesn't

have because everything he earns already goes into her and the upkeep of this house.”

“He should sell it,” I cut in. “Place is creepy as fuck and falling apart. He’d be better off using the money to get Alisha into rehab and then buying her a smaller home that’s more manageable.”

“It’s been in his family for generations,” Theo says.

“So what?” I shrug. “It’s only bricks and mortar, and from where I’m sitting, it’s brought them nothing but misery.”

“I doubt Sinner would let her part with it considering he’s using it to stash his guns and drugs,” Saint says.

“Let him buy it off her,” I say even though I know he’d never do that. He’ll demand she keep it and continue using it to suit his own ends. He contributes toward the upkeep of the house, but it’s pennies, and Galen covers most of that cost, including paying Mrs. Murphy’s salary. We’ve offered to help countless times, but he refuses to take our money.

Stubborn fuck.

We round the corner, and the maze comes into view. “Wow.” Saint whistles under his breath. “This takes me back.” I’d forgotten how intertwined Galen’s and Saint’s childhood memories are.

“Our girl did good.” Theo’s voice oozes pride.

“She did.” I smile as he turns to look at me, and we share a heated look, one that’s growing with intensity by the day.

Up ahead, Galen is swinging Lo around, and she’s laughing, happy it’s brought a smile back to his face.

“She makes everything better,” Saint murmurs, and I’m not sure if he realizes he said that out loud.

“She fucking does,” I agree.

“Come on, man,” Galen shouts, urging Saint forward with his fingers. “Let’s explore together.”

We watch the three of them disappear into the maze

together, and neither of us makes a move to follow them. My chest heaves the longer we stand here side by side. I'm acutely aware of the heat rolling off Theo's body in waves and the blood rushing south to my cock. Electricity surrounds us, crackling in the air, strengthening the connection simmering between us. Every nerve ending on my body is standing to attention, and anticipation is rife.

A volt zips up my arm when Theo's fingers brush against mine. At first, I think it's accidental, until his fingers touch mine again, curling around the tips, sending bolts of desire threading through my body. I got in trouble the last time I reacted on impulse, but fuck it.

Life is about taking chances, and if I continue waiting for Theo to take control, I'll be old and gray before he takes that leap of faith.

I won't push him too fast, but there's nothing wrong with nudging him in the right direction.

I know what I want, and it's him. Deep down, I know he feels the same. I wouldn't risk our friendship otherwise.

Turning to face him, I grab his face, winding my fingers into his gorgeous hair, slowly lowering my head so I'm not ambushing him. His eyes pop wide in a mix of lust and fear, but he doesn't pull away when my lips land on his. Angling his head, he opens his mouth, letting my tongue explore.

Our kiss swiftly turns frantic, and we're clawing at one another, desperate to get closer. I grab fistfuls of his hair while he drags his nails through mine, making me purr like a kitten. My cock is a block of wood, straining behind my zipper, and he moans into my mouth when I pivot my hips against his.

Feeling his erection sliding against mine does weird things to my stomach, and I grab hold of his ass, yanking him flush against me as our lips devour one another with zero hesitation. My blood is on fire, and I long to drop to my knees, pull out his thick cock, and suck it into my mouth until I feel the tip touching the back of my throat. My cock leaks precum, and I growl into Theo's mouth, wishing we had time to turn my fantasy into reality.

Tinkling laughter forces us apart in a nanosecond, and we pull away with enough time to adjust ourselves and straighten up before the others emerge from the maze.

But nothing gets past our wife, and her eyes sparkle with happiness the closer she gets as her gaze roams intelligently over us, noting our joint flushed skin, tousled hair, and the bulges still evident in our jeans.

Ditching Saint and Galen, she loops her arms through ours, pulling us forward, far enough away from the Lennox cousins to murmur, "Well, my loves. Tell me what I missed." She beams at us, happiness radiating from her every pore, and I love how excited she is for us. There is zero jealousy or possessiveness. Lo is confident in our love, automatically knowing it changes nothing about how we feel for her.

I brave a look at Theo, prepared to see remorse and confusion on his face, like the last time we kissed, but I'm pleasantly surprised to see a genuine smile on his lips. "A gentleman never tells, Lo," Theo says, keeping his eyes locked on mine. A slow grin spreads across his fuck-worthy mouth. "Let's just say it was hot and leave it at that."

Chapter Thirty-Two
Harlow

"What happened?" I blurt the instant I'm inside Caz's Mitsubishi Eclipse. We wave at the others as they pile into Saint's Land Rover. We're going to collect my Lexus, and we'll meet them back at the barn then.

"With what?" He slants me a mock innocent look, and I thump his arm.

"Don't play dumb. With Theo back there!" I waggle my brows, more excited than is normal. "Did you blow each other?" I know that most likely didn't happen, because we weren't gone long enough and I'm pretty sure Theo will have to build up to that, but I can't contain my overactive imagination, and I squirm in my seat at the very idea of them sucking one another off.

Caz chuckles. "I wish."

"Aw." I kick my feet up onto the dash. "I so wanted it to be that."

"Then you should've stayed in the maze longer." Caz peels

out of the driveway, heading toward the less salubrious part of town. "Galen seems happy."

"He is. He loves it." I'm thrilled he does, because there was a small part of me that feared I'd overstepped the mark. The guys warned me he's funny about accepting money or gifts from them, so I didn't know if he'd feel the same about this. I'm happy he saw the gesture for what it was. Happy to see a smile on his face again. I seriously could've throttled Alisha for her insensitive outburst at the table. She ruined dinner and embarrassed her son, and that shit doesn't wash with me.

Alisha needs to get her act together or get the fuck out of his life. I know that's not my call to make, but doesn't she see what she's doing to him? I make a silent vow to never let Galen visit her by himself again. If she pulls that shit on him, I want to be there to make it better.

"But stop deflecting," I add, pulling myself out of my inner monologue. "Put a girl out of her misery."

"We kissed," Caz admits, and I bounce on my seat, squealing and clapping my hands like a toddler on a sugar high. "And it was fucking hot."

"He looked happy. Like he's turned a corner," I admit, because Theo had the biggest smile on his face. His eyes were alive, and he looked comfortable in his skin.

"Man, I really hope so." Caz casts me a quick glance as he pushes the car forward. "I really want this to work."

"I do too. I am so wet right now imagining you two sucking each other off. Like, you've no idea." I'm not lying, and I can only imagine what thoughts must be running through Caz's mind.

"If my buddy wasn't doing us a favor opening his garage on a Sunday, I'd pull over and shove you on my dick right now," he says.

"Fuck. I love your dirty mouth." I toy with a strand of my hair. "I've always loved sex, but since I met you guys, it's like I'm in overdrive. The more we fuck, the more I crave it. Considering all the shit we have on our plate, I probably should be less fixated on sex, but I'm obsessed."

Caz barks out a laugh. "You're like a dude trapped in a woman's body."

I slap him across the back of the head, and the car swerves a little. "That type of comment is beneath you even if I know you were joking."

"I love that you're sex-obsessed. It's one of the reasons it works so well with all of us. We've got sex on the brain pretty much twenty-four seven. Fuck whatever else is going on in our lives. Nothing is more important than caving to our carnal desires. We should implement a no-clothes rule at the house," he suggests, his eyes lighting up with devilish delight.

"As much as I like that idea, we would literally do nothing else but fuck."

"And that's a problem, why?"

I laugh, rolling my eyes. "So, who's this buddy?" I deliberately switch the topic before I say screw my car and force Caz to pull over and push himself inside me.

"He's the guy I told you about. I used to work for him in his garage. Everything I know about cars, he taught me."

We pull into a large warehouse-style garage on the outskirts of Prestwick five minutes later, and Caz cuts the engine outside. My Lexus is parked beside us, but we walk past it, heading toward the guy with dark curly hair and oil streaks on his cheeks, lounging against the door to a small office. He's dressed in grease-splattered overalls, and he's wiping his oily fingers on a dirty red rag. A wide grin creeps across his full mouth, and he steps forward, pulling Caz into a bear hug. I watch in amusement as they slap each other on the back. "Caz, my man. Good to see you, dude."

They step out of their embrace.

"You too, Rich." Caz takes my hand, pulling me into his side. "This is my wife, Harlow."

"Your wife?" Rich almost chokes on the words. "What the fuck, man?" His eyes pop wide. "When the fuck did that happen?"

Caz chuckles. "A few days ago."

"Well, good for you, man." He turns his sharp gaze on me. "Nice to meet you, Harlow. And congratulations on your wedding."

"You too, Rich, and thanks."

"Your Lexus is ready," Rich confirms, handing me the keys. "She's a beauty. Took a hammering, but I'm glad we were able to repair her."

"It looks brand-new," I say, glancing over my shoulder. "You did a great job." I whip my wallet out of my back pocket. "What do I owe you?" I ask, sliding my platinum card out.

"Your husband already took care of it."

I narrow my eyes at Caz. "You shouldn't have done that."

"We all chipped in," he confirms, slinging his arm over my shoulders, earning a puzzled look from Rich.

They shoot the shit for a few minutes while I take the opportunity to text Diesel. Mom just arrived safely at the house in Europe, and it's a load off my mind. I thank Diesel, telling him we're still waiting for Bry to confirm details of the meeting time with his DEA agent brother. Diesel insists on being there. He thinks the guy is unhinged, and he doesn't want me near him unless he's there too, so he's already on a plane on his way back to the US.

"Can't you hack into the school system and fix it so we can all graduate already?" I grumble to Theo the next morning as we get ready to leave.

"You think we haven't tried that before?" Galen says, stuffing his feet into his boots and lacing them up.

"Theo's too honorable to do anything so underhanded," Caz says.

"Ask him to blow up our enemy? No problem," Saint adds. "Ask him to doctor our grades, and it's like we've asked him to assassinate the president of every country in the world."

Theo flips Saint the bird. "We attend to our responsibilities seriously, and that includes school. You'll thank me one day."

I push my body against his. "Just think, if we didn't have to go to school, we could still be in bed." I lick a line up the side of his neck. "Think of how much more enjoyable that would be." I press my mouth to his ear. "You could tag team me and Caz," I whisper, ensuring only he hears.

Theo's eyes blaze with warning as he holds me at arm's length, but I know he's not mad. While I won't push him, because I promised, I've decided to help nudge him in the right direction, because I think he needs it. And okay, I might be a little more enthusiastic today, because they kissed last night and there was no guilt, no remorse, no second-guessing.

"Your seductive tactics won't work either," he says, adopting an affable tone. "Now get your sexy butt in the Lexus. We don't need any more tardy slips on our records."

Morning classes drag, but I have one free period I use to

catch up on some homework, while ignoring requests from the career guidance counselor to meet in her office. I know she wants to discuss why my attendance has taken a nosedive these past couple months, and I really don't want to lie to her, because I've always respected Mrs. Horkan, and she deserves better. It's not like I can tell her exactly what's been going down, and I don't want to give her vague half-truths either because that would be an insult to our relationship. So, I've been dodging her attempts to corner me, feeling like a coward but accepting it's minor in the grand scheme of things.

The cafeteria buzzes with gossip as news of our wedding has reached the masses. Envious glances follow me as I walk across the room with my tray. "I hear congrats are in order," Emmett says when I claim the seat across from him.

"I'll accept your congratulations if you mean it," I say, popping a piece of bread in my mouth.

"I didn't say I understood it, but I was sincere because I can tell they make you happy." He slurps on his Coke, slanting me a lopsided grin. "Guess there's no accounting for taste," he quips on purpose as Saint arrives at the table.

Saint slams his tray down, sitting beside me, drumming his fingers on the table. "Careful, ass face. Being friends with my wife doesn't give you concessions. You'll treat me with respect like the rest of this fucking school."

"I see your ego is alive and well and living on its own planet," Emmett replies, no longer scared of pushing his buttons. He knows I'd never let them do anything to jeopardize Lynn's treatment at the hospital. "And I don't answer to you. I'm friends with your wife. You're nothing to me." He jabs his fork in the air, making his point clear.

Saint's lips tug up at the corners in begrudging admiration.

"Be nice, Emmett," I warn, because he can't disregard Saint

in public like this. I slide my fingers between Saint's. "Saint is my husband, and I expect you to treat him the same way I'd treat your wife or girlfriend—with respect and like an extension of you."

"The other Saints are fair game now, right?" a feminine voice says from behind, cutting into our conversation. I twist around in my seat, watching a small dark-haired girl with big boobs and beady eyes drape herself all over Galen.

Galen meets my eyes, urging me to go for it. Saint smirks while Caz chuckles and Theo quietly observes.

I take my time getting out of my chair, my rage expanding every time the bitch paws at my man.

"Who are you?" I ask, towering over her. Menace drips from my tone, but she's either too dumb or stupidly brave because she doesn't even flinch, continuing to run her long nails up and down Galen's arm. His lips twitch in amusement as he waits to see how I'll handle it.

"I'm Josie." She juts her chin out, as if I've offended her because I haven't a clue who she is.

"Well, Josie." I push myself right into her personal space. "It seems you're laboring under a misconception. Allow me to set you straight." I grab her arm, yanking her away from Galen. "What part of *we're married* do you not understand?"

She attempts to wrench from my grip, and that pisses me off, so I tighten my hold on her arm and force her to the ground, pinning my boot on her calves to keep her there. She glares up at me, and her cheeks darken with a mixture of anger and embarrassment. But she gets the message, and she stops fighting. "You're married to Saint. What's that got to do with Galen?" she hisses.

Her belligerent tone irritates me, and I'm already getting bored. "I married all of them. Check their hands." I project my voice across the now silent room, ensuring everyone gets the message. All four guys lift their hands, showcasing their black wedding bands. Low murmurs descend across the cafeteria.

"I...I didn't know."

"Clearly." I narrow my eyes to slits, slicing her with imaginary daggers before letting her go. "Next time you touch what belongs to me, I won't be so charitable." She gawks at me, her expression a mix of shocked disbelief and jealous anger. "Now fuck off before I change my mind and decide to make an example of you."

Her nostrils flare and her eyes darken with pure venom as she scrambles to her feet. She looks two seconds away from lunging at me, so I pull my Strider from its sheath, tracing my finger along the sharp blade. "This isn't an accessory." I pin her with a deadly look. "And if you're still here in three seconds, I'll happily demonstrate just how skilled I am with a knife."

Caz howls with laughter when she hightails it out of the cafeteria like she's got a bee up her butt. Guess she's not so dumb after all.

"That was cruel, Lo," Sean says, joining the conversation for the first time.

"It was," I admit, reclaiming my seat. "But it was necessary. The guys don't have time to fend off hordes of drooling women. I've just resolved the issue."

"That shit still turns me the fuck on," Saint admits, making no effort to lower his voice.

"Want me to suck you off in the bathroom?" I offer.

"Hell yeah," Caz replies.

"She wasn't offering to blow *you*," Saint smugly retorts.

"And you got your rocks off in the bathroom at my house yesterday," Galen interjects.

Emmett almost chokes on his soda. "Is that all you do?"

"Fuck?" Galen smirks, popping a brow.

"Pretty much," I confess, grinning. "I've got four guys to please. It's a tough job, but someone has to do it."

We all burst out laughing, and it's a much-needed tension reliever.

"Have you heard from Bry?" I ask Saint as we exit the cafeteria later, making our way to class.

"No, and he's starting to piss me off. How long does it take to talk to your brother?" Saint says, sliding his hand into the back pocket of my jeans as we walk.

"You think he's still lying?" I ask.

"I think Diesel is correct," Theo says before Saint replies. "His brother is the issue. Not Bryant."

"I agree," Galen says. "Bryant appeared to be telling the truth."

"Let me call him after school. See if he'll meet with me. I'll get to the bottom of it." I have a good relationship with Bry, and if he's going to divulge anything to anyone, it'll be me. If there's a problem with his brother, we need to know now. Not after he's gone to the authorities and handed our asses to them on a platter.

"Okay," Saint relents, kissing me when we reach my classroom. His cell pings in his pocket, and he groans. "Is Sinner still hounding you?" I inquire because he's been blowing up his phone nonstop since Mom disappeared Saturday night.

Saint nods, rubbing a hand across the back of his neck. "I can't ignore him forever. We need to discuss how we're going to handle him."

"Let's deal with Bryant and then agree what to do about Sinner," I propose.

He pecks my lips. "Okay. Later, queenie." He smirks, and I flip him the bird behind his back. He walks off laughing.

Asshole.

I'm going to kill Caz if that nickname sticks.

The others kiss me, one at a time, and I'm conscious of eyeballs glued to my back as I saunter into the classroom and take my seat. I know the general populace has questions and that we're feeding the gossip mill with our PDAs, but I've got zero fucks to give.

They are mine, and I am theirs, and everyone needs to learn that irrefutable truth.

I make an effort to focus in class, determined to find some time this week to catch up on my homework, but I lose the battle with my bladder ten minutes before the bell is due to ring, gathering up my books and standing.

"Get back in your seat, Ms. Westbrook," Batshit Branning demands, rapping her knuckles on the top of her desk.

"It's *Mrs.* Westbrook," I correct before anyone dares to call me Mrs. Lennox. Because that shit will *never* happen. I've talked to Saint about it, and he understands. I jokily suggested he legally change *his* surname, shocked when he actually appeared to consider it. I think Saint Westbrook has a nice ring to it, and I wouldn't be opposed to it at all.

"And I need the bathroom. It can't wait." I stroll past her, ignoring her threats of detention and write-ups, walking the eerily quiet hallway with a new spring in my step.

I am *so* over high school, and I can't wait to be finished. Only six more months and we're done. By then, the Sinner problem will be dealt with, and we'll be free to go where we want, do what we want, and I literally cannot wait.

I attend to business, wash my hands, and grab my book bag, pushing through the doors of the bathroom, back out into the empty hallway.

He's on me the second I step foot in the corridor, and there's no time to react, because he's caught me completely unaware. A large, manly hand wraps around my arm the same time a black bag is lowered over my head, and the sharp sting of a needle penetrates my skin. I sway on my feet as the enemy liquid swirls through my veins, blurring my vision and clouding my head. The world turns black, and I collapse against him, completely at his mercy.

Chapter Thirty-Three
Harlow

I come to, alone, in a darkened room, sometime later. Pain stabs me through the skull, and my butt is numb from the wooden chair I'm tied to. My hands are pulled behind my back, secured with layers of strong tape. Fuck. If it was rope, at least I'd stand a chance of getting free. As my eyes adjust to the darkness, I scan my surroundings.

The room is on the small side with a double bed and a single cot pressed against the back wall. Dark navy curtains cover the window, blocking out any natural light. A side door is partially open, offering a glimpse of the tacky bathroom with lime-green fittings. A scuffed mahogany desk rests against the wall in front of me, weighed down by a bulky old-fashioned TV that has seen better days. Peeling paint on the walls, the threadbare patterned carpet, gaudy flower-print comforter, and the musty smell of piss mixed with weed and stale cigarettes confirms I'm in some seedy motel.

Ignoring the dry taste in my mouth and the persistent pounding in my head, I piece together what happened. Some asshole waited until my guard was lowered to snatch me. So much for the new security measures in school.

What's the point of having guards and cameras when someone could snatch me so easily?

I'm guessing he had assistance, and whoever it was will fucking pay.

I didn't see who took me, because it all happened so fast. All I know is, it was definitely a man, and my money's on Sinner. He's pissed at Mom—frustrated she got out from under his clutches—and annoyed that his son and other junior members are ghosting him. This is his way of forcing Saint to confront him.

I'm not scared though, because I'm wearing the necklace Diesel gave me, so I know the guys can track me. I also know Sinner won't hurt me. He needs me to eliminate the commissioner, so I'm safe, at least until then. All bets are off after the assassination though, and I don't know what he has planned after he has no more use for me. But I refuse to worry about that now. Focus on one problem at a time has always been my motto.

I cast my gaze over the entire room, checking to see if there's anything sharp I can use to potentially cut the binds around my wrists, but there is literally nothing in this room. I hate sitting here like a damsel in distress, waiting for my guys to rescue me, but I'm low on options.

I jump as the door to the room swings open and my captor strides into the room. My eyes revolt as bright light filters into the room from outside, and I blink a few times. It's still daylight, which means I can't have been out cold for too long. School should be out by now, so I expect the guys to show up at any moment.

Stepping into the room, he slams the door shut with his

boot, depositing a paper bag on top of the desk, before switching the main light on.

"You?" My brows knit together. "What the hell is this?"

"Hello, Harlow." Bry's DEA agent brother shucks off his jacket, throwing it on the end of the bed. "Allow me to formally introduce myself. I'm Howie Young. Bryant's brother."

"I know who you are, asshole. Was Bry involved in this?" I grit my teeth, anger rippling through my aching limbs.

"My brother wanted a little meet and greet, and he got one."

His flippant tone grates on what little patience I have left, and I snarl, gnashing my teeth. "I doubt he requested for you to hurt me."

"Oh, come now, Harlow." He removes some paper boxes from the bag. "Let's cut the dramatics. You're not hurt, and as soon as I get what I want, I'll let you go."

I tilt my head to the side, putting a leash on my anger. "What is it you want?"

"You really don't know?" he asks, stepping toward me with a bottle of water.

"I wouldn't ask a question if I already knew the answer to it."

"Open wide." He uncaps the water, holding the bottle to my lips. I clamp my lips shut, glaring at him defiantly, because who the fuck knows what he's put in the water. "You just watched me open the bottle," he says. "I haven't tampered with it."

I continue glaring at him, and he sighs before slanting the bottle to his lips, taking a healthy mouthful of the clear liquid. "See? It's safe. I'd hardly drink it if it was poisoned."

"Why should I trust anything you say? You already drugged me once."

"I'm sorry about that." He almost looks sincere. "I don't like hurting women." His jaw tightens, and pain glimmers across his eyes. "But it was necessary."

"Why?"

"Just drink, and we'll talk then."

I let him tip water into my mouth this time, because my throat's as dry as the Gobi Desert, and he hasn't keeled over yet. However, I shut my lips after a couple of mouthfuls, just in case.

"Why am I here?" I ask again.

He sits on the edge of the bed, opening a couple of paper cartons. Delicious, aromatic scents waft around the room, and my tummy rumbles appreciatively, reminding me I barely ate anything at lunch.

"I'll make you a deal. You eat and I'll answer one question at a time." Like with the water, he eats first, and then he lifts a second, clean fork to my mouth, shoveling spicy chicken rice into my mouth. "I know Saint Lennox wants to meet. That he sent Bryant as his little messenger boy. Well, I don't answer to anyone. Least of all that asshole's offspring."

"So, this is a powerplay?" My face pulls into a grimace. "That's pathetic," I scoff.

"I don't expect you to understand," he hisses, pushing another mouthful of food into my mouth. "But Saint Lennox needs to learn up front that he has no control in this," he seethes.

"In what?" I ask, watching him chew slowly as anger literally vibrates from every taut muscle in his body.

"It will make sense when they arrive. I expect they won't be much longer."

"You'll be lucky to make it out of this room alive," I say, speaking nothing but the truth. "It seems rather foolish to have pulled a stunt like this. If you wanted a meeting on your terms, you just had to tell Bry that, and we could've worked something out."

"You say that like he's reasonable."

"Saint's...not unreasonable, some of the time," I admit. "And you talk like you think you know him. Why is that?"

"I know his prick of a father, and he's grown up in his shadow."

"Saint is nothing like that bastard! Nothing!" I yell. "You don't know a damn thing about him!"

The door crashes inward, and Howie dumps the takeout on the floor, standing behind me and pressing a gun into my head.

Saint barrels into the room like a raging bull, brandishing guns in both hands, wearing a ferocious expression that would terrify most normal men. But the guy keeping me captive is definitely unhinged and not normal.

The rest of my guys race into the room, followed by Bry at the rear. Bry has a large gash in his forehead, and fresh bruises linger under the skin on his cheeks, courtesy of my guys, I'm guessing.

The guys point their guns at the man holding me hostage while Howie keeps the gun pressed to my temple. "Put your weapons down, or I'll put a bullet through her skull," Howie says.

"What the fuck are you doing?" Bry roars, throwing his hands in the air. Theo closes the door while Galen and Caz rake their eyes over me from head to toe, checking to ensure I'm not harmed.

"Something you were too weak to do," Howie snarls. "Taking back control."

"Are you okay?" Saint asks, restraining his bristling anger.

"I'm fine." I'm not admitting I'm a little groggy or that I've got a monster headache, thanks to whatever he injected me with, because it'll only turn into a bloodbath, and I want fucking answers.

"I haven't hurt her," Howie says. "And I don't want to. I want to talk. See if what my brother says is true."

"Which is?" Saint asks, still keeping his gun trained on Howie.

"That we're on the same side. We both want to see Sinner pay."

Saint and Galen trade guarded expressions, and I know what it means. They're wondering if he can be trusted, and it's a big ask given the current hostage situation.

"Why don't we all put the weapons down," Theo says. "You untie our wife, and we discuss this calmly like adults."

Howie snorts. "What kind of fool do you take me for? Why do you think I did this? I don't trust any of you punks not to shoot me the instant my guard is lowered. Or to record me and trap me into some admission. I know the way that bastard Sinner works, and he's trained you all."

"Howie, you're making a big mistake," Bry says, attempting to negotiate with his brother. "I know them, and I vouch for them. Put the fucking gun down and let Lo go. Please. Jess would not want this."

"You didn't fucking know her!" Howie screams, waving the gun around. "Because that bastard stole your sister's life before you were even born."

"I know enough about Jess from what you've told me, and she wouldn't want to see any woman hurt because of her."

"I haven't hurt Harlow. I've taken care of her."

He's got a warped sense of how to treat a woman.

I'm betting he's still single.

Bry steps forward. "Give me the gun, Howie."

"You don't tell me what to do, little brother."

Bry exhales heavily. "I'm telling you that if you don't give me the gun, and let Lo go, you won't live to see the next hour, because there's a pissed-off VERO assassin on his way here and he will shoot first and ask questions later."

"What are you talking about?"

"That guy who's been after you about the recording. That's who."

Howie tsks. "He's not with VERO. He's ex-FBI. A PI hired by The Sainthood to get that tape back."

So that's why he's holding onto that footage. He thinks it's of some worth to Sinner. I know Diesel was trying to help, and that he can't blow his cover, but he's unwittingly sent out a completely different message.

"That's a front," Theo says. "But he is who Bryant says he is and every bit as dangerous."

"And he's not the only one," Saint adds. "Because the longer you keep my wife hostage, the less I care about what you have to say and the more I dream about riddling your body with bullets."

"Shut up, Saintly," I hiss, because he's going to get us all killed. "We want to hear what Howie has to say, because he hates Sinner as much as we do. This is stupid, and we're wasting valuable time. We are not enemies, and I'm not hurt." I arch my neck, looking back at Howie. "I promise no harm will come to you if you untie me and put your gun down. Look into my eyes, and see the truth there."

I'm not expecting it to work, so I'm as shocked as the others when he removes the gun, tucking it into the back waistband of his jeans. "Your turn," Howie says, eyeballing my guys.

I stare them down until they've lowered their weapons and the threat in the air has dissipated. Howie crouches behind me, pulling out my knife, using it to cut the tape around my wrists.

My legs are wobbly as I push myself to standing, and Saint

darts forward, scooping me into his arms while growling at Howie.

Flipping my palm up, I bore a hole in Howie's skull until he sheaths my knife and hands it back to me. I grip it in one hand as I cling to Saint, wrapping my arms and legs around him, because I don't trust him not to lose the plot and start World War Three in this motel room. Saint sits down on the bed, and I reposition myself so my legs are dangling across his, in a more acceptable manner. I place my knife on the bed beside us.

"Call your VERO agent off," Howie says. "I didn't agree to any meeting with him."

"Already done." Theo confirms what I already know, because there's no way Diesel has made it back from Europe yet. Plus, the guys would only call on him if they needed backup, which they don't.

Bry was calling his brother's bluff, and it paid off. I nod in Bry's direction, conveying my thanks.

"You should know," I say, eyeing Howie from my seat on Saint's lap. "That Sinner doesn't care about that recording. We are the ones who want it back. If you hand it to the authorities, he'd probably pat you on the back and thank you for getting rid of a problem for him."

Bry folds his arms across his body, leaning back against the wall, fixing his brother with an "I told you so" look.

Howie shakes his head. "Sinner would do anything to protect his flesh and blood. It's why..." He stops himself midsentence, leaning forward on the back of the chair, stabbing Saint with a curious look.

"Why what?" Saint grits out.

"Why wouldn't he do everything to protect his only son?" Howie asks instead of answering Saint's question.

"He's never cared about me," Saint admits, his voice devoid of emotion. "Even now, he only tolerates me because he's arrogant enough to want someone carrying his name to continue a tradition of leadership within The Sainthood."

"I've heard stories. I know what you guys do."

"We do what we have to, to survive," Galen snaps. "That doesn't mean any of us like it or choose it."

Chapter Thirty-Four
Harlow

"Don't you get it?" Caz says. "We were born into this world. All of us, but Theo. Even then, he had little choice when his parents disowned him. Sinner preys on those who are vulnerable, and he manipulates people into carrying out his will."

"He's very good at it," I add. "And he traps people into corners so there is no way out. That's why he's able to get the wider membership to agree to test-drive sex trafficking as a new business model." My tone drips with disgust, and the air is heavy with tension.

Howie's jaw flexes as he stares at Saint in a way that's starting to make me uncomfortable. If he makes one move against my man, I will flatten his ass to the floor and slice his skin to shreds before he's even blinked.

"My brother has told me you're a prick. How are you any different from your father?"

Saint turns his head to Bry, arching a brow, seemingly nonplussed about the comparison, but we all know the rage bubbling under the surface, because there is nothing Saint hates more than being compared to that sick psycho bastard.

Bry levels Saint with an earnest look, not shying away from the truth. "You know you're a prick. I didn't tell any lies, but my brother seems to have misinterpreted it." Bry walks over to Howie, standing in front of him. "Yes, Saint's a prick. So is Galen. So am I. Lo is a complete bitch at times."

I grin, because I take that as a compliment.

"But I never said Saint was like Sinner, because that's not true," he continues. "Saint isn't like his dad. He isn't a cold-blooded murdering bastard of women and torturer of children." He looks over at us, waggling his brows. "He loves Lo, and he'd take a bullet for his cousin and his friends. His loyalty may be hard-earned, but it's steadfast. Sinner doesn't know the meaning of that word, and he's incapable of anything even close to love."

"Is it true?" Howie asks, clutching the back of the chair.

There's a pregnant pause as we all wait to see how Saint responds. I'm wondering why we're so focused on him and where this is leading, but I'm trying to summon patience. Saint slowly nods. "I hate him. He's a bully and a psychopath, and I want to put him in jail where he can't hurt me or anyone I love. He needs to be removed as Sainthood president before his poison infects every part of the organization." His Adam's apple bobs in his throat, and I know this is tough for him. Frankly, I'm surprised he's being so open, but there's a weird vibe in the air, something I can't put my finger on.

"When I was little, I was his punching bag," Saint adds. "Now that I'm older, I'm a minion he pushes around to do his bidding. I've always been a means to an end for him. That's all. I've never meant anything else."

A crack appears in my heart, and I bleed for my broken man. Inside, I curse Sinner for the damage he's caused, and I curse his mother for running off and leaving him with a monster.

A strangled sound rips through the air, and I eye Howie curiously when he drops to his knees on the floor in front of us. Bry stiffens, his brow puckering. Saint goes rigidly still underneath me.

"I had no idea it was like that for you growing up. I should've stayed here. I should've taken care of you and Bryant," Howie says.

"What the fuck are you talking about?" Bryant snaps, rubbing his temples.

Howie gulps, looking up at his brother. "I didn't tell you the whole truth."

Tension is so thick you could slice it with a knife. I cling harder to Saint, because I sense a whirlwind is coming.

"What are you saying?" Bryant asks, his gaze dancing between his brother and Saint.

"Sinner didn't murder your sister because she knew too much," Howie admits.

My eyes lift to Galen's, and I see the moment it registers with him too.

Holy fuck.

Howie turns to Saint. "Sinner knocked my sister up when she was just nineteen. She was so sweet, so pure, until she met that bastard," he hisses.

My heart is lodged in my throat as I look at Saint's shell-shocked expression. I can tell he's connected the dots too. "He ruined her. Abused her. Beat her. Forced her to take drugs even when she was pregnant. Now that I know about his history with Giana, it makes sense. He knocked Jess up on purpose after he found out Giana was expecting Harlow. It was some sick retaliation. I knew Sinner was dangerous the first time I met him, and after I checked him out, I was even more worried.

I begged Jess to leave him, but she refused. She loved him up until the end, when he told her point-blank he never loved her, that Giana was the only woman he would ever love."

I hold Saint tight, and his body trembles as anger rolls off him in waves. Tears prick my eyes, and I want Howie to be wrong about this, but my gut says he's telling us the truth.

"What happened?" Theo asks. "What did Sinner do?"

Howie eyeballs Saint. "Jess realized what a monster he was, and she planned to run away with her baby. I helped her to get a new ID, and she fled to Texas a couple of weeks before she was due to give birth. I helped her get settled in the little two-bedroom house she found, but I had enlisted by then, and I was gone a few days later." He swipes at the tears pooling in his eyes. "I should never have left her alone. She wouldn't let me call our mom because Mom was still grieving our dad plus she was pregnant with Bryant."

Bry is as white as a ghost, and it's obvious this is the first time he's hearing this.

Howie maintains focus on Saint. "Sinner found her, and he refused to let her leave until she'd had the baby. Jess gave birth to you in that house, and he took you from her the second you were born." Tears stream down his face, and I'm fighting to keep my emotions in check. "She never even got to hold you. That bastard listened to her scream and cry and plead for you." Murderous rage washes over his features. "He killed her right there and then," he sobs. "Burned her body, and buried what was left of her in the backyard."

Saint's left eye ticks repeatedly, and I rub my hands all over him, trying to get warmth into his cold bones.

"Why didn't you tell me this?" Bry demands with his chest heaving.

"Because I thought it was too late to save Saint, and I knew if you realized who he was that you'd try. I assumed Saint was his father's son. The stories I'd heard about him seemed to confirm it. I believed that the part of him that shared DNA with us was too deeply buried." Howie wipes his tears away, standing.

"How could you leave him with Sinner knowing that?" I cry out.

"I couldn't do anything for him from overseas, and my mother was too fragile. Then she killed herself. She was heartbroken when Jess died. I couldn't tell her she'd been murdered, and she never knew she had a grandson, because I lied. I told her Jess and the baby died in a car accident. I also knew if Sinner murdered my sister because she tried to take his son away from him that there was nothing I could do to rescue him."

He hangs his head, and I want to pummel his cowardly body until he's not breathing.

I cup Saint's face, forcing his eyes to mine, but he stares vacantly at me, shielding his emotions, because it's his usual go-to coping mechanism. My eyes seek Galen's, and he wears the same concerned mask as me. This might tip Saint over the edge, and I don't know if any of us can stop him from wreaking havoc.

"How do you know about the birth?" Bry asks. "What else aren't you saying?"

Howie worries his lower lip between his teeth. "I didn't know exactly what had happened for a long time. It was only after I'd retired from the military and came back to the area that I sought vengeance. I used my contacts and the tools at my disposal as a DEA agent to dig into Sinner's background. That's how I found Alisha Lennox."

Oh hell to the no.

Galen freezes, and Saint digs his fingers into my hips, but it's the only outward sign of emotion.

"Alisha was there?" Caz asks what we're afraid to.

Howie nods. "She told me Sinner forced her to be there. She was pregnant, and he threatened her baby if she didn't help with the delivery. He blackmailed her into keeping silent about it after, but it tore at her conscience. She wouldn't talk to me at first, because she was scared, but I followed her one night to a party, and I got her to admit it when she was high."

Galen buries his face in his hands, and my heart is rupturing behind my rib cage. My guys are in a world of pain, and we need to get out of here. We need to be alone to process all this. *How many times will the sins of our parents continue to hurt us?*

"This is a lot to take in," I say. "And I know we have other stuff to discuss," I tell Howie, "but it has to wait. We need to go." It's an effort to keep my tone civil when I want to rip that sniveling bastard limb from limb, but I do it for Saint and for Galen, because they need me to be strong right now.

I climb off Saint, taking his hand and pulling him upright. He hasn't said one word. Hasn't made eye contact with anyone, and I'm scared for him. I get that he never knew his mother and he came to terms with her loss long ago, but this has still got to hurt. Sinner lied to him, and now he's discovered his father is the reason he grew up without his mom. Without love in his life. Saint already despises Sinner, and this will only compound it. He's a boiling pot of rage waiting to explode, and I'm fearful for what he might do.

"I'm sorry," Howie says, but it's a little too late for apologies. "By the time I found Bryant and I got my act together, I had heard enough about you to know it was too late. I thought you were just like him. I was wrong. I should've reached out, tried—"

"Shut your fucking face," Saint spits, whipping his hand from mine. He prods Howie in the chest, pushing him back. "I don't want your apologies or your pity or your help." His furious eyes swing in Bry's direction. "That goes for you too. Stay away from me. Both of you!"

I'm not surprised he's lashing out or that his natural reaction is to push them away. Bry isn't at fault. He was in the dark too. But Howie left Saint with a monster. He didn't fight for his nephew, choosing to believe the worst of him instead of giving him the benefit of the doubt. And Saint has survived without them this long, I'm guessing he figures he doesn't need them in his life.

If I was Saint, I'd be furious, hurt, and disappointed too.

Saint pushes past me, heading for the door.

"Cousin." Galen reaches for Saint, but he slaps his hand away.

"Don't!" Saint hisses. "I want to be alone." He yanks the door open and storms outside.

I race after him. "Saint, wait!"

"Leave him, Lo." Galen pulls me back as Saint climbs behind the wheel of his Land Rover. "He needs to process this his way."

Pain stabs me in the chest. "I don't want him to be alone."

"He isn't." Galen bundles me into his arms. "He has us. He knows that, and he knows we'll be waiting for him when he's ready to talk."

Chapter Thirty-Five

Harlow

"Lo. Stop pacing and come sit down," Galen says, patting the empty space on the couch beside him.

"He should be home by now." I ignore Galen, continuing to wear a line in the floor. "It's almost eleven. I don't like him being there by himself."

"We know where he is, and he'll come back when he's ready." Theo attempts to reassure me, and the more they attempt to calm me down, the more irritable I become.

"You're sure he's still at the bar?" I inquire, walking to the table where Theo is seated.

"Yes. Look." He points at the little red dot on the screen. "That's where his cell phone has been for the past few hours. He hasn't moved from Molly's Bar."

"This is how Saint processes," Galen explains.

"And it's better than him going after Sinner because who the fuck knows what he'll do to him now he knows the truth," Caz adds.

"Stop it!" I roar, losing the tenuous hold on my emotions. "Stop making excuses. Stop acting like this is okay, because it's fucking not okay! Ugh!" I pound my fist on the table repeatedly until Theo bravely intervenes.

"We know you're worried, and it's not that we're unconcerned," he says, uncurling my clenched fist.

"It's just what Saint does," Galen adds.

Drawing a deep breath, I try to calm down. "I understand it. I do, because that's what I usually do too, but things are different now. He has me, and he doesn't need to be alone with his destructive thoughts." I never should've let him leave by himself. I should've listened to my gut. I knew it was a bad idea.

"I can't believe your mom has known all this time and she said nothing," Caz says, deliberately sidestepping the topic. He tosses a couple more logs on the fire, fanning fresh flames.

"It's clear Alisha knows a lot more than we realized," Theo adds, kissing my knuckles before sitting back down in front of his tablet.

"Whether she remembers is debatable." Galen kicks his socked feet up on the couch when he realizes I'm too wound up to sit still.

Even after a lengthy run around the grounds, I'm still a mass of restless energy, and I won't relax until I know Saint is okay. This edgy, anxious feeling is disconcerting and new. I don't think the guys get it—this is as much about me, as it is about Saint.

Saint's pain is *my* pain.

I share in his frustration and his rage. My heart hurts in sympathy, my soul is bruised, and my mind is clouded with disappointment and uncertainty. I've never loved any man—besides my dad, and that was a different kind of love—before I met my guys, so these reactions, these emotions, are different for me too, and I hate feeling so helpless, so powerless, to support him in his time of need.

"And I'm not defending her," Galen continues. "I'm fucking pissed. At Sinner. At her. At my dad, because presumably he was there too, but she's fucked in the head. Drugs have fried her brain. Most times, she talks gibberish, and I never know whether to believe what comes out of her mouth."

"Or maybe she blocked it out because it was too painful," I suggest.

I know I've buried shit rather than face up to it in the past. Before I realized that is how tormentors continue hurting their victims. The only way to take back power, to regain control over your life, is to face your demons head-on. Alisha has spent her life denying the things she's been witness to and the things she's done. She's weak, and it's no surprise she's turned to alcohol and drugs to blot reality and fuel her addictions.

"Or she realized the truth would only hurt Saint more," Theo suggests, setting his tablet down.

"In her own fucked-up way, she thought she was protecting him," Caz adds, running with Theo's train of thought.

"She doesn't know the meaning of the word." Galen roughly exhales. Resting his head back on the arm of the couch, he closes his eyes. I know this is hard for him too. It's one thing for Alisha to hurt him. Quite another to hurt his cousin.

"It doesn't matter now," I say, because the time for talking is over. "We can't change the past. But we can deal with the here and now, and I'm done waiting." I snatch up the keys to my Lexus and head toward the door. "I'm getting my husband. You can come with or stay here, but I'm not twiddling my thumbs a second longer. Saint needs me. Needs *us*. Whether he knows it or not."

Still wearing my yoga pants and running top, which is no protection from the elements, I snag a hoodie from the hooks by the door, sliding my arms inside the long sleeves. Saint's scent swirls around me as I zip up his hoodie, rolling the sleeves up until my hands are poking out. The guys trail me as I step out into the icy-cold night air, and no words are spoken as we pile into the Lexus and hightail it out of there.

The bar is busy for a Monday night, packed to the rafters with bikers, laborers, and scantily clad women of all ages. Molly's is located on the other side of Prestwick from the grungy biker bar Darrow favors, which is a blessing, because if I ran into my asshole ex tonight, in the mood I'm in, I'd probably slit his throat.

Disregarding the eyeballs glued to my body, I push my way through the people crowding the bar, searching for Saint's head. My lips curl into a possessive snarl when I finally spot him sitting on a stool at the end of the bar with a bottle of JD and several empty glasses in front of him.

Two girls are vying for his attention, one on either side of him. Saint is ignoring them, shoving the brunette's hand off his arm when she tries to latch on, keeping his head down, his fingers gripping his drink so tight it's a miracle the glass doesn't smash. The woman with the bright blue hair thrusts her tits in Saint's face, smirking at her friend over his head, as if it's a competition and he's the prize.

Charging my way through the people in my path, I have singular focus. Anger rises like a tidal wave inside me as I watch the woman smush Saint's face into her chest before he even realizes what's happening. A snarl rips from my mouth, and I lunge for her.

Grabbing a fistful of blue hair, I yank the bitch away from my husband, slamming her face into the counter and pressing my arm across the back of her neck to keep her in place. She cries out, and it's music to my ears. "You fucking dare to touch my husband without his permission?" I press down on her head when she attempts to straighten up. Blood flows from her nose, and tears leak from her eyes as she whimpers in pain.

Saint tips his head up, fixing me with a look loaded with dark intensity. Raw aggression exudes from his every pore, and his sexy ass radiates danger by the bucketload.

It's no wonder these women were drawn to him, and I doubt they are the first ones to hit on him tonight.

None of them stood a chance, because he's fucking *mine*, and he has zero interest in other women.

I trust Saint completely, and I'm secure in his love. I feel the same about Theo, Galen, and Caz too, and I'm one hundred percent loyal to them in the same way. I know Saint being here is about suffocating his anger until he's too drunk to act on it and nothing else.

"We didn't know he was taken," the other woman protests in a pouty tone, attempting to come to her friend's aid.

Saint's lips kick up a little, and his eyes command me to handle her. Keeping my gaze on the woman, I lean down, licking along the seam of Saint's mouth with my tongue. He grabs my ass, and his eyes burn with lust. Turning the full extent of my hatred on the brunette, I straighten up, gnashing my teeth, preparing to put her in her place. "Tip for future reference. If a man has a ring on his *wedding finger*, it means he's taken." I tip my chin up, piercing her with a dark glare. "*No one* touches what's mine."

"You can do better than her," she tells Saint, eyeing me with disdain, and I'm done playing nice. Slamming the blue-haired bitch's head into the counter one more time—because

I'm fucking pissed now—I release her, stomping toward the brunette to deal with her next. Thrusting my fist out, I hit her square on the nose, leveling her with a couple of quick, successive punches. She stumbles on her skyscraper heels, squealing like a pig as she tumbles to the floor, clutching her nose, and it's enormously satisfying.

A bunch of guys rises from a table close by, eyes narrowing on me as they make a beeline for us. Most guys get off on bitch fights, but these ugly fuckers clearly have a different agenda. Either they've some beef with my guys or these women mean something to them—a sister perhaps.

"Fuck." Caz grabs me back as Saint slides off his stool.

Theo slams a couple hundred-dollar bills down on the counter.

"We want no trouble," Galen tells the bartender when he produces a sawed-off shotgun, pointing it in our direction. "You know who we are, and the women were out of line. They disrespected our wife."

The bartender glances at my rings and nods at Galen before hiding the gun back under the counter. "We want no beef with The Sainthood," he says, shooting a warning look at the guys circling us. "But it's best you were on your way."

I slide my arm around Saint's waist as his arm encircles my shoulders, and he leans into me. "We're out of here."

"I like it when you're jealous." Saint's breath is warm on my face, and I inhale the smoky sweet fumes of whiskey, wishing I'd gotten drunk with him.

"No one touches what belongs to me," I supply, following Galen and Theo as they clear a path through the bar. Caz guards our rear, ensuring we're not assaulted as we leave. Hostility trails us, and I welcome the frigid night air when we step outside. The sudden downpour, not so much.

Rain falls in dense sheets from the sky, pummeling my

body like a thousand tiny stones pelting me at once. Wind lashes the rain, sending it in all directions, and my clothes are rapidly soaking. "Let's get you into the car." I tug on Saint's arm when he stops suddenly.

"I want to walk."

"You'll get fucking pneumonia in this weather." I pull the hoodie up over my head, shivering as biting wind knocks into me. "Come on." I curl my hand around his elbow, but he shakes his head, pushing me away.

"I need to walk this off." Grabbing my face in his slippery hands, he plants a whiskey-tinged kiss on my lips. "Stop worrying. I'll be fine."

Theo pulls the car keys from my pocket, running toward the Lexus with Galen and Caz in pursuit.

"No." I grab Saint's wrists when he attempts to pull away. I didn't come out here to leave empty-handed. "You don't get to tell me that. That's not how this works." I point between us. "I'm your wife. I'm entitled to my concern."

"I don't fucking want it or need it!" he roars, as wind and rain batter his face.

"Tough fucking shit." I shove my face in his. "You don't get a choice. That's not how love works."

"Neither does forcing me to do shit I don't want to do. Leave, Harlow. Go home. I'll see you later."

He walks off, and I grab hold of his shirt, yanking him back.

His nostrils flare as he swings around, staggering a little. Balling his hands into fists at his side, he clenches his jaw. Rain has plastered his shirt and jeans to his body as the skies open, liberally dumping water on top of us. Fighting a shiver, I tuck my hands in under the sleeves of Saint's hoodie, craving warmth. His chest heaves as we stand there glowering at one another before he forcibly relaxes his fists, taking a step back. "I don't want to hurt you, and I'm still too fucking mad. Just go home, Lo. Please."

His face contorts in pain, crumpling in desperation, and my heart bleeds for him. He's so used to doing this alone he doesn't know how to react when support is offered.

Without waiting for my reply, he sprints off in the direction of the woods behind the bar, and I immediately give chase, because fuck this bullshit.

He's not dealing with this alone.

Period.

The others don't attempt to stop me, because they know it would make no difference. Saint needs to understand he's not an island anymore. I've given him enough space to get out of his head, and it hasn't worked. He's seriously delusional if he thinks I'm leaving him now.

He can hate me.

Scream at me.

Lose his temper.

I don't care.

He can do whatever he needs to do to work through his emotions, but he doesn't get to shut me out, and the sooner he realizes this is the way things are going to be from now on, the better it'll be for all of us.

Chapter Thirty-Six
Harlow

I run after him, slipping in the mud as rain hammers me from all sides. Cursing my stupidity at racing off without changing into more suitable clothing, I focus on staying upright as Saint disappears into the forest in front of me. Wind whips the hood off my head as I give chase, plastering stray strands of hair—that have come loose from my ponytail—to my brow.

Anguished shouting greets my ears when I dip under the shelter of the trees, welcoming the slight reprieve from Mother Nature. Rain still spills between the gaps in the branches, and tiny rivulets flow underfoot as I walk toward Saint, but the blanket of trees offers some respite. His fists pummel the bark of a tree while he roars and curses.

Slowing my pace, I observe from a few feet back, watching him take his aggression out on the poor tree with a pain in my heart. The skin rips across his knuckles, but still he continues to pound away, lifting his leg and kicking the bark when that's not enough.

I step up beside him, pulling his hand back. "Stop. You're hurting yourself."

"I don't fucking care!" he yells, yanking his arm free of my hold.

Swiping hair out of my eyes, I level him with a stern look. "Look at me!" I grab his arm before he makes contact with the broken bark. "You need to vent. I get that. But you vent *with me*." Grabbing his hand, I place it over my heart. "You own part of this, and every time you hurt yourself, you hurt me." He tries to wrestle his hand away, but I don't let him, gripping his wrist tight, forcing his hand lower until he's cupping my breast through the hoodie. "Take me. Right here. Let me help you work it out."

Grabbing the nape of my neck with his free hand, he yanks me toward him, forcing my head back at an awkward angle. "You want me to fuck my anger out, queenie? Is that what you're saying?"

"Yes." There's no hesitation in my voice.

The hand around my breast squeezes, and he slams me back against the tree. "You want me to hurt you?"

"If that's what you need," I calmly reply, dropping my hand between us and grabbing his erection through his jeans.

His eyes flash manically, and the grip on my neck tightens to the point of pain. He arches my head back farther, kneading my tit through the hoodie. "No." The word contains finality, and he pulls back, his hands leaving my body bereft. "I won't do that to you. I *can't* hurt you. Not like this."

If this was any other scenario, I'd tell him I'm proud of how far he's come, but that sentiment has no place in this moment. Taking a risk, I close the gap between us, slapping him across the face. "You don't tell me no. Not now. Not ever. And you don't get to fucking push me away." I rip at the button of his jeans as he stares at me in shock. "You hurt, *I* hurt. That's the way it's always been from the moment we met and our connection flared to life," I remind him, shoving my hand down the front of his boxers, wrapping my fingers around his hard cock. Stretching up, I crush my lips against his, forcing my tongue into his mouth. When he doesn't kiss me back, I rip my lips from his mouth and pull my hand from his boxers.

"I love you." I grip his chin. "I. Love. You." I peer into his eyes, beseeching him to let my love in. "I know your head is going in a million different directions, and I know you're used to dealing with shit on your own, but you don't have to do that anymore. I'm your wife, and your pain is my pain." I unzip the sodden hoodie, throwing it to the wet forest floor, ripping my training top and sports bra off next. "Pain and I are acquainted on an intimate level," I add, kicking off my sneakers next.

Saint stands transfixed, watching me like I'm some foreign creature he's never encountered before.

Warmth blossoms in my chest as the truth of those words finds a home inside me. I should be cold, because a storm is raging around us, but there's a different storm raging inside us, and it's more powerful, more destructive, more vivid, consuming us in an inferno of flames, heating every part of me. My skin itches with a craving to touch, and from the way Saint shudders, I know he's feeling it too.

He's just too fucking stubborn and too angry to admit it.

"Give in to it with me." I shove my yoga pants down my legs, bracing one hand against the tree as I yank them off my feet. Straightening up, I push my chest out and bare my soul, standing before him completely naked with rain bouncing off my pale, scarred skin, begging him to let go and give in to his instincts. "Lean on me and know that you never have to face anything alone again."

"Lo," he croaks, his voice cracking along with his resolve.

"I'm right here," I whisper, placing my hand on his heart.

"I'm here for you. Always," I add on a whisper, feeling that truth sink beneath my flesh, lodging bone-deep.

Any lingering concern evaporates as Saint lunges at me like a wild beast set free from captivity. His arms band around me as he hauls me against his body, and his lips descend like the thunderous crash of a stormy wave. Our mouths collide in a frenzied kiss, and our tongues battle for control as we ravish one another while the storm outside continues to swirl around us.

One hand trails up my spine, tugging on my ponytail, arching my neck. Biting down on my lower lip, Saint rocks his hips against mine, and I claw at his shirt, ripping it apart with my hands, buttons flying everywhere. His lips graze my jawline, nipping, sucking, and biting, while I shove the wet material off his chest and move my attention to his jeans. A primitive moan escapes my throat as his teeth break the skin along the column of my neck. He bites and sucks, leaving a trail of pleasure-pain in his wake, and I arch my neck farther, granting him greater access, forgetting about his jeans, as I lose myself to his punishing touches.

His hand is still wrapped firmly around my waist, but as he dips me back, he loses his footing and we fall. Twisting around, he bears the brunt of the impact while I land unceremoniously on top of him. "Are you—"

His mouth suctions on mine, trapping my words inside. Three fingers spear inside my pussy, and I scream into his mouth at the sudden intrusion. I attempt to sit up, to pull his jeans down so I can free his dick, but my foot sinks into the soft mud, and I lose my balance, toppling off him, landing sideways in the muddy sludge. His fingers slide out of me, and I mourn their loss. Using my elbows, I push up on my knees, helping him to pull the sopping-wet denim down to his knees.

"Climb on my cock," he demands, gripping my arms and helping me to get resituated.

Rain cascades down my spine as I lower myself over his cock, and I tilt my head back, closing my eyes, welcoming the droplets of water as they fall onto my face, washing some of the mud away.

Saint thrusts up inside me, and I groan, moving my hips as I start bouncing on him. Nimble hands roam my body, painting streaks of mud along my stomach and over my breasts, and his skillful fingers tweak and pull at my nipples, sending a flurry of pleasure to my core. Liquid warmth floods my cunt, and I whimper as every nerve ending on my body electrifies.

He curses as I clench around his cock, picking up my pace and riding him harder and faster. Outside the forest, rain crashes in voluminous sheets to the ground, and thunder rumbles angrily across the sky. A flash of lightning streaks across the sky, illuminating the Lexus in the distance. I knew the guys wouldn't leave or intrude, because they understand how much Saint needs this. How much *I* need this.

Saint sits up abruptly, pulling my legs around his waist, while his arms secure around my back. Resting my hands on his shoulders, I lean in and kiss him, adoring this position because I can hold him close as he ruts inside me. "I love the way you fuck me." I cry out as he slams into me, drilling his point home, plunging his cock in deep, hitting the perfect spot from this angle.

"I will never get enough of this, of you." He moves his hands to my hips and controls our thrusts. We rock against one another in perfect sync, and the crescendo is building in intensity inside me. He bites at my neck and my collarbone, leaving teeth marks all over my breasts. I welcome the sting, followed by the soothing brush of his tongue as he laves at the bruised, broken skin, and I dig my nails into his back, clawing a path up and down his muscled torso.

His lips return to my mouth, and the sound of skin slapping against skin and the feel of his hard cock claiming me over and over, sends me over the edge, and I come gloriously, squeezing his dick as he roars, spilling his hot cum deep inside me.

We cling to one another as we come down from our high. His dick softens inside me, but he doesn't pull out, and I don't want him to. Cradling his head against my chest, I run my hands all over him, needing him to feel my love soul deep. He hugs me tight, nestling his head against my boobs and closing his eyes, letting me touch him and love him and soothe away his pain.

I don't know how long we stay there, with our arms wrapped around one another, still joined, in our own little world, while the storm rages outside.

But inside, the storm is fading. Glimmers of sunshine burst through the dark clouds and the rain dries up, leaving a serene sense of calmness in its place.

Chapter Thirty-Seven
Harlow

Strong arms encase me from behind and Saint's large palm rests on my belly when I eventually stir from sleep. We fell into bed together last night, exhausted, not bothering to dress or dry our hair after a quick shower. I can already tell I have a bird's nest on my head and that I'll need another shower. Warm breath tickles my eardrum, and a shiver works its way through me as I nestle against him, and his tempting morning wood presses against my ass. "Keep doing that and I'll shove my dick inside," he murmurs in a sleep-drenched tone.

Reaching around, I grab his erection and pull it to my pussy, easing the tip inside. "Fuck me like this. I need you," I rasp, my throat dry from the effects of last night.

Saint slides inside me in one slick move, and I push my ass back into him, holding his palm on my stomach, as his shaft glides in and out of my cunt. Arching my head to one side, I offer up my neck so he can kiss it. We fuck slowly, never changing position, and he drives into me from behind in measured strokes while lavishing kisses along my neck.

After we come, I turn around in his arms, pressing my face to his chest, while his arms pull me close. The barn is quiet, and although I don't know the time—because I haven't looked at my cell yet—I know it's way past time to get up. I'm guessing the others went to school, deciding to let us sleep in.

"Thank you for last night." His gruff tone sends a rake of fiery shivers cascading over my heated skin.

Lifting my head, I look at him through hooded eyes, tracing swirling patterns on his chest with my finger. "We're a team. All of us. And you and I." I press a kiss to his skin, and his chest rumbles with pleasure. "I'm not saying you can't take time for yourself when you need it, but please don't push me away. I love you, and I want to be there for you."

"I know that, and it wasn't about you." He cups my face, smiling at the knotted mess that is my hair. "I don't want my darkness to infect you."

"Darkness is a part of who you are. And it's a part of me too. Your darkness sings to my darkness," I tease, wanting to lighten the mood. "Your darkness doesn't scare me," I add, feeling instinctually this is what he thinks. "If anything, it turns me on." I run my fingers along the stubble on his chin and cheeks. "I love every part of you, and you never have to hide anything from me."

He sits up straighter against the headrest, pulling me with him. "I never dared imagine this for myself," he says, trailing his fingers up and down my arm. "I scoffed at love."

I snort, snuggling in closer to his side. Tell me something I didn't know.

"I didn't purposely shut you out, Lo." He tips my face up with one finger. "I just reacted on autopilot. The others are used to me. They let me lick my wounds, and then Galen is usually the one bandaging me up after."

I sit up fully, palming his beautiful face. "They can still do that, but you need to make room for me."

"I don't have to make room, my queen." He takes my hand, placing it over his heart. Steady beats thrum under my fingertips, soothing any leftover frayed parts of me. "You're already there."

"How are you feeling today?" I ask, peering into his slightly bloodshot eyes.

"Like I drank my weight in whiskey and my wife rode me raw in the middle of a storm on a muddy forest floor."

My grin is instant and wide. "It was hot as fuck."

He tugs on my earlobe, and I shriek. "*You're* hot as fuck."

I peck his lips, moving my hand up to his face again. "Seriously. Are you okay? About what you learned?" He needs to talk about this, not bottle it up.

"I'm pissed," he admits. "I grew up thinking my mom abandoned me. That I wasn't worthy enough of her love. That shit hurt, but I never allowed myself to think about her, because she hadn't earned that right." Air whooshes out of his mouth, and his lips pull into a grimace. "Then Sinner started dropping hints, suggesting there was more to the story, but I didn't indulge it. I couldn't. We have too much shit going on. But last night changed all that."

His Adam's apple bobs in his throat. "She cared enough to risk her life by running away when she was pregnant with me." His chest lifts in a shuddering breath. "That changes everything. She's not the pathetic, weak bitch I'd built her up to be in my mind." Tears well in his eyes, before he brushes them away, and a cold, hard glint replaces the emotion. "That bastard stole my mother from me. And why?" He shakes his head, shrugging. "It's not like he ever wanted me."

"No one takes anything from him," I quietly say. "It's always about power and control."

Saint nods, absently dragging his fingers across my collarbone and the swells of my breasts, stirring desire in my belly again. "I hate him, Lo." His baby blues pin me in place. "Like really loathe him."

"I know, baby." I knead the knotted muscles in his shoulders.

"I stopped myself from going after him about a hundred times last night. I want to fucking end him," he says, through gritted teeth. "But I can't fuck things up. There are too many balls in the air. I'm just worried I won't be able to hold back, because I want to rip him apart. I want to stab him over and over and over again. To hurt him in all the ways he's hurt me."

"We have even more reason to make him pay now. And he will, Saint. He's going to pay for all the ways he has hurt us."

"Are you sure this is wise? Maybe we should drop by school and pick the others up?" I suggest, glancing at Saint from the passenger seat of my Lexus. He insisted on driving, and I didn't argue, because he needs to take back control, and I'll do what I can to help him feel more secure in himself.

"Sinner's issue is with you and me. Let's leave them out of it."

I nod, trusting him to play this the right way.

Sleek, freshly washed and dried hair falls over my shoulder as I peer out the window, watching the landscape flash by. The rain eventually stopped in the middle of the night, but large puddles fill the potholes in the road, and moisture clings to the grass and tips of the trees as we drive the long way around Prestwick Forest.

Saint parks directly outside Sainthood HQ, cutting the engine. "Follow my lead in there, but...intervene if I lose my temper."

I stretch over the console and kiss him. "I've got your back, and you'll keep your cool."

We walk hand in hand inside the enemy's lair, taking the stairs two at a time until we reach the upper level where the offices and meeting rooms are.

Saint raps on his father's office door twice before opening it.

A naked blonde with giant fake tits is bouncing on Sinner's cock like it's a new sport. Glancing over her shoulder, she licks her lips as her gaze roams Saint. "Wanna join in?" she asks, deliberately ignoring my presence. "I've always wanted to fuck a father and son."

Sinner sits back in his chair with his hands folded behind his head, flaunting that shit-eating grin I hate so much.

Saint smirks, slinging his arm around my shoulders and pulling me in close. "Nah. I don't fuck nasty whores. Got my queen right here, and she's the real deal."

"Unlike your plastic tits," I deadpan, while she continues bouncing on Sinner's dick like they don't have an audience. Sinner makes no move to get rid of her, grabbing her hips and slamming her down harder on his cock. She moans on cue, and I roll my eyes. "Welp, it seems you're over my mother." I grace him with a sickly-sweet fake smile, knowing this will push him into action. "So, we don't need to talk." I move to turn around. "We'll let you get back to her piss-poor replacement."

"Ow!" The woman cries as Sinner flings her off his dick, sending her tumbling to the ground.

"Get the fuck out," he roars, not even looking at her as he stands. His gross dick is still hard, bobbing against his toned stomach. The woman grabs her clothes from the floor, clutching them to her chest, shoving against us in her haste to exit the room. Saint slams the door shut after her with his booted foot.

Sinner stares at me as he slowly bends, pulling his jeans up his legs, taking his sweet-ass time tucking his disgusting cock away.

I honestly think he thinks I'm into him.

There are no words.

Plastering a bored look on my face, I hold his stare as he gets dressed, refusing to let him get to me.

"Sit," he snaps, thrusting his dirty-blond hair back off his face before reclaiming his seat. We take seats in front of his desk, side by side, leaning back casually, both eyeballing the bastard, waiting for him to make a move. "Where is your mother?!" he shouts. A vein throbs in his neck, and his muscles strain with tension.

"I don't know," I truthfully reply.

The desk rattles when Sinner thumps his fist on the wood. "Stop. Lying. I know you know. That you helped her." He glares at Saint. "And you!" He jabs his finger in his son's direction. "Have you forgotten where your loyalties lie, boy?"

Saint digs his nails into his thigh. "Hardly. We took care of the scene, didn't we?"

That was for Mom's benefit, but Sinner's arrogant enough to believe that falsehood.

Spit flies out of Sinner's mouth, and his nostrils flare as he leans across the desk, pinning me with a lethal look. "I'd put money on you being the one who put ideas in Giana's head. She'd never pull a gun on me without provocation."

Laughter spills from my lips. "You clearly don't know my mother at all, because I had nothing to do with that."

"You should be thanking Lo," Saint says. "She's the one who stopped Giana from pulling the trigger."

Sinner scoffs. "Giana would never have pulled the trigger. She loves me."

I don't correct him, because that will only cause an argument. I want this conversation over so we can get out of here before his son pulls the trigger. Saint promised he would cage his rage, but his pain is raw, and coming here today was risky. However, we knew Sinner would only come to us, and it's better to be in control and prepared. I'm also hoping to manipulate him a little so he doesn't go searching for Mom.

"If you love her as you say you do, you should give her some space. She'll come back to you when she's ready," I lie.

Sinner's eyes narrow suspiciously. "Why would you want that?"

"I never said I wanted it. She's my mom, and I want her to be with someone who respects her. Not someone who hands her to his perverted friends to rape." I shrug my shoulders, granting him another sugary-sweet smile. "But she's an adult. She makes her own decisions. And for some unknown reason, you're what she wants."

An arrogant smile spreads across his mouth. I'm not surprised he's fallen for the bullshit because he really does believe his own press.

"You said you had an update in relation to the commissioner," Saint says, gripping the armrests hard. "Let's hear it."

"Always so impatient." Sinner tut-tuts, reaching into the top drawer of his desk, removing a pair of plastic gloves. He puts them on before extracting a small brown envelope from the same drawer, passing it across the desk to me. "The instructions are in there. The commissioner is opening a new wing at the Lowell Public Library on Saturday afternoon. A friend owns a private apartment building directly across from the library, and the rooftop garden is the perfect vantage point. You can take him out and then escape through the rear access gate which is only for employees. I've included the codes to his security system so Theo can disable it."

I tuck the envelope in the back pocket of my jeans, nodding.

"Go to the warehouse and take whatever weapon and artillery you need," he adds, directing that statement at his son.

"Lo has her own equipment," Saint confirms.

"I bet she does." Sinner taps his fingers off his chin, staring at me. "Don't fuck this up. And don't even think about double-crossing me."

"I wouldn't dream of it," I lie.

"Lo is done with initiation when she kills him," Saint reminds him, gripping the armrests tighter.

"That's already agreed," he says, as if his word can be trusted. We all know he can change his mind in an instant.

"What's happening with The Arrows?" Saint asks.

"The shipment is due in tonight. We have a crew lined up to tail them. Then we hit the warehouse Friday night. I expect all of you to be there."

"We'll be there," Saint says, standing and pulling me to my feet.

"Tell your mother she can't hide from me forever." Sinner scrubs his prickly jawline. "I'll give her some space, but if she takes too long, I'm coming for her. There is no place she can hide that I won't find her."

A nasty shiver crawls up my spine, and I don't even dignify that with a response.

Saint has his hand on the door handle when Sinner calls out one final time. "Son?"

Saint grits his teeth before hurriedly composing himself. He turns around, feigning disinterest.

"Let's make Saturday a family affair." He grins manically. "Take Bryant with you."

Chapter Thirty-Eight
Harlow

"How the fuck does he know about me?" Bry rubs a hand down his face while pacing the floor in front of the fireplace. We updated Theo, Caz, and Galen, when they arrived home after school, while we were waiting for Bryant to show up. It's his first time at the barn, but we're low on places to meet. Besides, everything is out on the table now, and he shares a bloodline with Saint, so the trust issue is pretty much a non-issue at this point.

"Sinner has informants everywhere." Theo crosses his feet at the ankles.

"Then how come he hasn't found the Leydon evidence that was stolen from him?" Bry asks.

"Maybe he's perpetuating that lie because it suits him. Maybe he already has it back in his possession," I suggest as the thought occurs to me.

"And you killing the commissioner ends the threat once and for all," Saint adds, dragging his hands through his hair. "Fuck, you could be on to something."

I place my hand on his thigh, squeezing in understanding.

Trying to figure out who is playing who and why is starting to give me a permanent headache too.

"Does he know about Howie?" Bry inquires. Concern stretches across his face.

"That's probably how he made the connection," Saint surmises.

"Howie is pissed you wouldn't let him come with me." Bry props his butt against the arm of the couch.

"I don't fucking care," Saint snaps, pinching the bridge of his nose.

"He knows he fucked up, but he's genuinely sorry."

"He left me with that monster," Saint snarls. "It's not something I'll forgive overnight, if ever."

Bry gulps. "Fair enough." He wets his lips, clearing his throat. "But I hope you and I can start over. Wipe the slate clean."

Caz walks between the couches, setting a plate loaded with sandwiches and wraps down on the coffee table as he chuckles. "Aw, does Unky Bryant want a play date with his cute little nephew?"

Saint leaps from the couch, tackling Caz to the ground. Bry looks on in amusement as they roll around, throwing a few punches and jabs. Grabbing a chicken wrap, I munch on it while I watch the big kids play-wrestle on the ground. "Will you tell Howie that Sinner knows?" I ask when Caz and Saint quit messing around, climbing to their feet with matching grins.

"I should, so he's in the loop, but he's a bit of a loose cannon right now. He's completely obsessed with taking Sinner down, in a way that's not healthy, and I'm becoming more and more concerned. He'll go crazy if I tell him, and I don't trust he won't do something reckless." Bry reaches into his inside pocket, handing me an envelope. "I almost forgot. That's the McKenzie recording. Howie said there are no other copies and he's wiped all trace of it from his computer."

I hand the envelope to Theo, and he immediately tosses it in the fire.

Saint flops down on the couch beside me, snatching a wrap and biting into it, swallowing half of it in one go.

Bry coughs, reclaiming my attention. He's holding a silver-plated tin box in his hand, looking a little apprehensive. "I have something else I thought might come in handy." He hands it to me, and I place it on my lap before opening it.

"What is this?" Galen inquires, peering at the two guns inside. They are sealed in a plastic bag on top of a dried blood-soaked rag.

Bry's features soften, and he lowers his voice. "The guns are the ones used to kill Sariah Roark's family."

I can barely breathe over the messy ball of emotion clogging my throat. A hush descends over the room, and the only sound is the crackling of the fire.

"What?" I splutter, tears instantly stabbing my eyes. "How do you have this?"

"I stole it from Archer Quinn's safe last night," he confirms, and all the blood drains from my face.

"Fuck." Saint stares at him with newfound respect. "Was that smart?"

He shrugs casually. "I broke in, in the middle of the night, wearing a full disguise. I disabled the camera feeds before destroying the one I'd installed. There is no trace it was me. The Arrows will know come Friday night, but by then it'll be too late."

"The Arrows murdered Sariah's family? She always thought it was The Sainthood." I rub the ache tightening my chest. Her entire family was gunned down in a drug deal gone wrong. Sariah only survived the massacre because she played dead.

"I overheard a conversation Archer had with a couple of his board members last night. They're onto Diego. They know he's an FBI informant. I watched Archer place that tin in the safe. After the board left, his number two asked him why he kept such incriminating evidence. He said it ensured loyalty because most of the board had been involved and their fingerprints were on the weapons. I figure he plans to use that against Diego."

"So, if they go down, he does too," Caz says, filling in the rest.

"They're gonna put a bullet in his skull," Saint says. "That's usually the way these things go down. That evidence is insurance in case the FBI decide to prosecute on the grounds of Diego's testimony, even if he's dead. They'll use that to discredit him."

"We should let Diesel know about Diego so the FBI can protect him," I suggest. "He was due to reach out to them anyway. Might as well give him something to extend an olive branch with."

"I'm on it," Theo says, his fingers already flying over the keypad of his tablet.

Galen wraps his arm around me, pulling me into his side, while Saint grips my hand on the other side, squeezing my fingers. "What do you want to do with it, Lo?" Saint asks.

"I want justice for Sariah's family. I want her grandma Lorna to finally see the men responsible put behind bars."

"We can't interfere with Friday, or Sinner will murder us all in cold blood," Galen says, eyeing Saint over my shoulder.

"Why don't we let Friday go down as planned and ask Diesel to give this to the FBI on Saturday morning," Theo suggests, and it's a good idea. I nod, giving him a sad smile.

"The Arrows will be dead in the water by the time this weekend rolls around," Caz says.

"Two enemies down, one left to go," Saint adds, squeezing my hand. "Payback can't come soon enough."

We're busy the rest of the week, making last-minute plans with Diesel for the fake assassination and scheduling a time to hand over the package from Bry to the FBI. I'm not sure what's happened with Diego, but I don't really care. We passed on the intel. Whether the FBI acts to protect their informant is on them.

On Friday night, Saint, Galen, and Caz go with the rest of The Sainthood to ambush The Arrows warehouse. Theo and I sit it out, primarily because the guys don't want me anywhere near the showdown. Plus, we want to prepare for tomorrow. I need to take a few practice shots, and Theo wants to test hacking into the apartment's security systems in a dummy run before tomorrow. That excuse should appease Sinner, but one can never be sure where that psycho is concerned.

The guys return in the early hours of Saturday morning, exhausted but uninjured, and my taut muscles finally relax. Their clothes are covered with blood splatters, so they strip in the living room, throwing the tainted clothing in the fire while telling us about the successful ambush.

The Sainthood had the element of surprise, and they cleaned out The Arrows warehouse, before sending them an anonymous tip that sent the rival gang racing to protect their supplies store, only to find they were too late. It was a bloodbath, according to Saint, ending with most of The Arrows either injured or killed.

The news is all over the TV screens a few hours later, and we watch reports of the carnage as we quietly eat breakfast. Chaos has erupted on the streets of Prestwick as protesters take to the streets, calling on the governor and the commissioner to take a firm hand in tackling the increasing gang violence.

Diesel calls a couple hours later to confirm the FBI has the evidence and he expects arrests to be made in the coming days, as soon as they have verified the evidence is legit.

Galen comes with me to Lorna's house, because I want to deliver the news to Sar's grandma in person. Lorna collapses in my arms, sobbing with relief, and I only wish my bestie were here to witness justice being served.

When we return to the barn, Bry is there, helping Caz to prepare a late lunch. Although Saint didn't answer Bry the other day, there's an unspoken ceasefire between them, and they are mostly making the effort to get along. To be honest, it's shocked the hell out of me, but it only further highlights how far Saint has come. I've been telling him all along that Bryant isn't a bad guy, and I'm glad he seems to have accepted him now.

After we've eaten and loaded up Saint's Land Rover, we make our way to the northern end of Lowell, parking in the staff parking lot of the apartment building owned by Sinner's friend. Bry follows in his Chevy, pulling into the empty space alongside Saint.

Having an extra pair of hands helps, and we are set up on the roof in next to no time with plenty of time to spare before it all kicks off.

Although there is a small, enclosed greenhouse up here, this isn't a functional rooftop, and the apartment residents don't have access to it. We've been told it's occasionally used by staff, but we don't have to worry about unexpected guests at the wrong moment today.

Theo distributes earpieces he got from Diesel. "Check to ensure they're working," he says as he hands them out, and we test it back and forth for a couple minutes. "I'll be in an office on the first floor," he confirms. "The Wi-Fi signal is stronger there. I've disabled the cameras inside the building, but I can't deactivate the cameras out on the street until the last possible moment in case we tip the cops off."

The commissioner will have a team with him today, as is usual, but none of them are privy to the plan, because this needs to look real.

"Break a leg, babe." Theo pecks me on the lips before exiting the roof.

"I'm gonna take a piss before shit goes down," Caz says.

"I'll come with." Galen strides across the roof toward the door, spinning around at the last second. "You need anything from inside?"

"Grab a few bottles of water," I say, kneeling on the cushion and bringing my eye to the lens of the AR-15 rifle, checking the angle again.

"He's coming from the Lott Lane direction, right?" I ask Saint, double-checking because you can never go over the plans enough.

"Correct," Saint assures me, dropping to the ground a few feet away. He leans his back against the small wall that rims the perimeter of the roof, bending his knees. At this height, we shouldn't be spotted or heard, but we're not taking chances.

"I'd like to learn how to use one of those," Bry says from his position at my side, nodding at the mounted rifle.

"I'm sure Diesel could show you when all of this is over."

"You really trust that guy, huh?"

I lift my head, arching a brow in his direction. Saint toys

with the gravel, tossing a few stones across the roof, feigning nonchalance, but he's paying attention to every word. "I do. Is there any reason I shouldn't?"

"Howie doesn't trust him."

Saint snorts. "Of course, he doesn't."

Bry shifts uncomfortably, but he doesn't snap at Saint like he previously would have. They are treading on eggshells around one another, and it's kinda funny to see.

"There are rumors of corruption within VERO," Bry continues. "He suggests that you should be cautious."

Now it's my turn to scoff. "Every fucking organization is corrupt, especially the ones at the top. That doesn't surprise me, and Howie doesn't know Diesel like I do. He wouldn't betray me."

"I hope you're right."

Saint throws a few stones in the air. "I can't stand the prick, but—"

"Why doesn't that surprise me?" Bry chuckles, turning his head around and grinning at Saint.

Saint flips him the bird. "I was going to say, before I was so rudely interrupted, that he's come through for us. He—"

The door to the roof crashes open with force, the metal creaking as it slams against the wall. "No one fucking move or you're all dead," a familiar voice says, and I internally groan.

Chapter Thirty-Nine
Harlow

You have got to be kidding me. Darrow Knight has the worst fucking timing. Or the best if you're him, I suppose.

"Turn around slowly, bitch," a familiar female voice says from behind, and I cast a quick glance at Saint.

Oh, hell to the no. This is not going down now.

Determination zips through me as I pull out the dagger strapped to each side of my thighs, and I spin around, aiming both at Taylor Tamlin as I let them fly. My fast reaction doesn't give her enough time to retaliate, and she's also distracted by the commotion at her side as Caz and Galen burst onto the roof, a split second later, wrestling Darrow to the ground.

Taylor screams as a dagger embeds in each of her shoulders, automatically dropping her gun as her hands fly to the entry points, and her fingers touch the blades stuck in her flesh and bone.

Saint darts forward, snagging Taylor's gun while Caz and Galen easily subdue Darrow. He's sprawled across the ground on his stomach, and it's embarrassing how quickly they gained the upper hand.

Galen presses down on Dar's wrist as he stretches his arm, fingers straining for his gun. Bones crunch, mingling with Dar's agonizing roar. Bry stalks across the roof, snatching the gun and pointing it at his ex-buddy's head. "Shut the fuck up, Knight."

Theo is screaming in my ear, blind without any cameras, and I take a second to reassure him we are okay, and we have the situation under control.

"Fuck you, traitor!" Dar hisses, and Bry hits him across the back of his head with the gun. The blow lacks intent, because Bry knows not to knock him out yet.

Saint has Taylor's arms pinned behind her back, and with his free hand, he presses the muzzle of her gun against her head. Blood oozes from the wounds in her shoulders, and it's a glorious sight. Taylor emits a frustrated screech, glowering in my direction. I stalk toward her. "Shut up, bitch." She spits in my face, and I backhand her a few times. Ripping the end of her shirt, I use the material to wipe her gross DNA from my face before shoving it into her mouth, ensuring her screams don't carry in the air, alerting anyone on the ground below. "Time?" I ask aloud, knowing Theo will respond.

"ETA in fourteen minutes. Wrap it up quick," he says in my ear.

Smiling maliciously, I grab the handles on both daggers, rotating them in Taylor's shoulders, digging the wounds deeper. Tears leak involuntarily from her eyes as her screams of pain are muffled by the obstacle in her mouth. "You know, I thought you were smarter than this." I punch her in the stomach. "We gave you a lifeline, and you chose to throw it back in our faces." I punch her in the face, and blood spurts from her nose. "You don't get another chance."

Dismissing her, I crouch down in front of Dar, lifting his

chin and arching his head back at an awkward angle. "Now you, on the other hand, are *not* smart. But this is still disappointing. Did you seriously think you could sneak up on us and get the upper hand?" I stand, hovering over his pitiful form. "Turn him over." I shake my head. "I'm embarrassed for you, Dar. How the fuck did you end up junior chapter leader when Bry is worth a million of you?"

"Fuck you, whore," he hisses as Galen and Caz dutifully flip him over.

Galen kicks him in the head. "Watch what you say to my wife, dipshit."

Caz presses down on his foot, and Dar screams like a pussy. The sound of more bones breaking is music to my ears. How dare that asshole think he could show up here and thwart our carefully laid plans. And with that murdering bitch too?

Idiots. The pair of them.

Placing my booted foot on his crotch, I lean over him. "How did you know we would be here?"

He grins, because He. Is. A. Fucking. Brain-dead. Idiot. "Screw you. I'll never tell."

I kick him swiftly in the nut sack, and he cries out, trying to curl into a ball, unable to move his body properly with Galen standing on his wrist, Caz standing on his foot, and my boot pressed to his groin.

"Eleven minutes," Theo says in my ear.

As much as I'd love to take my time, we're all out of it. Whipping my knife out, I yank Dar's head back, placing the sharp blade to his neck. "You have three seconds to tell me the truth before I slit your throat."

Spittle flies into my face, for the second time in minutes, and I'm so done. I ram my knife into his thigh, in a similar place to the last time, reminding him of who he's dealing with. Tears flow from his eyes, and his face contorts in pain, but I'm not finished with him yet. Sticking the knife in the side of his neck, I clamp my other hand over his mouth to smother his screams. His eyes widen in panic, as reality finally dawns, and he realizes he could die here. The smell of urine filters into the air, and my nostrils revolt, scrunching up to ward off the stink.

"Dude, did you just piss yourself?" Caz asks, gagging.

How the hell did I put up with this pathetic prick for so long? Ugh. My previous choice of boyfriend was piss-poor—pun intended.

Bry smirks. "You're a mess, Knight." He grabs his face, losing all hint of humor. "Tell us now, or we'll let the lovely Lo gut you like the rodent you are."

I remove my hand from his disgusting mouth. "Don't kill me!" Dar pleads. "I'll tell you, and I've other shit I can tell you too."

"Now. Dar," I bark, losing my patience.

"I've had my suspicions about you for a while," he tells Bry, in between pained pants. "I followed you this week. Knew you were spying for the Saints, so I put a tracker on you."

"How long have you been working with Taylor?" I ask. When he doesn't answer straightaway, I kick him in the balls again. Galen covers his mouth this time, trapping his howls of agony. "How long?" I hiss.

"She came to me a week ago, suggesting we team up to take you all out."

"Does anyone else know you're here?" Galen inquires, exerting additional pressure on his broken wrist.

"No," he whimpers. "Archer is out for my blood." He stares up at Bry. "He thinks I was working with you because I didn't show up at the warehouse last night." Course, he didn't. Dar doesn't like to get his hands dirty, and he always gets someone else to pick up his slack. This little nugget of information is interesting though. Perhaps, it can come in handy.

Out of the corner of my eye, I watch Taylor wriggling in Saint's grip. He looks to me, and I nod. We can't deal with them right now, and we need to get them off this roof ASAP because we can't have any loose ends hanging around when this goes down.

Taylor crumples like a sack of potatoes when Saint slams the butt of the gun into her head. Caz punches Dar a couple times in the face, and he's out cold in a flash.

"Tie them up in the trunk and stay with them," I instruct Caz. "We'll deal with them back at the house after we get this over and done with."

"Galen, help Caz get them downstairs, and then I want you out on the street," Saint commands. "Stay in the alleyway beside the main entrance to this building. We don't want any more surprises."

Galen salutes Saint before heaving Taylor over his shoulder. Caz does the same with Dar, and they leave while I reposition myself on the cushion, taking deep breaths to get my head back in the game.

"Here." Bry picks up a bottle of water off the ground, handing it to me.

Saint crouches on my other side. "You okay?"

"I'm fine. Just give me a minute to get my bearings."

By the time the cavalcade arrives with the commissioner, I'm primed and ready to go. Diesel just called, confirming everything is all set from their side, and that helps to settle any last-minute nerves.

Thankfully, it's only the head librarian and a couple of her staff waiting outside to greet their honored guest. Most of the crowd is cloistered in the new wing. A couple of reporters linger outside the building, but the event wasn't large enough to draw attention from any of the TV stations. It also helps the library isn't in the main thoroughfare, and there's only a couple of bystanders walking the sidewalk.

I wait until the commissioner gets into position, and then I pull the special goggles down over my eyes, point the rifle at the infrared X marked on his chest, and take my shot.

Bull's-eye. I hit my mark dead on.

Screams ring out as the commissioner drops to the asphalt, blood pooling around him from the pouches tied to the front of his bulletproof vest.

As much as I'd love to stay and admire my handiwork, we can't hang around. Saint and Bry work efficiently together to dismantle the stand, placing it and the rifle into the black carryall while I race around the roof, snatching up bottles of water and checking for any trace evidence we may have unwittingly left behind. Droplets of blood are drying where Taylor bled out, and I'm on my knees, ready to clean them up, when Saint calls out to me. "Leave them. We can use it to our advantage."

We exit the roof with the sounds of sirens blaring in the background. Taking the staff elevator to the parking lot, we slide the gun case into the bed of Bry's truck, securing a few boxes and a blanket over it. Caz revs the engine of the Chevy, and Bry jumps in the passenger seat while Saint and I climb into the back of the Land Rover. Galen is behind the wheel, and Theo has his head stuck to his tablet from the passenger seat.

Brakes screech as both vehicles peel out of there, using the rear entrance, and we encounter no problems as we journey the side roads back to Prestwick.

Chapter Forty
Harlow

"Holy fuck. That was nuts." Bry grins like a madman as we enter the barn.

"That's one way of putting it," I deadpan, jerking my head at Theo. "Put the news on. I want to hear what they're saying."

Saint hands out beers as we watch a man with salt-and-pepper hair reporting from outside Lowell Public Library. The headline flashes **COMMISSIONER LEYDON ASSASSI-NATED IN BROAD DAYLIGHT**, and we listen for a few minutes as they spout theories before nauseating eulogies to the commissioner start rolling in. Galen clicks it off because no one wants to hear that crap.

"That went smooth despite the unexpected interruption," Theo says, swallowing a mouthful of beer. "I almost had a fucking coronary when I heard Darrow's voice."

"Speaking of." Saint drains his beer, uncapping another one. "What are we going to do with dumb and dumber?"

"I've had an idea." I heave myself up onto the edge of the table, sipping my beer.

"Thought you might." Saint grins, and I blow him a kiss.

"Taylor has to die, because she won't stop coming after us." I was charitable after she tried to kill me, and look where that got us.

Everyone nods in agreement.

"I say we use Darrow's gun to kill her. Then we dump her on her father's doorstep with the weapon and let him connect the dots."

Bry's face scrunches up. "My fingerprints are on the gun."

I grin, waggling my brows. "I have two other guns belonging to Darrow with his fingerprints on them. We'll use one of those."

"Damn, he's a total moron."

"Yep," I agree, popping the P.

Saint traces his finger around the top of his beer bottle as he speaks. "I suggest we pin the commissioner's murder on Taylor and kill two birds with one stone."

Although the commissioner isn't actually dead, to the outside world and his police colleagues, he is. The cops won't rest until they make an arrest, so handing Taylor over is a smart suggestion.

"We can anonymously tip off the media," Saint continues. "Explain how she's been targeting gangs in the area in some kind of vigilante justice, because she blames local crews for her sister's murder. When that failed, she set out to eliminate the commissioner, the man responsible for failing to keep crime from the streets of Lowell and Prestwick." A smug grin appears on his lips. "With Diesel's police contacts, and her blood on that roof, we can make that stick. Open and shut case. So even if her father or The Bulls try to hang us for this, no one will believe them."

"Damn, your devious mind never fails to get me horny," I

admit, sucking one finger into my mouth while I drill him with a heated look.

Saint's eyes darken with lust, and the urge to climb him like a spider monkey is riding me hard. "Trust me, queenie. It's mutual." Saint winks, and I sigh, realizing I'm stuck with the queenie nickname for life.

Bry clears his throat, reminding us he's in the room.

"What about the moron?" Galen asks. "Do we kill him too?"

"Keeping him alive is more advantageous," I propose. "He told us earlier that Archer Quinn thinks he and Bry were Saint-hood spies. I suggest we cut out his tongue and cut off his fingers, then send him back with a note that says he ratted them out and he's the one who's been spying for us. We can say he double-crossed us so he's their problem to deal with."

"Damn, woman." Caz whistles under his breath.

"What if they don't believe it?" Theo asks.

"It doesn't really matter. They're hanging onto the ledge by their fingernails at this stage. And how can they disprove it if he can't talk and he can't write?" I smirk.

Saint stalks across the room, grabs the nape of my neck, and slams his lips down on mine while settling between my thighs. I wrap my legs around him, tilting my head to the side, as he shoves his tongue between my lips. Holding his waist, I let him plunder my mouth as I drown in pleasurable sensation.

"You have issues," Bry drawls when we finally come up for air.

"Aw, don't be jealous of your nephew," Caz pipes up. "I'm sure there's some law about that."

"Shut the fuck up." Saint points his bottle at Caz. "I'm fucking older than him, and all that uncle-nephew shit is creeping me out."

Bry chuckles. "You really shouldn't have said that." His lips twitch. "Now I'm gonna remind you every chance I get."

"Then your attendance at Lowell High will be short-lived, because you breathe one word about that shit at school and I'll knock you the fuck out. Don't care if we're related or not." Saint crosses his arms, glaring at Bry, but there's no real heat behind it.

We wait for nightfall before dragging our prisoners from the trunk. They wriggle and writhe as we haul them into the forest at the side of the barn and deal with them.

After, I head back to the house so I can get cleaned up because I've got Knight's disgusting blood all over me, and I need a shower. Galen volunteers to stay with me while the others head out. Caz and Bry are going to round up a couple of minions to help deliver the bodies while Saint and Theo are going to Sainthood HQ to update Sinner.

Galen and I shower together, taking our time washing each other, before he slams me into the tile wall, claiming my pussy and then my ass. We are passed out in our giant bed when the others eventually return, just before midnight, bringing Thai takeout with them. Bry isn't with them because he chose to go home, and Theo and Saint swung by his house to pick Caz up on the way.

"It's handled?" Galen asks as I grab plates and silverware from the kitchen, carrying them to the table.

"All done," Saint confirms, unloading tons of paper cartons from two bags.

"What did Sinner say?" I ask when we're all seated and digging in.

"He's fucking ecstatic," Theo replies. "You took out the commissioner. The Arrows are essentially no more, and he has The Bulls under his thumb. He rules the roost."

"And he intends to crow like a cock," Saint says, pursing his lips. I lift one brow. Air expels from his mouth as he heaps food on his plate. "He's throwing a celebratory party next weekend in our honor."

"Like that's not shady as fuck," I say over a mouthful of curry, sarcasm lacing my tone.

"I don't trust him for a second," Saint agrees. "He's up to something."

"How can you be sure?" Caz asks.

"The party is at Galen's house," Saint confirms.

"What the fuck?" Galen speaks over a mouthful of food. "Why the hell is he throwing a party there and not at HQ?"

"Because he's fucking with us," Saint grits out. "I knew he wouldn't let Lo off the hook after this, and he's pissed because we've sided with Lo over him, and helped Giana to escape his clutches."

"Then we should be nowhere near that fucking party," Caz says, shoveling rice in his mouth.

"We can't not show," I protest, sipping my water. "He'll only hunt us down. I'm sick of whatever game he's playing, and I say we go there and call his bluff. Let's see what he comes at us with next."

"It's dangerous as fuck," Galen says.

"Not if we prepare. It's your house, which means we have the home turf advantage. We can switch off his cameras, raid his secret stash, and line up the audio recording we have of him telling me to kill the commissioner, so if he tries anything, we have leverage."

"Diesel called me a few minutes ago," Theo says. "He agrees Sinner is planning something, and he thinks this is an opportunity we shouldn't pass up. He's setting up a meeting between all interested parties this week to discuss how to handle it."

"What, like with the FBI and VERO?" I ask, holding my fork in midair.

Theo nods. "And he wants Howie there too. He thinks a joint task force working together will mean we end this thing quicker."

Saint scowls, predictably.

"Having so many controlling dicks in one room should be interesting," I joke.

"Speaking of dicks." Caz licks the back of his spoon, leering at me across the table. "I think it's time we christened our new bed in style. Don't you?"

"Oh, God," I moan, arching my back as Saint inserts a third finger in my pussy.

"I prefer Saint, but God works." I hear the grin in his smug tone. Good to know his ego is still soaring above the clouds.

Caz snorts, tweaking one of my nipples while Theo sucks on the other one. Galen's lips descend on my mouth, and his hands dive into my hair, rubbing my scalp. I moan into his mouth as he kisses me while my other three husbands continue their skilled ministrations, plucking my body like the strings of a guitar. My eyes pop wide when Saint lowers his hot mouth over my clit, sucking hard while he pumps his fingers in and out of my pussy, coating them with my juices.

"Always so fucking wet," he murmurs in between licks. Galen drags my lower lip between his teeth, piercing me with dark-emerald eyes as my fingers trace a path over the stubble on his face.

Theo and Caz face one another across my naked body as

they continue playing with my tits. I'm not sure if Saint and Galen have noticed the lingering looks between them or the crackle of electricity in the air, but I have, and I'm silently encouraging them to be brave.

Galen grazes his teeth along the column of my neck, and I seize the opportunity to slyly watch the two men lavishing attention on my breasts.

Caz's eyes are glued to Theo's mouth as he dips his head and his tongue darts out, tasting the sharp peak of my nipple. I bite back a pleasurable sigh, not wanting to distract them. Theo stares at Caz as he licks my nipple, and Caz's grip on my other tit hardens. Both their dicks are pressed against my thighs, and they are as hard as rocks.

"Aagh," I call out as Saint drags me down the bed, nudging my legs wider to give him greater access. Galen crawls down to us, propping my head on a couple of pillows. Holding his long, hard, thick shaft in one hand, he directs it to my mouth. I open wide, and he slides between my lips, thrusting his hips and hitting the back of my throat.

Grabbing his hips, I widen my mouth, taking him fully as he slides in and out. Cries of pleasure rip from his chest as I fondle his balls and suck his dick. Pressure coils tight in my belly as Saint continues to work my pussy and my clit with his tongue and his fingers, and I come apart on a scream when he shoves two fingers into my ass.

"Fuck, you're so hot when you come." Galen fists a hand in my hair as he fucks my mouth harder.

Behind us, sounds of kissing tell me Caz and Theo have succumbed to their lust, and a bubble of happiness spreads across my chest. I want to watch, but I'm afraid if they catch us looking they'll feel self-conscious and stop. My eyes meet Saint's as he lines his cock up to my entrance, and I see the truth in his baby blues.

Tonight is a turning point.

We all recognize that.

Saint impales me on his cock, thrusting into me hard as Galen pulls out of my mouth with a pop. I moan his loss, and he grins, bending down to bite my lip. "I need to come inside you, angel." Pushing my hair to one side, he drags his lips up and down my neck, sucking hard in a way I know will leave marks.

I love when my guys brand me.

Love the envious looks I pick up from all the girls in school when they spot the regular hickeys on my neck.

I'm a lucky woman, and I know it.

Galen moves behind me, and Saint pulls me up onto his lap, wrapping my legs around him, in a mirror of our position the night we fucked outside in the storm. "I think someone has a new favorite position," I murmur, riding his cock.

"Every way I'm inside you is my favorite position." His piercing blue eyes pin me in place, and I'm lost for this guy.

"Who knew my cousin was such a closet romantic," Galen quips, teasing my ass with his slick fingers.

I arch my head back as I bounce on Saint's cock, looping my arm around Galen's neck and pulling him closer as he inches into my ass. My eyes roll back in my head at the sense of fullness. Of complete ownership. I let go, trusting my pleasure to the Lennox cousins. "Don't pretend you're not romantic too. You gave me my angel daggers," I purr, licking at the seam of his lips as he rocks in and out of my ass.

"Because nothing says romance like daggers," Saint deadpans, and a giggle bursts from my chest.

A loud moan erupts behind us, followed by a slew of expletives, and I can't contain my curiosity anymore. Galen and I twist our heads around at the same time while Saint's jaw loosens as he stares over my shoulder.

Holy fuck.

Galen and Saint continue grinding inside me, albeit in a slower, less attentive fashion, as we watch Caz drive his cock into Theo's ass. Theo is on all fours, facing the headrest, and Caz is hugging his back as he thrusts inside him, over and over again.

It's the hottest thing I've ever seen, and my pussy floods with warmth. Theo moans and hisses while Caz whispers shit in his ear as his powerful body pounds into Theo with years of pent-up lust.

Reluctantly, I tear my gaze away, touching Galen's jaw to bring him back to me. This has been a long time coming for Caz and Theo, and they deserve some privacy. Saint swings his gaze to mine, examining my flushed cheeks, excited eyes, and parted lips. His mouth pulls into a lopsided grin. "That turns you on," he whispers, stabbing his hips into mine.

"Like you wouldn't believe." I decide to mess with them as they pick up their pace, fucking me in perfect sync. "You know what'd be the hottest thing ever?" I struggle to keep a straight face while I pose my question. Galen grabs my hips, drilling harder into my ass.

"I'm afraid to ask," Saint drolly replies.

"All of you fucking. That would be like a dream come true."

"You do remember we're cousins," Galen says.

"Well, duh. Not you two, obviously. But Saint could fuck Caz and you could fuck Theo."

"Not ever happening, queenie." Saint pinches my tit. "I'm not into dick."

"I could be persuaded," Galen blurts, trailing his fingers up my spine.

"Really?" My gleeful screech confirms how fucking excited

I am right now. I look back at him, eyes sparkling with anticipation.

"No." He smirks. "I was yanking your chain."

I slap his chest. "It's mean to get me all excited like that."

"We're addicted to pussy, babe," Saint says, rocking up inside me. "*Your* pussy, and that will never change."

Roars and shouts litter the air behind us, and I grin at Saint as Caz and Theo audibly come together. Saint leans in, kissing me softly. "I love that you support them. I know how much that will mean to Theo, in particular."

"Get the fuck away from me!" Theo screams, and the bed bounces behind us.

All the blood freezes in my veins.

"Theo." Caz's anguished tone slices through me. "Did I..." His choked voice trails off.

Galen and Saint stop thrusting, and we share a concerned look. I don't know whether to intervene or leave them to work it out themselves.

"Don't touch me!" Theo shrieks, and the headrest bangs against the wall. "Just leave me alone!"

"Don't do this," Caz pleads.

"I. Said. Don't fucking touch me!" Theo screeches before a pained cry erupts from his throat.

I slide off Saint, communicating with my eyes. He nods, jerking his head at Galen. Climbing off the end of the bed, I pad around it, heading for Theo.

His back is flattened to the headrest, and his head is in his hands, his hair shielding his face, as his shoulders heave. Caz is standing beside the bed, looking dejected and full of remorse. I touch his arm, looking up at him, asking him to trust me with my eyes.

To let me talk to Theo and help him get out of his head.

The pained expression on Caz's face guts me, and my heart

hurts for him. "It will be okay," I mouth even though I've no idea if it will. He stares at me with so much emotion, confusion coexisting with hurt and pain. Sweeping my fingers along his cheeks, I plead with my eyes, begging him to let me handle this.

Reeling me into his arms, Caz holds me tight. I squeeze my eyes shut to ward off the tears that are building when I feel his strong, powerful body tremble against mine. His mouth wanders to my ear. "Tell him I'm sorry," he whispers, his voice steeped in raw agony. Abruptly, he lets me go, not looking at either of us as he walks out of the room with Saint and Galen.

Chapter Forty-One
Theo

Blood pounds in my head, and my skin itches with an almost incessant need to crawl from this shell and inhabit a different body. I didn't think it was possible to feel so lost and so together at the same time. To battle heart-soaring happiness, soul-crushing pain, and mind-skewing panic as if they are three parts of the same whole. But that's how I feel in this moment. Powerful emotion crashes into me from all sides, battering me relentlessly, like an angry wave ravishing everything in its path, hell-bent on destruction, just taking and taking, until it feels like I'm drowning.

"Theo." The bed dips as Lo joins me. "The others are gone. It's just us." Her silky, sultry voice swaddles me like a comfort blanket. "Please talk to me."

Unshed tears stab the backs of my eyes, and my chest heaves as intense emotion presses down on me, constricting my airwaves, making breathing difficult. Lo places her hand gently on my arm, and that soft touch breaks the fragile walls around my heart, unravelling me. I fall apart as sobs wrack my chest, and my entire body trembles with a host of conflicting emotions.

"Oh, Theo." Banding her arms around me, she holds me tight as I expunge years of pent-up longing, fear, and self-loathing.

I bury my face in her neck, clinging to her toned curves, allowing the heat from her body and the familiar spicy scent of her perfume to soothe me. She presses kisses into my hair, holding me close, supporting me with her empathic silence, her unspoken words.

When I'm all cried out, I finally face her, feeling both burdened and freer at the same time. I'm suffocating under a pillow of contradiction, and I can't clear the haze from my brain long enough to make sense of everything churning inside me.

"Baby." She brushes knotted strands of hair away from my face. "Please talk to me. What is going through that beautiful, compassionate, intelligent mind?" Cupping my face, she dots tiny kisses all over my chin and cheeks.

"My head is a mess," I admit in a hoarse voice, my throat scratchy from crying. "I'm feeling too fucking much." I gulp over the lump in my throat.

"Do you regret it?" she tentatively asks, caressing my face with her fingers.

I immediately shake my head. "No. No, I don't." I can't regret something I've craved for years or deny that it more than lived up to my expectations. The act itself isn't the issue. It's the aftermath of wild, uncontrollable emotion I'm struggling with.

"Then what?" Compassion shimmers in her eyes. "Did it hurt? Or you didn't like it or…"

"Fuck, no. It was …" I'm struggling to find the right words to describe all that I'm feeling, but I'm not sobbing on this bed like a basket case because Caz hurt me or I didn't enjoy it.

Lo and I experimented a lot when we were together, and

she's used dildos, butt plugs, beads, vibrators, and prostate massagers on me. Tools I've continued using by myself because I wanted to be prepared to seize the opportunity if it arose. "I liked it. A lot," I truthfully admit, because nothing compares to a warm, hard, *real* dick sliding in and out of my ass. Or the guy in charge of it, ensuring he took care to make it enjoyable for me. Honestly, I wouldn't have wanted any other guy taking me for the first time but Caz.

This confusion isn't physical. It's emotional and psychological. My brain is clear enough to figure that part out.

Her shoulders relax, and she smiles. "So, it was a good experience?" Lo gently probes my troubled mind.

"Yes. He made it good for me, and he made sure I came too."

"Then what's the problem?" She threads her fingers in mine, and her touch helps to ground me.

"I wasn't expecting to *feel* so much," I croak, rubbing a hand across the tightness in my chest. "And it hit me all at once, almost knocking me off my feet."

"That's kind of understandable." She looks contemplative. "You've thought about this, fantasized about this, for a long time, Theo."

"So why did I freak out?" I look to her for answers I can't find. "Why did I shut down?" The look on Caz's face when I pushed him away, as he reached to hug me after we'd fucked, will stay with me for a long time. He was devastated, and I hate that I did that to him. That I ruined what was an otherwise perfect moment.

"Only you can answer that, Theo." Lo widens her legs, gesturing for me to sit in front of her. I move into position, nestling between her long, slim legs, leaning my bare back against her naked chest. Resting my head against her collarbone, I sigh as her fingers wind into my hair, massaging my scalp. "You know I'm a judgment-free zone, Theo. Try to relax and just tell me the thoughts in your head. We'll figure this out together."

Reaching up, I clasp her wrist, angling my head so I'm looking at her. "I love you, Lo. For so many things and in so many ways, but this right here is one of the biggest reasons. I'm not sure I'd have even gotten to this point if it wasn't for you."

She leans down, pressing a tender kiss to my lips. "Sure, you would have. It might've taken a little longer, but you'd have gotten there."

I twist my head, staring straight ahead, trying to untangle the thoughts in my head as Lo gives me a scalp massage. "I've never been so exposed. Stripped bare in every sense of the word," I admit after a few minutes of amicable silence. "I feel... vulnerable. Uncomfortable in my skin, yet comfortable at the same time, and proud of myself for trusting him like that."

Lo's fingers drag through my hair, kneading my scalp, and I close my eyes for a moment, enjoying the sensation.

"Let's unscramble that, because there's a lot beneath the surface of that sentence." She stops kneading my scalp, angling my chin up with her fingers. "Is it true you've never been that exposed before? That you've never passed trust over to another?"

I don't have to think about it for long to understand what she's getting at. "I did that with you."

She nods, still holding my chin as her eyes penetrate mine. "You trusted me enough to let me use all manner of sex toys on you. You even let me fuck you with a strap-on a few times. Yet you only knew me for a few months. You've known Caz for years."

"I feel like a fraud," I admit in a whisper.

"Why?"

"Because I still don't know who I am or what I am."

Her lips purse, and heat flares in her eyes. "This better not be about labels, Theo, because we've already had this discussion. You are *you*." She slides her hand down to my chest. "One of the smartest, kindest, most loyal people I know."

"You forgot sexiest," I quip.

Her lips kick up. "That goes without saying." Her smile softens. "We are who we are at any given moment in time, but it's always evolving, because that's in our nature. And we're only at the start of this journey called life."

"I love how you own who you are. No apologies or fucks given," I admit.

"That." She prods my chest. "That is exactly what I'm talking about. I knew that Theo one time. A boy who was excited to explore possibilities. What's changed?"

I dig deep to unroot the truth I've always known these past couple of years. "My parents are in my head. They cast me away for being me. Maybe that's when I stopped owning who I was and the image of who I wanted to be."

"Fuck those motherfucking assholes," Lo hisses, fire dancing in her eyes. "They are such hypocrites. They defied your mom's parents for love, but now their heads are so far up their asses they can't see how they are doing to you what her parents tried to do to them."

It's a true assessment. A truth I've told myself many times, but their words cut deep, slicing at the very core of who I was becoming. "The logical part of my brain agrees with you, but there's an innate part of me that thinks everyone else will react the same if I show them who I truly am."

"I know who you are. So do the guys. And we all love you for being you. We will support you, no matter what. No questions asked."

"Is that why Saint and Galen haven't said one word to me?" I've seen the knowing looks these past few weeks, confirming they've seen the attraction between Caz and me. I expected Saint to come knocking on my door, but their silence has been deafening.

"Like me, they didn't want to interfere," Lo says, adding, "unlike me, they're not so comfortable speaking about feelings and emotions."

"This will complicate things." It already has.

"We'll uncomplicate it." She shrugs as if it's that simple. "Together. Like we have with every other situation we've faced." Pressing her lips to my cheek, she adds. "I'm sensing there's more."

"I'm scared. Everything I've ever wanted is within reach. I have you, and maybe him, and a real shot at happiness. What if the reality doesn't live up to the fantasy?"

"We make our own reality, Theo. Others may try to control us, but they don't. Why can't you make your fantasy your new reality?"

Man, she really does make it sound so simple. I'm not naïve. I know it's not. But Lo is helping me knock down the obstacles, one at a time, and my heart is already steadier, a serene sort of calmness lapping at the embers inside me, helping me feel more like me.

"What if I'm no good at it? What if I fuck everything up for all of us?"

A mischievous glint shines from her eyes. "Trust me, you have this sex thing nailed down tight." She presses her mouth to my ear, and her warm breath raises goose bumps all over my skin. "You're a fucking God in the bedroom, Theo. You just need to believe in yourself."

"Thanks for the vote of confidence." I grin, sitting up, the scalp massage long since forgotten. "And you may be biased because we were always straight fire between the sheets."

"Just so you know, you're making me wet, and I didn't get

off because someone I love had a bit of a meltdown before I got there."

I clasp her hip. "Don't worry, my queen. I'll make sure you're looked after once I complete the meltdown mode." A shuddering sigh releases from my mouth, as I let go of everything tethering me to fear. "But I wasn't talking about sex. We're building something special here, Lo. Something permanent and long-lasting because you're our forever and we are yours. I don't want to fuck that up."

"You can't carry that burden entirely on your shoulders, Theo. You aren't responsible for our happiness. We're each responsible for our own happiness. And we're a team. We'll figure this out together."

"My dad said I ruin everything. That I'm a massive disappointment," I admit, hearing the words in my ears as if he's here whispering them to me. "What if he's right? What if I ruin this?"

Holding my shoulders, she repositions us so we're facing one another. "Fuck your dad. He's an asshole for planting that doubt, and he's wrong. You could never be a disappointment. Never." She cups my face, inspecting my eyes as understanding sweeps across her features. "That's why you like to be in control. Why you are always planning and organizing and making sure everything is in place. To ensure nothing goes wrong. To prove your value." She lowers her voice. "Am I right?" I nod, because deep down inside, I know that's the truth. "Do you feel in control now?" she asks.

I snort out a laugh. "I've never felt less in control."

"Then it's no wonder you're scared. I don't think this is about Caz at all. Not really."

Slowly, the last of the fog clears as her words penetrate deep. "I want to live my life freely. But that's the antithesis of control, so how do I marry the two?"

She shakes her head, and her breasts jiggle with the movement. Lust stirs in my loins, and my cock starts thickening, only now remembering we're both naked, on a giant bed, with the heady scent of sex still permeating the air. "I don't agree," Lo says. "You can be free and still be in control. Isn't that what freedom is? Having control over your life to live it as you please?"

I know exactly what I need to do. Scrambling off the bed, I extend my hand to her. "I need to talk to Caz. I want you there."

Slowly, she crawls off the bed until she's standing beside me. "Are you sure you don't want to talk to him alone?"

"Yes. You are the center of our world, and if Caz and I are to have any kind of relationship, we need to work out how to do that without affecting what we share with you."

I pull on sweats, and Lo pulls Saint's T-shirt on over her head. It hits her mid-thigh, and she looks hot as hell with her sex-tousled hair and those gorgeous long legs I daydream about. Reeling her into my chest, I plant a passionate kiss on her lips, holding her close. When our lips part, I press my forehead to hers. "Thank you."

"I didn't do anything but coax the truth from your mind." Her hands land on my hips.

"You did more than that, and you know it." Lifting one of her hands, I bring it to my lips, placing a kiss on her knuckles. "You've been my anchor for a long time, Lo."

"As you are mine." Stretching up, she kisses my mouth. "And I'm excited for you. Your happiness means the world to me. Same for Caz, Galen, and Saint."

"You're truly okay with this?"

She nods vigorously, her smile expanding. "So much, yes. I tried to respect your privacy, but I sneaked a few glimpses, and the two of you fucking was like *my* every fantasy come to life."

She nips at my jawline. "So. Fucking. Hot." My answering smile is so wide it threatens to split my face in two. "I tried to persuade Saint and Galen to hop aboard the D-train, but they shut that shit down pretty fast."

I throw back my head, laughing. "Yeah, no. That will never happen." I love the Lennox cousins, but I'm not attracted to them sexually or romantically. Not in the way I am drawn to Lo and Caz.

"Come on. Let's go put Caz out of his misery." She tugs on my arm, and a last-minute bout of nerves attacks me.

"I hope I haven't fucked it up before it's even begun. He was so hurt."

"Just be honest with him. Caz loves you, and he's probably as scared as you are for a lot of the same reasons."

"I never want to hurt him."

"I know, babe." She laces her fingers in mine. "Let's go tell him."

We walk downstairs, but the place is empty. Galen and Saint have made themselves scarce, so I figure they have relocated to the workout barn to give us space to work through this. Ascending the stairs on the other side of the barn, we find Caz lying on his side on his bed, staring off into space.

I clear my throat. "Caz. Can we talk?"

Slowly, he turns his head in our direction, examining my face carefully. He nods, hauling himself into a seated position with his back against the headrest. He's wearing clean black boxer briefs that cling to his shapely hips, mold against his cock, and hug his muscular thighs, leaving little to the imagination. Carved abs that look painted on, chiseled shoulders, and rippling biceps complete the tempting package, and I've never been more attracted to any guy in my life.

Lo crawls up the bed beside him, leaning her head on his shoulder, while I perch on the side of the bed in front of him.

"I'm sorry for pushing you away. I got all up in my head, and I freaked."

Pain tightens his features. "Do you regret it? Did I...hurt you?" He chokes out the words, and I hate he's been beating himself up over something that's entirely my fault.

"No." I slide my hand in his. "Not at all. It was everything I had hoped for and more. That's the problem."

His brow puckers, but he doesn't pull his hand away. "I'm not following."

Lo lifts her head from his shoulder, rubbing his arm as she smiles encouragingly at me.

Nerves prickle my skin, but I open myself up, exposing my vulnerability, because I owe him at least that much. "I'm scared, man. Of feeling too much. Of fucking everything up. Of hurting you. Of getting my heart broken." The words rush out in quick succession, but at least I got them out.

"Theo." He sits forward, palming one side of my face. "You think I don't feel those things too?"

"You do?" I'm surprised because nothing seems to faze Caz. He owns who he is, and he's fearlessly brave.

"I do, because this is *you*." He grips the back of my neck, staring into my eyes. "I want you as more than just a friend. I love you as more than just a friend. But I don't want to fuck things up either, because I can't lose you."

Lo swipes at the tears pooling in her eyes as I lean forward, pressing my forehead to Caz's. "We can be scared together," I whisper over his mouth, peering into his warm, honest brown eyes. "And I love you too," I add before my lips meld against his.

Chapter Forty-Two
Harlow

"Can I talk to you both?" Theo asks Saint and Galen the following morning as we eat breakfast at the table.

Saint squirms on his seat. "If this is about last night, you don't need to say anything."

"We're cool with it," Galen adds. "As long as you've worked your shit out."

"You're seriously okay with it?" Theo asks, color blooming in his cheeks.

Caz is grinning from ear to ear, contributing nothing to the conversation, spooning cereal into his mouth while he watches it going down.

"Yup." Saint slurps coffee from a mug.

"It's not like it was a big secret," Galen adds, stuffing the last piece of toast into his mouth. "We could tell you were hot for each other." The words are muffled over his chewing, but the sentiment is clear.

Caz stands, rounding the table and clamping his hand

down on Theo's shoulder. "They're cool with PDAs and live porn reenactments too. In case you were wondering."

Theo's cheeks get redder while Saint spits coffee all over the table.

"You're such a shit-stirrer," Galen says, licking his bowl clean. "Pun intended." He waggles his brows, his mouth stretched into the biggest grin.

"Okay." Saint stands abruptly, throwing his hands up. "Enough. We're cool for you to do your thing. End of story."

And just like that, our leader has spoken, ending the conversation, much to Theo's obvious relief.

We leave school early on Wednesday to attend the meeting Diesel has set up with the various interested parties. Not gonna lie, I'm on edge for a whole heap of reasons, but if we can do this—if we can work together—it means Sinner's end is close, and that's all that matters.

Galen blares the music as Saint drives my Lexus to the secret meeting. Following the coordinates Diesel sent us, Saint drives into an industrial park on the outskirts of the bustling town of Grenlow, coming to a halt in front of a small hardware store.

Saint's lips pull into a snarl as he parks beside Diesel's Land Rover, and I smother a smile. The back door opens abruptly, and Diesel leans inside, arms stretched overhead as he holds onto the door frame. "A few things before we go inside," he says without bothering with formalities. His eyes drop to the necklace on my chest. "You're wearing it, good. Only activate it once we are in the room. They have mad security here, and I don't want it to trigger any system."

"You don't trust these guys," Saint says, spinning around in the driver's seat.

"I trust few people and definitely not a group of this size. Many of these men are unknowns, so tread carefully." His somber gaze roams between us.

"What else do we need to know?" I ask.

"Don't mention the recording we have of Sinner and the board instructing you to kill the commissioner."

"Because you don't trust everyone or it's something else?" Theo asks, leaning forward on his elbows.

"We need to be cautious, and until this goes down, I don't know if we can trust anyone with that intel."

"We keep it to ourselves. Got it," Galen says.

"What about the FBI agent? He'll be here, right?" Diesel nods. "Did you meet him the other night?" I inquire.

"Yes. He's a good guy, and I believe him when he says he's on our side. He was only assigned to this case eight months ago, which is a little unusual for a man who's been an agent for less than four years. But I did some digging, and he graduated top of his class from Quantico, and he continues to impress his bosses, so they gave him a high-profile case in the hopes he would crack it."

"Why didn't he tell you Giana was recruited as an FBI informant?" Galen asks.

"There was a good reason for that, but I'm not at liberty to disclose it."

I exchange suspicious looks with my husbands before clearing my throat and focusing on Diesel. "I thought we agreed to share everything? That we're a team?"

"We *are* a team." He lets his gaze fall on each one of us. "And I've told you things that could get me fired. This is political, and it doesn't impact what we're doing. If I felt you needed to know, I would tell you."

I peer into his earnest eyes, and I believe him. The guys are all staring at me, letting me decide. "Okay. If you say we don't need to know, we don't need to know."

His shoulders relax in obvious relief. "Thank you."

"Anything else?" Saint glances at the time on his cell.

"Let me do most of the talking, and only speak if you're asked a direct question."

"Then why the fuck are we here?" Caz asks, checking his weapon.

"You're here because I insisted you play a part, but that doesn't mean any of these people trust you or respect you."

"Wow. That's reassuring," Galen snarks, twiddling his brow ring.

"I'm telling you how it is." Diesel's tone brooks no argument. "You're all members of the very organization we are trying to take down."

"We're fucking helping you do it," Saint barks, glaring daggers at Diesel like this is his fault.

"And that is how I secured your presence here and got overall agreement. But you are still kids, and—"

"We're fucking eighteen," Saint hisses, leaning forward in his seat. He jabs his finger at Diesel. "We're adults, not kids."

"Galen is only seventeen," Diesel reminds us. "And it wasn't meant as an insult." He stabs Saint with a serious look. "I know your value. I know you are not like normal eighteen-year-olds. I know you are all razor-sharp and that your reasons for taking The Sainthood down are legit and why. I trust you." Tension splinters the air. "I trust *all* of you, but that's because I'm around you and I've learned to trust you."

That statement is fucking monumental, and I could kiss Diesel for his loyalty.

"Thank you," Theo says. "And we trust you too."

Diesel's eyes lift in challenge, pinning in one obvious direction.

"We do," Saint agrees after a few silent beats. "Because you've proven that to us too."

"Can I just say how fucking proud I am of all of you." I beam like a gratified mother hen. "And you've no idea how happy it makes me that you're all getting on."

"Don't throw a party yet," Saint drawls. "We won't be holding hands and singing "Kumbaya" around the campfire anytime soon."

"Challenge accepted." I fold my arms and purse my lips, fighting a smile.

"Entertaining as this is, we need to move our asses," Diesel says, dropping his arms and straightening up. "And don't bother carrying weapons. They'll just confiscate them."

Saint is grumbling over the no-weapons order as we stash our guns and knives in the trunk.

"Don't worry, dude," Caz says, cracking his knuckles and flexing his biceps. "This body is the best weapon known to man. I'm all you need."

Saint rolls his eyes, a hint of a smile threatening his lips.

We trail Diesel into the hardware store, following him as he crosses the room toward the single door at the rear. He punches in a code on the keypad, and we walk through the door in single file, moving along a narrow corridor and down three flights of stairs.

A man wearing military fatigues with a rifle strapped across his shoulder escorts us into the underground facility hidden beneath the industrial park. It's massive down here, and we go through various security checkpoints before we're escorted, on electric carts, to a conference room where the others are waiting.

A deathly hush descends on the room as everyone stops talking when we enter. My fingers curl around my necklace, in what I hope is a natural nervous gesture, and I subtly press down on it to activate the recording software.

Diesel introduces us to the men sitting around the table, before we claim seats alongside Howie. Bryant isn't here because Howie insisted his brother stay away. VERO, Homeland Security, and the FBI aren't aware of his involvement, and we all agreed it was safer to keep him out of this. We'll update him after the meeting has ended, so he's still in the loop.

"On behalf of my boss, I would like to thank you for returning the missing intelligence files to Homeland Security," a small, thin man with a mop of dark reddish-brown hair says, opening the conversation.

We nod, as a group, in acknowledgment.

"The purpose of today's meeting is to plan operations for the party on Saturday night," a tall man with wavy brown hair says. Diesel introduced him as the head of VERO and his boss. We were only given job titles. No names. To protect the privacy of these important pricks. "We will need details of the security systems on the property in Thornton Heights so our people can deactivate it to gain entry."

"That won't be necessary," Diesel says. "Theo will handle it securely and safely from inside the house." He jerks his head at Theo, urging him to speak.

"I'll disable the exterior cameras, to mask your presence, while leaving the interior ones active to record proceedings. I'll deactivate the security system when you are en route, and Diesel will provide the codes to access the front gate and the entrance doors."

Sinner has upped security at Galen's house in the past few weeks, but there isn't much Theo can't do, and it took him less than three minutes to hack into the system last night and get everything he needs to ensure this happens smoothly.

"What is the stated objective of the operation?" the FBI representative asks. He's the youngest person in the room, besides us, but Diesel did say he's a relatively new FBI agent so it's not all that surprising.

"The objective is to take Neo 'Sinner' Lennox and the board of The Sainthood down. To force the organization to its knees. To stop the supply of drugs and illegal weapons on the streets. To halt his sex trafficking plans," Diesel's boss says, confirming he's up to date on his intel.

"How do you see this going down?" Saint asks, earning a warning look from Diesel.

"We will surround the property while the party is in full swing and wait for the right time to intervene and arrest them."

"On what grounds?" I ask, ignoring the heated stare Diesel sends my way. I get that he wants us to be quiet—he's probably afraid we'll mouth off—but he knows us well enough by now to know we won't stay mute.

"We'll raid the house and *discover* the illegal stash he's hiding in the ballroom." He uses little air quotes with his fingers, and it just looks weird on a man of his age.

"He'll say that it's not his," Galen cuts in.

Diesel exhales heavily, sitting back in his chair with a resigned look on his face. If we weren't surrounded by these pricks, I know he'd roll his eyes or call us out for blatantly disregarding his instructions.

"And you can be damn sure you won't find any fingerprints on any of the supplies," Saint says.

"He'll pin it on my mom," Galen adds. "I don't want her caught in the crosshairs."

"If you'd let me speak," the VERO boss man snipes, clearly agitated. "It's a two-fold strategy. We're relying on you to manipulate him into incriminating himself. Get him to admit he killed Daphne Leydon and he conspired to murder the commissioner." From the lack of surprise on everyone's faces, it's clear they are all aware of what went down.

Commissioner Leydon's state funeral took place yesterday, but the people in this room know it was a ruse. That the commissioner is alive and well and hiding in a government safe house until Sinner is arrested and he can come back from the dead.

"And what if they can't get him to fess up?" Howie asks. There's another DEA agent with him, because Howie is still officially on extended leave from the Drug Enforcement Administration, or maybe they know he's a bit of a loose cannon and they don't trust him to represent them alone today.

"They must," Diesel's boss says. "Otherwise, what the fuck are we doing here today?"

"We'll get him to admit it," Saint says, confidence blistering in his tone.

"And what then?" the FBI agent asks, drilling a look at Diesel's boss.

"The drugs and guns seizure will enable us to detain them while we search The Sainthood properties and gather enough evidence to pin him for the murder and conspiracy to murder charges," he says. "Then we build a solid case and put him away for life."

"We want possession of the drugs and firearms," Howie's DEA colleague says.

Diesel's boss nods. "That's already agreed." He throws a bunch of pages down in the middle of the table. "VERO and Homeland can't have fingerprints on this. As far as the public will know, this was a joint effort between the FBI and DEA to take down the country's most notorious criminal organization."

A muscle clenches in Saint's jaw, and Galen's hands grip

the armrest on his chair tight. Theo remains impassive while Caz rubs his hands along his thighs.

"What if we don't find the Leydon evidence?" the FBI agent asks. "A confession alone may not be enough to convict him. I thought you wanted to wait until the missing evidence was located?"

"We don't have time for that now. Sinner is expanding his business, and the last thing we need is the streets flooded with kidnapped sex slaves. He is too dangerous to sit on this any longer. Especially now he's wiped the board with his competition. If we must put him away for the drugs and firearms charges while we build a more stable case for other crimes, so be it." He puffs out his chest. "The objective now is to get him off the streets. By any means necessary."

Chapter Forty-Three
Harlow

News of The Arrows arrest is all over TV screens and splashed across internet headlines on Saturday. While full details are only emerging, the reports confirm that several members of the board were responsible for the brutal Roark family slaying all those years ago.

Caz comes with me to visit Sean after breakfast, and I explain how Bry had the evidence proving involvement of The Arrows and how a friend helped us get it into the right hands within the FBI.

But the arrest is not just for the cold case.

When FBI agents raided The Arrows warehouse, they found a ton of dead bodies—casualties from the shootout with The Sainthood. Although The Arrows didn't kill their own guys—and they are no doubt pointing the finger of blame at The Sainthood—with no weapons and no traceable bullets, there is no evidence to haul The Sainthood in for that.

Darrow's body was among the bodies found in the warehouse, but I feel zero remorse. Darrow dug his own grave.

It plays out how we planned it with reports confirming

Taylor Tamlin assassinated the commissioner and ended up dead when her partnership with Darrow Knight turned sour. Media speculation suggests The Arrows retaliated by killing one of their own because he risked the entire crew through his actions.

"The power these men have is sickening," Theo says while we lounge in the main living room in Galen's house on Saturday afternoon.

"It's scary as fuck," Caz agrees, helping Galen to load more logs on the fire. Galen spends a fortune on heating this old house, and it's still cold as fuck. I'd wager it's colder inside than outside today. My pebbled nipples prod against my hoodie, and I pull the blanket higher over my body, snuggling closer to Saint on the couch.

"What we're doing tonight is risky as fuck." Saint peers distantly into the flames. "Who's to say they won't arrest us too?" he adds before taking a swig from his beer.

"Diesel won't let that happen," I reply, plucking the beer from his fingers and lifting it to my lips.

"I trust Granddad, but—"

"That's a sentence I never thought would leave your lips," I admit, cutting across him.

"Pay up." Caz shoulder checks Galen. "Told ya."

I arch a brow as Galen plops down on my other side. He leans forward, glaring at his cousin. "Fuck you, Saintly. You've just cost me a fifty."

Saint glares at him, because he doesn't like to be reminded he's changing. Also, he fucking hates being interrupted midsentence, and Galen is bearing the brunt of that frustration.

Saint's jaw tenses and then loosens. "As I was saying, before you all decided to be buttheads, I trust the perv, but we don't know the others won't double-cross him. His boss is a self-serving prick who'd throw anyone under the bus if it got him what he wants."

"I don't disagree," I say. "I didn't like him either, but what choice do we have? This is our best opportunity to end this, and no plan is without risk."

"We have to trust in Diesel and the plan," Theo says. "It will work."

"What are you doing with your mom?" I ask Galen.

"Locking her in her room until it's over. Mrs. Murphy will stay with her. I'll warn her not to come out, no matter what she hears."

"Maybe we should move them to the barn," I suggest.

Galen shakes his head. "We can't be sure Sinner doesn't know about our place, and I'd prefer to keep her near."

"You don't trust her not to ditch Mrs. Murphy and look for a good time," Saint says, and Galen nods.

"We should check the ballroom," Galen suggests, rubbing a spot between his brows. "Make sure the stash is still there."

"I thought you checked yesterday." I hand the beer back to Saint.

"We did, but we weren't here last night. We should double-check to be sure it's still there," Galen adds, standing.

"Sit," Theo says, his fingers tapping over his tablet. "I'll check the camera feeds for the last twenty-four hours."

We absently watch the TV reports while Theo works his magic, and I run my hand over the ink on Saint's hands while snuggled into his side.

"Holy. Fuck."

We all sit upright at Theo's outburst, sharing wary looks. "What is it?" I ask, almost afraid to look. "Is it gone?"

Theo lifts his head from his tablet, shock splayed across his face as he shakes his head. "It's worse. Look." He turns the screen around, and we watch with mounting horror as at least twenty young girls are frog marched into the ballroom and shoved into the hidden compartment under the floor. The time-stamp on the screen shows this happened at four a.m.

The girls are disheveled—their clothes torn, skin dirty, and hair greasy and knotted. Their fear is palpable as they cry out in Spanish, their bodies trembling, lips wobbling, and tears streaming down their faces, as they cling to one another, clearly terrified.

I jump up, and the blanket falls to the floor. "We have to get them out of there."

Saint tugs on my arm, pulling me back. "Babe." Strain etches across his handsome face. "We can't."

"They could die!" I don't know if there's enough oxygen down there, and from the state they are in, it's obvious they haven't eaten or drank in some time. "We need to help them."

"Angel." Galen cups my face as Saint pulls me on his lap. "The best way to help them is to let the FBI find them tonight. They can identify Sinner and his men as the ones who put them there. It helps solidify the case against him."

"They can still do that even if we release them now!" I argue, needing to do something.

"Sinner could check before the party, and if they're gone, it will tip him off," Caz says, pinning me with a sympathetic look.

"I know this kills you, Lo," Theo says. "It's killing all of us, but they will be free in a few hours. We've got to let this play out."

"We should at least give them some water and food." I plead with my eyes.

"We can't risk it. They might try to escape if we open it up." *Or they could already be dead, and I don't want you to see.* That's what I read in Saint's eyes as he begs me to understand.

I climb off his lap and pace the floor. "This feels wrong."

Caz stands, wrapping his arms around me from behind.

"We know, queenie. But we can't risk everything at the last minute. We will get those girls out of there as soon as we can, and then we'll take care of them. The authorities will see they are returned home. This is the best way of handling it."

I can't stop thinking about those girls trapped and scared, in the hidden compartment in the floor of the ballroom, as I get dressed for the party that's about to kick off in an hour. Caterers and other staff hired by Sinner showed up a couple of hours ago, and we watched as they wheeled furniture, food, and booze into the ballroom, decorating it like it's a genuine celebration instead of some carefully orchestrated effort at putting us in our place.

I pay extra attention to my hair and makeup, wanting to look and feel the part when we emerge victorious tonight. While I don't have a crystal ball, I'm confident we will prevail, because no other outcome is acceptable.

I'm building the kind of life I dreamed about, and that psycho bastard is not ruining it for me.

Sinner is going down tonight.

That is the mantra I'm sticking to, and I'll do whatever is necessary to ensure it happens.

Galen slips into his bedroom as I sit in my black strapless bra and panties on the side of his bed, strapping my knife and one of my daggers to my thighs. He flattens his back against the door after he closes it, breathing deeply as his striking green eyes roam my semi-naked body.

"We don't even have time for a quickie," I warn him, continuing my task.

"I know. Doesn't mean I can't admire the view." His lips kick into a smirk, and I grin.

"Any sign of Satan yet?" I ask.

He shakes his head. "Not so far, but I'm sure he won't be long. He'll want to be here to greet his guests."

"Do we know who's coming?"

"Sainthood members and their women, I'm guessing, although he seems to have been selective with the invitations, because there are only seats for thirty."

"Is your mom okay?" I inquire, standing as he walks toward me.

He nods. "She's in her room with takeout, wine, Netflix, and Mrs. Murphy to ensure she stays there."

I palm his cheek. "We won't let anything happen to her."

"I know." He reels me against him. "But I'm more worried about you." He softly clamps a hand over my mouth when I open it to speak, careful not to press too hard and ruin my makeup. "I know you can handle yourself. I know you could take out most of that room single handed if you needed to. Still won't stop me from worrying." He presses his delectable mouth to my ear. "Husbands worry about their wives. Get over it."

"I love hearing those words," I admit, running my finger back and forth across the black band on his ring finger. "And wives worry about their husbands too—even if they are fucking badass."

His hands slide to my ass, slipping under the lace. "Sure we don't have time for a quickie?" He slaps my ass, and I shake my finger at him as liquid lust coils in my belly.

"You are such a bad influence, and coming from me that's saying a lot." I shimmy my panties down my legs and kneel up on the bed. I glance over my shoulder while he unbuttons his jeans, grinning wickedly as he zooms in on my pussy, licking his lips. "You have five minutes, Romeo. Do your worst."

"He's up to something," Theo says when we join the others in one of the guest bedrooms ten minutes later.

"What's happened?" I ask, my sex hangover instantly cured when I meet Theo's troubled gaze.

"He's turned the cameras off inside the ballroom."

"What about outside?" Saint asks as we all huddle around Theo, peering at his laptop, pretending we know what we're looking at on the screen.

"They are still intact."

"What the fuck are we going to do?" Caz asks, pulling a black shirt on over his head.

The guys are all dressed in their Sainthood attire. Black shirts, black jeans, and black leather cuts. Their freshly washed hair is styled to perfection, and they all smell divine. I wish we were going to a proper party, where I could get drunk and grope them on the dance floor.

"Such little faith you have." Theo's fingers dance across the keys, like a skilled pianist playing a piano. "I planned for this eventuality." He sets the tablet down with a flourish. "The exterior cameras are off and the interior ones are on, like we agreed, but if Sinner checks, it will look the opposite, because I've hidden the feed behind fake images."

"Fuck, that's hot." Caz slams his lips down on Theo's mouth, and I swoon, like I do every time they touch each other. It's still early days, but they are slowly opening up to one another, and it's a beautiful thing to bear witness to.

"Careful you don't come, queenie," Saint drawls, noticing my expression.

"I've already taken care of our girl," Galen replies. "Lo just came twice on my cock in six minutes."

Saint eyeballs him like he's lying, but he's not. Galen is just that good, and he's earned bragging rights, but now isn't the time to gloat. "Stop talking about sex." I pin them with a warning look. "We can't afford to get distracted."

"Lo is right," Theo says, breaking his lip lock with Caz. "Like always."

"You are such a suck up." Galen rolls his eyes.

"We should never forget that Sinner is smart as fuck, and he has a way of being ahead of the game. We're prepared, but so is he." The troubled, haunted look returns to Theo's eyes, making me nervous. "Don't lose sight of that tonight."

Anxious energy filters into the room. We all get what Theo's saying, and we agree, but it's worth the risk to end this once and for all.

My fingers slide across the metallic silver belt on my dress and strengthen my resolve. Sinner *is* going down. No other outcome will do.

"Let's do this." Saint offers me his arm, and I loop mine around it. "Sinner will be here any second. Let's roll out the red carpet."

"By the way, queenie," Caz says, slapping my ass as we make our way out of the room. "You look fucking hot."

I blow him a kiss over my shoulder. "Thank you, husband. I chose leather so we match."

That sexist pig Sinner hasn't supplied me with a fitting Sainthood wardrobe, so I improvised. Not that I'd ever wear anything that came from him, especially not something bearing The Sainthood logo I despise so much, but it's the principle of the thing.

I smooth a hand down the front of my black dress, knowing I look good. This is one of my favorite dresses. The top is a fitted leather corset with straps that crisscross over my shoulders and down my back, showcasing some of the ink on my skin but not low enough to be indecent. The bottom half is black silk, and the skirt flares out in billowy pleats, allowing me to hide my knives underneath.

Theo's phone pings in his pocket, and he glances at it as we make our way downstairs. "Diesel said they are in situ, and they'll move into place outside as soon as we give them the word."

We must wait for all the guests to arrive before we can signal the team to sneak on to the property.

"Did you tell him about our discovery?" I ask under my breath as we descend the stairs.

"Yes, and he agreed we were right to do nothing," Theo adds, squeezing my hand.

Loud clapping greets us as the lobby comes into view, and bile rises in my throat at the sight of Sinner.

He's dressed in a tuxedo.

As if he's attending a movie premiere or a high-society gala.

Behind him, his board members are in their Sainthood cuts, so they clearly didn't get the memo.

Tension bleeds in the air as we walk down the last few steps. Heated eyes pin me in place and all the tiny hairs prickle the back of my neck. I'm glad I chose to wear my hair up in a high ponytail, because this house is suddenly as hot as a furnace, and little beads of sweat gather on the nape of my neck.

Sinner whistles, doing nothing to disguise his blatant ogling. "You have grown into a very sexy woman, Harlow. My son is a lucky man." His wolfish grin does nothing to calm my growing trepidation, but I put a lid on it, forcing my body not to react to his sickening gaze and his disgusting words. I plaster a sociable smile on my face. "Thank you for the compliment." I almost puke on the words.

"Allow me to escort the lady of the moment into our ballroom." He offers me his arm, and I cling tighter to Saint's arm, discreetly rubbing my necklace to activate the recording device.

"You mean *my* ballroom," Galen says with a glare.

Sinner chuckles. "Let's not split hairs, nephew. We both know you'd be living on the streets if I hadn't intervened to save you and your mother." He casts a glance around. "Speaking of the junkie whore, where is she?"

"Mom is not here," Galen lies. "And don't call her that."

"Pity," the bald dude with the ink on his face says, crudely grabbing his crotch. "I could use her mouth."

"I wanted to stick my dick in her ass," the dude with the scraggly beard says.

"Be patient, friends." Sinner's lips tug up. "There will be plenty of hot, young pussy available tonight. And lots of nice, tight ass. Just how I like it."

I know exactly which young girls he's referring to, and I fucking hope Diesel and the team intervene before it gets to that part of the night, because I will slaughter every single one of those sick perverts before letting them lay a hand on those poor women. "You're disgusting pigs." I dig my nails into Saint's arm and mentally count to ten in my head.

"You just don't know what it's like to be with real men," Sinner says, yanking me from Saint's grip.

"And you don't know the English language," Saint hisses, yanking me back. "She's my wife. *Our* wife. And we're not sharing her." Saint pushes his face up in his father's. "I don't know how to state it more clearly."

"Oh, I got the message loud and clear last time, son." Sinner grabs Saint's chin, but I push him off.

"Don't fucking touch him."

Sinner laughs. "You're all so uptight." He throws his hands around. "It's a time for celebration. We're the Kings of the world." He hoots, and his cronies join in, whooping and hollering, and the urge to murder them all in cold blood is riding me hard.

One of the hired staff mans the front door, letting more Sainthood members inside. So far, I haven't spotted a single woman, and my unease grows.

"You're the belle of the ball, my dear," Sinner adds. "Enjoy your moment. You've earned it." He flashes me that obnoxious shit-eating grin of his, and a nasty shiver rockets up my spine.

Dread blossoms to life in my chest, because there's no mistaking the double meaning.

Chapter Forty-Four
Harlow

Bry is one of the last to arrive, and he plops into the vacant seat at our table. "This looks cozy," he murmurs, surveying the room with sharp eyes. "And like an ambush."

"Thanks for that, Captain Obvious," Saint says, slowly raising the beer bottle to his lips.

Not drinking would look suspicious as fuck, but we're wary Sinner may have spiked our drinks. So, the guys have switched out the beers in the bucket in the middle of the table, and we're only sipping our drinks, giving the illusion we're getting drunk along with the degenerates, when we have every intention of remaining sober. We need clear heads to beat Sinner at his game tonight.

"I was wondering how long it'd take you to revert to form, *nephew*." Bry plucks a bottle from the bucket with a smug grin, leaning back in his chair.

"Stop it," I hiss, subtly glaring at them. "I know we're all on edge, but sniping at one another will only distract us. Save your venom for the person who truly deserves it."

A muscle pops in Saint's jaw, and I drape myself around his taut body, kissing him until I feel him relax underneath me. When we break apart, Sinner is staring at us in a way that unnerves me. But I plaster a fake smile on my face, settling back in my chair, raising my bottle in mock salute to the devil.

"There are no women here," Bry murmurs.

"Why do you think I'm so pissed?" Saint grits out, tearing strips off the label on his bottle.

Galen fixes his cousin with a fierce look. "He's not touching Lo. And you need to get your shit together."

Galen is right. It's unusual to see Saint like this, but I know it's because he's worried for me. He's not used to having to protect someone and it's throwing him off his game.

Sinner taps a fork on the side of his glass, claiming everyone's attention. The room instantly mutes. "Welcome, close friends and family." He drills a look in our direction. "Thank you all for being here tonight. Please take your seats and let the celebration begin."

Waiters descend on the room, delivering mountains of food. Sinner sits at a long table in front of the window, lording over proceedings, like he's American royalty. I snort at the thought, because I bet the asshole truly believes his shit doesn't stink. The seats on either side of Sinner are empty, which is weird, because I didn't expect him to serve dinner if he's still waiting on some guests.

Out of the corner of my eye, I spy Theo sending a pre-prepared message on his cell to Diesel under the table, and he must have deactivated the security system too. He's clearly not waiting around, and I'm glad. There's comfort in knowing we'll have a team of highly-skilled government operatives outside to wade in when shit goes down.

We move food around our plates, without eating—because

we wouldn't put it past Sinner to spike our food too—and I will Sinner to hurry the fuck up and get on with it.

After the tables have been cleared and more alcohol is dispensed, Sinner calls the room to order. "I'd like to make a toast." He watches Baldy and Scraggly Beard exit the ballroom into the house, and I don't miss the wicked gleam in his eye.

I shift uncomfortably in my seat, bile swimming up my throat, as trepidation starts mounting.

Saint and Galen share a silent communication across the table. "Go after them," Saint says, and Galen rises, striding across the room, his long legs eating up the distance in no time.

"Nephew." Sinner calls out after him, but Galen ignores him, making a beeline for the double doors. Sinner jerks his chin at the two men standing on either side of the entrance, and they shut the doors, blocking Galen's exit with their arms crossed and menacing smiles on their faces.

Galen spins around, narrowing his eyes at his uncle. "You can't leave just as I'm about to toast your beautiful wife." Sinner smiles, but it doesn't meet his eyes. "Return to your seat, Galen." The smile drops off Sinner's face, replaced with a sinister warning.

"I need to piss," Galen argues, folding his arms and not budging an inch.

"I don't give a fuck," Sinner snaps. "Sit. Down." His tone is cold. His expression is hostile.

Galen looks to Saint, and Saint nods, knowing it's futile to protest further. Galen's face is like thunder as he returns to the table. "I don't like this," he hisses, rubbing a hand back and forth across the back of his neck. "He's going for Mom. I just know it."

"We should've put guys in there with them," Caz says.

"We agreed not to drag any of our extended crew into this." Saint's hands clench into fists at his side. "We can't be sure they'll side with us over Sinner." He glances at Galen. "We should've gotten Alisha out of the house."

"There's no point talking about what we should have done," I say as Sinner calls my name. "We'll deal with whatever he throws at us. We need to focus on the here and now."

"Come up here, my dear." Sinner gestures me forward with his fingers.

"You can toast Harlow from here," Saint says, his voice projecting confidently across the room. I know they want to keep me close so they can intervene if needed.

"I wasn't asking, son." Sinner's tone is clear and unyielding. Two goons appear at my back, casting dark shadows over the table. One of them drags my chair back, the legs screeching in the process.

Saint goes for his gun, but I plant my hand on his thigh. "Don't." We can't show our hand too early.

I stand, staring straight ahead as I walk toward Sinner, flanked by the two perverts. Eyeballs glue to every part of my body as I step closer to the enemy, and I swallow back my distaste.

"Here she is." Sinner yanks me into his side. His arm wraps around my shoulder, his nails digging into my exposed skin. "The woman of the hour. Don't let this sexy exterior fool you. Harlow Westbrook takes no prisoners." He raises his glass, pressing me in even closer to his side.

Everything about him irritates me to no end.

His cologne. His good looks. His fake praise.

But most of all, his touch.

His fingers on my bare skin sends me back to my thirteen-year-old self, and I long to whip out my knife and stab him in the gut.

Man, it would be so satisfying, and I hope I get to stab him at some point during the night.

My guys are rigid and on guard at the table, wearing neutral expressions to disguise their true feelings, watching and waiting with bated breath for the moment when this will turn real. Galen locks eyes with me, and his reassuring gaze helps to keep me grounded.

"To the woman who single-handedly assassinated the commissioner, eliminating one of our most powerful enemies. To Harlow Westbrook." Sinner's voice booms out across the room, and goose bumps break out along my arms. The longer his fingers are on me, the more I want to scrub at my skin and remove every hint of his DNA.

The room full of assholes stands, lifting their glasses in a salute to me. Invoking all my acting prowess, I smile and act gracious when all I want is to firebomb every single one of them, after first gouging out their eyeballs with their forks.

"Yes," Sinner says, digging his nails in deeper, drawing blood. "Harlow has done well, but that doesn't excuse her other sins."

Everyone sits down, and I can almost taste the anticipation in the air.

Here we go.

The men at the table surrounding us lounge in their seats, puffing on blunts and cigarettes, knocking back beer and whiskey, sharing knowing grins as they eye me like I'm dessert.

Sinner sits down, yanking me on his lap, instantly banding his arm around my chest to keep me in place.

Chairs fall to the floor as my guys stand, ready to wade into battle.

Cold metal presses into my temple, and I hold still.

"Sit your asses back down," Sinner barks. "Or I'll pull the trigger." A clicking sound bounces off the walls in the now deathly silent ballroom as he readies his weapon. Five of Sinner's men surround Saint and the guys, patting them down and quickly disarming them before shoving them back into their chairs.

Saint's jaw is as hard as glass as we make eye contact while the senior members of The Sainthood restrain my husbands and Bry, tying their hands behind the backs of their chairs. Rope is secured around their ankles, ensuring they can't move.

I hope Diesel and the team are in place and that he's listening to every word so he can move in at the right moment.

Sinner stands, keeping his arm around my chest and the gun pressed to my head while he moves us forward. When we reach the guys' table, he hands me off to that bald prick. Baldy's arm replaces Sinner's across my chest, and he grabs my boob, cupping it as he presses a gun into my temple.

"Get your fucking hands off my wife!" Saint snarls, his chair jumping, making a loud screeching sound, as he attempts to stand while strapped down.

Sinner slams his hand down on the back of his son's chair, yanks his head back, and jabs his gun into Saint's neck.

All the air escapes my lungs as I silently plead with Saint to play the game. Sinner is completely unpredictable—and a cold, ruthless killer—so it wouldn't take much provocation for him to pull that trigger.

"You're in no position to make demands." Sinner shakes his head, and a look of pure evil washes over his face. "You think you can tell me what I can and can't do, boy!" he yells. "You let that fucking slut hold a knife to my throat! You helped her steal my fiancée from me!" He slams the butt of his gun into Saint's temple. Saint's head jerks with the motion, but he makes no sound.

"Leave him the fuck alone!" I shout, ignoring how my skin crawls as Baldy prods his hard dick against my ass and his fingers fondle my breast through my dress. "Your issue is with me. Leave Saint and the guys out of it."

"Leave Harlow out of this," Galen cuts in, gritting his teeth. "She did what you wanted. You asked her to assassinate the commissioner, and she did it."

"And now she's bound to me. If you don't cooperate, I'll hand her ass on a silver platter to the cops. Explain how Taylor Tamlin is a plant to hide the real assassin. I doubt your precious *princess* would ever make it to trial. Cops despise cop killers," Sinner says, switching his attention to his nephew. He points his gun at Galen's chest. "It's cute you all think you saved her, but I don't give a fuck if she's married. She is mine to do with as I please."

"It's our most sacred tradition," Saint hisses, pointing at Scraggly Beard. "You said so."

The asshole smirks. "I say a lot of things I don't mean. No one in this room gives a fuck about the old traditions. We're making our own rules."

"In case you're too dumb to understand, that means your wife is ours to fuck," Baldy says, slipping his hand underneath the top of my dress and into the cup of my bra, kneading my bare flesh.

Saint roars, and Galen curses. Caz growls. Theo pins remorseful eyes on me.

I hate this ugly fucker, but I won't give him the satisfaction of knowing how much I loathe his hands on me, because pricks like him get off on that shit.

My guys need to keep it together.

I stare stoically ahead, remembering the end game. Sinner has only fessed up to ordering the hit on the commissioner. He hasn't admitted to Daphne Leydon's murder yet, so this needs to continue.

I retreat to that numb place within myself. One I've relied upon for years. A place I haven't gone to in months. Brick by brick, the wall goes up around my heart, and I tune out my emotions, focusing on the mission—destroying Sinner and bringing The Sainthood to its knees.

"No one gets away with betraying me," Sinner adds, punching Caz in the face. "And you have all betrayed me." He yanks Theo by the hair, pulling his head back, stretching his neck at an awkward angle. "You think I don't know what you've been doing behind my back?" He spits on Theo's face, and my fingers inch toward the hem of my dress, ready to go for my knife. "You are traitors, and traitors need to pay for their sins."

Sinner walks back to Saint, crouching in front of him. "Your mother tried to betray me, and I gutted her until I was swimming in her intestines."

"You did her a favor. Death is preferable to sharing a life with a sick fuck like you." Saint's tone is clinical although his eyes seethe with rage.

Sinner punches him in the stomach before ramming his fist into his face. Blood spurts from Saint's nose, and my fingers inch closer to my knife. I can't stand by and watch him hurt my husbands, but I can't end this too soon either. Not before we get what we came for.

The only way he'll fess up is if I can get him to talk.

"You say we're traitors. What are our crimes?" I jut my chin up, piercing Sinner with a haughty look. "Because it can't be my mother. She chose to leave you, and you can't blame a daughter for helping her mother to escape a monster. And I fucking killed a man because you asked me to. The commissioner is dead because you ordered it. What more do you want?"

He stands, patting his son on the head in a patronizing fashion. My fingers still at my side as he stalks toward me, but it's too late—he's noticed.

Clasping my chin in one hand, he tugs my dress up to my waist in the other. "Remove her weapons," he commands, and two men step forward, unstrapping the knife and the dagger secured to my thighs. Their fingers brush against my skin, like vipers taking a little taste before sinking their teeth into my flesh, but I don't flinch, reinforcing my walls and blanking out their touch.

Sinner lets go of my dress, and the silky material glides down my thighs, covering my exposed skin. Slowly, his hand eases up my thigh, under my skirt, and he cups my pussy through my lace panties, licking his lips as he eyeballs me. "You think I don't know you're working with the FBI?" He pushes my panties aside, spearing my cunt with two fingers, and I wriggle in Baldy's arms, unable to stop myself from fighting against his vile touch.

Saint roars at his father, and I stop fighting, focusing on my husband, comforting him with my eyes, pleading with him to keep it together. I stare at Saint, letting myself drown in his blue eyes, using his face to ground me, helping me to blot everything else out, to distract me from his father's disgusting assault.

When I'm satisfied Saint is more in control, I switch my attention to the game, deciding to play along, because keeping Sinner talking is essential to getting out of this nightmare. "What gave me away?"

"Do you know how long I've been looking for those files?" Sinner asks, sliding his fingers in and out of me.

Bile churns in my gut, but I hold myself still, not letting myself react in any way. I run with the opportunity presented to me. "I don't have the Daphne Leydon files. If the FBI has them, they didn't get them from me."

"I'm not talking about that."

"You're not?" I feign confusion, ignoring his fingers inside me. "I thought you wanted to find out who'd stolen the evidence from you. Or are you no longer worried about being caught for Daphne's murder now the commissioner is dead?"

"I'm talking about the Homeland Security files," he snaps, withdrawing his fingers and evading my question. My body wants to slump in relief, but I freeze my muscles in place. "Do you know how long I've been trying to find those fucking files?" Shoving his fingers into his mouth, Sinner moans while licking them clean. "Salty as fuck."

I want to sucker punch that disgusting grin right off his hideous face.

"Why am I not surprised." He casts a glance at my husbands over his shoulder. "Think I might have pussy for dessert tonight."

"Why do the Homeland files matter to you?" I ask before my guys lose it. "What do they have on you?"

The doors to the ballroom ease open, and Sinner's irritating grin expands. "Always so eager for answers." He yanks me from Baldy, but there's no relief in being traded from one perverted psycho to another. "And I'll give them to you, but first we have a little surprise. A couple of additional guests." Keeping his gun at the back of my head, and his arm tight around my waist, he walks me back to his table in time to see his "guests" being hauled into the room.

"Mom!" I scream, bucking in Sinner's arms as my mother is led into the room by two of Sinner's men.

Oh my God.

How the fuck did this happen? Diesel said she was in Europe, secure in one of his safe houses, so how the hell did Sinner find her?

An unsettling thought lodges in my brain.

Did he do this? Has Diesel been working for Sinner this entire time?

Chapter Forty-Five
Harlow

Pain stabs me through the heart and my lungs, working its way through every vital organ until I can barely breathe. If Diesel has betrayed us, then that means there is no rescue in sight.

No!

I don't believe it.

Diesel hates Sinner, and he's proven his loyalty to me time and time again. He last checked in with Mom a couple of days ago, and she was fine.

Someone must have betrayed him.

That's the only explanation that makes sense.

My heart rate steadies, and my panic dials down, because I know, deep down inside, that Diesel hasn't lied. That he's on our side.

A strangled sob rips through the air, pulling me out of my head. Tears pour down Mom's face as she's flung into a chair, sobbing.

Dressed in a low-cut red and black ballgown that trails the

ground with her hair and makeup professionally done, she looks beautiful on the surface—until you see the anguish in her eyes, the tears coating her face, and the fresh bruises mushrooming under the skin of her arms and around her neck.

One of Sinner's goons secures her to the chair, and we stare at one another, silently conveying so much.

"Get your hands off me." My head whips up in time to see Alisha slap one of the men manhandling her into the room. Unlike Mom, she's *not* party ready. They have stripped her to her underwear, and her small boobs and skeletal frame are on display, making her seem even more vulnerable. Matted hair frames her makeup-free face, but there's no disguising her sunken cheekbones and gaunt eyes. My gaze darts to Galen's, and my heart breaks at the devastated look on his face.

Sinner sits down beside Mom, hauling me onto his lap. Lifting her head, Mom pierces me with a look loaded with regret and guilt.

"Shut your face, whore." The man holding Alisha's skinny frame grabs her by the hair, pushing her toward the table. She screams, arms and legs flailing as the man throws her forward, slamming her head down on the table with force.

Galen shouts and curses, screaming at the asshole to leave his mom alone. His body contorts when he tries to move his chair, pain spreading across his face. One of Sinner's men punches him in the face, and it's killing me to stand idly by while this happens. Rage flows through my veins, and I'm seconds away from saying fuck the mission.

Alisha is dumped unceremoniously in the chair on the other side of Sinner, and she's not looking so hot. Her eyes are rolling back in her head as she curls into a ball, bending her knees against her chest. Blood trickles from her nostrils, dripping down over her chin, and a nasty lump is already swelling on her forehead.

I purposely ignore looking at the guys, focusing on doing what needs to be done.

"Now that everyone's here," Sinner says. "We can move things along." When he shifts underneath me, his disgusting erection digs into my ass, and I almost lose it. Acid licks a path up my throat, but I keep it together, forcing a full-body shudder to retreat.

"As I was saying, I know you and your mother are working with the FBI in an attempt to take me down." Sinner clucks his tongue. "Such stupid, stupid girls." Reaching out, he grabs the armrest of Mom's chair, pulling her in close. "You were my everything, princess," he says to Mom, gripping her chin.

His gun is still pressed to my head, but the arm around my waist is gone now, and I could make a move, but my gut tells me to hold firm.

"Why'd you have to ruin everything by leaving me for that prick Trey? Everything would be different if you'd just stayed."

Dry tear tracks streak Mom's cheeks, and her eyes are clear and targeted. Her chin juts up as she eyeballs her ex-fiancé. "You're a thug, Neo. A criminal. A serial murderer. A rapist."

He slaps her cheek, and her head whips back.

My fingers inch up my stomach.

Mom smiles at him, her cheek bearing the imprint of his hand. "Falling in love with Trey Westbrook was as easy as breathing, proving what we shared was *nothing*." She points between her and Sinner. "You mean *nothing* to me."

Sinner slaps her again, yanking her head back, and I warn Mom to tone it down with my eyes. If she continues pushing him, he'll kill her.

I've already lost one parent. I am *not* losing another on my watch.

"Your love was a death sentence!" Sinner roars. "He'd still be alive if you hadn't left me. That's on your conscience."

"No," I speak up, needing to deflect him from Mom. "It's on yours. You murdered my father so you could clear a path to my mom, because you knew there was no way she'd ever look at you as long as Trey Westbrook was alive."

"You think you know everything, little girl, but you know nothing." He jabs the gun into my crotch. "I didn't kill your father."

"Liar," I hiss. "You've already admitted it."

He flashes me that stupid-ass grin. "Because I wanted you to believe it."

"Now you're saying you didn't kill Trey? You expect us to believe it?" Mom asks, lifting a brow.

"I was getting ready to kill him, and my plan was way more fun than a staged car accident, but Homeland beat me to it."

Genuine shock splays across my face. "Why the fuck would Homeland want to kill my dad?" I ask although my brain has already started connecting the dots. Sinner grips my chin tighter, grinning as he waits for me to work it out. "They were looking for the files."

"Ding, ding, ding." Sinner swipes a beer, knocking it back, while Mom and I trade concerned looks.

"What was on those files?" Theo asks, speaking louder so his voice carries from his table.

"You mean your little FBI contact didn't tell you?" Sinner gloats. I'm glad he doesn't seem to know about Diesel, or the fact the commissioner isn't dead, but he could be bluffing to draw me into telling him the truth. Mom's face is immobile as she goes along with it too.

I shake my head. "No. Care to enlighten me?"

"You know, Harlow, this would've turned out differently if you'd just trusted me." He caresses my face, keeping his gun pressed against my pussy, ensuring I can't make any move.

I snort. "You're fucking joking, right? You're the least trust-worthy person I know."

"Then you've been hanging around the wrong people." He rubs his thumb along my lower lip.

Mom flinches, but I warn her with my eyes. Now that we've got him talking, we don't want him to stop.

"I'm one of the most loyal people you could meet—as long as you don't betray me." His eyes are like poisonous laser beams as he stabs his gaze in Saint and Galen's direction. His hostility toward Theo and Caz isn't as severe, because they're not blood, but there's no doubt whatever punishment he has in mind is for all of us.

"Maybe if you'd told me about the files, I would've admitted I had them," I bluster.

"Then I would've had to tell you everything, and you'd done nothing to earn my trust."

"I killed the commissioner for you."

"You did, but I know there was some ulterior motive. And we'll get to the bottom of that before the night is done."

Alisha moans on our other side, blinking as she falls in and out of consciousness.

Sinner grabs one of her bare breasts, squeezing hard. "Worthless junkie whore."

I want to snatch his hand back, but he's got a gun pressed to the most precious part of my body, and I'm taking no chances. "Tell me what was on those Homeland files, and I'll tell you about the commissioner," I lie.

"We were hired by Homeland Security to retrieve those files. A disgruntled employee had stolen them. Apparently, he was planning on releasing them to the public and he had to be stopped." Sinner has the undivided attention of every person in the room, and it's obvious that even the board members weren't fully aware of the situation.

Of course, Sinner is lapping up the attention, grinning as he continues explaining. "The files contained details of a terrorist plot against the US. The terrorists were stopped when they were on US soil, and Homeland ensured nothing was leaked to the public because they didn't want anyone to discover that a US-owned private company was the one to supply them with weapons and artillery."

"Why the fuck would Homeland hire *you* to stop one of their own?" Saint spits out.

"They wanted this done off the record, with no trace back to them, because the head of Homeland and the head of VERO are both on the board of the private company who sold the weapons to terrorists."

"Oh my God." The words slip from my mouth. "This is so fucked up."

Sinner barks out a laugh. "For once, we agree on something."

"How did my father end up with those files?" I wonder if he knew what was on them. If that's why he hid them. Why he didn't tell anyone. And fuck. *Does Diesel know about his boss? Is this what's happening here? Is he trying to protect him?* My mind churns with endless possibilities.

"We were supposed to hand over the files after we stole them, but I didn't trust Randall not to screw us over. The deal was we would have protection for life. That any and all future charges would be buried. We would be free to build our empire with police protection and support at the highest level, but I only had his word for it. My plan was to hold the files ransom until the deal was put in writing." He slams his bottle down on the table. "Then Trey fucking Westbrook stole them from us, and everything turned to shit."

"Who's Randall?" Galen asks.

"The head of VERO," Sinner confirms.

My brows pucker. "I thought you said you were hired by Homeland?"

"We were, but it was via Randall, because VERO does this kind of shit for the government and private corporations all the time. Randall was the one who reached out to me."

"What happened after my dad stole the files?"

"We didn't know who had taken them although, after Homeland had Trey murdered, I suspected it was him."

"That's why you wanted me back," Mom says. "So you could find those files before Homeland did."

Sinner nods, smirking. "Making you pay for leaving me was an added bonus."

"I fucking hate you," Mom snaps.

He slaps her, and I'm losing control of the tenuous hold on my emotions. "Not as much as I hate you." He rips the front of her dress, exposing the swells of her breasts to the carnivores in the room.

I've no doubt, when story time is over, he fully intends on starting the orgy part of the night. I've zero plans to participate, and hell will freeze over before I let them touch Mom or Alisha or any of those girls trapped underneath this room.

"Anyway, the gloves were off when we failed to deliver the files," Sinner continues, needing little encouragement now.

The psycho loves the sound of his own voice, and he loves the adoring attention from the captive audience.

"Randall went apeshit. A couple of our shipments were seized by the authorities in a clear warning, and I knew it was only a matter of time before they found something to pin on us, so we needed leverage."

"Daphne Leydon," I say, and he nods.

"How exactly does the commissioner fit into all this?" Saint asks.

"The commissioner was Randall's lackey, and he also

owned shares in VERO. When we failed to show up with the Homeland files, Randall sent the commissioner after us. We had to stop him, so kidnapping his wife was a no-brainer. That she was also the niece of the US president was the cherry on top. We knew that would keep them at bay. The plan was to hold on to her until the files were recovered and we had our deal in writing. But we enjoyed her time in captivity a little too much."

Sinner grins, and a chorus of hoots and hollers rips across the room, making me feel ill.

"Her death was accidental." Sinner shrugs. "But it helped serve a purpose. Daphne had blurted a ton of helpful shit before her untimely passing, and Randall knew if we were taken in for her death that it would all come out so they couldn't do anything to us."

Now I get why everyone has been searching for the recording showing Daphne being murdered. VERO wants to use it to keep The Sainthood in line and The Sainthood wants to use it to force VERO to give them a deal. However, without the evidence, VERO has the upper hand now they have the Homeland files back in their possession.

Thanks to us.

That was an epic fuckup on my part.

One I'm now regretting.

But I can't change the past—we are where we are.

My mind continues processing all we've learned. It's better for VERO if they don't find the Leydon evidence, hence why that smarmy fuck reacted like that at the meeting on Wednesday. Getting Sinner to confess to the murder serves their ends much better. I doubt Randall plans on putting Sinner away. I'm betting his plan all along has been to bust in here and kill them all so everything dies with them. Then he has the audio and camera feeds confirming the truth.

Motherfucking asshole.

I doubt he plans to let any of us out of here alive.

Except Randall didn't plan for Sinner spilling his guts.

Why has he? Does he know they're outside? Or that we're recording everything?

Fear prickles the back of my neck as I realize we're way more in the dark than we knew. Another troubling thought enters my mind. *Diesel is listening to all this, and we have more than enough now to put his boss and The Sainthood away, so why the fuck haven't they busted their way in here?*

My eyes meet Saint's across the tables, and I see the same concern in his gaze. Theo is restrained, like the rest of them, so he can't even check in with Diesel.

OMG. What a fucking epic clusterfuck. Either Diesel is a part of this and he's protecting his boss or his boss knows his days are numbered and he's done something to Diesel and the other men. Neither scenario is reassuring, and a blanket of dread washes over me.

"Why murder the commissioner?" I inquire.

"To send a new message. So they know we aren't to be messed with. Also, it gives me leverage over you." Sinner removes the gun, tucking it in the back waistband of his pants, so his hands are free to push my dress up to my waist. I knew he'd get arrogant, and now I just need to bide my time for the perfect moment to strike.

"Get your filthy hands off my daughter!" Mom screeches, panic clear in her tone.

"Such a pretty young pussy," he says, cupping me through my panties. "I've traded you in for a younger, hotter, sexier model," he tells Mom, sliding his fingers back and forth across my crotch. "Jealous?"

"Why are you telling us all this?" Theo shouts in an attempt to get him back on track.

Sinner licks a path up my neck, deliberately eyeballing my guys as he does. I breathe a sigh of relief when his hands withdraw from my crotch and my skirt pools over my thighs, covering me.

Tears shine in Mom's eyes, and her face is pale with guilt.

"Always so inquisitive." Sinner tips his bottle at Theo. "I don't trust that weasel Randall. He helped reunite me with my backstabbing fiancée, and he says he wants to put our relationship back on an even footing, but I don't buy it."

That fucking bastard Randall double-crossed Diesel. We've been two steps behind the entire time.

"That conniving cunt is only keeping me on his side because he doesn't want the truth coming out. Until we find that Leydon evidence, he's our biggest threat." Sinner's gaze roams around the room. "You are here tonight for a couple of reasons. One being I trust you. Should this get ugly, I wanted you all to be aware of the facts so you can do what is necessary to protect the sanctity of The Sainthood. And I have a new plan for retrieving that evidence, one you will play a part in."

I stare at the heavy curtains blanketing all the windows, wishing I could see through them, to know what the fuck is going on outside because the team should be here by now.

"Why are *we* here?" Saint asks. "We know you don't trust us."

"Tonight is about repentance, my son." He fists a hand in my hair, tugging my neck back. "I was going to slaughter you all." He shrugs casually, like it's no biggie. "Let's be honest, you deserve it for daring to betray me. But I gave it more thought, and I believe a better punishment is having you watch me claim what is yours."

Sweeping his hand across the table, he sends silverware and glasses crashing to the ground. "I'm going to fuck what's yours right here in front of you. Then every man will stick his dick inside *your wife* while you watch." He cups my breast through my dress. "I'm going to keep her for a while, until I've broken you down. Then you either recommit to The Sainthood and me or you can fucking die with your whore."

Chapter Forty-Six
Harlow

Sinner grabs my neck, thrusting me forward over the table as he hikes my dress up to my ass. Mom screams, thrashing about in her chair, while Alisha stares absently into space. I'm not sure how much she heard or if she's with us at all.

"Time to party, dudes," Sinner roars. "Go forth and mingle."

Terrified screams rip through the air as the underground section of the ballroom is uncovered, and men grab petrified young girls, dragging them up the stairs.

"Get the fuck off me!" Mom screams when Baldy straddles her chair, tearing at her dress while grazing his teeth along her neck.

It's now or never.

Sliding my hand around my front, I unclip the metallic belt on my dress, removing the two daggers stowed there. I wait for the telltale sound of Sinner lowering his zipper before I swing into action, thrusting my arm back, embedding my dagger firmly in his thigh.

Sinner roars, stumbling back, and I spin around, yanking my dagger from his thigh, blood immediately spurting from the wound. Sinner doubles over, pressing his fingers to the wound to stem the blood flow. Baldy hollers, moving to climb off Mom, and I react on instinct, tugging his neck back and dragging my knife across his throat.

Mom screams as he falls forward on top of her, blood spilling everywhere. Shots ring out behind me, mingling with girlish screams and cries as the room descends into chaos.

Windows shatter, in perfect uniformity, raining glass on the ballroom as commotion outside in the hall confirms the cavalry has finally arrived.

"You fucking bitch," Sinner yells, lunging at me.

A shot whizzes past his ear, narrowly missing him, and he dives under the table as I sidestep him.

"Fuck." Alisha's hands shake as she holds Sinner's gun, pointing it wildly around the room. She must have stolen it from him when he was bent over, distracted by his injury. "Aagh." She cries out as her ankle is yanked from under the table, and she goes down hard. The gun flies across the room, but there's no time to go after it, because Sinner has Alisha in his grasp, and that spells nothing good.

Lowering to my knees, I crawl under the table in time to see Sinner pull a knife from his calf. He drives it into Alisha's chest, and I scream for help, moving toward Sinner as Saint and Galen drop to their knees on the other side of the table. "Alisha needs help," I shout as Sinner scrambles off to one side, making his escape. Shots pepper the air, mixed with screaming and crying. "Help her," Saint yells, pushing Galen under the table, while he climbs to his feet, going after his father.

I want to stay with Galen, but I don't know if Theo, Caz, and Bry have managed to free themselves, and Mom is still tied to her chair. Gunfire echoes around us, chilling my bones.

Innocents are going to get caught in the crossfire if this continues.

"Keep your head down," Galen roars as I scoot back on my heels, crawling out the way I came.

Cautiously, I poke my head out from under the table. Mom is where I left her, but her head is down, chin lying on her chest. Baldy is slumped at her feet, his glazed eyes vacant and his throat a bloody mess. I flick my attention back to Mom, anxiety ratcheting up a level when I notice blood pouring from a bullet wound in her shoulder. Fuck. That shot Alisha fired must have hit Mom. Panic bubbles up my throat, but I force myself to remain calm as I crawl around the back of her chair, dodging the bullets whizzing back and forth across the room.

Casting a furtive look around the space, I hurry to cut the bindings on Mom's legs and arms. I don't see Theo or Caz, but Bry has Scraggly Beard in a headlock as they fight for possession of the gun in the bastard's hand. I cut through the rope securing Mom's ankles while I watch Bry, fear creeping up my spine. Until Scraggly Beard visibly weakens, his eyes shuttering, body slouching, and Bry pries the gun from his loosening fingers. Without hesitation, Bry pumps two bullets in his chest before joining the general melee.

Diesel's crew is fighting The Sainthood as scared young girls huddle under tables and along the side of the room, trying to stay out of the line of fire.

A couple of women wearing FBI vests are handing girls to people outside through the broken window frames. A few men with DEA stamped across their backs are trading punches with some of the Saints over by the hidden section of the room, stopping them from gaining access to the guns stored there.

I don't spot Howie among them, and I'm wondering where the fuck he and Diesel are.

Other men, wearing plain black military garb, are eliminating members of The Sainthood in a shoot-first-ask-questions-later mentality.

"Lo!" Theo comes racing across the room as the rope breaks on Mom's feet.

"Is Caz okay?" I ask as Theo slides around the table on his knees.

"He's gone after Saint. He chased Sinner out into the hall."

Fuck. I want to go after them, because I don't trust Sinner, but I can't leave Mom.

Theo instantly senses my dilemma. "Go. I'll look after your mom."

"She's been shot." My voice wobbles.

"Harlow." Mom lifts her chin, blinking her eyes open. "I'm okay. Go do what you need to."

I grip Theo's arm. "Check on Galen. He's under the table with Alisha. Sinner stabbed her."

Grabbing Sinner's gun off the floor where it landed, I crouch down, flattening myself to the wall as I make my way out of the ballroom and along the dark hallway.

A couple of guys in leather cuts lie motionless on the floor, eyes staring blankly at the ceiling. I step over their corpses, inching forward carefully. Gunfire dies out behind me as the authorities gain the upper hand, and a thin layer of stress leaves my shoulders, but it's marginal, because two of my guys are out here with the devil incarnate and Mom and Alisha are injured back in the ballroom.

I pass through the lobby, glancing out the open entrance door at the trucks and vans parked haphazardly across the front lawn. A few men wander around, talking into mouthpieces, but for the most part, everyone is inside.

Carefully, I pick my way along the far hallway, checking each room in turn, growing more and more anxious as I encounter empty spaces. This monstrosity is huge, and I'm despairing of ever locating them when a gunshot goes off on my left, from the direction of the rear gardens, and I take off running for the back door.

All is quiet when I step out onto the stained gray stones, creeping around the house, in the direction of the maze, with my back flat to the wall.

"Fucking fuckity fuck!"

My heart stops beating. "Caz," I hiss, sneaking around the bend with my gun raised, unsure of what I'll find.

"Lo. Thank God." Caz runs toward me.

"Are you okay? Are you hurt?" I scan his face under the faint glow of the outside lamps.

"I'm fine. It's Saint. He's in the maze somewhere with Sinner, and I can't find them."

I grip the gun tighter. "Saint knows that maze better than Sinner. If anyone has the upper hand, it's him."

A shot rings out from inside the maze, followed by shouting. "I'm going in. Stay here in case we need help." I wish I had my cell with me, but it's sitting in my purse back at the table.

"Do you even know where you're going?" He holds on to my waist, not wanting to let me go after them.

"I went over the plans with the gardener." I tap my temple. "It's memorized in here." I stretch up, pecking his lips. "Don't worry about me. I can take care of myself."

"I'll always worry." He kisses me hard. "And I'm not letting you go in there by yourself. We'll find Saint together."

I don't bother arguing, because there's no time to waste.

We run toward the maze, and Caz stops me at the entrance. "That motherfucker can't leave here alive today." His eyes drill into mine, and I nod, already realizing that truth.

The initial plan had been to get Sinner locked up. To ensure justice was served, but that's not going to happen now. Sinner would never make it to trial. Randall or the head of

Homeland Security or some other corrupt bastard within the very organizations supposed to champion justice would ensure he "committed suicide" or had an unfortunate accident before he ever stepped foot in a courtroom.

That bastard deserves to die *at our hands*—not anyone else's.

"Stay down and stay behind me," I whisper as we enter the maze.

Working off gut instinct, I veer left, hoping my memory is serving me well and that I'm heading in the direction of the place Galen loves most. He took me here that one time when we were kids, explaining how it was his favorite part of the maze because it had a wooden bench, a small water feature, and a stone toy chest his grandma had installed just for him and his sister. Galen and Saint were practically joined at the hip growing up, so if Saint is hiding anywhere in here, staking out his dad, I'd bet my left tit he's there.

My arm whips out, holding Caz back when voices tickle my eardrums up ahead.

"Drop it, or I'll kill you right now," Sinner says, raising all the hairs on my arms.

I point right to Caz, cautiously slithering around the other side of the neat shrubbery so we can scope out the scene.

"You won't get away with this," Saint spits out. "The place is crawling with Feds, DEA, and VERO."

"You think I haven't planned for this day?" Sinner chuckles. "I've known this day would come, and no crooked motherfucker is taking me out. You'll like where we're going. The ocean is crystal clear, the sky a cloudless blue, and there's untapped pussy for the taking."

"You're insane. You won't make it out of this house alive."

Slowly, I poke my head around the corner, sucking in a

sharp breath when I see the predicament Saint is in. Sinner has him in a firm headlock with a knife at his jugular.

"You have such little faith," Sinner says, moving them forward a few steps. "I have a crew waiting at the back of the property and a private jet being fueled at a private airfield as we speak."

"Then leave me here and go," Saint says.

Sinner chuckles. "I'm going nowhere without you, son. Contrary to what you think, I love you."

This is such bullshit. Sinner must be bluffing, unless Randall tipped him off, but that doesn't make sense. It's probably a ruse to attempt to get Saint to leave with him.

"What a crock of shit," Caz whispers, mirroring my thoughts. I nod while computing solutions. I can't shoot Sinner from this angle without risking Saint, but if we move around and he spots us, he could kill Saint before I get to end him.

"Well, I don't love you." Saint slams his head back into his father's skull while simultaneously elbowing him in the ribs. It's enough to free him from Sinner's hold, and it's most likely our only opportunity.

I race toward them. "Get down," I roar, raising my gun. Saint dives on the ground as Sinner grabs at him, and I take my shot. The bullet lodges in Sinner's shoulder, and an animalistic howl rips from his mouth. Stalking toward him, I plant another bullet in his other shoulder and one in his knee. He drops to the ground, screaming in agony, as Caz rushes to Saint, helping him stand. I press down on Sinner's hand to loosen his hold on his knife, but he's already dropped it somewhere. Bones crunch under my foot, and Sinner roars, rolling on his side and clutching his knee.

I offer the gun to Saint, and we stare at one another. The kill shot belongs to my love, but I'll understand if he doesn't want to do it.

The choice is his.

Caz stomps on Sinner's ankle, and more screams litter the air.

The sound of approaching footfalls increases the urgency.

It's now or never.

Saint curls his fingers around the gun, and I nod. Without hesitation, and without uttering a single word, he aims the gun at his father's head and pulls the trigger.

The screams instantly stop. Sinner's eyes glaze over as his chest heaves his last breath, and his body stops fighting. Silence descends, blotting out all other sounds.

It's a profound moment.

As if a calming wave has blanketed the Earth, quieting all the noise, rolling over any resistance in its path, soothing the land and restoring peace.

I hook my fingers in Saint's, squeezing his hand, as we stare at the motionless body of the man who gave him life.

"Jesus." Galen slams to a halt, his eyes instantly meeting Saint's. Theo materializes beside him with Howie, Diesel, and Bry taking up the rear. We stand around Sinner's lifeless body, staring at a man we all hated, as the realization sinks in.

He's dead.

And we're free.

A shuddering breath leaves me as relief floods my system. "Thank fuck, you're all okay."

"You killed him," Diesel asks, glancing between Saint and me.

I nod. "We did. He had to die."

Now it's Diesel's turn to nod.

"I hope he's rotting in hell," Galen says, viciously kicking his corpse a couple times.

"Amen to that," Howie adds, crouching over him and punching him repeatedly in the face.

"Where were you?" I ask Diesel.

His eyes roam me from head to toe, checking I'm intact. "Dealing with a snake."

"Randall?"

Diesel bobs his head.

"You knew he was dirty?"

"Not until recently. I—"

"This'll have to wait," Galen says, cutting across us. He eyeballs me with a solemn expression. "Our moms have been taken to the hospital in an ambulance. I said we'd follow."

"Okay." I move to walk off, but Galen steps in front of me.

"Hang on. I need to check something first." Taking my hand, he strides with purpose toward the stone box nestled alongside the freshly painted wooden bench with Theo following suit. My brows pucker, and I throw a look at Theo. His shoulders lift, his puzzled face conveying he knows as much as me.

Galen opens the lid, and expletives rip through the air.

"What is it?" Saint asks, staying where he is while Diesel, Howie, and Caz all step forward to join us.

Galen lifts a large wrinkled brown envelope from the box, spinning around to face us with a mad grin on his face. Opening it, he removes the contents. "It's the Leydon evidence," he confirms, holding up the clear plastic bag containing a bloody knife and a USB key.

"What the fuck, man?" Theo steps forward, shock splayed across his face.

Diesel and Howie share a grin. Bry lounges against the armrest of the bench, taking it all in.

"Mom stole it," Galen confirms, and I almost keel over.

"*Alisha* had it all this time?" My tone betrays my disbelief.

Galen grins. "She told me the truth under the table before the EMTs arrived," he explains. "She followed Sinner and his men one night. Climbed in the trunk of one of their cars. She planned to capture them doing something illegal. Something she could use as insurance, but she found this tucked under the spare tire well of the trunk. She didn't know what it was until she watched the video footage. Then she knew she'd struck gold."

"So why the fuck didn't she use it to put those bastards away?" Saint blurts, his voice a little breathless.

My head whips to his, noting how he sways a little on his feet. I frown, keeping an eye on Saint. "Why didn't she use it to save herself?" I ask.

"She was scared because she knew it was dynamite. She didn't trust handing it to the police after what Daphne admitted on the recording. She gave away trade secrets. Secrets that would destroy a lot of powerful people. Mom decided to hide it. To keep it in reserve until she needed leverage with Sinner. She knew he'd come for me at some point, and she was going to use it to bargain for my life."

My eyes seek out Galen's. His gaze is brimming in emotion. He's always thought his mom didn't care. This gesture shows she did, in her own fucked-up way. She was trying to protect him the only way she knew how.

Silence engulfs us.

So much bloodshed could've been avoided if Alisha had just come to us, but I understand her concerns, and she was right not to turn it into the police, because then it would've just ended up in the commissioner's hands and the corruption would've been buried forever.

Galen hands the evidence to Diesel. "Nail their asses to the wall, man."

"Fuck!" Bry yells, claiming our attention. He darts forward to catch Saint as he falls. Saint's eyes are closed, his face is pale, and there's a thin layer of sweat on his brow. Bry holds Saint's unconscious body in his arms, and my heart is trying to escape my rib cage. Racing over to them, I almost fall when my shoes slip in something wet on the ground. Horror washes over me as I realize it's blood.

And it's oozing from a large gash in Saint's side.

Chapter Forty-Seven
Harlow

"Is he okay?" I ask, jumping out of my seat the second the doctor steps into the waiting room. He stopped by before Saint was taken into the operating room to update us. I can't believe that bastard Sinner stabbed his own son, just before I shot him, and I didn't see.

That Saint said nothing isn't a surprise, because martyr is basically his middle name. When he's well enough, I'm going to slap the shit out of him for saying nothing until it was almost too late.

Walking right up to the doctor, I fold my arms, preparing for whatever the news is.

"The surgery went well, and your husband is in the recovery room now," he says, and a layer of stress lifts off my shoulders.

"Is there any permanent damage?" Galen inquires, stepping up beside me. His arm slides low around my back, and I lean into him, welcoming his support.

"The knife missed his spleen and his liver, so I expect he'll make a full recovery. We've cleaned out and stitched up the wound, and we'll keep him here for a few days until the antibiotics are in his system and we know there's no infection."

I slump against Galen as relief courses through me. "He's going to be fine?"

The doctor smiles, patting my arm. "He'll be back to himself in no time."

Caz chuckles. "Oh joy."

"He'll be brought to his private room within the hour. You can visit him then, but he'll be very groggy for the next few hours so don't expect much."

"Thanks, Doctor," Theo says, stretching his legs out and shifting his butt on the chair.

We've been here for hours, and it's almost five a.m., but there's still no sign of Howie or Diesel. Diesel promised to stop by and fill us in, but they had to attend a meeting at FBI HQ in the city.

Mom had surgery to remove the bullet from her shoulder, and she's sleeping now. Her doctor told me she'll be fine after some rehabilitation. Alisha hasn't fared as well. She's in a coma in the ICU, and we don't know if she's going to pull through. Galen has been moving between her room and here, waiting on news of his cousin.

"You should sleep," Bry says, handing me a blanket. "You look beat."

"I'm okay." I drop down beside Caz, resting my head on his shoulder as Galen plucks the blanket from my fingers, draping it over my bare legs. "I can't sleep until I've seen that he's okay with my own two eyes."

"Your love is endearingly nauseating," Bry admits, stifling a yawn and stretching his arms up over his head.

"Still jealous, Eccleston?" Galen smirks, flopping onto the chair beside him.

Bry flips him the bird, and warmth spreads across my chest for the first time tonight.

Everything is returning to normal, and it's going to be okay.

The door creaks as it opens, revealing two very tired men.

"Hey." I sit up straight as Diesel and Howie enter the room. "I wasn't sure if you'd make it."

"Sorry it took so long," Diesel says, gratefully taking the seat beside me when Theo vacates it. Howie sits beside Bry while Theo pulls another chair over. "There was a lot to discuss."

"We can do this later," I offer even though I'm dying to find out what's going on.

Diesel grins. "It's cute you think I don't know you. I'm here because you won't sleep until you know the truth." He presses a kiss to my head. "And I wanted to check up on the punk. I already checked in on Giana. How is Saint doing?"

"He's good. Just out of surgery. Doc says he'll make a full recovery."

Diesel smiles, tucking a piece of hair behind my ear. "I'm happy to hear it."

I can tell he means it, and I don't hesitate to fling my arms around him, hugging him tight. Tears prick my eyes, and a sudden flood of emotion accosts me. I ease back, holding his worn-out eyes in place. "Thank you, Diesel. For everything."

"No thanks is necessary. It was a team effort." His lips pull into a tight grimace, and remorse glimmers in his eyes. "I'm sorry for all you went through tonight. I wanted to tear into the room the second that bastard put his hands on you."

"But you couldn't," I blurt, not wanting him to beat himself up over this. "I understand, and it's fine. *I'm* fine. I don't want to dwell on it." I take my time locking eyes with Caz, Theo, and Galen, because this message is for them too. "He didn't break me, and we're sure as shit not going to let what he did tonight in any way affect our relationship. He's defeated. Gone from our lives. That is all that matters."

One by one, they nod.

"I'm glad that sick motherfucker is dead," Howie hisses. "I only wish I'd been there to see it."

"Saint did us proud," Caz says.

"About that." Diesel sits back, rubbing a hand over his head, stifling a yawn. "We told the FBI Saint shot him in self-defense after he stabbed him. It's best Saint corroborates that story when the FBI arrives tomorrow to question him."

"Consider it done," Theo says, lifting his eyes from his tablet.

"So, what happened with Randall?" Galen asks Diesel, leaning forward on his elbows.

"Did you know he was corrupt?" I add.

"I'd become suspicious, but it was more of an instinct than anything solid until I met with Doug, the new FBI agent assigned to the case. They had been investigating Randall for some time, and they knew he was dirty, but they had nothing concrete to charge him with. They knew he was knee-deep in this shit with the commissioner and The Sainthood. They were hoping either Giana or Diego would find something they could use to tie them all together. I wasn't approached, because they weren't sure if I was involved or not." He pauses, cringing a little.

"Apparently, your dad had vouched for me, but after Trey was murdered, they couldn't be certain I hadn't been involved, so I was deliberately shut out," he explains.

"Is it true Homeland and VERO killed my dad?" I didn't have time to process that revelation during the showdown in the ballroom, but it's been playing on a loop in my mind ever since.

"The FBI believe so although they have no proof. They

intend to question Randall about it. He's a selfish prick, and he might just throw his police and Homeland buddies into the fire to save his own ass."

"They must've known Dad had the files." I tug the blanket up, covering my shoulders, suddenly icy cold.

"Doug believes they did and that they approached your dad asking him to return them. When Trey denied all knowledge, they killed him. Or perhaps Homeland believed then that he *didn't* have the files and they had to kill him as they'd drawn attention to themselves, or they suspected he was lying and they murdered him before he could do anything with them." He shrugs. "It's all supposition, but our guess is it was something like that."

Caz slides his arm around my shoulders. "I'm sorry, queenie."

Diesel quirks a brow, and I smile. "My status has been elevated now I'm a married woman," I explain. Diesel rolls his eyes, but it's in good humor.

"Where is Randall now?" Theo asks.

"In FBI custody although I'm not sure if he'll remain there," Howie says. "You wouldn't believe the politics."

Galen snorts. "We'd believe just about anything at this point."

"Is he going down for this?" I ask.

Diesel nods. "Most definitely. The recording from the ballroom and the Leydon evidence are enough to put him away, and as soon as the FBI has a warrant to search his home and office, I expect they'll find more to charge him with. Plus, we have operatives willing to testify that he had planned to take everyone out tonight."

"I thought as much," I admit, yawning. Caz nudges my head toward his shoulder.

"We were prepared for it," Diesel explains. "We brought

Howie into our confidence last night, and we had a separate team lying in wait. As soon as Randall and his men swung their weapons on us, our guys moved into position."

"He was outnumbered, and we took them down," Howie confirms.

"It's why we were late to the party, so to speak." Diesel grimaces at his bad joke. "We wanted to ensure they were in custody and off the grounds."

"What will happen to the commissioner?" I ask.

"He's being taken in for questioning, and he'll be charged too," Diesel supplies.

"And what about the girls?" Caz inquires. "What'll happen to them?"

"They're being looked after, and they'll be sent back home in time." Diesel skims his gaze around the room. "You did good, guys. You've done a great thing."

"What about The Sainthood?" Bry asks, his leg tapping on the ground.

"Most of the members in the ballroom were killed, including all of the current serving board members. The FBI already has warrants to search all of their businesses and properties and permission to seize their assets."

"If there is anything left of them after this," Howie adds. "It will be a drastically altered organization."

"Is Lincoln all right?" I ask, because I've been worrying about him too.

Diesel's face pales. "He's in surgery in a Greek hospital. Randall's men left him for dead when they grabbed Giana and brought her back to the US."

"I'm so sorry." I grab his hands. "I'll organize a private jet to take you there. I know the company Dad always used."

"I'll make it happen," Theo says, his fingers already flying across the keyboard.

Diesel gulps. "That would be appreciated. Thanks, Lo."

A nurse pokes her head through the door, smiling at me. "Mr. Westbrook is in his room now, and he's asking for you."

My lips curve in amusement at her faux pas, but I don't correct her. "Thank you." I stand. "We'll be right there." I lean down, kissing Diesel on the cheek. "Keep me updated on Lincoln, and please send him my regards. I hate that he got caught up in this. If there is anything else I can do, just ask."

Diesel stands, kissing my cheek. "Stay safe."

"We're going to head out." Bry rises with his brother. "I doubt his lordship wants to see us."

If it was just Bry, I'd insist he stays, but I'm guessing Bry is leaving because Howie is here. Bry knows, as well as I do, that Saint would not want to see his older uncle. "I'll text you updates," I promise, waving them off.

We leave the waiting room together, the four of us going in one direction and the three of them in another.

I open the door to Saint's private room with my heart thumping loudly in my chest. I know he's okay, that he'll make a full recovery, but I'm still anxious as I slip into his room. Lighting is dim, and the blinds are closed. The steady *beep, beep* of a machine and Saint's heavy breathing are the only sounds in the room. We tiptoe across the tile floor, careful not to wake our Sleeping Beauty. Saintly may have been asking for us, but he's sound asleep now, so we take seats around his bed, waiting for him to come around.

Fingers curl around my hand, and I jolt awake, springing up, my gaze darting around the strange room until I get my bearings. Caz is snoring in the chair beside me. Theo is asleep, draped over his tablet at the end of the bed, and Galen's chair is empty. I'm guessing he's with Alisha. My gaze drifts to the man in the bed, the guy threading his fingers in mine, and my pulse races when I lock eyes on

Saint's tired, bright blue ones. "You're awake," I blurt, stating the obvious.

"It would appear so." His voice is hoarse, and I grab the cup of ice chips by his bed, tipping a few into his mouth.

"How do you feel?"

"Like I'm ready to get out of here."

I roll my eyes. "I already know you're going to be the grumpiest patient ever," I tease.

"Bite me." He grins, waggling his brows.

I lean in close, lining my mouth up with his. "I'll make you a deal," I whisper over his lips. "Stay here until the doctor discharges you, and I'll blow you the second we get home."

His fingers wind through my hair, and he pulls my mouth down to his, kissing me possessively. "How about I'll discharge myself now, and you can blow me the second we get home?"

I roll my eyes again. "You're incorrigible."

"But you love me." His eyes shine with the truth.

"I do." My smile fades. "You scared me. There was so much blood."

"You can't get rid of me that easily, my queen." He brushes hair off my face. "We're going to grow old and gray together."

"I love the sound of that." Happy tears well in my eyes.

"Hey, man," Caz leans forward, squinting to clear his sleepy gaze. "Glad you're awake." A frown mars his brow. "Why does it say *Mr. Westbrook* on the chart by your bed?"

"'Cause that's my name," Saint coolly replies.

My eyes pop wide, and my jaw slackens as I stare at the chart. I hadn't noticed it before now. "You're going to do it? You're seriously taking my name?"

His eyes probe mine. "Is that okay?"

"Yes! Of course," I splutter, as tears stab my eyes again. "If you're sure."

"I'm sure. I'm done being a Lennox."

I'm not in the least bit surprised. "You don't want to take your mom's surname?" I inquire, because that might seem more logical. Plus, I've no issue taking that name. It was Lennox I had the issue with because I want no ties to that bastard rotting in hell. But Mrs. Harlow Young has a nice ring to it.

"No." Saint goes quiet. "I don't want to share a name with another man who has let me down."

I know he's not referring to Bry. I nod, cupping his face, my eyes wet with tears of the emotional kind. "Then Mr. Westbrook it is."

Epilogue

10 Months Later

Theo unlocks the front door to our two-story beachfront property, stepping aside to let me walk in first. I drop my keys on the hall table, kicking off my sneakers, as Theo and Galen follow me into our new house. "What time did Caz and Saint say they'd be home?" I ask, strolling into the large open-plan kitchen and dining room, heading toward the French doors at the rear.

"They're planning to leave the garage early. Caz said he'll grill steaks." Galen snakes his arms around me from behind. "Where do you think you're going?" Brushing my hair to one side, he nips at my neck with his teeth.

"It's still warm outside. I thought I'd study by the pool until my other two husbands get home from work."

It's only been one month since Theo and I started at Brown, but I'm already drowning in assignments, and I intend to stay on top of my studies.

"Boring," Galen singsongs in my ear, his hands trailing lower on my body, igniting a furnace inside me.

"Don't tell me you're caught up on your assignments already, because I'll never believe that," I murmur, fighting a moan.

Galen applied to Brown too, but he wasn't accepted, so he's studying business at Providence College. Most days, he drives the forty-minute journey with Theo and me although we brought all our cars with us to Rhode Island, even my dad's Gran Turismo.

"Nope, but I've one word for you." His fingers slide beneath the waistband of my jean shorts. "Priorities."

I twist around in his embrace, circling my arms around his neck. "I think I like where this is going."

"Me too," Theo adds, dumping his book bag on the island along with his tablet. He saunters toward us with a lopsided grin, sliding his body behind me, grinding his hips into my ass.

"Fuck, you two don't play fair," I groan, as Galen pops the button on my jeans, dragging my zipper down.

"Don't pretend you're complaining," Galen teases, sliding his hand into my panties and cupping my bare pussy.

"You can't get enough of our cocks," Theo adds, squeezing the cheeks of my ass.

"Guilty as charged," I moan, riding Galen's hand.

Galen chuckles when I pout as his hand leaves my heat to slide my shorts down my legs. Jumping up, I wrap my legs around his trim waist. "Ravish me, gentlemen." I angle my head back, finding Theo's mouth warm and welcoming. His tongue sweeps into my mouth, and I groan. "And I'll pretend you're my assignment."

"I expect full dedication, Mrs. Westbrook." Theo yanks his shirt over his head and unbuttons his jeans.

"You can expect nothing less," I call out in a teasing tone as

Galen walks me into the living room.

"Get naked, angel," he demands, shucking out of his clothes. "I need to be inside you."

Theo steps into the living room, completely naked, holding lube in his hand, and liquid lust floods my pussy as I make quick work of the rest of my clothes.

Galen lies down flat on the large leather sectional, pulling me down over his face. I scream as his tongue goes to town on my cunt while Theo hovers over us, playing with my tits as he makes love to my mouth.

Galen brings me to orgasm in record time, and I'm a mass of quivering cells as he slides me down his body, lowering me over his hard erection. Deep-seated contentment washes over me as he fills me up. Theo presses his body against me from behind, raining kisses on my face and my neck as I ride Galen's cock. Teasing my puckered hole with two slick fingers, Theo continues kissing me until I'm literally putty in his hands. He eases slowly into my ass, and I sigh a happy sigh.

I still love sex, and I can't get enough of my guys. I hope it never ends.

Hands, lips, and cocks adore me as we fuck on the couch in the living room with a familiarity that comes from intimate carnal knowledge. It's been over a year, and my lust for my husbands hasn't faded at all. If anything, I'm hornier than ever.

Things are good. We've settled into our new life here in Newport. Caz and Saint are overjoyed to have their own garage, and it's already picking up steady business. Caz is in control of the workshop while Saint is running the business side of things. Both are attending courses at the local community college a couple of nights a week.

The front door slams. "Honey, I'm home!" Caz calls out, like he does every night, and a humongous smile graces my mouth.

"You're early," I say, over a moan, looking over my shoulder as Caz and Saint step into the living room.

"You started the party without us. No fair." Caz mock pouts, striding toward me with purpose. He plants a hard kiss on my mouth. "Looking sexy as fuck, queenie."

"Hurry up and get naked," I demand, eyeballing Saint as he strips.

"Hey, babe." Caz kisses Theo, and I melt, like always. Things are really good between the guys now. While I'm their main focus, and they never leave me in any doubt, they usually spend one night a week together, doing couple stuff by themselves, and I'm A-Okay with that. The sight of them together still turns me into a puddle of liquid arousal.

"Open wide, queenie." Saint approaches, stroking his hard length, desire heavy in his gaze.

I lick the drop of precum at his crown, eyeing him intently as I take his cock into my mouth. Galen digs his nails into my hips, slamming me up and down on his erection until he comes explosively. Saint slides into my pussy then, and I blow Caz while Theo continues to fuck my ass. The only sounds in the room is skin slapping against skin and mutual moans and groans, and it's the sweetest symphony.

"How was work?" I ask Saint an hour later after we've all showered and changed. Caz and Theo are grilling steaks out by the pool while Galen stands with his back to us at the end of our garden, facing our private beach. Saint watches his cousin with hawk eyes while sipping on a beer.

Taking his hand, I lead Saint over to the outdoor dining

area. "Busy, but good," he replies. "I still managed to fit some online study in." He sits on a chair at the table, pulling me down on his lap.

Theo walks over with a cool glass of wine. "For my wife." He pecks my lips. "Dinner won't be too long."

"You need me to make anything?"

Saint arches a brow, and I slap his chest. "I don't burn everything. I can make a salad."

Theo laughs, pressing a kiss to my cheek. "Don't sweat it, babe. We have it under control." He walks into the house, and I lean back against Saint, thinking about how lucky I am. The guys dote on me constantly, and they love me so good.

Honestly, life doesn't get much better than this.

"You seem preoccupied," I say after a few minutes of silence. "Anything I can help with?" I take a sip of the crisp, chilled wine, enjoying the taste of it gliding down my throat.

"Do you think he's okay?" Saint asks, jerking his head in Galen's direction.

I reposition myself on his lap, careful not to knee him in the balls. "He's okay." I caress Saint's prickly jawline. "He talks to me regularly. He might get a little melancholy from time to time, but he assures me he's okay."

"I'm glad he has you. I never expected Alisha's death to hit him so hard."

Alisha died twenty-four hours after being brought to the hospital. Perhaps if she hadn't been so fragile from years of abusing her body with drugs and alcohol, she might have survived Sinner's knife wound, but we'll never know.

"You should talk to him if you're worried." We're all close, but sometimes, getting the guys to talk about their emotions is as painful as a root canal.

"I think he prefers to tell you that shit."

I rest my case.

"It's more than just his mom dying. It's the realization his family is gone, and I think it's only hitting him now that his grandma's house is sold."

"You think he regrets selling it?" Saint asks, tipping beer into his mouth.

"No, but that doesn't mean he isn't sad. Galen has a lot of memories tied up in that house."

"Not all of them good," Saint says, speaking the truth.

Two months ago, Galen sold the house and half the grounds to a property developer, because he didn't want to live in a home where so many had died. He made a deal that gave him the maze and enough land to build his own house, including a separate entrance via the rear of the property, so if we want to build a house there in the future, we can.

The developer is building high-quality condos, catered for the upper end of the market, and he's already walled off the property, so the part Galen still owns is completely private and inaccessible until he decides what to do with it.

Right now, none of us has any burning desire to return to Lowell, but who knows what the future holds? We have the barn, I still have the cabin and Galen has the land, so we have options, which feels good.

"Did you hear anything from David Jennings?" Saint asks, rubbing his fingers up and down my arm.

I shake my head. "No, but I don't expect to. He owes me nothing."

Lincoln helped Mom and me free David Jennings from prison with assistance from Diesel, who has been promoted to the head of VERO.

David Jennings is the man who was convicted of kidnapping and torturing me as a kid—an injustice I needed to set right. Luckily, Dad left me a large inheritance, and I hadn't dipped into the compensation fund David was forced to pay me—one I received when I turned eighteen—so I transferred it back to Jennings. With interest, it has grown considerably over the years, and I hope it helps compensate *him* in some way, for all the years he spent languishing in a jail cell.

Saint clicks his fingers in my face. "Earth to queenie. Where'd you go?"

"I drifted off, *Saintly*." I poke him in the chest.

"You okay?" Concern stretches across his face.

"I'm perfect. I was just thinking of everything that's happened since you guys left The Sainthood, we graduated, and we moved here."

He tilts my face around as Caz approaches, carrying a platter of steaks. "You have any regrets?"

I tweak his nose. "Not a single one. I love my life."

"Life is good," Caz agrees, setting the steaks down as Theo materializes with an overflowing bread basket and a generous salad bowl.

Caz inserts two fingers into his mouth, shrilly whistling, drawing Galen's attention. Galen strolls across the garden with his hands shoved deep in his pockets.

I slide onto the seat beside Saint as Theo and Caz distribute the food. They're the unofficial chefs in the house, because the rest of us can't cook for shit. I lower my face to the plate, sniffing the succulent chargrilled aroma. My tummy rumbles appreciatively. "This smells delicious."

"Only the best for our queenie." Caz cheekily grabs my boob, and I shoot him a faux glare.

"Hands off the girls." I pin him with a seductive grin. "At least until we've eaten."

"Fuck. Now I'm hard again." He rubs at his crotch, rounding the table to sit beside Theo.

"You're always hard," Saint drawls, popping a piece of steak in his mouth. "You should get that checked out."

"Nothing wrong with my dick." Caz leans back, grinning smugly. "Maybe you should seek medical assistance for your erectile dysfunction."

Theo almost chokes on his food. Caz chuckles while running a gentle hand back and forth across Theo's back.

I pat the seat beside me when Galen approaches. "Sit here, babe."

Waves of dark messy hair fall into his eyes as he ambles toward me, and my heart swells with love for my broody guy. Galen drops into the seat, and I grab his face, kissing him softly. "I love you," I whisper, knowing he needs to hear that right now.

He pulls me to his chest, cradling me against him, his hand finding the nape of my neck as he holds me close. "Love you too, angel. More and more with every passing day."

Fuck. These guys slay me in all the best ways.

"I don't have erectile dysfunction, dipshit," Saint growls, flipping Caz the bird.

"Are you forgetting that time you couldn't get it up?" Caz grins, cutting vigorously into his steak.

"Are you forgetting I'd just come out of the hospital and had a reaction to the meds I was on?" Saint swiftly replies.

"How long are you going to keep reminding him of this," I ask after chewing a piece of delicious steak. "Because Saintly's likely to murder you if you don't drop it, and I'm quite fond of your face."

I know why Caz does it. Nothing insults my grumpy alpha husband more than questioning his manhood, and Caz just loves pushing his buttons.

"My face or my dick?" Caz asks, and Theo rolls his eyes.

"You have dick on the brain, dude," Galen says. "Saintly's right. You should get that shit checked out."

Caz molds his mouth into an O shape. "Galen siding with his cousin. Shocker."

"No one is taking sides; although, if you continue to poke the beast, I might need to incentivize you into toeing the line," I add, patting Saint's thigh.

Caz relents, like I knew he would. He throws up his hands. "No need to invoke the cockblocking strategy, babe. You know I'm only yanking Saint's chain." He grins at Saint. "You know I love you, man."

Saint rolls his eyes, and Caz chuckles.

"And I've always got your back," he adds with a mischievous glint in his eye. "Next time it happens, we'll fulfil conjugal duties on your behalf."

Saint throws a bread roll at Caz's head, and Caz's chest rumbles with laughter, knowing he's won this round.

Never a dull moment, but I wouldn't have it any other way.

The conversation flows freely as we eat dinner after Caz quits winding Saint up, focusing on different topics.

"I heard from Diesel today," Theo says, and Saint, predictably, scowls.

He can pretend he still doesn't like him, but we all know the truth. There's a begrudging respect between them now.

"Is he still overseas?" I ask, spearing a piece of lettuce with my fork.

"Yeah. He sounds as busy as ever."

"What'd he want?" Caz asks, pushing his empty plate away and rubbing his toned flat stomach.

"To offer me a job." Theo beams.

"Get the fuck out." Grinning widely, I stretch across the table to high-five my super-smart, super-sexy guy. "That's awesome. I'm proud of you."

"It's only part-time, but it's all stuff I can do remotely, and I want to contribute to the household finances."

The only disagreement between us these past few months has been over money. Which I fucking hate, because it shouldn't matter where the money comes from as long as we have enough. And we do. Between my generous inheritance and the sizable sum Galen got for the sale of his grandma's house and land, we have more than enough to last us a lifetime even after purchasing this house, the garage business, and paying college tuition.

The guys donated all their savings to charity, because they didn't want money that had come from illegal activities. They split their funds between a leading addiction support center with branches in Lowell and Prestwick and a new charity called Moonlight that provides a safe haven and support services for victims of sex trafficking.

"Plus, I can start paying you back," Theo adds, challenging me with a look.

"Cool." I don't give a rat's ass that I paid for Theo's tuition —especially since Mom insisted on paying my tuition—or need him to pay me back, but I'll take his money if it makes him feel better.

Initially, Theo tried reaching out to his parents, hoping they might support him financially after he landed a place at Brown, but after the media coverage of what went down with The Sainthood, they want even less to do with him now.

Fuck them. It's their loss.

"Did Diesel mention anything to you about Christmas?" I ask Theo, and he shakes his head.

"We only talked business."

"Work on him please." I know it's months away, but we'll need months to convince him to join us, because Diesel *never* takes a break. "Mom and Lincoln are coming here to celebrate with us, and I'd really love him to come. I miss him."

Saint harrumphs, and I slap his thigh in warning.

"I'll do my best," Theo says, cutting his steak into even pieces. "But I wouldn't get your hopes up. He's a total workaholic."

I'm so proud of Diesel, and his promotion was well-deserved, but I hate that I never see him anymore because he's so busy. He makes the effort to keep in touch by phone, but I really hope he can celebrate Christmas with us.

I'd love Bry and Howie to join us too so it's a real family affair, but Saint vetoed that idea the second I suggested it. While he's made an effort to bond with Bry and he's in regular phone contact with him, he's still on the fence about Howie. I'm hoping, in time, Saint will be able to find it in his heart to forgive him.

Howie wants to make it up to Saint, and, according to Bry, he craves a relationship with his nephew, but he's realistic enough to know he hurt him by abandoning him as a baby and that he can't rush him.

Bry graduated high school by the skin of his teeth, and he's now working at a tattoo parlor in Prestwick. Emmett and Sean both got football scholarships, and they're now happily settled in the dorms at the University of Southern California. I make a point of checking in with all three regularly, and I hope we never lose contact.

"How is the lovely Giana?" Caz asks, interrupting my thoughts.

I focus on his wolfish grin, already knowing where he's going with this. Caz is in a playful mood tonight, and it's a manifestation of the happy place he's in.

"Still denying her and Lincoln have a friend with benefits thing going on?" he adds.

"The official line she's still feeding me is they are best friends."

"It could be the truth," Theo says, always quick to defend.

"So pure," Caz teases, and Theo stabs him with a dark look. Caz chuckles. "They're bumping uglies, for sure."

"She says she wants to help him set up his new law practice because she feels responsible for the fact he's in a wheelchair now, and maybe that's true, but she's happy, and that's all I care about."

Mom and Lincoln moved to Arizona six months ago, because that's where Lincoln and Diesel's family lives. Mom is setting up the law office they bought together, as business partners. When it's open, she will manage it while Lincoln will provide legal services to the local community. Mom sold our family home, and she's bought a new sprawling mansion in a nice, exclusive, gated community in Arizona, which Lincoln shares with her.

"Shit, I forgot to mention this," Galen says, setting down his silverware. "I saw a report online today. Finn Houston and his sidekick Brooklyn Robbins were arrested on drug-trafficking charges in Texas last weekend."

"So that's where they were hiding out," Saint muses, finishing his food and shoving his plate away.

"I'm not surprised they were arrested. Neither of them is smart enough to sell drugs and not get caught." I take a sip of my wine.

"Let's hope *they* make it to trial," Galen supplies.

"I doubt there are higher powers who need to silence those two idiots," Saint says.

Silence descends as we remember how Randall Solice was found hanging in his cell just before he was due to stand trial on multiple charges.

The FBI didn't have enough evidence to charge the head of Homeland Security, but the doubt it cast on his reputation was enough for him to retire early under a cloud of suspicion.

Commissioner Leydon was sent to prison, convicted on

multiple counts of treachery and murder. He'll spend the rest of his days behind bars.

Diesel says he was the scapegoat, because someone had to publicly pay, but they buried half the stuff that happened in the process, which I fucking hate. It means the man who ordered my father's murder is walking around with a generous pension and not a single care in the world. I could go after the ex-head of Homeland Security, but there has to come a point where you draw a line under something, and we made a call, collectively, to let it go.

Maybe, I'll feel differently in the future, but right now, we're enjoying our new lives and the freedom we have to choose our own path.

Diesel says the new head of Homeland Security is a good guy and together they are hoping to clean up both organizations, but it's a tall order because corruption is hard to completely weed out.

Caz and Theo enjoy beers on the patio while the three of us clean up after dinner. Then we join them outside, taking a few quiet moments to appreciate all we've fought so hard for.

Although nightfall is creeping in, the weather is unseasonably warm for September, and it's still suitable for swimming. Something we indulge in regularly, thanks to our own private beach. I stand, pulling my cotton sundress up over my head and tossing it on the lounge chair. "Last one in the water gets cockblocked for a month." I giggle as I race toward the shore in my bra and panties.

We all know I'm lying, because I can't even go twenty-four

hours without dick, but that fierce competitive streak that burns bright in each of my husbands—and their perpetual willingness to pander to my every whim and need—has them all jumping up and shedding their clothes like it's an Olympic sport.

Water splashes me as I plunge into the ocean, wading through the waves, counting the seconds before one of them catches up to me. I shriek when strong arms lift me up like I'm weightless and I'm flung over broad shoulders.

Galen slaps my ass. "Naughty, naughty, angel. You know we'll punish you for that."

"I'm counting on it." As I watch Theo, Caz, and Saint plow through the water, with a full heart and a giant smile on my face, I know I can always rely on my husbands to deliver what they promise.

Want to read a sexy scene with Lo, Caz, and Theo? Scan your phone below:

Check out **Revere** the final book in the series. This is an epilogue novella, set 12 years in the future. I have also included a bonus Valentine's Day scene.

Harlow Westbrook's life is the stuff of dreams. Married to her four soul mates and with a family she adores and a fulfilling career, she should be blissfully happy. Except she can't give Saint the one thing he craves—a biological child of his own.

When cracks appear in their relationship, impacting the entire family unit, it threatens everything they have fought so hard for.

But Harlow has never been the type of woman to give up when things get tough.

Especially when her happily ever after is at stake.

Available now in ebook, paperback and audiobook.

About the Author

Siobhan Davis is a USA Today, *Wall Street Journal*, and Amazon Top 5 bestselling romance author. **Siobhan** writes emotionally intense stories with swoon-worthy romance, complex characters, and tons of unexpected plot twists and turns that will have you flipping the pages beyond bedtime! She has sold over 2 million books, and her titles are translated into several languages.

Prior to becoming a full-time writer, Siobhan forged a successful corporate career in human resource management.

She lives in the Garden County of Ireland with her husband and two sons.

You can connect with Siobhan in the following ways:

Website: www.siobhandavis.com
Facebook: AuthorSiobhanDavis
Instagram: @siobhandavisauthor
Tiktok: @siobhandavisauthor
Email: siobhan@siobhandavis.com

Books by Siobhan Davis

KENNEDY BOYS SERIES

Upper Young Adult/New Adult Contemporary Romance

Finding Kyler

Losing Kyler

Keeping Kyler

The Irish Getaway

Loving Kalvin

Saving Brad

Seducing Kaden

Forgiving Keven

Summer in Nantucket

Releasing Keanu

Adoring Keaton

Reforming Kent

Moonlight in Massachusetts

STAND-ALONES

New Adult Contemporary Romance

Inseparable

Incognito

When Forever Changes

No Feelings Involved

Still Falling for You

Second Chances Box Set

Holding on to Forever

Always Meant to Be

Vengeance of a Mafia Queen

Reverse Harem Romance

Surviving Amber Springs

MAZZONE MAFIA SERIES

Dark Romance Mafia

Condemned to Love

Forbidden to Love

Scared to Love

RYDEVILLE ELITE SERIES

Dark High School Romance

Cruel Intentions

Twisted Betrayal

Sweet Retribution

Charlie

Jackson

Sawyer

*The Hate I Feel^*

*Drew^*

THE SAINTHOOD (BOYS OF LOWELL HIGH)

Dark HS Reverse Harem Romance

Resurrection

Rebellion

Reign

Revere

The Sainthood: The Complete Series

DIRTY CRAZY BAD DUET

Dark College Reverse Harem Romance

Dirty Crazy Bad - A Prequel Short Story

Dirty Crazy Bad # 1

Dirty Crazy Bad #2

ALL OF ME DUET

Angsty New Adult Romance

Say I'm The One

Let Me Love You

Hold Me Close

All of Me: The Complete Series

ALINTHIA SERIES

Upper YA/NA Paranormal Romance/Reverse Harem

The Lost Savior

The Secret Heir

The Warrior Princess

The Chosen One

*The Rightful Queen^*

TRUE CALLING SERIES

Young Adult Science Fiction/Dystopian Romance

True Calling

Lovestruck

Beyond Reach

Light of a Thousand Stars

Destiny Rising

Short Story Collection

True Calling Series Collection

SAVEN SERIES

Young Adult Science Fiction/Paranormal Romance

Saven Deception

Logan

Saven Disclosure

Saven Denial

Saven Defiance

Axton

Saven Deliverance

Saven: The Complete Series

^Release date to be confirmed

www.ingramcontent.com/pod-product-compliance
Lightning Source LLC
Chambersburg PA
CBHW051309190726
48290CB00001B/65